Praise for Steve

"James delivers first-rate characters, dazzling plot twists, and powers it all with non-stop action."

> —JOHN TINKER, Emmy Award-winning screenwriter

Synapse

"A complex and riveting thriller that invites you to ponder the deepest questions of existence while at the same time leaving you on the edge of your seat."

> —JAMES L. RUBART, five-time Christy Award-winning author of *Blood from a Stone*

"Animated by themes of hope, love, and belief in the afterlife, James's thrilling story of greed and corruption will win over readers."

> —*PUBLISHERS WEEKLY* STARRED REVIEW

"A groundbreaking, mind-bending adventure. *Synapse* is next-level suspense that keeps the pages turning combined with next-level writing on par with the great literary masters."

> —JAMES R. HANNIBAL, award-winning author of *The Paris Betrayal*

"Steven James once again delivers a perfect amalgam of character and plot, totally immersing the reader in an irresistible narrative."

> —SIMON GERVAIS, international bestselling author of *The Last Sentinel*

"James . . . delivers a thought-provoking look at the definitions of humanity, belief, and faith in this timely near-future sf thriller."

> —*LIBRARY JOURNAL* STARRED REVIEW

"Suspenseful and profound. A mind-bending thriller with a taut storyline filled with the added tension of existential questions and ethical dilemmas we have no answers to today—but may find ourselves wrestling with in the all-too-near future."

> —TOSCA LEE, international bestselling author of *A Single Light*

Every Deadly Kiss

"James brings complexity and intrigue to his latest Patrick Bowers thriller, layering plotlines and unfolding characters in a way that keeps readers on the edge through the very end. . . . Fans of the Bowers Files will not be disappointed."

—RT BOOK REVIEWS

"Unnerving and laced with breathtaking suspense, *Every Deadly Kiss* is a surprising and complex thriller that will keep readers obsessed to the final page."

—FRESH FICTION

Checkmate

"A perfectly crafted hard-hitting, intense thriller that takes readers to the top of the cliff and dangles them over the edge. James is an author that every thriller reader should have on their bookshelf."

—SUSPENSE MAGAZINE

The King

"His tightly woven, adrenaline-laced plots leave readers breathless."

—THE SUSPENSE ZONE

"With a multidimensional quality, Steven James writes with a confident, assured ease. Just good old-fashioned, gimmick-free storytelling that pushes the envelope to the edge and beyond."

—STEVE BERRY, *New York Times* bestselling author of *The Kaiser's Web*

The Queen

"A masterpiece of a thriller."

—SPECIAL AGENT R. WAYNE SMITH, FBI (retired)

"With a brilliant strategy, James manages a checkmate, and he seems to have many more moves in store."

—*PUBLISHERS WEEKLY*

The Bishop

"Breakneck speed doesn't even begin to describe the pace . . . Absolutely brilliant."

—JEFF BUICK, bestselling author of *The Krubera Conspiracy*

"Steven James's *The Bishop* should come with a warning: Don't start reading unless you're prepared to finish this book in a single sitting. An intense, intelligent thriller with characters as real as your next-door neighbors, *The Bishop* goes beyond the exploration of good and evil to what it means to be human. Riveting!"

—KAREN DIONNE, #1 international bestselling author of *The Marsh King's Daughter*

The Knight

"Page after page, the suspense never ends. This book is highly recommended."

—MIDWEST BOOK REVIEW

"I'm continually in awe of Steven James and his mastery of story. If you are looking for top-notch thriller writing laced with suspense, action, mystery, and emotion, then look no further. Steven James is your guy."

—FICTION ADDICT

The Rook

"Fans of *CSI* and *Law & Order* will enjoy the police work and forensics, but this jacked-up read feels more like an explosive episode of *24*; it's a wild ride with a shocking conclusion."

—*PUBLISHERS WEEKLY* STARRED REVIEW

"Readers will be on the edge of their seats."
—*ROMANTIC TIMES* TOP PICK

The Pawn

"An exceptional psychological thriller."
—BOOKSHELF REVIEW

"Riveting."
—*PUBLISHERS WEEKLY*

"Seriously intense."
—POP CULTURE TUESDAY

"Steven James writes at a breakneck pace, effortlessly pulling the reader along on this incredible thrill ride."
—ARMCHAIR REVIEWS

"An exhilarating thriller that will keep readers up late into the night . . . In a word, intense."
—MYSTERIOUS REVIEWS

Opening Moves

"*Opening Moves* is a mesmerizing read. From the first chapter, it sets its hook deep and drags you through a darkly gripping story with relentless power. My conclusion: I need to read more of Steven James."
—MICHAEL CONNELLY, #1 *New York Times* bestselling author of *Desert Star* and executive producer of *Bosch*

"Steven James has created a fast-moving thriller with psychological depth and gripping action . . . Full of twists and enjoyable surprise, *Opening Moves* is a blisteringly fast and riveting read."
—MARK GREANEY, #1 *New York Times* bestselling author of *The Gray Man*

BROKER OF LIES

Also by Steven James

—⁂—

SCIENCE FICTION
Synapse

SUSPENSE
THE BOWERS FILES
Opening Moves
The Pawn
The Rook
The Knight
The Bishop
The Queen
The King
Checkmate
Every Crooked Path
Every Deadly Kiss
Every Wicked Man

THE JEVIN BANKS EXPERIENCE
Placebo
Singularity

YOUNG ADULT
THE BLUR TRILOGY
Blur
Fury
Curse

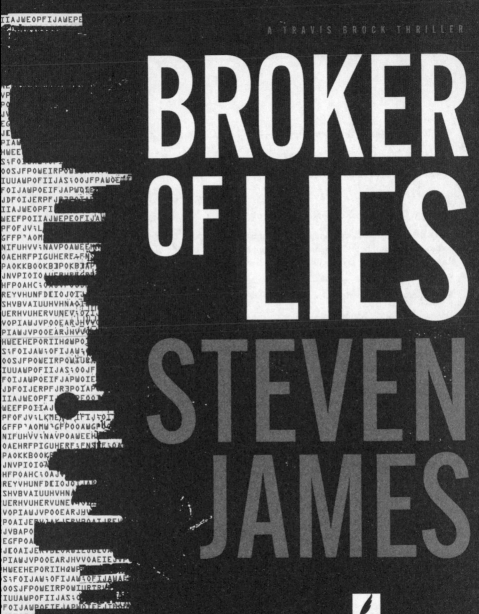

A TRAVIS BROCK THRILLER

BROKER OF LIES

STEVEN JAMES

Tyndale House Publishers
Carol Stream, Illinois

Visit Tyndale online at tyndale.com.

Visit Steven James online at stevenjames.net.

Tyndale and Tyndale's quill logo are registered trademarks of Tyndale House Ministries.

Broker of Lies

Designed by Ron C. Kaufmann

Published in association with the John Talbot Agency, Inc., a member of The Talbot Fortune Agency, LLC, 180 E. Prospect Ave. #188, Mamaroneck, NY 10543.

For information about special discounts for bulk purchases, please contact Tyndale House Publishers at csresponse@tyndale.com, or call 1-855-277-9400.

Library of Congress Cataloging-in-Publication Data

A catalog record for this book is available from the Library of Congress.

ISBN 978-1-4964-7330-1 (HC)
ISBN 978-1-4964-7331-8 (SC)

Printed in the United States of America

29	28	27	26	25	24	23
7	6	5	4	3	2	1

Facilis descensus Averno.

VIRGIL
The Aeneid

CIAJWEOPFIJAWEPE

JF
O
M
G
JE
PIAW
HWEE
S;FO
OOSJFPOWEIRPO
CUUAWPOFIIJAS;OOJFPAWOEMF
FOIJAWPOEIFJAPWQIE
JDFOIJERPFJR3POIA
CIAJWEOPFI
WEEFPOIIAJWEPEOFIJAW
PFOFJV;L
GFFP'AOM
NIFUHVV;NAVPOAWEEHO
OAEHRFPIGUHERE;FN
PAOKKBOOKBJPOKBJAP
JNVPIOIOA
HFPOAHC;OAJ
REYVHUNFDEIOJOIJ
SHVBVAIUUHVHNAOI
JERHVUHERVUNEV;O
VOPIAWJVPOOEARJHVV
PIAWJVPOOEARJHVV
HWEEHEPORIIHQWPO
S;FOIJAW;OFIJAW;
OOSJFPOWEIRPOWIUB
IUUAWPOFIIJAS;OOJF
FOIJAWPOEIFJAPWOIE
JDFOIJERPFJR3POIA
IIAJWEOPFI   OEOO
WEEFPOIIAJ
PFOFJV;LKME;   ;FIJ;OI
GFFP'AOMW;GFPOOAWGP
NIFUHVV;NAVPOAWEEH
OAEHRFPIGUHERF;ENS;E;OA
PAOKKBOOKE
JNVPIOIOA
HFPOAHC;OAJ
REYVHUNFDEIOJO;IA
SHVBVAIUUHVHNA
JERHVUHERVUNE;V;
VOPIAWJVPOOEARJHV
POAIJERUJAK;ERVPOAIJRE
JVBAPO
EGFPOA
JEOAIJERVBLOAWIEJGLO
PIAWJVPOOEARJHVVOAEIE
HWEEHEPORIIHQWF
S;FOIJAW;OFIJAW;OFIJAWA
OOSJFPOWEIRPOWIURTR
IUUAWPOFIIJAS;O
FOIJAWPOEIFJAPWOIEF;AINW
JDFOIJ
IIAJW
WEEF
IIA
WEER
PFOF
GEF
N
H

PART I

Fresh Corpses

CHAPTER 1

Zoë Hughes eyed the door. "He's in there?"

A nod from her supervisor, a nurse who'd been working in the burn ward for nearly twenty years. Kathleen Capron had seen it all. More than anyone should see.

"Is it true?" Zoë asked. She was just one semester out of college. Still adjusting to it all.

"About?"

"His wife."

Neither woman moved toward the room. Kathleen shuffled one foot. "You mean that she was still alive?"

"Yes."

"That's what they're saying."

Zoë caught herself swallowing hard.

Kathleen placed a reassuring hand on Zoë's forearm. "I know this is your first time, but follow my lead. And don't look into his eyes when it happens."

"Why do you say that? Will it frighten him?"

"It'll frighten you."

Zoë nodded quietly.

Kathleen rapped gently on the patient's door and, without waiting for

3

an answer, announced herself. "Mr. Brock? It's Kathleen, your nurse." There was no reply from inside. She nudged the door open. "It's time to change your bandages."

She angled through the doorway with Zoë behind her. "Today I have Nurse Hughes with me. She'll be assisting me."

Zoë smelled the man's wounds before she ever saw him. The stench of burnt flesh lingered in the air despite the cleaning agents the custodial staff had used in the room.

She knew from reading the thirty-five-year-old man's charts that the burns covered over a third of his body, from his left leg up and across his torso to the side of his face. Though the wounds were mostly on the left side, both of his arms had been burned when he reached into the flames.

She also knew that with severe-enough full-thickness, or third-degree, burns—when the nerves were damaged—the patient didn't feel any pain. But this man's burns hadn't affected his nerve endings. He would feel it when they removed the bandages sticking to him.

He would feel it all.

They say it's one of the most painful experiences a person can go through. Like peeling off your skin whenever it's time for fresh bandages. And debridement—scrubbing the burns when necessary to keep them clean and free from infection—was perhaps the worst part of all.

"How are you doing today?" Kathleen asked him, a question that Zoë thought could not possibly bring a favorable response.

The man said nothing, but nodded faintly. Only one of his eyes was visible; the other had been bandaged over.

"Good." Kathleen consulted his chart. "We need to give you something to dull the pain."

This time, instead of nodding, he shook his head and whispered a single, coarse word, the swelling in his throat no doubt making it hard to vocalize: "No."

"It's necessary."

Now his reply was firmer, more adamant. "No."

"Don't worry, it also serves as an amnesiac. It'll help you forget all this when it's over."

"Can't forget." His voice cracked as he replied.

"Mr. Brock. It's protocol for us to give patients—"

"No drugs." There was steel in his response.

Zoë waited to see what Kathleen would do. With what this man was going through, why would he be refusing pain medication? Maybe he was delirious. Probably that's what it was. He wasn't thinking clearly.

Still, they needed to clear this up. She couldn't imagine what it would be like trying to change his bandages without him being medicated.

Kathleen stared at Mr. Brock for a moment, then signaled for Zoë to come with her and told the man, "We'll be right back."

Zoë followed her into the hall, closing the door half-shut behind her.

"He expressly stated his wishes," she said softly to Kathleen.

"But he's in no state to understand what he's asking."

"How do we know that? I mean, how—?"

"He's not in his right mind, Zoë. He wouldn't deny the pain meds, not if he knew what was coming. We give them Veldexin for a reason."

"Yes," Zoë said, "to forget the pain, I know, but—"

"That's not the only reason. It's also for the next time."

"The next time?"

"If we didn't give it to them—if they remembered everything—when we returned to change their bandages, they would fight us off. Believe me, I've been there. The last thing you want to have to do is strap someone down while he writhes and screams for you to stop as you prepare to peel the bandages off his burns."

Zoë gulped. "Then what do we do?"

"We go back in there and we do our job."

"But—"

"We do it." Kathleen raised an authoritative finger. "And don't question things once we get started. Remember who's in charge."

"You are."

"Yes."

Back in the room again, the man muttered as they approached his bed, his words breathy and forced. "Don't touch me until I speak to a doctor."

"It's time to change these bandages, I'm afraid," Kathleen told him sternly.

Zoë eased closer to him, and all at once he reached out and grabbed her wrist. "A doctor."

He stared into her eyes with arrant determination and clutched her with unnerving strength. She wanted to pull away but didn't want to hurt him, and she knew that if she jerked her arm, it would definitely jar him, maybe rip some of his wounds open again.

At last, Kathleen sighed. "Fine."

—⁓—

In silence, I watched the two nurses walk away. Because of the bandage covering my left eye, I had to turn my head in order to do so. When my neck flexed, the burns on it sent tight streaks of pain shooting down my spine, and I had to stop and stare upright again, trying to catch my breath and quiet the pain stabbing through me. Beyond the open doorway I heard the incessant beeping of a monitor in another room and the irregular sound of a squeaky cart being rolled down the hallway.

Then the door closed as they left me alone in the room. Sterile and stark. A bone-white tomb. As I lay there waiting for the doctor, my senses seemed to become keener. The charred smell of my burns hadn't gone away, and I wondered how long it would take before it did, or if the odor would be locked in my memory forever.

Probably locked in.

Forever.

It made me think of the fire, and though I tried my best to forget—something that never worked and seemed to always bring the opposite result instead—I remembered it all as if it were happening right here, once again: Awakening to the smell of smoke. Sitting up and feeling beside me on the bed, but finding it empty, my wife gone. Smooth sheets. Cool to the touch.

"Sienna?"

Instinctively, I'd fumbled for my glasses on the nightstand, but they fell to the floor behind it.

I rushed to the door and felt the wood.

Blazing heat.

Flames snaking in beneath the door.

"Sienna!"

No reply from the hallway, just the crackling hiss of the blaze.

Wrapping my T-shirt around my hand to protect it from burning on the doorknob, I opened the door just enough for a strip of flames to lick in at me, hungry for fresh oxygen.

I pushed it shut, sealing them out.

With the fire trapping me in the bedroom, the only way out of the house was off the balcony beyond the French doors.

I hurried through them and peered down into the night. It had to be at least twenty-five feet to the downward-sloping hillside, but there she was, standing beneath the oak tree in the front yard. *Thank God, thank God, thank God.*

But why didn't she wake you up?

Trying not to overthink things, I glanced behind me. Through the gathering smoke, I could see the fire already trying to climb up the inside of the bedroom door.

I faced the neighborhood again and took a deep breath.

And leapt.

And dropped through the air, sliding through the narrow slipstream of time before impact. The descent seemed somehow both brief and long, and when I finally hit the ground, my left ankle buckled.

I collapsed to the grass, then pushed myself awkwardly to my feet and hobbled toward her. "Sienna? Are you okay?"

However, when the woman turned, I realized that it wasn't my wife but one of our neighbors, Claire, standing there in pajamas. She held a cell phone to her ear and looked shocked and terrified.

"Have you seen her?" I gasped. "Is Sienna out here?"

A wide-eyed headshake.

I turned toward the house again. By the intensity of the flames shooting out the windows, I could judge which rooms were already ablaze and which ones weren't yet fully engaged. It appeared that, although the fire had found the upstairs bedrooms, the east side of our home was still mostly intact.

Go.

Find her.

A fire truck raced toward me down the street and turned onto our drive-way, its siren pulsing, screaming in the night.

"Tell them I went after her!" I yelled to Claire as I limped toward the garage, mentally reviewing the layout of the house, trying to calculate where Sienna might be.

Go through the garage. Then check the kitchen. The living room. The basement if you need to.

The garage's side door was locked. Obviously, I didn't have the key, so I punched in the entry code and the garage door rattled open, taking forever, smoke pouring out and circling around my legs as it did.

"Sienna!"

The word echoed sharply off the garage walls, but brought no reply.

I pressed forward, rounded the car, fought my way through the smoke, and burst into the kitchen.

Fierce heat. Acrid air that made it tough to breathe, tough to think. I tugged my shirt up over my mouth and scanned the room, searching for Sienna through the shimmering, hypnotic skin of the flames.

Nothing.

Our fire alarms. Why aren't they going off?

No time to worry about that. The living room. Go!

As I stumbled into it, the front door flew open and a firefighter appeared. He gestured for me to join him, but I waved him off as I scrutinized the other side of the room for her and, there, yes, there, there, there, through the flames, I made out a vague form, prone on the steps, maybe fifteen feet away.

As I rushed toward her, a ribbon of fire caught hold of my sweatpants' left leg, but I kept going. I felt the fireman's heavy hand on my shoulder, but I pointed to the steps. When he shook his head, evidently believing it was too late for her, I tore free and started toward the stairs.

She'll be okay. She'll make it. You've got this.

I brushed away a flurry of cinders singeing the back of my neck, then covered my face the best I could with my blistering arms and dashed toward the stark wall of flames separating us, but my foot snagged on the edge of the carpet and I went down hard in the heart of the blaze. The firefighter grabbed one of my ankles and pulled me back.

"No!" I cried. I struggled to tug free, but I was weak, dazed, coughing, gasping for breath.

And then, as the man hefted me up into a fireman's carry, I saw movement on the stairs as she raised her head and reached a trembling, scorched arm toward us. A woman burned beyond recognition, now engulfed in flames.

She's alive! You can save her! It's not too late!

But he was carrying me out the door.

I tried to tell him to stop, to take me back, but if the words actually came out, even I didn't hear them. I was plunging into a pit of confusion and terror as the world spun in a dizzy, bewildering arc around me.

Someone helped me to the ground and threw a thick blanket over me to quell the flames on my clothes. The firefighter who'd carried me outside removed the mask he'd been wearing to keep the smoke out of his lungs and knelt beside me.

"Go back!" I shouted. "You can save her!"

"Is there anyone else in the house?"

"Just her, just Sienna on the steps. You have to go!"

"It's too late, sir."

"No. Please."

"I'm sorry." He sounded like he truly was.

"No!"

This couldn't be happening. It wasn't. My love for her would keep her alive long enough. It had to. I could do it. I could rescue her.

I tried to push myself to my feet, but didn't have the strength. Adrenaline must have been masking the pain earlier, but now its effect began to fade. I felt my consciousness wavering. As I collapsed backward, I couldn't tell if the firefighter was sending others into the house to try to get to Sienna or not.

All the images overlapped like dark waves pounding against the shore of my awareness—a tide of agitated currents passing across each other: the pain, the smoke, the questions, the image of a burned arm reaching toward me, a shade of unspeakable grief already edging in. I tried to think, to process things, to reason my way to a solution, but death was the only conclusion. There she was on the stairs, in my memory, in my heart, being burned alive.

You were too late. You could have gotten to her.

Desperate, I prayed that somehow God would rewind time and bring her back to me, but no miracle split the day in favor of Sienna's life and our love for each other. Instead, I was left with the simple, brutal, jagged truth of my loss.

Before I passed out, I saw the fire eat the roof and lift a triumphant fist toward the black sky, and the last thing I thought of before unconsciousness overtook me was Sienna and how I had failed to save her.

So now, here in the hospital, I did not let the nurses give me any drugs. The pain would be part of my penance, reminding me of Sienna whenever they changed my bandages.

Also, because of my job, I couldn't in good conscience allow the medical personnel to give me any drugs that might negatively affect my memory. I needed to trust it implicitly. Forgetting anything could prove fatal to the people I served.

I was blessed with the curse of an eidetic memory. It was why I had the job that I did.

And now it would make the memory of this day my constant companion. My constant enemy.

It took me a while to convince the doctor, but finally she acquiesced regarding the drugs. "Alright, Mr. Brock, I'll let the nurses start, but as soon as the pain gets too intense, let them know immediately and they'll give you something for it."

Then the nurses bent over me, fresh bandages in hand.

And they did what they were paid to do.

And as they set to work, though a tear leaked out of my right eye, I somehow managed not to cry out. With clenched teeth, I held back. I held it all in. Even when the scrubbing began.

In the aftermath of the fire, while I was recovering from one of the skin grafts, I met with a detective from DC's Metro Police Department and my supervisor at the Pentagon, Colonel Oden Clarke.

"It was arson, Mr. Brock," Detective Caruso told me gravely. A keen-eyed Black man with a stocky frame, he looked to be in his early thirties. All business. Always arrived with a notebook and pen in hand. "We found evidence of accelerants."

"But who?"

"We don't know yet."

Then Colonel Clarke, a true Scotsman through and through, who was career military and probably twice as old as Caruso, spoke up and said to me in his gruff and direct manner, "We're moving forward with the hypothesis that it's because of your job."

"No one's supposed to know about my job."

"It looks like someone found out."

Monday, April 25

SEVENTEEN MONTHS
AFTER THE FIRE

CHAPTER 2

THE PENTAGON

ARLINGTON, VIRGINIA

6:51 A.M.

Well?" the Pentagon Police officer asked me. "Do you have a number for me?"

I was at the security checkpoint near the south entrance, and she had a smile on her face. A cloudless steel-blue sky stretched wide and bright above the capital city.

"Hmm," I said. "I didn't know we were doing this today."

"Then that'll play to my advantage." She was relatively new on the job. Just four weeks and one day. Dark, captivating eyes. Confident. Slender and, at five ten, she was as tall as I was.

"Twenty-one vehicles," I said.

The Pentagon Police served as part of the Department of Defense's Pentagon Force Protection Agency, or PFPA. The patch on her uniform read *Semper Vigilans.* Translated: Always Vigilant.

It was a good motto for them.

It would've been a good motto for me too, come to think of it.

For some reason another connection came to mind: *"Vigilans" is also the root word for "vigilante." It means "to stay awake."*

And a mental reminder: *Always stay awake, Travis. Awake and aware.*

Vigilante.

Always awake.

After a quick, somewhat cursory examination, she handed back my computer bag and blue-level clearance ID badge. "Alright, give me the fifth vehicle from your car."

"Ford Focus. Virginia plates. BXL-1482."

"And what about number sixteen?"

"Toyota Prius. DC plates. BH-9405."

"You could be making these up, for all I know."

"That is true."

A slight headshake and another smile that might've bordered on being flirtatious, but I wasn't positive. Given the extent of the scars covering half of my face, I was used to people staring at me for that telling moment too long—and then abruptly averting eye contact. Shock. Dismay. Sometimes they would dry swallow, gulping back their revulsion. But not this woman. No, not her. Not from the start.

She wore an engagement ring, so maybe I was misreading things. I'd never been the best at picking up cues like that from women, and had somehow become even worse at it since losing Sienna. A lot had changed since then. I'd retreated into myself, the first four stages of grief slowly gnawing their way through me, leaving raw wounds I wasn't sure would ever heal. Actually, I was still waiting for the fifth stage—acceptance—to really settle in.

"I'll have to start making you remember the years of the different models," the officer said.

"I'm not that good."

She shook her head once again. "I was watching you, Mr. Brock. You didn't even seem to be studying the vehicles."

I thought about confessing that she was right; I hadn't been studying them as I'd passed by, but had been distracted, lost in thought about why I'd had such a slow time for my five-mile run earlier. And now, my mind was somewhere else again, dwelling on that word *vigilans* and its implications.

"Well," she said, when I failed to reply, "tomorrow I want you to park at the far end of the lot. Give yourself an actual challenge."

"Sounds like a plan."

There were five above-ground levels to the Pentagon. Even many of the people who worked here didn't know how many levels lay beneath it.

I did.

I knew those sublevels all too well.

The Department of Defense used a number of random access measures of security, or RAMs, throughout the building. Offices were often moved, many rooms simply had a door number with no indication of whose office it might be, and hallways were endlessly being remodeled. If you didn't know what you were looking for, you probably weren't going to find it. Additionally, cameras constantly monitored every corridor, elevator bay, and stairwell, and anyone who appeared to be walking around aimlessly was detained and questioned.

Another good example of a RAM was the sharp bends in the hallways beneath the building leading to the DOD archives. The twisty halls were meant to keep potential attackers from sprinting full-speed down them. Little details, but those were often the ones that made all the difference, which was something I tried to keep in mind every day as I came to work.

Back in the 1940s when the Pentagon was being constructed, the goal was for an employee to be able to walk to anywhere in the building within fifteen minutes—a daunting task, considering there were more than seventeen miles of hallways. Over the last fifteen years, I'd found that, at a brisk pace, nine minutes was the norm for me, but that usually required cutting through the inner courtyard.

However, in truth, I didn't need to get around all that much. Mostly, I spent my ten- to twelve-hour workdays in a tiny, secluded office far underground. Alone with my markers and filing boxes. Six days a week. Year in and year out.

In a job like mine, there was always more work to be done, and scheduling personal time wasn't exactly one of my specialties. The only hobbies I really had were playing chess against myself, shooting for personal bests in half-marathons, watching classic movies on TV before climbing into bed, and collecting coffee mugs from memorable places I'd visited—if that even counted as a hobby.

And, of course, searching for answers regarding the arson, which still remained unsolved. I'd spent countless hours doing so and was ready to spend countless more. Whatever it took.

I guess that wasn't really a hobby, though. More of an obsession.

Just past security, I paused.

If I walked any farther into the building, blocking technology would jam cell signals, so this was my last chance to check my messages until lunchtime at the earliest.

I glanced at my phone and saw that, just two minutes ago, a notification had popped up—an automated message informing me that another FOIA, or Freedom of Information Act, request had come in and was waiting in the queue. I already knew of eight others that'd arrived yesterday, so it looked like today was going to be another long day.

The Department of Justice received thirty-two thousand requests a year, with more than a million pages of released documents out the door as a result. Here in the Department of Defense, I certainly had my hands full, but at least I didn't need to deal with that many.

With my memory and equipped with 4,652 days of experience working with DOD secrets, I tended to work much faster than my counterparts at NSA. For them, a typical FOIA request response time was fifty days. More complex requests could take as long as five hundred days. However, no matter how fast I could work, there was always more to do, and this request caught my attention right off the bat.

It'd been routed through the Department of Homeland Security. Since most requests that came to my office were from the private sector, this was a bit unusual. Also, the date wasn't listed in the automated message. I would've anticipated today's date to appear, but none came up. Maybe a glitch or oversight of some sort. But it was flagged as a priority message, so that seemed unlikely.

My curiosity piqued, I pocketed the phone and headed toward my office.

Over the years, I'd noticed that it typically took people a while to get oriented to the way the Pentagon was laid out—that is, what the room numbers meant. For instance, 1E453A: 1 was the floor, E was the ring, 4 was the corridor, and 53A was the room. Though somewhat confusing at first, the system was logical, and after a while, navigating through the building became second nature—even though it was the largest office building in the world, employing nearly twenty-six thousand people.

From inside the Pentagon, it was obvious that the windows were tinted yellow. It wasn't something a person would necessarily notice from outside the building. It was just something you got used to when you worked inside it.

When you were in the rooms that actually had windows, that is.

As I passed through the corridor toward 1A447A, I recalled my first day on the job when I was twenty-two and fresh out of law school, when Colonel Clarke was showing me around the building.

"The A ring is in the middle," he'd said. "The E ring is on the outside, and the further out you go, the higher the rank, so the most important people work on the E ring—which has the coveted windows."

"So, by being on the E ring, the most senior officials get the best view?"

That was where his office was.

"Yes."

"Making them the most vulnerable to an attack from outside the building."

"What can I say?" he grumbled. "It's the government."

The windows were bulletproof, of course. That wasn't surprising. But the glass was also specially treated to withstand any number of other undisclosed threats.

Sometimes I thought about that on my way to my office, three floors underground, where there were no windows to peer out of. Nothing much to see in there, either. Just a bank of computer screens, pockmarked cement block walls, a dated photocopy machine, and stacks of overstuffed cardboard bankers boxes filled with files.

And a cluttered desk with four coffee mugs from different state parks where I'd been hiking with Sienna, stuffed with black, chisel-tipped permanent markers.

Yes, there were apps I could use to black out text, but I preferred markers, partly because many of the documents I had to refer to had never been digitized. Scanning them in would not only have taken up precious time, but would've also increased the likelihood that they could be hacked into, viewed by bad actors, or downloaded. Better to avoid all of that in the first place.

But I also used markers because, whenever possible, I chose to work from a printed page rather than a computer screen. I was old school that way, probably because, for some reason, with actual, physical printouts, I noticed more of what needed to be noticed.

And what needed to be redacted.

When matters of national security were at stake, when people's lives were on the line, I couldn't take the chance that I might make a mistake. Not one. Not ever.

Well, not ever again.

Only once in my career had I failed to redact some information and had it turn out badly. That was just over four years ago, on a project regarding the Active Denial System, or ADS—a nonlethal means of crowd control for use in riots. It wasn't something I liked to think about. Yet I did. Every day. It kept me vigilant.

Always vigilant.

When I came to room 1A447A, I swiped my ID to badge myself in. Leave it to the military to turn the word *badge* into a verb, one that I was used to now after all these years on the job. I was actually a civilian—or a GS as they called me—a government service employee. I'd been working for the government since graduating from college. Back then, I'd thought I would be in court most days arguing cases, so this was not the life I'd anticipated. Then again, I didn't know too many people whose lives ended up going according to plan.

Another Pentagon Police officer waited in the room beside a retinal scanner on the wall. "Good morning, Mr. Brock."

"Morning, Tony." Though he was only in his early thirties, he'd already lost most of his hair and sometimes joked with me, warning me that my time was coming, getting nearer every day. "How's the birthday girl getting along?" I asked him.

A blink. "Excuse me, sir?"

"Your daughter, Jamie." No PEDs, or personal electronic devices, were allowed on the level where I worked, so I secured my cell phone in the small locker with my name on it. There wouldn't have been any reception down there anyway, but I might've used the phone to take photographs or to record what I was doing, which was obviously strictly forbidden and might have resulted in decades in prison. "She turned five on Sunday, right?"

"How did you—?"

"You mentioned it to me."

"I did?"

"Sometime last year." I recalled the date but didn't specify it. I shrugged. "Maybe I'm wrong."

"Oh. Right. Um . . . Yeah, no, she had a princess party with her friends. That girl loves being a pretty little princess."

"Good for her."

"Tiaras everywhere. They even got me to wear one. I *seriously* hope those photos never make it onto social media. You got any kids?"

"No." I caught myself glancing at my empty ring finger. "No kids."

When I was burned, the doctors had needed to remove my wedding ring—snipping it off so they could save my finger. With Sienna gone, I'd had no reason to replace it.

So much was lost that day—not just the woman I loved, but also a deeper sense of anticipation that life could get better, would get better. With a loss like that, you can become numb. Eventually you find ways to move forward, but that doesn't necessarily mean you're moving on. The numbness follows behind you, always keeping you within reach. And it taunts you, inviting you backward into its "fatal embrace"—a term my counselor had used back when I was still trying therapy before I gave it up last year. "Look forward, not backward," she'd told me. "Focus on the healing to come, not the pain of the past."

Easier said than done.

That fatal embrace was tough to escape from. I'd say it was even comforting at times, in a dark and imprisoning sort of way. You retreat into what's familiar, even though it's a place filled with heart wrenching pain, because it's what you know. Moving forward would mean letting go—and finding a way to let the past let go of you. And most of the time, that doesn't even seem like an option.

But maybe the pain is a way of connecting us to our loss, evidence of the depth of our love for those we've lost. A cord back through time that was best held onto rather than forgotten.

Now I thought of a clutch of five-year-old girls with tiaras and birthday cake on their faces.

My four-year marriage to Sienna hadn't brought us any children, something I was at times thankful for and at other times deeply regretted. Knowing what I knew, being so intimately aware of the secrets that were trafficked in the name of national security, I understood how dangerous our world truly was and that raising a child in it would be a monumentally difficult task. How could you do it right? How could you keep them safe?

But that's not the point, is it? You can't keep everyone safe. Not all the time. Not in the end. You couldn't even keep Sienna safe. Not from the fire.

Unsettled by that reminder, I stared into the retinal scanner. It beeped, the elevator doors whisked open, and after nodding goodbye to Tony, I headed down to my office in the third level underground.

Officially, the government acknowledged that there were two underground levels—the mezzanine and the basement—but when the Pentagon was attacked on 9/11, damage reached below those two and word leaked out about a third sublevel. However, the DOD's public affairs department mostly contained those reports by linking them to discredited conspiracy theories. There were some things, after all, that the government *was* good at—and disinformation in the interest of national security was one of them.

—⚭—

THREE MILES AWAY

Ilya Vasiliev carefully secured the gag in the mouth of the unconscious man who was restrained in the chair in front of him. The Russian didn't want his captive to make any uncalled-for sounds when he came to and realized where he was and what was about to happen to him.

Ilya had done this before. He knew his job well.

"Brock has photographic memory?" he said to his partner, Sergei Sokolov.

"Let's just say it's 'uninhibited,'" Sergei replied. "He's like no one you've ever met."

For today's conversation, Sergei had chosen a mechanics garage on the outskirts of DC. The isolated location was ideal for what they had planned for the man in the chair, and the extensive array of tools here allowed for a certain amount of creativity in their work.

Sergei had been born in Moscow but raised in the States by adoptive parents. He spoke English without even a trace of the language of his motherland. Ilya's Russian accent, on the other hand, was evident in everything he said. The tattoos on Ilya's arms, back, and neck identified him with the Russian mafia, or *Bratva*, chronicling his two decades of activity with them and revealing his status and allegiances.

However, the current job was more of a freelance project.

"And Brock can give us information we need?" Ilya asked.

Sergei nodded. "If anyone can, he can."

"But you said he works in Pentagon. How to get to him?"

"We have someone on the inside."

"They can help us?"

"They already have."

Their captive groggily opened his eyes and stared around the garage, his gaze landing on the assemblage of tools spread across the workbench in front of him. He gulped perceptibly and tried to yank himself free and rise from the chair, but that only served to tighten the knots in the ropes that held him down.

Sergei gently patted the bound man's shoulder. "Welcome back, Detective Caruso. It appears that we have a few things to discuss regarding a certain fire. Shall we get started?"

CHAPTER 3

The elevator doors dinged open and I traversed the nondescript, labyrinthine hallway to the dim, cell-like enclosure where I spent the majority of my life.

In the days following the revelations of Snowden, Manning, and Assange, the Department of Defense had decided that the fewer people who knew its secrets, the fewer could be compromised, blackmailed, or turned into whistleblowers—or traitors, depending on the term you preferred. So, the powers that be had cut the number of redactors in half.

And then, two years later, halved it again.

The process continued, winnowing down the number of my peers, until I was left alone to deal with requests related to the DOD's most closely guarded top secret programs.

At the time, Colonel Clarke had told me that they needed just the right person, one who could evaluate vast amounts of data—someone with a memory sharp enough to notice underlying patterns and see the relationships between them, the things most people miss.

"We need someone with discernment." He tapped the air in front of him thoughtfully. "Someone with an eye for detail who can determine what needs to remain secret and what would be safe and acceptable to release to the public, and when—or if—that should ever occur. And I need someone I can trust. Implicitly."

As it turned out, he chose me.

My job as a redactor consisted of four steps: *Analyze* the information carefully, *confer* with others when necessary, *evaluate* if the request met one of the nine exemptions to the Freedom of Information Act that would require me to keep the information from the American people, and *decide* how much material I needed to redact. ACED.

Put simply, I would assess Freedom of Information Act requests and decide what could be declassified and what needed to remain secret. In my role as a redactor, or "censor," as they sometimes referred to me, I had operational knowledge of top secret Department of Defense programs dating back decades—programs that even many of my supervisors hadn't been briefed on.

I knew about the biological weapons tests that two of our allies continued to carry out, and that we monitored, for six years after we signed the 1972 treaty prohibiting their use and experimentation.

I could recite details about the development of the latest strategic initiatives in cyber intrusion and hypersonic weapons, the history of our research into the development of space-based weapons, the schematics of the newest generation of underwater drones, plans for radiological dispersal devices, and the names of operatives in three black ops programs that didn't officially exist.

If there was a DOD program that needed to be protected or kept secret, odds were I'd read about it—and, consequently, remembered it.

With the Department of Homeland Security request that'd just come in this morning on my mind, I settled in at my desk and logged in to my computer. Before tackling that particular request, however, I needed to at least take a look at the other ones I'd received since Saturday. Protocol.

Over the last decade, because of exponential advancements in artificial intelligence, machines had taken over more and more government analyst jobs. However, at least for the time being, AI was still unable to decide when a secret should no longer remain a secret and what information could safely be released to the public while still maintaining national security. For these tasks, a human needed to be in the loop.

Discernment is tough to teach to a machine. Besides, if a computer were programmed to do my job and it got hacked into, the military's deepest-held secrets would be compromised. So, Colonel Clarke and his team exchanged the efficiency of a machine for the judgment of a human being, as flawed and imperfect as we were. Well, as I was.

The overall classification of a document was equal to the highest classification for any part of that document, and that classification appeared in the header or footer of every page.

Everyone who worked with or had access to top secret information knew what those initials meant: *U* for unclassified, *C* for confidential, *S* for secret, and *TS* for top secret. It wasn't just that the person's job depended on it. The very lives of others did too—soldiers, operatives, informants. Breaches could cause exceptionally grave damage to national security, and it wasn't uncommon for a single page to have numerous words, phrases, or even paragraphs blacked out when I was done with it. A patchwork of the truth, meticulously edited for public consumption.

Secrets.

My specialty.

All in the service of protecting the innocent.

It'd always been obvious to me, even back in law school, that our government needed to keep secrets. Of course it did. The only way countries survive is by keeping secrets. In truth, secrets don't diminish our freedoms; they protect them for our children. Those who demanded more "transparency" often forgot that they wouldn't want their own lives to be transparent. And it was even more vital that the government kept its secrets to protect the lives of its citizens than it was that those citizens kept their secrets simply to protect their reputations.

"But why can't we all just trust each other and get along?" some people might say.

Because human beings, by nature, are not very good get-alongers. As much as we might want our world to be a Kumbaya campfire sing-along kind of place, it's not. Because, right in the middle of the hugfest, someone's going to sneak up from behind with a stiletto and slit your throat. And we are, each of us, both the dancers by the fire and the assassins with knives drawn, lurking in the shadows. Because that's the kind of world we live in. The inimitable word *agathokakological* summed it up best: consisting of both good and evil. The paradox of human nature. The enigma of our morality.

We are indeed agathokakological beings . . . with agathokakological hearts . . . living in an agathokakological world that we have shaped in both good ways and bad ones. Torqued it and warped it at times, healed it at others. We have, within us, the potential to swing to either extreme, to either end of the pendulum. And sometimes we go back and forth between them on the very same day.

In order to protect the good from the evil, secrets must be kept. Winston Churchill famously said, "In wartime, truth is so precious that she should always be attended by a bodyguard of lies." I protected the truth in my own way, apportioning it out to the public as needed. Others, like Colonel Clarke, oversaw that necessary bodyguard of lies. I left my colleagues alone to do their job while I did mine.

The first three FOIA requests were easy enough to handle—they all dealt with top secret programs that DARPA, or the Defense Advanced Research Projects Agency of the Pentagon, currently had in operation or development. I couldn't release any of that information yet. In fact, it probably wouldn't be wise to make those files public for several years, if not decades. I dealt quickly with those requests, denying them entirely for national security reasons, then sent two of the others to a Department of Justice redactor since they concerned FBI programs, and the requests should have gone over to her in the first place.

Internal routing issues.

A frustratingly common problem.

That left three FOIA requests from yesterday for me to address. Normally, I would tackle them in the order in which they arrived, but none appeared particularly pressing, and since the Homeland request had been priority-flagged, I turned my attention to it instead.

The request related to a series of weapons programs with a long history stretching back to the Manhattan Project in the 1940s, which had led to the development of the atomic bombs that ended World War II. The applicant was researching the Department of Energy's Y-12 National Security Complex in Tennessee, its evolving role in our national defense posture, and its relationship to a private defense contractor, Paraden Defense Systems. Currently, Y-12 housed the nation's supply of enriched uranium and was one of the most tightly guarded military complexes in the world.

Oddly, this request wasn't just sent to the Department of Defense, but was addressed to me personally, which, though not unprecedented, was quite unusual. I was supposed to be invisible here, doing my job in the background. As far as I knew, even many of the staff at Homeland wouldn't have known to address a request like this to me.

Even more curious now, I printed it out and directed my focus to the specifics of the request.

At first it seemed like a straightforward inquiry involving information that had recently been declassified during the seventy-fifth anniversary of the project and the opening of the Manhattan Project National Historical Park, which uniquely had sites in three locations spread across the country: Oak Ridge, Tennessee; Hanford, Washington; and Los Alamos, New Mexico. I'd been handling more and more requests regarding those sites over the last five years. But why would Homeland turn to me for information they could look up on their own?

In particular, the request's closing two paragraphs gave me pause:

Past problems are indicative of future ones, so based on the history of Y-12 and the programs it has been involved with, I would like to request all information be released regarding its current research initiatives with Paraden Defense Systems. As a concerned citizen, these partnerships are worrisome. They need more transparency. Many projects regarding this contractor deserve to be more closely monitored. Otherwise, they'll remain hidden to the detriment of democracy. Secrets and knowledge of this type must immediately be released to the public.

Let the truth be known! Answer this request today, before it's too late! Now is the time to let the American people understand the implications of what is going on. Don't let another afternoon pass by without taking action—lives depend on it!

This was all odd.

Very odd.

Since the nature of FOIA requests varied so much and could relate to thousands of different federal programs, there wasn't any specific submission form. It just wouldn't have been feasible for a single form to cover all the necessary ground. Instead, people could format their questions in whatever way seemed most applicable to the information they were asking us to release.

And there was a lot to unpack in this one.

First, the fact that it was addressed to me and had been routed internally from Homeland, rather than coming through the normal channels.

Second, the mention of a private sector organization, Paraden Defense Systems. I recalled that another FOIA request had come in during the first week of February regarding Paraden as well. It'd been submitted by a representative of a religiously based antinuke activist organization called the Pruninghooks Collective. Actually, FOIA requests from that group weren't particularly uncommon, arriving on my desk every few months. The Collective was relentless about unearthing information related to nuclear weapons development and storage. However, what Paraden had to do with Y-12 and why it would come up here again was a mystery to me.

Third, that last paragraph ended with more of a demand than anything else. It didn't close with the same respectful tone as most of the requests that came in—especially those from Homeland. And it read like a warning— perhaps even a threat. It emphasized the need for a response today, by the end of this afternoon, even.

I took a careful look at the request's routing number, and that's when, for the first time, I located the date on it.

My heart seemed to crash to a stop in my chest.

For a moment I thought I must have misread it, but there it was, in black and white.

It should've been today's date, but it wasn't. Despite the fact that the request had just arrived this morning, the date that appeared was November 19 from a year and a half ago.

This request was backdated to the night I was burned.

The night I lost Sienna.

I stared in shock at the printout. It made no sense. Why would someone at Homeland postdate a FOIA request to me, personally, with that specific date? It couldn't just be a coincidence, could it? I mean, what were the odds of something like that happening?

Could this have something to do with the fire? Could Paraden or Y-12 somehow be connected to what happened to Sienna?

I tried to move forward with my analysis of the request, but found myself flooded with memories. My hand shook slightly as I recalled my loss all over again.

The fatal embrace.

The cord of pain tugging me back toward her once more.

CHAPTER 4

With a job like mine, it was difficult to maintain a lot of friendships, and I wasn't the most outgoing person in the world, so the entire relationship had come as a surprise to me. Sienna worked as a linguist for the intelligence community—mostly translating Russian documents and intercepts for the CIA—and we tended to move in the same circles.

She first introduced herself to me at a benefit event for a children's cancer charity. Even though I was slow on the uptake that she liked me, she was persistent, and I'd finally come to my senses after she asked me out for coffee.

Sienna had a quiet, reflective nature, often reading Tolstoy's and Dostoevsky's masterpieces in their original language. She was very studious and cerebral, but not uptight or judgmental of people who weren't. She'd never been married, had few relatives, and tended to keep to herself, so when we were together, there weren't many distractions.

I'd never been with a woman who made me feel so comfortable being myself around her. No pretense. No judgment. Just acceptance. She was a doorway that let the real me through, and I realized after only three months that I wanted to do more than simply spend time with her. I wanted to spend my life with her.

When I decided to propose, I mentioned it to Colonel Clarke and then said, "You and your wife have been together for quite a while, right?"

"Thirty years. Going on thirty-one next month. Fingers crossed."

"Congratulations. What's the secret, sir?"

He considered that for a long moment before replying. "Be honest, but not always open."

"What do you mean by that?"

"Be open when it serves her, but hold back when it protects her. Kinda like your job—no lies, but not always the whole truth. Whenever someone says, 'I'm just being honest with you,' he's not. He's just being *open*—and more open than he needs to be. Never wield openness as a weapon disguised as honesty. Intimacy depends on honesty, but that doesn't include sharing every time you're tempted to look at another woman, for instance."

The advice was sincere and I promised I'd take it to heart. Then I said, "How did you propose—if you don't mind me asking?"

At that, he smiled reminiscently. "It happened at a gun range. I had the ring hidden in one of her boxes of ammo. When Katherine opened it up, there was the ring, and I got down on one knee—that's vital. It might seem outdated, but do the one-knee thing. And flowers won't hurt your case either, by the way. Anyhow, I laid my weapon on the ground, took her hand and said very simply, 'Would you be mine? Would you marry me?'"

"And she said, 'Yes'?"

"Not quite. She said, 'Let's shoot for it.'"

"You're kidding me."

"I'd swear on my mother's grave if she were dead." He held up a hand to confirm that he was being straight with me. "Katherine hit the bullseye. I was so nervous that I missed the target completely."

"What did that mean?"

"I asked her the same thing, and she said, 'It means I get to call the shots from now on. And I say yes.'"

I knew the gun range angle wouldn't work for me—I was no sharpshooter; I hadn't even held a gun since deer hunting with my uncle when I was in high school. Because of that, I wasn't sure there was a whole lot in the colonel's account that I could apply to my particular case—except the one-knee advice. And the flowers. Those I could use.

He must have realized how nervous I was, because he put a reassuring hand on my shoulder. "You'll be fine. But just be ready for anything. Remember, she might say, 'Yes,' and she might say, 'No.' Or, 'Not yet.'"

"Or, 'Let's shoot for it.'"

"Knowing her," he said, "it might be, 'Let's translate for it.'"

"Let's hope not."

When the time came, I took Sienna to Sabatino's, a high-end foodie restaurant that we'd been to once before and that she'd really seemed to enjoy.

An hour beforehand, putting the colonel's flower advice into practice, I'd gone to the restaurant, handed a dozen roses to our server, and requested that he deliver them to the woman I was with when he brought our food.

He smiled. "Absolutely."

During a college semester abroad in Moscow, Sienna had acquired a taste for caviar. We almost never had it, but tonight I wanted to splurge, to show her how much I cared about her, so I ordered golden Ossetra caviar as an appetizer, which she assured me was worth the price. For her main dish, she went with Moghrabieh and vegetable pilaf with an herb cheese crust. I chose the flaxseed-dusted North Carolina rainbow trout.

As I waited for the server to bring out the entrees and the roses, I was more nervous than I'd ever been in my life.

What would she say? Was she ready for this kind of commitment? I had no idea how I would react if she said, "No," or "Not yet." Maybe retreat into my work. A turtle going back into his pentagon-shaped shell.

And then, in one swooping, unforgettable moment, it happened.

The food came. The server handed Sienna the roses. "This is from your thoughtful date," he told her with a grin. As she accepted them, her jaw dropped and then she gave me a slightly shy but radiant smile and said, "How romantic of you."

Without a word, I went to one knee, right there in the restaurant as the patrons at the nearby tables looked our way in surprise. I took out the ring box and opened it. Then, as she raised her hands to her mouth in a silent gasp, I said the words I'd rehearsed a hundred times: "I can't imagine living without you. Would you make my life complete? Sienna Haven Turner, would you marry me?"

Or, at least that's what I wanted to say. That's what I'd planned to say. Only later did she tell me I'd actually said, "I can imagine living without you. Would I make your life complete?"

However, she overlooked the fumble and whispered, "Yes. Oh, yes."

I slipped the engagement ring onto her finger, the people at the neighboring tables applauded, I stood, took her in my arms, and we kissed beside the elegantly adorned table, the wine flutes, and the delicate, aromatic roses.

Because of our jobs, we couldn't really discuss work at home, so we made the most of our mutual interests and our free time together instead—running in the mornings before work, hiking to waterfalls in West Virginia on the weekends, and watching old Alfred Hitchcock movies and *Twilight Zone* episodes together while sampling select lagers from local microbreweries.

She loved traveling, and since she specialized in Cyrillic languages, she invited me to go with her a couple of times on business trips to Saint Petersburg. But with my job, traveling to Russia wasn't really an option, even if I was only tagging along with someone who'd been vetted as much as I had. If Russia's intelligence services found out who I was, they might come after me to try to recruit me. And I couldn't afford even the slightest hint of a breach of trust.

Sienna. My love. My life.

Then, seventeen months ago, the fire stole her from me. The scaffolding of my dreams collapsed in on me. Work became everything. The shell won.

Now she was gone, and the date on this FOIA request regarding Y-12's top secret mandates matched the night of the fire.

Whatever the significance of the date and the request's content, I needed some answers. If this had anything at all to do with Sienna, it would be my first clue in a year and a half regarding who might've been behind the fire—a person I'd vowed to find and vowed to bring to justice.

Vigilans.

Vigilante.

Same root word.

Always awake. Always ready to act.

Hoping that uncovering more about Y-12 would help, I studied the scope and parameters of its mission during the month of the fire, and then worked my way forward, pulling up the information on its current research, keeping a close eye out for any ways it might relate to Paraden Defense Systems, all while the request's afternoon deadline, promising dire consequences, hung over my head.

CHAPTER 5

There's a call for you on your private line, sir."

"Thank you, Allison. I'll take it in my office."

Senator Cliff Richardson, the newly elected Democrat from California, strode through the reception area toward his office, slipped inside, and closed the door behind him.

Locked it.

Only a few people had his private number. Even fewer would've felt comfortable using it.

He took a seat at his mahogany Parnian desk—one that'd cost him a small fortune. He valued quality, but a desk this expensive wasn't the sort of thing he would've put taxpayers on the hook for. Instead, he'd purchased it himself with some of the money he'd gotten when he sold his tech company during his election campaign, a decision he'd made in order to avoid any future conflicts of interest or the appearance of malfeasance.

Fifty-two years old. A tech millionaire turned politician and ready to make a real difference in the world. A progressive. An idealist. A fighter.

A true believer in all that America could be.

He picked up the receiver and tapped the blinking button on the phone's base. "This is Senator Richardson."

"Senator, it's Joshua. I just got word. It looks like the vote should happen at your subcommittee meeting this afternoon."

"And your gut? What's it telling you?"

"I'm optimistic. It took a little convincing, but I think Presnell will tilt in your favor."

Cliff didn't ask what kind of techniques Joshua had resorted to while doing the convincing. From his work on the Senate Armed Services Committee, Cliff knew an acronym that was common in the business. Intelligence and law enforcement agencies used it as a way to remember the top five ways to induce a person to work with you or become an asset or confidential informant: C.R.I.M.E.

C—Compromise. Find out someone's secrets and use them as leverage. Will his affair ruin his career or cause him to lose custody of his kids? Then remind him of that fact when you ask for his help.

R—Revenge. Discover who has hurt him and appeal to the base desire for vengeance. Promise that, with your resources, you'll be able to accomplish more in the line of revenge than he ever could on his own.

I—Ideology. Uncover someone who wants to work for the United States and give him the opportunity. What does he believe in? His religious or political leanings can be invaluable for using him to accomplish something that he considers to be for the greater good.

M—Money. Give him the desires of his heart. Yes, sometimes cash, but not always. Sometimes it was drugs. Sometimes prostitutes. Find out what he covets most and you'll find out where he's the most vulnerable.

E—Ego. Everyone likes it when their ego is stroked. So, when you want something from someone, compliment him, show interest in what he does, flirt with him. Take things as far as necessary to get what you need.

Often, a combination of approaches was necessary, so Cliff wouldn't have been surprised if Joshua had turned to more than one of them in his interactions with Senator Presnell.

"And the conference in Oak Ridge?" Cliff asked him.

"I'll be there. Might not be until the morning, though. I have a couple of things to take care of before I can leave for Tennessee. What time does Dr. Yong's speech begin?"

"It kicks things off at ten o'clock. I'll see if I can get some podium time. Otherwise we'll go with a press conference in the afternoon to make the announcement."

"When do you get there?"

"I fly down tonight."

"Alright." Joshua's tone shifted; it sounded like he was ready to wrap up the conversation. "We'll talk more then, at the hotel."

After ending the call, Cliff sighed and rubbed his forehead. Even though he wasn't a particularly religious man, he offered up a prayer that things would work out.

He could picture Joshua—just shy of six feet tall. Caucasian. Medium build. Brown hair. Brown eyes. No visible tattoos or distinguishing marks. He was fit, yes, but he could disappear quickly and easily into a crowd. The man was a ghost.

Or a monster, depending on how you looked at things.

And now, here they were, joined at the hip.

On his desk beside his laptop, Cliff kept a picture of his brother, Keith, who'd been a Marine captain when he was killed in Afghanistan because of an intelligence failure—compromised intel that hadn't been properly vetted. Now, Cliff picked up the picture and looked at it, reminding himself of why he was doing what he was. Why he was working with someone like Joshua at all.

Because of a hero.

Because of his brother.

Cliff had never had any aspirations of serving in the military himself, but after Keith's death, he'd wanted to do something meaningful for his country like his little brother had. Instead of just procuring more wealth for himself, he'd figured he could honor Keith's sacrifice by making one of his own.

So he'd made a decision. He'd sold his Silicon Valley business to, as it turned out, one of the richest women in the world—a real estate investor and tech billionaire named Janice Daniels—and moved into politics, hoping that there, he might be able to make a lasting difference in people's lives.

His experience in the tech industry had made it clear to him that there were technological vulnerabilities in the US infrastructure, particularly when it came to supply chain management.

As a result, he was deeply worried about America's nuclear energy sector being compromised by a hostile group—either a nation state or a private entity. Infiltrating the supply chain could bypass other security measures and allow unfriendly actors access to top secret programs. He'd chosen to dedicate his career to making sure that didn't happen.

After getting elected, he'd tried sharing Department of Energy studies with his associates and offered numerous policy recommendations to the Subcommittee on Energy, all to no avail. Finally, he realized he needed to do something drastic to wake people up. That's what led to procuring the microchips, which had been shipped to Tennessee from India three months ago. Once he revealed their presence, it would get the attention of the sub-committee. It would get the attention of everyone.

The decision in regard to the chips was entirely for his country, to address security concerns. Future generations would recognize that, even if his peers and coworkers failed to see the big picture now.

When you're in a position of authority, you sometimes have to make the tough choices. As he set Keith's picture down, Cliff reminded himself of that, of his campaign promises regarding national security, and of his calling to serve the American people, to place them first—as his brother had—no matter what the personal consequences of that decision might be.

Yes, sometimes pursuing a higher ideal required sacrifice.

And sometimes it required working with someone like Joshua.

A man capable of the unthinkable.

A monster in business attire who was always ready with a quick disarming smile.

CHAPTER 6

I found nothing to indicate that Y-12 was working with or had ever worked with Paraden as the FOIA request indicated. Also, there didn't seem to be any programs or initiatives at Y-12 that correlated to the date of the fire.

All I could locate in the Y-12 files was a deeply buried reference to Project Symphony, a top secret research program that DARPA was involved in regarding air gap hacking, a technique developed by the Israelis which allowed operatives to hack into computers that weren't online.

I'd studied Project Symphony briefly last year in reference to another FOIA request, but it was such a highly guarded initiative that I'd never even had a FOIA request regarding it. The secret had been well-kept from the public. The bodyguard of lies doing its job.

When a computer is "air gapped," it isn't connected to other computers by any sort of hardware or wireless connection. It's completely offline and isolated. If that's the case, how can someone hack into it? Eight years ago, Israel's elite Defense Force Unit 8200 began tackling this seemingly unsolvable problem by investigating ways to hack in through the heat waves of computers, through sound waves if the computer was playing music, even by using magnets in ways that I still couldn't wrap my mind around, even after reading the technical papers delineating the process.

Apparently, Paraden had bid on the Project Symphony contract. The files I'd been able to pull up weren't complete, so I couldn't tell if Paraden had provided any components for it. I'd need to check the archives down the hall to know for sure.

As far as I knew, Y-12 wasn't involved in any type of research relating to Project Symphony, unless perhaps the site was a place to test the prototypes that DARPA had come up with. If so, that might explain the mention of it in the Y-12 files.

But what about the possible connection to the date of the fire? Who might be behind all of this?

I turned my attention to the Paraden Defense Systems angle and the antinuke organization that had mentioned them in a FOIA request earlier this year—the Pruninghooks Collective.

I wondered if Paraden had anything to do with Y-12's history with anti-nuke groups—specifically, the incident with the nun at the Highly Enriched Uranium Materials Facility, or the HEUMF, back in 2012. The facility had been constructed after 9/11, and was serviceable, but not nearly as secure as it needed to be. In fact, Y-12's security had been breached at least three times in the last fifteen years. The most famous instance occurred when Sister Megan Rice, who was eighty-two at the time, and two of her male co-activists—a handyman and a Catholic pacifist—made it past four fences to the HEUMF and started sledgehammering the corner of the building.

They splashed human blood on the outer wall to symbolize "the death of the innocents," spray-painted "WORK FOR PEACE NOT WAR," "THE FRUIT OF JUSTICE IS PEACE," and "WOE TO the EMPIRE of BLOOD," then laid out roses and Bibles and sang hymns while they waited to be arrested—which didn't happen for nearly half an hour.

The three protestors were part of an activist group known as the Plowshares Movement, a sister organization to the Pruninghooks Collective—a more radical arm of the antinuke movement.

Congressional inquiries followed that site intrusion and, to put it mildly, there were a few personnel changes after the hearings. To avoid similar incidents in the future, the Department of Energy's National Nuclear Security Administration was constructing a 6.5-billion-dollar complex at the site of the Y-12 Security Complex in Oak Ridge—the costliest building project in Tennessee's history. When completed, the Uranium Processing Facility would be one of the most secure buildings in the world. It needed to be, since it was the place where our enriched uranium would be stored and where Cold War nuclear weapons would be dismantled so that the enriched uranium could be recovered.

But Paraden wasn't involved in the site's construction. Mostly, they designed detonators and explosive devices for the Army.

Frustrated, I studied the request again, analyzing the sentences themselves, taking a deep dive into the wording to see if there was anything I was missing.

At first I found nothing, but then the beginning words of the sentences in the last two paragraphs caught my attention: *Past . . . As . . . They . . . Many . . . Otherwise . . . Secrets . . . Let . . . Answer . . . Now . . . Don't . . .*

Huh.

Interesting.

The first letters of each sentence spelled PATMOS LAND. I checked the rest of the request for other acrostics, but finding none, I tried to determine the significance of this one.

Patmos was a Greek island in the Aegean Sea, probably best-known for being the place where John the Apostle was banished and had his visions of heaven and the end of the world that he recorded in the Book of Revelation.

What would that island have to do with Y-12?

Is this some kind of apocalyptic threat? That the end of days is starting because of the work at Y-12?

That was certainly reading too much into it.

Still—why that acrostic? And why was the request backdated? And what did any of this have to do with me or the fire?

A hive of questions. Poke it and who knew what might come out.

I was going to poke it.

As I thought of secrets held and hidden agendas, for an unsettling moment I wondered if whoever sent this might've found out about my own secret that I'd been carrying around since the night of the fire.

Because of what I was privy to, I underwent monthly lie detector tests to assure I hadn't been turned or compromised in any way. My finances were regularly inspected to make sure I hadn't been bribed. My personal correspondence, including all texts and email, was closely monitored. I wasn't on social media—that would have created more problems than it was worth. The DOD was skilled at getting people to give up their secrets and they strove to confirm that I wasn't keeping any from them.

And yet, I did.

I kept one.

My private project would not have pleased Colonel Clarke, but I couldn't help but pursue it. Sienna, the woman I'd fallen in love with beneath the blossoming cherry trees in DC, was gone. The woman who'd made me laugh at myself while she tried to teach me words in each of the five languages she spoke and I struggled to even say, "Hello," had been torn away from me.

Despite me not being a life-of-the-party sort of guy, she'd welcomed me into her heart. I'd loved her while she was with me, yes, of course, but only after she was gone did I realize that her love and commitment to me had been the truest, purest part of my life.

Accelerants were used. Someone had started that fire. It wasn't an accident.

For nearly a year and a half, I'd known that I couldn't move on, not until her killer was identified and the scales of justice were balanced once again. Her life was worth it. Her death demanded it.

Detective Caruso's investigation hadn't led to any results. No suspects. No trail. One day last year I finally had to recognize that, for all practical purposes, it was going to be up to me to find the answers on my own.

And so, I'd made room in my schedule whenever I could to search for the identity of the arsonist. I'd spent hundreds of nights online poring over obscure articles after work, scouring the Internet for any connection with other arsons or with people who might have wanted me dead, but found nothing solid.

Until perhaps now, here, today.

Over the years, I'd seen justice succeed and I'd seen it fail. The system wasn't perfect, and often those who fell through the cracks were the ones who could least afford to or had the most to lose.

That's what happened with my mom.

Dad was a mean drunk with a violent streak, and I was too small to know what to do about it.

One time when I was nine, he grabbed Mom by the hair and threw her across the kitchen headfirst and into the refrigerator so viciously that it gave her a concussion. A week later when he was drunk, he shoved her toward the countertop, and she snatched up a knife and stared him down. I watched from the doorway, hoping that despite all she'd taught me about avoiding violence, she would use it.

She might've cut him when he came at her, but she held back. He grabbed her, grinned with a malevolence I'd never seen before—even from him—and I knew something terrible was about to happen. So, as scared as I was, I ran toward him and tried to push him away from her. He backhanded me brutally across the face, sending me crashing to the floor. Then, he wrenched the knife from my mom and threw it aside, clattering it across the linoleum, barely missing my leg. Instead of letting her go, he twisted her arm, torquing it so severely that it fractured in two places and never healed properly, even with three surgeries.

That was the time she actually went to the police—maybe because he'd struck me that day too. She trusted the system, that the authorities would put him away and protect her—and me—but found instead that his lawyer got him free on bail. He skipped out, disappeared, and neither Mom nor I ever saw him again. Nearly thirty years of silence. For her, thirty years of fearing he might one day return.

What if she'd protected herself? Taken justice into her own hands? Killed him in self-defense? I didn't know. But at least he would be gone and she wouldn't still be living in fear that he might show up and finish what he'd started.

Maybe that was why I studied law in the first place, to seek punishment for those who deserved it and justice for the rest of us. Possibly, although that might've been reading too much into it all.

Regardless, with my law school training I knew plenty about how well-meaning but flawed our justice system was.

I wasn't ready to let my wife's murderer slip through the cracks. I wasn't certain I trusted the system, but I did trust myself.

I would find my answers and I would do what was necessary to see justice meted out. Some might call it vengeance; I called it a necessity. And I was ready to see things through to the end, whatever that might require of me.

That's what I thought of now as I tried to discern the meaning of the unusual FOIA request before me and what significance the acrostic PATMOS LAND might hold—and why the request said that lives depended on taking action today.

Turning from Y-12, I concentrated on the Paraden angle and searched for any connection between their defense contract work and the island of Patmos. Maybe, just maybe, there was a clue lurking in those files, and—if the date on the request was any indication—there was.

CHAPTER 7

Adira Halprin just needed to get the suitcase through security. Once she was past the checkpoint, her assignment would be complete.

Well, actually, once she had the gun ready.

Then her job would be done.

She touched up her makeup in the SUV's flip-down mirror. In her line of work, she'd learned long ago that when you look like a professional, people treat you like a professional. That was as true of going through airport security as it was of presenting quarterly earnings reports in corporate boardrooms.

The look she was going for today was that of a young professional on her way to a trade show. Her hair—blonde, short-cropped. A pixie cut. Her blue shirt accentuated her azure eyes. The driver's license she was using today put her at thirty-one, three years younger than her actual age.

Knowing that TSA agents were just as human as anyone else reassured her. Of course they weren't impartial or objective. No one is. They could be impressed. Distracted. Intimidated. Manipulated. And yes, seduced. From the reports she'd read, others from her team had used all of those tactics. When there was something as important as their work on the line, it would have been foolish not to take into account human nature and all the ways of leveraging it to your advantage.

As she was exiting her vehicle, a message came through on her phone, asking her status.

She texted back, **I'm in the parking garage now**.

Then, being careful to avoid being picked up on the garage's southeast corner CCTV camera, she strode toward the airport entrance.

Sneaking a weapon past airport security checkpoints wasn't nearly as difficult as most people imagined it might be.

Adira knew this from personal experience.

Hiking boots worked well. Some already came with a steel shank, and a blade could be placed beneath it easily enough to get it through, or a retractable curved blade could be hidden inside the heel. Russian spies in the seventies and eighties often used that tactic. High-heeled shoes could easily hide a ceramic puncture blade.

The edges of credit cards—especially the newer metal ones with a chip—could be sharpened, turning them into blades. Affixed to the end of a pen, they could create a makeshift knife that could do some real damage. TSA agents never checked the edges of the credit cards in passengers' wallets. It wasn't even on their radar screens.

Electronics were always a possibility. It was amazing what you could do with the inner workings of a laptop computer, and with a little ingenuity, explosive devices could be matched to a typical laptop's hardware. Technically, TSA agents were allowed to ask you to power up any of your electronic devices to make sure they worked, but they almost never did. With the number of devices people carried these days and the speed at which the agents needed to get each person through the checkpoints, it just wasn't feasible.

In Adira's line of work, when you could identify a safety measure that wasn't implemented because of time or money constraints, you had yourself a vulnerability that you could use to accomplish your mission.

Belts worked well for concealing paperclips, bobby pins, or safety pins for picking locks. She always carried several bobby pins—today she had one on the front of her belt, another in the back, just in case.

Hair dryers could be modified to fire cartridges when they were powered on. That was an alteration she'd come up with last year. She hadn't loaded the cylinder, however. She'd simply constructed the prototype to prove that it could be done.

The curling iron she had with her today was also one of her designs. By twisting the metal tube, a retractable blade either protruded from the tip or disappeared back into the casing. All she had to do was get it through security.

That, and the printer in her carry-on bag.

Last night she'd checked in online and downloaded her boarding pass to her phone. She didn't have any suitcases to check, just her carry-on bag and purse. She preferred it this way—fewer people to interact with at the airport. Fewer factors in play. Fewer things that might go wrong.

For the most part, TSA agents looked for what they'd seen before. There were weekly updates sent out with lists of objects that'd been confiscated at airports nationwide, but obviously the items that'd gotten through didn't make the list, so no agents knew about those, what they were, or who'd managed to sneak them through.

The Knoxville airport capitalized on the idea of being the gateway to the Smokies. A cascading waterfall in the middle of the main lobby greeted people as they approached the security checkpoint. The susurrant sound of flowing water and the gentle scent of spring filled the concourse.

Over the years, Adira had found that getting prohibited items through security at regional airports was easier than at major or international ones. It simply came down to experience—since there were fewer people passing through the checkpoints, there were fewer threats to assess and fewer questionable items to evaluate.

Now, bypassing the airline check-in counter, she went directly to the TSA checkpoint. There were nearly three dozen people in front of her, but with two security lines open, she guessed that her wait would be ten minutes or so. Fifteen max.

Yeah, that would work.

Even though TSA agents dressed like cops, they didn't carry weapons or handcuffs and they weren't authorized to arrest anyone. However, they could—and would—call in law enforcement whenever they deemed it necessary. Even at an airport this size, Adira knew that someone from the sheriff's department would be on-site at all times.

She reminded herself to act naturally. If you're in a situation where people would normally be nervous, show how nervous you are. If you're in a place where you should have nothing to worry about or nothing to hide, don't fidget, don't repeatedly check the time or anxiously scan the area.

Fit in.

Never call attention to yourself. Avoid making a fashion statement or trying to stand out. Don't express yourself. Express what those around you are expressing. That's how you vanish. That's how you avoid getting caught.

She came to the bored-looking TSA agent at the initial checkpoint and handed over her driver's license and boarding pass. The woman, whose name tag simply read *Noland*, glanced momentarily at the license, then at Adira's face, then back to the license.

Though she'd been through this type of situation dozens of times before, Adira did what she always did and reminded herself to remain calm: *Breathe. Don't appear too rushed, too nervous. You're just here to board your flight to Atlanta. That's all. Nothing special.*

Noland scanned the license, then, disinterestedly, scribbled her initials on the boarding pass. She handed it, along with the license, back to Adira, then gazed past her to the people in line behind her. "Next."

As the line shuffled forward, Adira moved closer to the X-ray machine and the body scanner.

With recent advances in 3D printer technology, it wasn't necessary anymore to sneak a gun past airport security.

You could simply print one after you were through.

It depended on the type of weapon you wanted, of course, and the intricacy of what you were printing, but you didn't need a very elaborate design to create a cylindrical device that could be held in one hand and fire a lethal projectile. There were plenty of free designs online, but she'd come up with her own, one that took into consideration the limited time she had to get the weapon printed.

In an airport X-ray machine, books, because of their size and density, looked surprisingly like plastic explosives. There was no need to raise any red flags or draw unnecessary attention to what her bags might actually contain, so apart from the occasional paperback romance novel in her purse, Adira avoided bringing books on her trips.

The line edged forward again, bringing her to the X-ray machine bins. She kicked off her shoes, then set them, along with her purse, into a bin on the conveyor belt. She placed her carry-on bag behind it and waited to pass through the full-body scanner.

The TSA agent standing just beyond the scanner signaled for her to step forward, and Adira entered the unit, held her hands above her head, and waited the obligatory three seconds while the scanner swept in a semicircle in front of her.

The agent motioned for her to exit, then held up his hand as she left the machine, indicating that she wait until he could verify the scan. "Just a moment. Alright . . . and . . . you're clear."

"Thank you."

Almost there.

Just retrieve the items and print the gun.

However, as she walked to the conveyor belt to collect her things, the agent on the other side of the belt paused it while her carry-on bag was still under the X-ray machine. He appeared to be studying his screen carefully.

Adira's heart began to flutter in her chest.

Be calm. Be patient. It'll be fine.

The man sent her bag onto an alternate track on his side of the X-ray housing, then hoisted it up. "This yours, ma'am?"

"Yes."

"I'm going to need to take a look inside. You can gather your other items first."

She did, then joined him at a nearby counter, where he carefully set the bag down and snapped on a pair of nitrile examination gloves.

"Are there any sharp objects in here that could harm me in any way? Needles? Anything of that nature?"

"No."

He unzipped the suitcase, set aside the curling iron and plastic toy dinosaur, and lifted out the miniature 3D printer. "What is this?"

"It's a printer. A prototype. I'm a rep. It's for a trade show."

She directed his attention to some business cards and brochures in the bag, ones she'd had printed up just in case.

The TSA agent rotated the printer in his hands. "Looks like a juicer."

She smiled lightly. "I get that a lot. But it's actually for 3D printing."

"Huh." He studied it curiously. "You hear about these things. Never seen one before."

"I know, it's fascinating, right?"

He grunted admiringly. "You never can tell what they're gonna come up with next."

"No. You can't."

At last, he nodded, put the printer back in her suitcase along with the toy and the curling iron, and zipped it shut. "You have a good day, ma'am."

"You too."

She accepted the bag from him, walked to a nearby chair, and put on her shoes.

Go.

Slow and easy.

She toted her bag to the family bathroom where she could have some privacy and where there wouldn't be any security cameras. Once inside, she opened the suitcase, turned the printer on, put the plastic dinosaur in it, programmed it, padded her wig and change of clothes around it to quiet the noise, and then sent the message to her contact: **I'm in. I'm prepping it now.**

It took a moment, but then a reply came through: **11 am tomorrow. Be aware.** The significance of the time didn't mean anything to her, but she figured that whatever the message meant, more information would be forthcoming.

Leaving the restroom, she circumspectly rolled the suitcase behind her to a deserted corner of the seating area near her gate.

By the time her flight began to board, the gun would be ready to use.

CHAPTER 8

I found nothing regarding the defense contractor and the island of Patmos, so I questioned my initial assumption that the PATMOS LAND acrostic referred to the Greek island and searched for other things it might stand for. Could the formation of the words be coincidental? Random letters that just happened to appear in that order? Unlikely. I was no statistician, but that seemed like a veritable impossibility.

I decided to cast my net further out, and when I did, it didn't take long before I came across another, more promising possibility: an equity firm operating here in the United States called Patmos Financial Consortium.

By following up on public records, I learned that the group had real estate holdings all across the country. Recently, they'd applied for permits on some remote tracts of land in North Dakota and Texas—which made me think of crude oil, but the paperwork didn't point in that direction. The relationship of the contents of the request to the date of the fire remained murky, however, as I wasn't able to identify any direct connection between the equity firm and the defense contractor.

The FOIA request urged action today, indicating that lives were at risk. Though I wasn't sure exactly why, I took that seriously and felt a tightening sense of pressure to make some progress.

Pushing back from my desk, I stood and began to pace—although there wasn't much room in my cramped office to do so.

As far as I knew, neither Sienna nor I had ever had any investments tied to this Patmos Financial Consortium. If this request was related to the fire, what was I missing here?

Don't assume. Analyze. Investigate. Evaluate.

I was inferring that the Patmos reference was significant, but what did I actually know here?

The request specifically mentioned Y-12 and Paraden.

You studied Y-12. Look up any past FOIA requests that include Paraden and you might find the answers you're looking for.

Because of the Y-12 connection, I realized that I might have to consult with someone at the Department of Energy's National Nuclear Security Administration, but because of the repeated security failures, the DOD had recently taken over security at the site. Additionally, the Nuclear Regulatory Commission and the Department of Homeland Security also played a role in developing cybersecurity protocols there.

A tangled mess of oversight.

Nothing surprising there. All part and parcel of government work.

In order to verify the dates and details regarding Paraden, I needed to look at some printed files that'd never been digitized, so I grabbed a copy of the index, left my office, and followed the twisting hallway to the Department of Defense's archives.

Inside the vast, capacious room the shelves seemed to stretch on forever, packed from floor to ceiling with endless rows of bankers boxes filled with nearly two hundred and fifty years of government secrets.

The place reminded me of the massive warehouse at the end of *Raiders of the Lost Ark* when they store the Ark with all of those other crates in that nameless government facility. In addition to DOD files, there were records down here from the Department of Energy and many of the federal agencies that made up Homeland before they were all combined after 9/11.

The overstuffed boxes were brimming with hundreds of millions of pages, including collections of personal correspondence of presidents, congressmen, and Supreme Court justices—vast troves of information that museums, historical sites, and presidential libraries didn't have the authorization to display. There were blueprints to covert military programs and installations, specs for nuclear bombs and any number of Department of Defense vehicles and planes—ones that had been developed and ones that'd never been built. Some of the boxes contained personnel files and military service records from soldiers dating back to the Revolutionary War.

Much of the material would probably have been safe to release, but in many cases, the secrets were so well buried beneath the years and inhumed by reams of bureaucratic red tape that people in the public sector didn't even know to ask about them.

The files needed to be stored somewhere, so they were split between here and Fort Meade, where the National Security Agency, or NSA—known lightheartedly by those who worked there as "No Such Agency"—had its own archives. It made sense to keep two and a half centuries' worth of secrets under two of the nation's most impregnable buildings.

The date. The arson. Sienna's death.

The answers to it all might very well lie right here, on the shelves surrounding me.

Consulting the index, I walked down the P aisle and set to work pulling up everything I could on past FOIA requests mentioning Paraden Defense Systems.

CHAPTER 9

"We recognize the gentleman from California," the chairperson of the Subcommittee on Energy announced. Senator Augustina Harris, a Georgia Republican, was a brisk and bristling woman who, it seemed to Cliff Richardson, hadn't taken kindly to the implications of what he was saying about the inaction of the committee she chaired.

Well, so be it, he thought. At least today he had the chance to address those present and maybe get a vote that would bolster the security of the national infrastructure and make the work he'd done on the project from India moot.

The other seventeen men and women seated in the conference room, including Senator Presnell, whom Joshua had indicated would vote in Cliff's favor, turned their attention to him as he rose and cleared his throat slightly.

After thanking Senator Harris for the floor, he addressed the room. "Distinguished committee members, I want to reiterate that the time to act regarding cybersecurity at our Department of Energy sites is long overdue. We have the research before us. We have the documentation necessary to make our decision here, now, today. Our country is at imminent risk of having our infrastructure hacked into and compromised and, as I'm sure you're aware, that could mean disabling energy grids, interrupting food and medicine deliveries. Emergency services disrupted. Blackouts affecting millions of people. Looting. Riots. Insurrection. We cannot forestall action."

Maybe that was too much, too melodramatic, but he wanted to make the stakes clear right off the bat. This mattered. More than anything he'd ever given his life to before, this work could actually make a lasting difference.

The room was dominated by the behemoth slab of a table that everyone was seated around, and now he plopped the latest report onto it. "Here we have yet another study. More findings. More warnings. More recommendations. But I'm afraid that unless we show some backbone today, this report will have the same effect as the ones that came before it—last year, and the year before, and the year before that."

"And what effect is that?" Senator Harris asked icily. She had her touch-of-gray hair pulled back into a severe bun that could not possibly have been comfortable to wear. She scratched her right temple with the tip of a pristinely sharpened pencil.

"To provide more fodder for landfills and recycling bins," Cliff said bluntly. "If I may be frank, no one listens to reports anymore. We are suffering from the old problem of paralysis by analysis. Look at history—when do gun laws get passed? Only after a mass shooting. When did the Patriot Act get passed? Only after 9/11. The day to make a decision has arrived. We don't need another study. We don't need more research or more documentation of the problem. We need *implementation*. Action. The American people deserve our best and . . ." He let his voice trail off as he gazed directly at the chairwoman. "You have not been giving it to them."

"I find that comment personally offensive since I'm the one who makes the call on—"

"Good. Then you're finally listening to me. I finally have your attention."

"Oh, you have it, Senator." She held the pencil upright but deathly still against the table. "I am listening quite intently to what you're saying."

"Disasters result in action, but this matter must be addressed before a disaster occurs. The consequences of this are so grave that 9/11 would pale in comparison."

"You're implying we need a tragedy in order to make progress? That's a troubling assertion."

"Yes. And yet, sadly, it's all too often the case."

She held up her hands, palms to the ceiling. "And your point with all of this is . . . ?"

"We are vulnerable to a cyberattack on our infrastructure, and one of the most pressing concerns involves potential risks to the nuclear Triad and to our nuclear power plants. Cyber intrusion has happened at least twenty-three times since 2000 at nuclear facilities worldwide—and those are just the publicly acknowledged incidents. It's a near certainty that there were additional incidents that haven't been reported—and current intrusions we aren't even aware of."

Senator Presnell spoke up from the other side of the table. "Do you have any examples?"

Cliff shifted his attention to him.

A freshman Republican senator from Wisconsin, Bill Presnell had been a nationally ranked flatwater canoeist before getting elected, and still raced throughout the Midwest when he had the chance. A stellar athlete and a scholar too: a University of Wisconsin, Madison, *summa cum laude* grad. Joshua had filled Cliff in about Presnell. It was all in his report.

"In 2011," Cliff said in reply to Presnell's question, "the Oak Ridge National Laboratory in Tennessee was the victim of a spear-phishing campaign. In 2014, the Korea Hydro and Nuclear Plant in South Korea was hacked into, most likely by North Korea. In 2016, Germany's Gundremmingen Nuclear Power Plant and Japan's Toyama Hydrogen Isotope Research Center were both compromised. In 2021—"

"Okay, okay," Harris said curtly. "We understand. You've done your homework."

Agitated by her tone, but more motivated than ever to make some progress, Cliff went on. "We must take responsibility now and not kick the can down the road for another group of Congress members to deal with. Because you know what? I have a name for people who do that."

"And what is that?" Presnell said half-jokingly. "Politicians?"

A light touch of laughter rippled around the room.

"No," Cliff said. "Cowards."

Any lingering laughter ceased.

You shouldn't have gone there, Cliff. Just stick to the issue at hand.

"I'm here today for one reason and one reason only," he said, "to get us to improve the security of our nuclear energy plants, which serve as a vital aspect of our infrastructure, providing us with nearly twenty percent of the nation's energy needs."

"Alright," Harris said. She went back to fiddling with her pencil, rolling it somewhat aggressively between her fingers. "What exactly are you proposing?"

Cliff didn't have a slide presentation, but he paced toward the video screen on the wall where he had a better view of the room. "Supply Chain Risk Management, or SCRM, is just as much a part of national security as antivirus protection at our nuclear reactor sites."

"Talk us through that—SCRM?"

"As the National Counterintelligence and Security Center puts it, 'Supply Chain Risk Management is the process of identifying, assessing, and mitigating the risks to the integrity, trustworthiness, and authenticity of products and services within the supply chain.' Basically, the supply chain is the most vulnerable point in the delivery system of getting parts to our nuclear reactors. We need to assure that our microprocessors are secure during their route from the processing plant to the final destination—all throughout production and shipping, where quality can be compromised, counterfeit or fraudulent products can be introduced, and malicious software can be inserted. And there's always the risk of stolen data and reverse engineering. All the steps in the supply chain, from start to finish, need to be secured."

Harris stabbed the printed report with the pencil that she just couldn't seem to leave alone. "You mean when we outsource electronics? Is that where you're going with this?"

"Yes. Most of the time the lowest bid is accepted for new projects, and the bids are low for a reason. The security clearance and background checks of those producing microelectronics are rarely taken into consideration, and the production of the components often happens in countries whose interests are not aligned with those of the United States."

"China, for instance?" Presnell inquired.

"Yes."

"That's a big 'for instance,'" someone at the far end of the table mumbled.

"That's right," Cliff replied. "It is." Maybe he *was* getting somewhere with this group. "Malware can be introduced into and embedded in systems before they're ever installed at our facilities. The supply chains of all critical systems should be regulated and, in some cases, classified. We're dealing with asymmetrical threats that are unabashedly seeking the exfiltration and manipulation of critical data."

As Cliff gauged the room, the air conditioner kicked in, louder and more noticeable to him in the silence than it would normally have been.

It looked like he had everyone's attention. Maybe he'd been worried about this for no reason. He was making progress. This might be all that was necessary, here, today. Here, with the vote.

Richard Atkins, a New York Democrat who'd been serving in the Senate longer than anyone else in the room, leaned forward attentively. "What about firewalls?"

A burst of cool air blasted down from the overhead vent onto Cliff's face, causing him to inadvertently shiver.

"Useless against this type of threat," Cliff explained. "If you already have the malware in place, you don't need to hack your way in or take down a firewall. It happens from the inside. And with the projected development of MRAM embedded memory and more nanowire transistors, we're looking at even more potential vulnerabilities on the horizon."

"But," Atkins countered with a hand flagged in the air, "how do we identify counterfeit microelectronic processors or compromised components?"

"There are any number of tests we can conduct—from laser scanning and acoustic scanning microscopy to mass spectrometry to visual and X-ray fluorescence inspection—but they all take time and money, neither of which have been adequately allocated for this purpose."

Cliff assessed things again. Yes, he'd gotten a bit technical there, maybe too technical, but he trusted that he was addressing the questions appropriately, that he hadn't lost anyone. Yes. Things were going to tilt his way.

Harris spoke up. "And to that end, you're proposing that we initiate . . ." She consulted the paperwork in front of her. "A ninety-four million dollar increase in the budget? And where will this money come from? Let me guess: raising taxes."

"If we increase taxes on the super-rich—those who make more than a hundred million dollars a year—by just a fraction of a percent, we can—"

"Uh-huh. I had a feeling this was just another Democratic ploy to raise taxes."

"This is a bipartisan issue," Cliff emphasized. "It deals with national security. We need to act. I'm willing to give ten million dollars of my own money just to get this program started."

"Everyone here is aware of your net worth. You don't need to flaunt—"

"That's not the point. I—"

"Paying for a program that will benefit you personally constitutes a conflict of interest." Her voice was filled with iron shavings. "It might even be a criminal act."

You need to rein this in. Things are getting away from you.

"You're not listening," he said. "It would benefit all of us, not me personally."

A stiff silence. "Alright. I'll take everything you've said under advisement."

"No." He found himself speaking his thoughts, not holding anything in. "That's not enough! Not anymore. Advisement is not what we need. We have a fleeting opportunity to mitigate this threat before something catastrophic happens. Legislation before lightning strikes. We need to get out ahead of this rather than playing catch-up after something unspeakable happens."

"All of this appears in your budget request?"

"Yes." Cliff scanned the room, trying to read the faces of those present and gauge whether they would vote in his favor or not.

His gaze landed on Presnell, who said, "I move that we table this discussion until our next meeting. That will give us each the time we need to take a careful look at Senator Richardson's proposal."

"I second that," a senator from Michigan said.

"No, listen," Cliff said, "it's been tabled before. This is the—"

"Senator Richardson," Harris interjected. "We have a motion that's been made and seconded to table this discussion until our next meeting. It's time to take a vote."

"I'm telling you, we need to move on this!" Cliff exclaimed adamantly.

But she just continued, "All in favor?"

And they voted.

And the *ayes* had it.

Again.

Cliff pounded the table. He couldn't hold himself back. He glared at Presnell. When the man avoided eye contact, Cliff stormed out of the room.

He hated that he'd lost his patience, but things had finally come to a head. Both China and Russia's cyber espionage capabilities were five to seven years ahead of those of the United States. With Y-12 as vulnerable as it was, he couldn't sit this one out. For the good of the country, for the sake of the future, the time for debate was over. Now was the time to act. Now, before it was too late.

After locating a quiet, isolated landing in the stairwell, he put a call through on his encrypted phone to tell Joshua they needed to move forward.

"They tabled it again," Cliff told him angrily. "Presnell didn't come through for us."

"That's unfortunate to hear."

"What happens now?"

"Do you really want to know?"

A pause. "Just tell me when it's over. I'll have the rest of the money transferred to your account tomorrow, after everything goes down."

"Alright. I'll see you in Oak Ridge at the summit."

"Yes. I'll connect with you in the morning."

After the call, with a cable of anxiety tightening inside of him, Cliff left to wrap up the day's work before his evening flight to Knoxville.

It was all in play.

No turning back.

Although members of Congress were protected by the Capitol Police while in DC, when they were in their home districts or traveled, they didn't always receive security details, and in order to stay more accessible to his constituents and the public at large, Cliff, just like many of his colleagues, chose to travel without a protective detail.

Consequently, the only security he would have in Tennessee would be Joshua, who could pose as his aide.

Cliff reviewed his agenda: His plane would land tonight at seven thirty-one. That should get him to Oak Ridge by eight or eight fifteen, giving him just enough time to get settled in before meeting Dr. Yong for drinks at nine.

He'd never crossed paths with the Nobel-winning physicist before, but they shared a passion for protecting the citizens of the world from the results of a radiological event, so based on their common interests and mutual goals, he'd set up the meeting.

Hopefully, even though the subcommittee vote hadn't resulted in any forward progress, Dr. Yong would agree to give him some of his podium time tomorrow morning so he could use the opportunity to get his message out to the world. That could settle this. That might be all that was needed.

If not, the message that he and Joshua had designed with the help of the computer technician in Hyderabad, India, would definitely get the job done.

The microchips were already installed in Y-12's Highly Enriched Uranium Materials Facility. The announcement regarding them would upend the industry and finally ensure more safety for the American people, whom Cliff had committed his life and his future to serve.

It would all work out—as long as things in Oak Ridge went according to plan. And it would make a difference in the end. Cliff told himself that his brother, Keith, if he were still alive, would've been proud.

But in truth, lately, in his most honest moments, he'd begun to wonder if that really was the case, or if Keith would've been ashamed of him instead.

He told himself it would have been the first response and not the second. Definitely the first.

CHAPTER 10

Making my way through the archives' stacks of papers and cardboard boxes, I came up with more than a dozen Paraden contracts. I also discovered that in December the Pruninghooks Collective had actually sent in a FOIA request to the Department of Energy regarding Project Symphony. Since Y-12 was a DOE site, it made sense and explained why I hadn't been the one to process this request.

Another link to Y-12.

Although Paraden typically focused on developing detonators, it looked like they actually had provided some key components for developing a prototype of a device being used in Project Symphony.

So, there was a connection to the air gapping research after all.

With a sharpened sense of focus, I collected the Paraden contracts and Project Symphony files and returned to my desk to try threading together the significance of the four Ps that seemed to be circling around each other here: Paraden Defense Systems, Patmos Financial Consortium, Project Symphony, and the Pruninghooks Collective. Was there some hidden significance behind that? Another, deeper connection? Hard to know, but if there was, I was going to bring it to light.

—∞—

McGHEE TYSON AIRPORT

TWELVE MILES SOUTH OF KNOXVILLE, TENNESSEE

Adira Halprin reassured herself that the gun had to be nearly ready by now.

As she listened to the printer whirring faintly in her suitcase, she gazed around the airport.

Situational awareness.

The plane that she was scheduled to depart on pulled up to the jet bridge and the sprightly, twentysomething gate agent opened the doors to the jetway so the passengers on board could deplane.

More passengers were passing through security and filling in the seats around Adira now in preparation for departure, but it was the two SWAT team members that caught her attention. The stockier of the two men carried an M4 slung in front of him.

Okay, these boys meant business.

They were scrutinizing the terminal, obviously looking for someone. It didn't appear that they were focused specifically on her—at least, not yet. However, she decided she couldn't take any chances that her cover might've been blown.

Nonchalantly, she unwrapped a block of strawberry bubble gum, popped it into her mouth, then tugged her carry-on bag back across the concourse to the family bathroom again.

Once inside, she locked the door, then dug through her purse and pulled out the whiskey-colored wig. Quickly, she slipped it on over her blonde hair, then found her pair of studious-looking glasses and put them on. Then, a quick change of clothes—and shoes, of course. When disguising themselves, most people forget to change their shoes. It's one of the most common mistakes in spy-craft. Never forget the shoes. And if you suspect someone of changing into a disguise, look at the shoes first, not the face.

A new and different look to fit a new and different driver's license, one that she produced from the secret, sewn-in pocket in her purse.

After a final glance in the mirror to confirm that her wig was positioned properly, she took a deep, calming breath, and then, a bit hesitantly, eased the door open a crack to check if the SWAT officers were coming her way. For the moment, they were facing the other direction.

In the bag she was rolling behind her, the 3D printer clicked off and powered down.

The gun was ready. If they searched her things, they would find it.

She needed to get out of the airport—but take the suitcase along or leave it here? If she left it, she might get away without being stopped, but it would mean taking the chance that someone else would find and acquire the weapon—and that wasn't something she could risk.

Take it with you. Get out. Get back to the car. Deal with things then.

She left the restroom and merged with the group of passengers who'd just deplaned and were heading toward baggage claim. The airport's exit lay less than thirty feet beyond it.

Just when she thought she might be in the clear, one of the SWAT guys eyed her and then gestured to his partner, who consulted a phone, no doubt with a photo on it, and nodded to him.

Immediately, they hastened toward her.

Well, so much for disguises.

Don't hurry. Don't run. Don't attract attention.

Adira's senses sharpened: She felt the gentle brush and swish of her clothes across her skin, smelled the touch of alpine cologne on the man walking beside her, tasted that inviting sweetness of the plump glob of strawberry bubble gum in her mouth.

Very, very berry.

"Excuse me, ma'am." The SWAT officers were four yards away. "We need you to come with us."

Here we go.

She paused and pointed to her chest. "Who, me?"

"Yes." The taller of the two men was doing all the talking. Mr. Chatty produced a TASER. She knew the model and it would not feel good to get stunned with that puppy. The other guy had his hand on the grip of his M4.

You don't want to do this, Adira.

Yes, you do.

She chewed her gum as indifferently as possible.

"Hands to the side where we can see them."

She held her hands out.

"Now, get on your knees."

If they took her in, they would surely discover her tweaks to the curling iron. And, of course, they would find the gun.

But how did they know to follow you in here? You made it through security. How did—?

She knelt.

You need to get out of here. Talk your way out of this. There's still a chance you can make it.

"Officer, what's going on? I don't understand."

As the SWAT guy with the TASER approached to cuff her, she visualized what was about to happen. If she dropped her left hand to the ground, she could spin backward, kick out his leg, go for the TASER, stun the other guy, acquire his weapon, and then—

It all played out in her head, and she knew she could pull it off, even anticipating how she would respond if things didn't quite go as planned.

Which, in situations like this, always seemed to be the case.

Too many people nearby. They could get hurt.

Harming civilians was not on the table, not today, so in the end she didn't act. She didn't move.

More roughly than he needed to, the officer shoved her to the floor and onto her stomach, pinned her beneath one knee, wrenched her arms back, and zip-tied her wrists.

Tell them now or wait?

They don't need to escort you out of here like this.

But you're already blown. At this point, it won't really make any difference.

The other SWAT officer spoke into his radio. "We have her. We're bringing her in."

"You don't understand what you're doing." Adira kept her voice low. "I'm a member of the Red Team. I—"

"Shut up."

"Listen to me," she said as he hoisted her to her feet. "I work for the government." The other guy retrieved her suitcase as she went on. "Call Nathan Lassiter at Homeland Security. I'll give you the number."

The two men exchanged a glance, but neither of them spoke.

"You need to believe me," she reiterated.

"It's not our job to believe you," the one who'd cuffed her said brusquely. "It's just our job to bring you in."

Fair enough.

She would've said the same thing if she were in his shoes.

Or boots, as it were.

5.11s too. Nice. The man had good taste.

She blew a bubble the size of a grapefruit as they hustled her through the airport and into a vehicle waiting out front.

CHAPTER 11

SPRINGFIELD, VIRGINIA

Nathan Lassiter, the Transportation Security Administration's Deputy Director in Charge of Special Projects, received the call from the authorities in Knoxville and, after a moment of deliberation, let it go to voicemail.

He'd been expecting them to contact him, but he was still trying to sort out exactly what to tell them.

Nathan had tried unsuccessfully to contact his friend Detective Sean Caruso from Metro PD three times since he'd failed to show up for their one o'clock lunch meeting, now nearly an hour ago.

Caruso tended to get lost in his work, so his lack of a reply wasn't a complete surprise, but after their conversation yesterday at the funeral home, Nathan had expected to see Caruso at the restaurant today or—at the very least—to hear from him about his change of plans.

They found you, Nathan thought. *Maybe they found him. Maybe they saw you speaking with him yesterday and went after him.*

Anxiously, he left one final message for Sean to call him, then escaped the diner and headed up Frontier Drive toward his TSA office. The afternoon was heating up, and he felt sweat dampening the collar of his freshly pressed Oxford.

Despite the training he'd had years before in the Secret Service, he found himself glancing around too much, something you don't want to do if you think you're being followed because then you give away your suspicions to your adversary, alerting them that you're onto them.

Take it easy. You're alright as long as you're out in the open or in your office.

Not knowing anything about his personal situation, his supervisor— Homeland's Deputy Secretary—had encouraged him to stay home this week following his dad's funeral yesterday, but Nathan had felt that it might be better, and safer, to come in to work today.

He'd been working with the Department of Homeland Security ever since it was first formed under the Bush administration following 9/11. At the time, he was in the Secret Service, but when the opportunity came for a move to TSA six years ago, he had accepted the position.

He'd appreciated the chance to lead the agency's Red Team, and felt that he'd genuinely contributed to the safety of the American people since starting there. However, he knew that he'd strayed off the path of doing what was right, and he honestly wasn't sure how to find his way back onto it again.

You've gone too far, Nathan.

No, you can solve this. You can make things right.

He caught sight of a young couple in retro 70s clothes chatting with each other, walking toward him, and he stepped aside to let them pass. They offered him a friendly nod. No other interaction. Good.

Not far away, a middle-aged woman with wiry gray hair was lighting up a cigarette while holding a cream-colored poodle outside a hair salon.

Nathan avoided eye contact with her and pressed on.

Last autumn when he'd first noticed the telltale signs in his father, he'd pretended it was nothing—the missed words, the memory loss, the confusion when doing things he'd done for years, losing track of where he was and what time it was. Nathan had told himself it was just normal signs of aging. But then came the forgotten names. Close friends. Family members. Finally, it was too much to ignore.

And too much to bear.

When the official diagnosis came through, Nathan wasn't surprised. Though devastating, maybe, on one level, he was relieved to have a name to hang all the questions on—Alzheimer's.

But money was an issue and the in-home care was expensive.

His father had worked as a missionary in Ghana for more than four decades and had no health insurance. He didn't believe in it. As he'd said, back when he was coherent enough to put words to his convictions, "I trust in the power of God rather than the provisions of man." In addition, he'd donated most of his life savings to pay for wells to provide clean water to the villages he'd been ministering to.

He'd foregone earthly treasures in favor of heavenly ones, but in the end he'd needed far more care than his remaining savings could provide for, and he hadn't been the one stuck paying for it.

Nathan knew what his dad's wishes were, but he couldn't stand to see him suffer alone at some second-rate care facility. So, in December when he was approached by the woman asking for his help, he'd faced a choice—but how do you balance out devotion to your country with love for your family?

She hadn't asked for much and had offered more than Nathan would ever have imagined in return. She simply wanted him to obtain and pass along the security access code to a defense agency subcontracted by the military— Paraden Defense Systems. Just one act. Since the company changed security codes daily, it would only be for one-time access. And for that information he would receive $500,000, enough to keep his father at home and comfortable during his final days.

Just one act. Just one access code.

Nathan had made his choice.

Now, glancing one last time over his shoulder to make sure he wasn't being followed, he passed through security at TSA's headquarters, and headed toward the elevator to his second-floor office.

You make a decision like that and you tell yourself that it won't matter, but deep inside you know that it will, that it already has. You try to justify it, but it doesn't work, not when you know you've betrayed everything you believed in and spent your life defending.

But you served the greater law of love, right? The law of devotion to your family. Isn't that enough?

For him, for a time, it had been.

Not anymore.

Nathan didn't know what the woman did with the access code he'd provided for her, and didn't want to think about it—didn't dare to. Yesterday at the funeral, when he'd said his final goodbye to his father, he'd also decided he was going to make things right, to straighten out what he'd done. And so, he'd put a series of events into motion, trying to stop the momentum of his choices. He'd hoped to have Detective Caruso help him, but his friend wasn't picking up.

Now, heaving a deep sigh, Nathan closed his office door and slumped into his desk chair. If he was right, the secret lay in the work a certain member of his team had done during a week last year when there weren't any Red Team duties to perform.

He typed in his password, bypassed the security protocols that he himself had helped design, and then began looking into the private calendar of the one person who might be able to get him some answers, a Red Team member known by the code name "Flower Girl."

CHAPTER 12

With the acrostic and what I'd been able to uncover, everything seemed to revolve around Y-12.

Someone from Homeland had submitted this FOIA request and now, though it took a little work, I traced it back and found the name of the person who'd sent it in—a former Secret Service agent and current TSA operative by the name of Adira Halprin.

Is it possible that she knows something about the arson?

It wasn't a question I could simply ask a supervisor.

I needed to speak with Ms. Halprin in person.

Using my clearance, I tracked her down and discovered that, just half an hour ago, she'd been arrested for trying to sneak a weapon onto an airplane in Knoxville using a fake name and driver's license.

Okay, that was interesting.

In addition, rather than deal with her in Knoxville, she was being transferred to a clandestine site about twenty miles outside of DC, which had been set up by the Department of Homeland Security in the aftermath of 9/11 and was still discreetly used for DOD and DOJ interrogations of high-value suspects. It wasn't a military base by any stretch of the imagination—more of a safe house, really. Still, taking someone there meant there was a clear and present threat that was being taken seriously.

Ms. Halprin was claiming to be a member of the Red Team, a classified DHS unit that tested the security and integrity of TSA checkpoints.

Their five members attempted to sneak weapons and bomb-making supplies past airport security—and they were remarkably successful, with a success rate of nearly ninety percent. Recently, because of mismanagement at the Federal Aviation Administration, oversight of the Red Team had been moved from the Department of Transportation to TSA. Consequently, it was now under the auspices of the Department of Homeland Security—the place today's FOIA request had originated.

The Red Team's monthly reports affected FAA guidelines, training programs, and personnel decisions, so putting them under DHS's authority made sense to me, since the move provided an additional level of objectivity to the team's work.

Though I wasn't intimately familiar with the ins and outs of exactly how the Red Team worked, last year I'd redacted information about a DOD program it intersected with and had met Nathan Lassiter, the TSA administrator responsible for overseeing it.

When he'd found out who I was and what had happened to Sienna, he'd mentioned that he knew Detective Caruso at Metro PD and had offered to assist in any way that he could to help us find some answers. As it turned out, that hadn't led anywhere, but it'd meant a lot to me that Lassiter had made the offer.

There were safeguards in place in case any Red Team members were caught, so the fact that Ms. Halprin had been arrested was conspicuous. If she really was part of the team, it shouldn't have raised any red flags when she was stopped. She should have simply been able to meet with the authorities, have them contact Homeland to confirm her identity and then release her. Clearly, something else was going on here.

Whatever that might be, right now it looked like she just might be the person to give me the answers I was looking for. And if she was being held in custody, who knew what kind of access I would have to her later on down the line. This might be my only chance to speak with her.

After scanning her personnel file, I returned to the Pentagon's first floor, retrieved my phone, and passed down the hallway to the other side of the building, where Colonel Clarke's office was located.

Since the Pentagon's inner courtyard was the only place in the building where people could get any cell reception, they tended to congregate near it. Reception was spotty, but at least it was available. Because of that, the tables beside the windows were almost always occupied, as they were now, even though it was long past lunchtime. The reason for the seating preference was another one of those little details that you wouldn't know unless you worked here in the building yourself.

While I was near the tables, I checked my phone and found a text from Detective Caruso, the Metro PD detective who was looking into the arson at my house. He'd messaged me at just a few minutes after seven asking me to give him a call at my earliest convenience. **I might have something regarding the timing of the fire,** he wrote.

Caruso knew about my *idée fixe* to find the answers behind the arson, and even if it wasn't exactly protocol, he'd gone out of the way to keep me updated on his progress in searching for the arsonist.

Trying not to attract attention, I surreptitiously texted him that I would call him as soon as I could. Intrigued and distracted by the message from Caruso, I continued to Clarke's office and less than three minutes later I arrived at the bulletproof glass doors shielding it.

In the military, glass doors typically signify the highest-ranking or most important personnel. So, when you're called behind the glass, it's often not a good thing. It's like getting sent to the principal's office.

However, I had a long relationship with Colonel Clarke, stretching back fifteen years, and this was something I felt like I needed to talk about with him face to face.

I badged my way past the glass doors.

After a receptionist showed me into his office, Clarke rose from behind his immaculate desk and greeted me cordially. "Travis, it's good to see you outside of the basement."

"Good to see you too, sir."

She left as he gave me one of his crushing handshakes.

Colonel Clarke stood a solid six three. At sixty-two years old, he'd served his country for nearly all of his adult life. A tad grizzled around the edges, he moved with purpose and poise and I'd never seen him lose his cool. He'd retired with benefits nine years ago, but that had only lasted a few months.

This guy wasn't meant for retirement, and at his request, the Secretary of Defense granted him a waiver and brought him back in. I couldn't see the colonel leaving again of his own accord anytime soon. He was a true patriot all the way to the bone.

In my job, it wasn't unusual for me to consult with others—not just military personnel, but also, in some cases, civilians—to verify data or analyze the consequences of the release of certain information. So, there was nothing particularly odd about today's request of him. The only unusual factor here was the limited time window.

"I have a FOIA request that's going to require a personal interview off-site," I said.

"What's it concerning?"

"Research at Oak Ridge."

"Would it make sense to kick it over to the DOE?"

Since the Oak Ridge National Laboratory was one of the sites managed by the Department of Energy, it was a natural question and one I'd anticipated.

"It looks like this is a joint project with them. Could go either way. But the timing is tight."

Clarke scratched at the side of his jaw. "Is this about Project Symphony? About the conference in Oak Ridge tomorrow?"

I didn't know about any relationship between Project Symphony and a conference tomorrow.

"It's possible," I said.

"What do you need?"

"Clearance to go to L & L Manufacturing."

Honestly, I wasn't sure he was going to give me the green light here.

"When is it happening?"

"Now," I said. "Today. The woman I need to speak with should be there within the next thirty minutes or so." I decided to leave it at that. He might wonder about the timing, but two things were in my favor: First, nearly everything I did was time-sensitive, and he knew that. Second, he trusted my judgment.

"Hmm," he said reflectively, then nodded. "Yes, okay. I'll sign off on it, but I want you to keep me apprised of the situation."

"Yes, sir."

I passed through those glass doors again, curious and slightly confused.

What conference was he referring to in Oak Ridge? Whatever it was, he was assuming I'd be familiar with it, and maybe I should've been.

I made a note to look into it after I'd had a chance to talk with Ms. Halprin.

To get to my car, I exited the Pentagon via the same security checkpoint I'd used earlier in the day, the one with the Pentagon Police officer who seemed at times to be hitting on me.

As I approached her, she cocked her head and looked at me with unabashed interest. "Mr. Brock? Leaving already?"

"Something came up that I need to take care of."

"Ah. Well, remember, tomorrow I want you to park farther back. Give yourself more of a challenge."

"Right. See you then."

A wink. "See you then."

—∽—

She watched him walk away.

When he was halfway to his car, she picked up her encrypted cell and made the call.

"He's leaving. You need to move."

"I thought he never left until after five thirty?"

During their first phone conversation, she'd heard the man on the other end speak Russian to someone else who must have been in the room with him, but other than that she had no indication of who the people behind this were. "He never has left early," she said. "Not as long as I've worked here. Look, I did what you asked—"

"You placed the tracker?"

"I attached it to his computer bag this morning when I inspected it. He had the bag with him just now when he left, so you should be set." Then she added concernedly, "I did everything you said."

"Good. Then we can consider our business in this matter completed."

"And my fiancé?"

"As long as this remains our little secret, he'll never see the pictures. Thank you for your kind cooperation."

CHAPTER 13

Adira didn't know what type of military transport plane she was in the back of, but it was something aging, musty, and wide-bellied. Two expressionless MPs flanked her. They hadn't spoken a word since the SWAT guys passed her off to the military's custody a couple of hours ago.

She also didn't know where they were taking her, but the fact that they hadn't simply transported her to the Knoxville Police Department told her that something much bigger was up here.

Not necessarily cause for alarm.

But certainly cause for a healthy dose of attentiveness.

Her ears popped as the plane began its descent.

A lieutenant colonel, or at least someone wearing a uniform with that rank insignia on it, had been very inquisitive during the flight: "Who are you working with? What's the name of your group? What do you want?"

And she'd told him the truth, but he just wouldn't accept it.

He started in again. "Explain to me one more time why you printed a gun and had a curling iron with a retractable blade at an airport. What were you doing with those weapons?"

"As I said, I work for Homeland Security." She held up her shackled wrists. "Is all this really necessary?"

He ignored her question about the handcuffs. "You're a member of their Red Team."

"Now you're getting it." She rested her hands on her lap again. "Good for you."

"Uh-huh. And if it's real, how come I've never heard of it before?"

"We're not a burger chain. We don't advertise what we do."

They'd taken her wig and glasses, which was fine by her. It might've been a pain to keep them on in case she had to fight her way out of here.

At least they hadn't taken her bubble gum.

Even though it was definitely true that she would've preferred a fresh piece by now, she wasn't complaining. Sometimes you just have to work with what you've got.

"And this Red Team of yours," the man said, "how many of you are there?"

"I don't know."

"You don't know."

"Listen, I went through all this earlier. We work independently around the country. Just call Nathan Lassiter at Homeland. He'll clear everything up."

"We're in the process of reaching out to him. In the meantime, why don't you tell me the names of some of the other people you work with."

"We use code names."

"Of course you do," he said patronizingly. "And what's yours?"

"Flower Girl."

A snicker. "Flower Girl?"

"My middle name is Chrysanthemum."

"You mean your *real* middle name? Because the names on the four driver's licenses you had in your purse were all fake."

Adira held back a sigh. "I'm telling you, call Nathan. I gave you his number."

She studied the man for a moment. Narrow face. Blond hair, trimmed almost to his scalp. Contacts. A pierced left earlobe, nearly healed over—must not wear earrings much. His fingernails were chewed down. A nervous habit maybe.

"Let's get back to your job for a second." He angled one of those chewed-on fingers at her. "You say you're responsible for testing the security at airport checkpoints?"

"Yes. And it's substandard at best."

He held up his palms. "And yet, here you are."

"Yeah, I've been wondering about that."

"About what?"

"How you found me. Who turned me in? Someone had to have tipped you off, so—"

"Listen to me, Adira—or whatever you want to call yourself—I want to know who you really work for and why you were targeting that flight."

"Where are you taking me?"

"I'll ask the questions here."

"I need to use the bathroom."

"If you work for the government, why aren't you carrying any official identification?"

"I mean, I really do. I need to pee."

"You're not listening to me. You have a whole slew of charges against you here—including resisting arrest."

"I didn't resist arrest, cowboy. If I did, you wouldn't have me in this plane."

He leaned forward. "You're in a lot of trouble and your attitude isn't helping you out at all here."

"Do you want me to pee all over the floor?"

"We'll hose it off afterward. It's nothing we haven't dealt with before."

She blew a bubble in his face, which, since the gum was anything but fresh, was quite an achievement.

He sat back.

"Check my phone," she said. "You'll find text messages from Nathan."

"We did check your phone."

"And?"

"And if we could verify any part of your story, you wouldn't be in here. Your most recent texts were sent to a number that's been linked to a Russian hacking syndicate."

She let his words sink in.

Didn't see that coming.

Someone was not playing by the rules here. Her texts hadn't been sent to a Russian hacker, but to her boss. She knew that much for sure.

"What's going to happen tomorrow morning?" He held up her phone, screen toward her. The last text from her contact stared at her, the enigmatic mention of 11 a.m. tomorrow.

"I don't know what that refers to."

"Uh-huh," the lieutenant colonel said. "We have your gun. The one you printed." He removed it from his satchel and held it up. "How do you explain this?"

"What? The plastic gun or your man purse? Because, seriously, that design is not very—"

He backhanded her across the face, cutting her off. He was quick—quicker than she anticipated—and she wasn't able to get her hands up in time to block him.

The ferocity of the blow took her by surprise. However, she was aware that one of the most effective ways to break people was by using random acts of violence and of kindness. Intermittent reinforcement. It's how you psychologically wore them down, and was a technique kidnappers and human traffickers often used to subjugate their victims.

She tasted blood on her lip. It didn't go well with the bubble gum, so she spit out the gum, along with a glob of bloody saliva, onto the floor of the plane.

"Hose *that* off."

He said nothing.

"Tell me where you're taking me."

"A place where there are some people who are very anxious to meet you."

CHAPTER 14

FAIRFAX, VIRGINIA

Having found out what he was looking for earlier, Nathan Lassiter had made sure Adira was going to be transferred back to the DC area, to a safe place where they could talk and clear everything up—and where, if he was right in what he'd assessed, she might lead him to the woman who'd approached him and paid him off.

He reassured himself that by the end of the afternoon he would have some answers.

Forty-five minutes ago he'd left TSA headquarters, and now, after battling some unwieldy traffic, he finally pulled into his driveway at home.

He parked and went inside, then closed the front door securely behind him, leaned his back against it, closed his eyes, and exhaled deeply.

Maybe his choices over the last twenty-four hours were solving things. Maybe they were just making them worse. In either case, he told himself that, in the end, things would work out, that he could fix his past mistakes and bring something worthwhile—something positive—to bear on the future.

On his way to his home office, he came to the room he'd converted into a bedroom for his dad five months ago, pausing now, near the base of the stairs, to look at the empty hospital bed.

With everything that'd been happening, he hadn't taken the opportunity to properly begin the grieving process, but he reassured himself that there would be time for that to happen later, once everything was resolved.

Once she gets to L & L you can talk to her, find out what she knows, get some answers.

Though Nathan wasn't sure what exactly might be happening in Tennessee this week, he'd found a time—eleven o'clock tomorrow morning—and he had his suspicions that the person who'd paid him off had ties to whatever it was that was being planned. He didn't have enough intel to go through official channels to start an investigation or contact his counterparts at the FBI, but it was enough for him to feel like he needed to take action of some sort.

If he was right, the fire at Brock's house was related to both the people who'd bribed him and the Red Team. Talking with both Travis Brock and Adira was essential.

There were a lot of possibilities right now, not a lot of answers.

He'd done some digging on his own, but had been careful not to raise any red flags, since he was worried that he was being monitored by the people he'd provided the access code to.

They're watching you. They might have others working for them. Others in Homeland. Maybe even in the Pentagon.

At L & L Manufacturing, he'd have the security to facilitate the kind of private conversation he would need. From there, he could drive to Dulles and catch the flight to Tennessee.

Going to his desk, he studied the printouts he'd brought with him from his office and drew his highlighter across the executive protection detail his protégé had worked in Belgium a year ago. It just might be the answer he was looking for—if he was right about who had arranged for the arson at Brock's house. But who'd actually started the fire? That was the thing.

Caruso might know—if he would ever return his calls.

If he's able to. If they haven't gotten to him.

To quiet those thoughts, Nathan started recording a device-specific, time-stamped voice message to Adira Halprin—it would only be available on her DHS tablet, and only today.

"Here's what I know," he dictated into his laptop. "Eleven o'clock, tomorrow. Knoxville. Something with Paraden. Look into them with Brock. I trust him and I trust you. Never doubt that. I'm not trying to hurt you; I'm trying to protect something bigger than all of us."

But then, the more he thought about it, he realized that since she'd been arrested in Knoxville, she wouldn't have access to her tablet and it might very well have been confiscated by law enforcement.

Rather than hit Send, Nathan deleted the message.

Tell her when you see her.

He'd done what was necessary to get her back to the DC area.

Find out what she can tell you about the group, then get to Tennessee. Once you're there, you can stop this.

He confirmed his flight, checked in online, then made sure his gun was loaded and went upstairs to pack for his evening flight to Knoxville.

CHAPTER 15

Earlier, at the Pentagon, I'd texted Detective Caruso that I would call him, but now when I did, he didn't pick up.

Phone tag.

Knowing that Adira claimed to be on Nathan Lassiter's Red Team, I put a call through to his office to tell him I was here to speak with her, but he didn't pick up either. I left a message for him to call me.

Phone tag, take two.

In my line of work, trust was both a necessity and an indulgence. You had to trust the people you worked with—yes, of course—but you couldn't afford to give them the benefit of the doubt either. You were always walking a fine line, and so were they. And right now, I wasn't sure whom to trust, or which side of the line I was even on.

The L & L Manufacturing site didn't appear on any maps as government-owned property. A rusted eight-foot-tall chain link fence encircled the languishing, overgrown twenty-acre property—just enough of a deterrent to keep curiosity seekers at bay, but not so over-the-top that it would attract undue attention or scrutiny.

Three cars were parked beyond the fence at the dilapidated office building that squatted beside the sprawling warehouse. From my research, I knew that, while there were currently only three security personnel here, a team of interrogators was on its way to question Halprin and would be arriving at any time.

I pulled up to the security gate, where a fit and trim man in his late twenties dressed in a rent-a-cop uniform held up his hand. Despite his innocuous outfit, his posture and demeanor betrayed him—this guy was military.

"Can I help you?" he said, but it wasn't really a question.

"I'm here on behalf of Colonel Clarke."

That's not exactly true.

It's true enough.

I added, "I came to talk to the woman."

"What woman is that?"

"The one brought up from Tennessee. Halprin. From Lassiter's team."

I produced my Pentagon ID and handed it over for inspection.

"Let's see your paperwork," the guard said stiffly.

"It's a bit of a last-minute thing. Call it in. It'll come up."

As he returned the ID to me, he tapped a button on his radio and told whoever was on the other end to run the verification passcode that I relayed to him. A few moments later, an affirmative answer came through from Clarke's office.

The man leaned close to me. "Was she really going to do it?"

"Do it?"

"The flight to Atlanta. Hijack it."

"I really can't say at this time."

A nod. "Gotcha. Be safe in there, sir."

"I will."

"Park by the office's side entrance. Francesca will show you to the basement."

—m—

From four hundred and fifty meters away, where he sat in the metallic gray electrician's van that was already prepped for what he had planned for Travis Brock, Sergei Sokolov observed the redactor through his field binoculars as the man drove onto the property.

"An old manufacturing plant?" Sergei muttered to Ilya Vasiliev, who was in the passenger seat beside him. "What is this place? Why did he come here?"

Ilya typed rapidly on his laptop, his fingers flying across the keyboard. "Running the name of the plant now."

Sergei processed the information they'd gleaned from the Metropolitan Police Department detective earlier in the day. Impressively, Caruso had held out longer than Sergei had anticipated, but in the end, when Ilya really got started on him, he'd given them the intel they needed about an arson investigation he was involved in and the search for a missing State Department employee named Lena Rhodes.

She worked for their Office of the Legal Advisor, offering recommendations on legal issues related to treaty proposals. Her disappearance and the fire at Brock's house had happened within two days of each other, and Sergei's employer had wanted to know if the detective had linked them in any way. As it turned out, he had, but had sworn to his final breath that he hadn't told anyone about his findings.

Although Sergei had been in favor of getting rid of the detective's body more discreetly, their employer wanted to make a statement, so they'd left it in the trunk of the detective's own car right in front of MPD headquarters.

Ilya stopped typing.

"What do we know?" Sergei asked him.

"Not much here. It was industrial manufacturing plant: bolts, screws, machine parts. Been here since 1971. Family-owned. Factory itself closed now. They just ship orders out from old inventory. Nothing suspicious."

"Except for the fact that Brock left the Pentagon earlier than usual and came directly here."

"Yes. But whatever is happening, if someone is trying to keep this place quiet, they have done good job."

Sergei considered the deadline they were under, as well as the isolated location. "I think we should take him now. Here."

"I agree."

They'd brought an assortment of tools from the garage after they were done with Detective Caruso, just in case they needed them for future conversation starters. Sergei asked Ilya, "Do you have any bolt cutters in the back? That fence doesn't look electrified."

Ilya opened his door. "I believe I do."

CHAPTER 16

A slight, ginger-haired woman carrying a handheld radio met me at the front door of the modest and unobtrusive-looking office building that was not much larger than a double-wide mobile home. "I'm Francesca."

"Travis Brock."

"Hands to the side."

I complied, and she patted me down. Finding no weapons, she invited me to follow her through a paneled reception area toward a dimly lit hallway. "Colonel Clarke sent you?"

"That's right."

"You a lawyer?"

"Yes." At least that wasn't a lie. I'd graduated from Boston College with a jurisprudence degree, even though it was one I'd never really used. I wasn't here in the official capacity of a lawyer, but it wouldn't hurt if she thought I was.

The hall terminated at a reinforced security door, which Francesca unlocked with a key that she wore on a braided lanyard around her neck.

Before us lay a basement stairwell with perforated steel steps, a stark contrast to the homey feel of the front office and hallway. "Better hurry," she said. "From what I've heard, the interviewers are going to be here soon."

Ah, yes. The term *interviewers* was so much more politically correct than *interrogators*.

"How soon?"

"Ten, fifteen minutes. And they'll want to have access to her right away."

"I understand."

Francesca led me down the stairs and through a drab observation room, where a young, eagle-eyed guard monitored an array of video screens and a two-way mirror the width of the wall. He nodded a greeting to me and I responded in kind.

A woman waited on the other side of the glass, her cuffed hands chained to a bar on the steel table in front of her.

Francesca dropped me off in the "interview" room. As she closed the door behind her, I took a seat across from the woman who, despite her penchant for fake identities was, in truth, named Adira Halprin.

Attractive. Athletic build. Midthirties. Short blonde hair. Incisive eyes.

She regarded me closely, then glanced at the video camera staring at us from a corner of the ceiling, its red operational light blinking metronomically, before appraising me again.

"There's just one of you?"

"Yes."

"I have to admit, you don't look like who I would've expected."

I adjusted my glasses. "Okay."

Once again, she flicked her eyes toward the camera. This time, it turned slightly to the side. "They're watching us."

"The audio is off. They think I'm your lawyer. They'll be monitoring us to make sure you don't attack me, but the camera is positioned away from our faces so they can't have lip readers decipher what we're talking about."

"And what *are* we talking about?"

"The FOIA request you sent through. I want some answers."

"The FOIA request?"

"Regarding research at Oak Ridge and Paraden Defense Systems."

She gazed at me with a look that was hard to read. "I don't even know who you are."

"I'm someone you can trust."

She waited.

"Travis Brock," I said. "I work at the Pentagon."

"So do twenty-five thousand other people. Why should I trust you?"

"Because I'm here and they're not."

At that, she tilted her head slightly back and forth a couple times as if she were weighing the merit of what I'd said. "That's a valid point."

Doesn't she know you? At least recognize your name? Her request was addressed to you personally.

"They're saying you were going to hijack an airplane," I said.

"They're wrong."

"Does the date November nineteenth mean anything to you? What about the Pruninghooks Collective?"

A beat. "What is this even about?"

"A year and a half ago," I said. "The nineteenth of November. A fire in DC. We don't have much time. I'm asking if—"

"Before what?"

"What do you mean?"

"You just said, 'We don't have much time.' Time before what?"

"Before your interrogators get here and get started."

"Aha. I see."

"You see?"

She leaned forward. "I know how this goes, Mr. Brock-From-The-Pentagon. You're working with them. You offer to help me, but it's a ruse, a way to get me to share information with you. Good cop, bad cop for the twenty-first century. Well, guess what? I don't have anything to share. I'm not who they're making me out to be."

"I believe you."

She tilted her head to the side and narrowed one eye at me. "What do you even know about me?"

"Really, Ms. Halprin, there isn't time for this."

She tipped back in her chair as far as the restraints allowed and fake yawned. "Hey, I've got all night."

"I'm telling you, they're on their way. You need to trust me."

"Earn it and I'll give it."

I spoke quickly. "You grew up in Jefferson, Wisconsin. Small-town girl. Gymnastics all the way through high school. Graduated in the top ten percent of your class. Then on to college at Georgetown: double major in poli sci and criminal justice. Accepted into the United States Secret Service's James J.

Rowley Training Center two months after graduating. But you didn't exactly play well with others and you quit three years after that—well, quit when you found out they were going to fire you. Now, when you're not working in international executive protection, you freelance as a Red Team member testing TSA checkpoints. So far, you've made eighty-nine attempts to get weapons or bomb-making materials past security, and have been successful all but once. Today."

She stared at me. "How do you know all this?"

"I saw your file."

"Which file? My time at the Secret Service is classified. None of that information is in the public record."

"I didn't get it from the public record."

"But obtaining access to—"

"None of that matters right now. I'm looking for answers, and you're the first person I've come across since my wife was killed who might be able to help me find them."

—⁂—

There were no bolt cutters after all, so Sergei turned to plan B.

From past experience, he knew that one of the best ways to get close to security guards, or at least to take them unaware, was to approach while shaking your head. Rather than raise suspicion, doing so changed the entire social dynamic of the encounter: Instead of asking what you're doing, the security worker will, out of instinctive concern, ask what's wrong.

And that's what happened now as Sergei walked up to the front gate shaking his head and heaving a deep, disgruntled sigh.

"What is it?" the guard said, leaving his shack.

"Can you even believe this?"

"Believe what?"

"Landon screwed up my paperwork again."

"Landon?" He straightened up slightly. "Who's—?"

A single shot to the head and the man went down. Sergei glanced back up the road to where he'd left Ilya with the SVDS Dragunov sniper rifle in the van nearly a hundred meters away. Now, Ilya rolled forward and met up with him.

"Nice shot," Sergei said.

"*Spasibo,*" Ilya replied in Russian: *Thank you.*

Sergei walked past the body, opened the gate, and then returned to the van and slid in beside Ilya. "Let's go find Brock."

—⁓—

While I was waiting for Adira Halprin to tell me why she'd sent in the FOIA request, I heard a *thwap* from the other side of the two-way mirror where the guard I'd passed on my way through the control room was seated. It sounded like it might've been someone rapping once, sharply, against the glass, but I couldn't be sure.

"What was that?" I said.

"Oh, that was a gunshot," Adira replied, staring at the mirror.

"How do you know?"

"Believe me. I know."

Curious, but also wary, I said, "I'm going to check it out."

"No, wait—"

"I'll be right back." Then I left to find out what'd happened, closing the door to the interview room securely behind me.

—⁓—

Adira swore under her breath and quickly repositioned herself close enough to the table to reach the bobby pin on the front of her belt.

First get free from the table, then get free from the handcuffs.

Then get the hell out of here.

CHAPTER 17

Adira had inserted the bobby pin into the lock mechanism and was trying to jimmy it open when a brawny man she didn't recognize burst into the room holding a Russian-designed PSM, a popular security forces pistol dating back to the seventies. Though a bit dated, it was still a lightweight, slim, easily concealable choice for a handgun.

He looked at her questioningly.

"Who are you?" he asked in a thick Russian accent.

"Don't shoot me!" she begged, playing the role of a helpless victim as she furiously worked the bobby pin in the obstinate lock. "I can help you!"

Just a little more. A little bit more. You've almost got it.

He lumbered toward her. "I asked who you are."

The click in the lock told her that she was free from the table's bar.

Okay.

Now, the cuffs.

He stood maybe four feet away from her, with the steel table between them.

"My name? You can call me . . ." As she leaned in against the table, she realized that it moved slightly. Using that to her advantage, she ducked her head, shouted, "Flower Girl!" and shoved it forward, driving the man backward into the wall behind him.

As he slammed against it, he redirected his gun toward her, but she dove across the tabletop at him. With her wrists still cuffed together, it was terrifically awkward, but she managed to grab his arm before he could fire and to angle the weapon away from her. The gun discharged, sending a bullet ricocheting off the ceiling.

Struggling against her restraints, she cranked harshly on the man's wrist to disarm him. The pain hardly seemed to register on his stoic face, and she had to really torque his hand—and must have been close to snapping his scaphoid—before he finally released the weapon, which clattered onto the table, spun away from her, and dropped to the floor.

He muttered something in Russian, grabbed her by the neck with his free hand, and threw her violently against the wall. Then, hefting the massive table aside, he went for the gun, but she scrambled toward it and kicked it across the room before he could retrieve it.

As he was straightening up and coming toward her, she planted both hands on the floor and did a cartwheel kick toward his face. Her heel connected with his right temple and he went down, but he wasn't out. It took another fierce kick to the side of his head before he dropped, at last, unconscious, to the ground.

Still cuffed, Adira snatched up the gun and rushed out the door to the observation room on the other side of the mirror, where she found a guard slumped over a blood-splattered computer keyboard.

Travis stood at the far end of the room, hands held up to his sides. A stout man about six inches taller than her held a handgun aimed at his chest and straddled the space between them, his back to her.

"Drop the gun," she ordered him. "Or I drop you."

—᠁—

When Sergei heard the woman's threat, he paused.

He'd been preoccupied with Brock, so he hadn't seen the entire fight through the two-way mirror to the adjoining room. However, she'd somehow bested Ilya and his gun had gone off. Now, looking through the glass, Sergei saw his associate lying prone on the floor.

No visible blood spatter, but still, it was possible that he was dead.

Even if he is, you can't compromise the mission. You need to bring Brock in alive.

Sergei realized that the woman could've easily shot him already if she'd had a mind to, but instead she'd held back. Clearly, she wasn't intent on killing him.

He debated risking it: spinning to face her, and trying to get a shot off before she could. But in the end, for the sake of the mission, he decided that if she'd taken Ilya out she obviously had skills and it would be better to comply and return for Brock at another, more opportune time.

He held his hands out, one to each side, leaving his finger off the trigger of his Makarov.

"Set the gun down," she commanded. "Do it slowly. Then kick it toward Brock."

―⁂―

The man obeyed her.

"Pick that up," Adira told Brock. "Aim it at his chest, and if he makes a move, squeeze the trigger. Do it as many times as you need to until he's no longer a threat."

She wasn't sure how Brock had managed to get himself in this position, but there were other things to worry about at the moment.

Watchfully and attentively, she eased past the man and joined Brock at the other side of the room. Although she'd lost hold of the bobby pin that she'd used a few moments ago to get free from the table, she had another one on the back of her belt. However, with her hands cuffed in front of her, it wasn't possible to reach it.

As she took over targeting the subject, she said to Brock, "There's a bobby pin behind me on my belt. Grab it for me. Then I want you to cover him again."

It took him only a moment to find it and hand it to her. Then, he aimed his gun at the man once more while she slid her gun under her belt and worked at the handcuffs.

She didn't know how long the thug she'd been fighting in the interrogation room would be out, or when the people Brock had mentioned to her earlier would arrive, but obviously, she needed to hurry. Knowing that they didn't have much time here put pressure on her to pick the lock quickly, but at least this time she didn't have a gun aimed at her face.

"Who sent you?" Brock asked the man.

No reply.

"Why did you kill this guard?" he pressed him. "What is it you're after?"

The man didn't respond.

The cuff clicked.

Ah, yes.

Good.

Adira unhinged the steel bracelets and freed her wrists.

After testing to make sure the filing cabinet that was inset in the wall was immovable and secure, she tossed the handcuffs to the assailant. "Cuff yourself to the drawer of that cabinet. Do it now."

"You have no idea what's happening here."

"Actually, I do. We're walking out of here and you're not."

"My friend in there—you didn't kill him, did you? You should have. Now he has a bullet with your name on it."

"Must be a small font."

"A small font?"

"I have a long middle name. Now, close that bracelet."

He secured one of the cuffs around his left wrist. "Believe me, it would be better for you both if you just came with me now."

"Yeah, well, I think we'll take our chances."

For a moment she thought about shooting the guy in the leg or something just to make sure he couldn't follow them if he did manage to get free, but her Secret Service training kicked in—as well as her conscience—and she decided against it.

A stupid idea, really.

Still, it was tempting.

After he snapped the other cuff around the file cabinet's handle, she directed Brock to join her and the two of them darted up the stairs.

—⧟—

The image of the dead guard in front of the two-way mirror was fresh in my mind as we came to the reception area and I saw that Francesca was also dead, shot in the neck. She lay crumpled on the floor, a savage stain of fresh blood soaking into the pale green carpet beneath her.

An icy tightness climbed into my chest. It wasn't so much that I felt sick to my stomach; it was more like a boa constrictor was encircling me, cutting off my breathing. Coming across dead bodies wasn't anything I was even remotely used to or trained for.

Process it later. Right now, just get to safety.

We sprinted outside.

Hoping that maybe the guard at the front gate had survived the facility's incursion, I scanned the road leading away from the manufacturing plant.

When I saw his motionless body on the ground, I felt another chill.

You saw all three of them alive only minutes ago. And now they're dead. For always and forever dead.

Like Sienna. The reason you came here. The reason you're—

"You okay?" Adira Halprin called to me.

"Yeah." I tried to focus on the situation at hand and realized that there might very well be more assailants on their way here. I indicated the passenger's side of my car. "Get in. Let's go."

She shook her head. "No. They'll track your vehicle. Is there a way we can get out of here on foot?"

"Not a good one. But a couple of miles down the road there's a strip mall. We can leave the car there."

We climbed in and I took off, with thoughts of the dead haunting me as I drove away from the property and the fresh corpses it contained.

PART II

Chloroform

CHAPTER 18

NINE MINUTES LATER

Former Army Ranger Gunnar Bane stepped out of the black Lincoln Aviator and into the cool spring evening settling over the L & L Manufacturing campus. At fifty-five, he'd been retired from the military for nearly fifteen years, but had found work as a civilian security contractor to be an even more satisfying career—especially with jobs like this one, in which his specific skill set could be put to use for the good of the country.

As a writer working on his first book, he heard the words even as he might've written them for his novel: *Bane folded up the navigator glasses he'd been wearing as he drove toward the setting sun, slipped them into the pocket of his weathered flight jacket, and scoured the area.*

"What do we know?" he asked the coterie of soldiers who were already at the site.

Major Díaz, a stout five-foot-six Hispanic man with a shaved head and ramrod straight posture, spoke up. "Three people down. The subject is missing."

Gunnar ran a hand across the sandpapery, salt-and-pepper stubble on his chin as he processed that. "A woman who was handcuffed and shackled to a table was able to take out three highly trained intelligence officers and escape?"

A tight pause. "Well . . ."

Impressive.

Maybe Ms. Halprin really was a terrorist.

Unless things were not as they appeared.

And, in this line of work, they rarely were.

Díaz studied Gunnar. "I understand Lassiter sent you?"

"From Homeland. Yes," Gunnar said. "Halprin works with him and he wants some answers." Then, getting back to the site analysis: "And the security video? What does it show?"

"The footage was deleted," the major told him. "The computers smashed. Our best shot is the digital forensics team at Quantico—they might be able to dig through it and recover some files, but other than that, we've got nothing."

The scene unfolded in Gunnar's mind: *Bane let his gaze travel across the property, taking everything in—the slain guard out front, the soldiers securing the area, the office building and warehouse in the background, the sun sinking down against the distant tree line.*

"I understand that a name was run by the guard beforehand," he said, "that someone else might've been present."

Major Díaz spoke into his radio, then relayed the information to him. "Travis Brock, sir. He came here on behalf of Colonel Clarke. DOD business."

Gunnar was familiar with Clarke, had worked two classified assignments for him in the past.

"And what do we know about Brock?" he asked Díaz. "Who is he?"

"A DOD censor. Works at the Pentagon."

That didn't seem right, but maybe Mr. Brock wasn't just a redactor.

Or maybe he'd switched teams.

"Expand the perimeter." Gunnar swept a steady hand through the air, delineating his order. "We have three casualties. Brock didn't walk here from the Pentagon. Locate his car. Do whatever you need to—track his phone, his vehicle's GPS, any PEDs; look for credit card use; contact his closest relatives. I want him found. Now."

He put a call through to Nathan Lassiter and brought him up to speed on what they knew so far about what'd happened here—which wasn't much.

"I don't think you need to come here tonight," Gunnar said to Lassiter. "There's not much we can do onsite right now."

"I see. Any idea where she might've gone?"

"No. But I'll find her."

After hanging up, and while the major put things into play, Gunnar routed a call through to speak with Colonel Clarke for himself to find out what this redactor was doing here when the shootings occurred.

CHAPTER 19

FOUR MILES AWAY

Inside the car at the strip mall parking lot, I found my hands shaking—probably a mixture of the effects of being fueled on adrenaline and then struck with grief from seeing those three bodies at the manufacturing plant.

What have you gotten yourself into?

Although I was tempted to call the authorities and tell them everything, I pressed pause on that idea for a moment. I needed answers, and if the cops or the military came and took Adira away, I might never get them. This was my chance, maybe my only chance, to find the answers and closure I'd been searching for ever since the fire.

Reviewing what I knew, we had at least two people after us who were ready to kill—and had already done so three times—to get to us.

Let this play out. See what you can learn from Adira and then, if you need to, go to the authorities later tonight.

I was studying the parking lot, evaluating our situation, when Adira said to me, "Time to procure another vehicle."

"How do you propose we do that?" I said.

"We borrow one."

"You mean steal."

"The word *steal* has such a negative connotation," she said. "It makes the borrowing sound so permanent. When you were a kid, didn't you ever learn that it's good to share your toys? Think of it as a toy we're letting someone share with us. We can always bring it back later."

A college-age woman wearing a loose-fitting gray Georgetown sweatshirt and torn blue jeans was leaving the strip mall, heading toward a beat-up, twenty-year-old Camry. She toted her purse as well as two bags of purchases and stared distractedly at her phone as she walked.

"How about we rent one?" I suggested to Adira, retrieving a roll of cash from my glove box.

"Rent one?"

I left my car and approached the young woman, with Adira in tow. "Rent one?" she was saying. "Seriously?"

"Trust me."

"Ma'am," I said to the woman, who'd pocketed her phone and was digging through her purse, presumably for her car keys. "I work for the government. I'd like to rent your car. You'll get it back at the end of the week—until then, you can use mine."

She eyed me suspiciously. "Rent it?"

"I'll give you a thousand dollars for one week."

She glanced briefly at her car and then looked at me again. "It isn't even worth that much."

I held up the bills. "Okay, then I'll buy it from you."

After seeing the money, she began playing with one of her chipped pink-painted fingernails. "Um . . . now that I think about it . . . a week's rental *does* come out to a thousand dollars."

Adira scoffed. "Gimme a break. I'll just go and—"

"No," I said to her. "It's okay."

I unpeeled ten one-hundred-dollar bills and handed them to the woman, and even though she'd watched me count them out, she did so for herself as well.

"Okay!" she exclaimed as she plunged the cash deep into her purse. "Let me just get my stuff outta there. Then it's all yours."

"We're in a bit of a hurry, so—"

"Give me just one hot second."

While she was retrieving her items, Adira whispered to me, "I know how to hot-wire a car. I'm telling you, I could've just borrowed one for us. It wouldn't have cost you anything."

"Don't worry about the money."

"And how come you're carrying around a wad of dough big enough to choke a dinosaur with, anyway?"

I wasn't certain how much to share with her, but I figured that if I wanted her to be up front with me, I needed to be up front with her as well. "In my job, everything I do is closely monitored. Credit cards, electronic communication, bank accounts. Over the years, I set some cash aside, just in case I ever needed to do anything off the radar."

Like find my wife's killer, I thought.

"And why would you need to drop 'off the radar' of people at the Pentagon?" Adira asked me pointedly.

"This isn't the best time to get into all that."

"Uh-huh. You know all about me from reading my files, but I don't know anything about you except that you're a lawyer who works at the Pentagon— and has been planning for years how to disappear. Is the lawyer part even true?"

"I studied law, passed the bar, but I've never practiced. I'm a redactor."

"For who?"

"The Defense Department."

She gave me a curious look. "You redact DOD files?"

"Yes. That's how I read your FOIA request and your personnel file."

She sent the request to you by name. She should know all this. What's going on?

Nearby, the woman finished with her car and clunked the rust-pocked door shut. "Okay, that's everything," she announced. "And you'll seriously get it back to me in a week?"

"If I don't, you can keep mine," I said. "I'll call you."

She looked at me quizzically. "You don't have my number."

"I'll find it."

"How?"

"Magic." After retrieving my computer bag and phone from my car, I threw her the keys.

She hurried off, probably hoping to get out of the parking lot before I could change my mind, then accelerated down the street, leaving Adira and me alone beside the Camry.

"We need to move," Adira said.

"First things first. We need to lose anything that might lead the authorities to us." I held up my phone. "There are certain NSA initiatives that will . . . Well, let's just say a phone doesn't need to be powered on for them to find it. They can even remotely turn on devices, listen in, track your movement. It's scary what they can do."

"I hate to be the one to break this to you, Dr. Oblivious, but that's not exactly a secret. Everyone knows that. Ever since Snowden."

"Oh. Right. Sure."

She studied me. "You don't get out much, do you?"

"Not so much."

I crushed the phone underfoot and then smashed my laptop on the pavement before tossing the computer bag into the backseat of the Camry in case I needed any of the papers in it later. "Let's put some distance between us and that manufacturing plant."

We climbed into the sedan, which smelled faintly of cigarette smoke and pine-scented air freshener, and I cranked the engine. It coughed twice, then died.

"Oh, that's encouraging," Adira muttered. "You should've read the fine print on the rental agreement."

"Come on, buddy," I urged the car, "you can do it."

Adira looked at me skeptically. "Seriously? A pep talk?"

"Hey, you never know."

Finally, after two more tries, the old Camry backfired harshly and chugged to life. Cautiously, I nosed onto the street and then eased up to speed as night began to crawl into the crevices of the waning day around us.

Leaving the parking lot behind, I drove past a baseball field where a girl and a man whom I presumed to be her father were tossing a softball back and forth beneath the park lights, which were just now blinking on in anticipation of the coming dusk.

The girl, who was maybe nine or ten years old, giggled and cried out, "Haha, Daddy!" when he missed a catch and had to go track down the ball near the fence. I thought of her innocence and how the only thing she had to worry about right now was catching throws from her dad.

No other pressing issues. No adult-sized problems.

She likely had no idea about the pain pulsing through the world all around her or the kind of tragedy we'd just witnessed at the interrogation site.

Oppression, injustice, murder—all so close, so prevalent. All just a heartbeat, a breath away. But right now, she could be content to play and laugh with her dad. Right now—

"So," Adira said, drawing me out of my thoughts, "what are you doing helping to free a person of interest in a potential terror attack?"

"I don't think you did anything wrong."

"And why do you care about that?" She looked in my direction. "Why do you care about me?"

"I care about the truth," I said. "And I saw a connection."

"Between?"

"Between something that happened to me and what's happening to you."

"What are you talking about? What happened to you?"

I knew it was going to be tough to say the words because they would bring back bitter and stinging memories, but once again I felt the need to be honest and open with her.

"Seventeen months ago someone burned down my house while my wife and I were inside it." A lump formed in my throat as I pictured that burnt hand reaching out to me, the flames enveloping her. "I survived but she was killed, as I mentioned earlier." I needed a second to regroup before going on. Finally, I said, "I'm searching for answers, for closure. This FOIA request contained an acrostic that I think refers to a firm called the Patmos Financial Consortium. Does that ring a bell?"

Adira shook her head. "Never heard of 'em. And I'm sorry about your wife. Honestly, I wanted to tell you that when we were in the basement."

Her words sounded genuine and heartfelt. "Thanks."

A beat of stillness. "So, what was this connection you saw?" she asked.

"The date of the fire. And your name was linked to the FOIA request."

"My name?"

"Yes." I merged onto the highway. "We need some answers here. Is there anyone you trust?"

"One person. My boss—Nathan Lassiter."

"Wait." I glanced her way curiously. "I know Lassiter. He's aware of what I do. He knows about the fire."

Could he have anything to do with the Y-12 connection? He directs Adira's team. Maybe . . .

"We need to meet with him," Adira said. "He can clear this up."

"Is he close by?"

"I don't even know where we are."

"Maryland," I said. "Just outside of DC."

"Well, that's perfect then. He lives in Fairfax, Virginia. Shouldn't be too far."

"With traffic, maybe an hour. Maybe less."

"Make it less." She directed her focus out the window toward the twilit evening. "I want to get all this straightened out as soon as possible."

CHAPTER 20

Two years ago, after more than four decades of research, Dr. Chia-hao Yong had won the Nobel Prize in Physics for his work in isolating the properties of the typically unstable uranium-233 isotope and developing its potential use as a nuclear fuel. Since then, he'd focused his attention on researching air gap hacking technology in order to help protect the systems he'd spent his lifetime developing.

Now, he walked to the front desk to check in to the newly constructed eight-story hotel attached to the Oak Ridge Tech Corridor Conference Center on Bethel Valley Road.

As he was collecting his room key, the manager, a congenial man in his late forties, emerged from the back room. "Excuse me, Dr. Yong?"

"Yes?"

"There's a package for you. Give me just one second. I'll be right back." The man disappeared into the room again, and then returned momentarily, carrying a shoebox-sized package. Plain brown wrapping. A return address that Chia-hao didn't recognize in New York City. His name printed in simple block letters.

"Do you know who sent this?" he asked as he accepted it. The box was light and almost felt empty.

The manager smiled apologetically as he shook his head. "I'm sorry. I just know it was delivered here by courier about half an hour ago."

"Oh. Okay. Alright."

After Chia-hao signed for it, the man asked, "Would you like someone to help you with your luggage?"

"No. I am fine. Thank you."

Rolling his suitcase behind him, the physicist headed down the lush hallway toward the elevator to his fourth-floor room.

This was the sixth International Nuclear Association Safety Summit since he'd co-founded the organization with one of his colleagues from Germany seven years ago. The INA had been organized to contribute to the global knowledge on current cyber threats to nuclear weapons, power plants, and production facilities. Its mission consisted of identifying, isolating, and eliminating cyber vulnerabilities to nuclear systems worldwide. It wasn't run by any governmental entity and wasn't aligned with any single country's politics or any political party, but was committed instead to preventing radiological incidents anywhere on the planet.

Unfortunately, this was becoming more of a challenge as more and more countries explored using nuclear in their search for safe, renewable, carbon-free energy sources.

At his door, Chia-hao placed his key card against the reader. After the green light blinked on, he entered and found the room to be well appointed, with a sleek, contemporary design that made the most of muted bluish light, gentle reflective surfaces, and obtuse-angled walls.

Normally, the summit would've been held on the campus of the Oak Ridge National Laboratory near the Spallation Neutron Source research facility. Researchers there studied nanoscience, the arrangement of atoms, and how to imbed numbers and security codes into credit card strips, as well as structural integrity and microfractures in the metals used in bridges and airplanes, with the goal of reducing their failure rate.

However this year, because of the traffic and security concerns as a result of the ongoing construction of the Uranium Processing Facility on Y-12's campus, the conference was being hosted just a few miles down the road at the Tech Corridor's sweeping new complex.

Tomorrow, to get the summit rolling, Chia-hao would be giving the opening address, speaking on current cyber threats to nuclear systems. He had an informal meeting scheduled with Senator Richardson later tonight at the hotel bar, and he also needed to review his notes for his talk in the morning.

A full evening.

He set the package on the bed, left his luggage beside the closet, kicked off his shoes, and sighed. It'd been a wearyingly long day. He'd left Taiwan twenty-two hours ago, but it already felt like it had been a week since he'd kissed his wife goodbye back in Taipei.

Now, before unpacking his suitcase, he turned his attention to the package. It was taped up prodigiously, and it took some effort to get to the cardboard. But, at last, after sliding the tip of a car key along the tape, he was able to open the box's flaps. Inside, he found an elegant, lacy white fabric folded over itself.

Even more curious now, he carefully lifted the cloth to the side.

And gasped at what he saw.

Staggering backward, he pressed his hand against his mouth in horror.

His wife's ring finger, with her cherished antique wedding band still encircling it, lay in the box. Not every married woman in Taiwan chose to wear a wedding band, but Su-wei had. The ring had once been his grandmother's, and had been passed down through the family. There was no mistaking it.

The shock of seeing Su-wei's finger sent Chia-hao dropping backward into the chair by the window, offering a desperate prayer for her safety.

A USB flash drive waited beside the finger.

That was all the box contained. No note. No demands. Just the delicate nest of fabric containing Su-wei's finger and the drive.

Chia-hao was well aware of the ploy used by hackers of giving someone a USB drive with malicious code hidden on it. Out of simple curiosity, most people would insert the drive into a computer. Once it was mounted, the code would do its work—infiltrating the system and installing self-replicating algorithms that could record keystrokes and obtain passwords or other proprietary information.

Yes, he knew that. He knew all of that, but the life of his wife was at stake. He needed to find out what was on this drive.

Chia-hao powered up his laptop, took a deep breath, and, trembling, mounted the flash drive.

She is alive, he told himself. *She has to be. Or else her captors would not be doing this.*

A message appeared on the computer's screen: *Mount this while you are connected to the center's system tomorrow during your presentation. Do it and she lives. Tell anyone about this and she dies.*

"Oh, dear God," Chia-hao muttered. "It has begun."

CHAPTER 21

Earlier, since Sergei hadn't had anything with him to pick the handcuffs in the basement, he'd ended up wrenching off the handle of the file drawer to get free.

Now, back at the mechanics garage, Ilya used a hacksaw to free him from the cuffs.

"How's your wrist?" Sergei asked lightly. "From when she disarmed you?"

"Fine," Ilya grumbled.

"And your head?"

"All good. Next time we meet, she will not get away so easily."

"We can worry about her later. For now, what can you tell me about the tracker on Brock's computer bag?"

Ilya finished with the cuffs, consulted his laptop, and then informed Sergei that Brock was about fifteen miles away, heading west.

"Well," Sergei said thoughtfully, "whoever was with him—that woman— she's the reason he went to the manufacturing plant. We should learn who she is before we make another move on him. She might be valuable to our employer as well." He took out his van keys. "I'll drive. You type. I want you to find out whatever you can about our mystery woman."

⁓

In the basement of L & L Manufacturing, Gunnar Bane evaluated the situation.

No surveillance video. No witnesses. No answers. Three dead intelligence officers. Two fugitives—a redactor and a Red Team member, both of whom knew enough secrets to do some real damage to national security if they fell into the wrong hands.

Gunnar knelt to study a file cabinet that'd had one of its drawer handles violently torn off. It didn't appear that any files were missing, but that would need to be confirmed. He was calculating how much force it would've taken to tear the handle free and if one person could've reasonably done so by himself when Major Díaz approached him.

"State Police found a nineteen-year-old woman driving Brock's vehicle," the major said. "She says some guy with a scarred face rented her Camry from her. He was with a blonde. Short hair."

"Brock and Halprin."

"Yes. We're running a background on the woman who was in his car, but right now it looks like she's telling the truth."

Gunnar cocked his head. "She said he *rented* it?"

"Gave her a thousand bucks for the week."

Gunnar straightened up and brushed off his hands on the front of his khakis. "Can we track her car?"

"No. No GPS. Nothing like that. It's too old."

"Brock knew that when he took it," he muttered. Then added, "And his phone? Computer?"

"Both at the parking lot where he met up with her, a couple miles from here."

"And both destroyed, I'm guessing."

"Yes, sir."

"Let's go." Gunnar led Díaz up the stairs and outside.

Dusk was rapidly descending—the gloaming, they used to call it. The dying of the day. The birth of the night. The writer inside of him recorded the moment: *Twilight shadows lengthened around Bane and the major in the ebbing, crepuscular light.*

Gunnar tried to enter Brock's mindset, or even Halprin's. But empathy was not his specialty. It was something he was working on, this idea of seeing things from another person's point of view. His therapist had suggested that getting in touch with his feelings more would help him not be so tense all the time. "Get a hobby," she'd said. "Go and write the Great American Novel and try to imagine what it would be like to be each of the characters."

He was currently working on that. Maybe not a *great* novel, but hopefully a good-enough one. Sell it. Make some money. Pay for his niece's college education. *Write later*, he thought. *Focus now.*

"How did Brock pay her?" he asked Díaz.

"Pay her?"

"The woman he rented the car from. A thousand dollars is a lot of cash to be carrying around. Anything we can learn from her, let's learn it. We need to find a way to track Brock's movement."

"Who is this guy?" Major Díaz asked, a tinge of concern in his voice.

"Someone we need to make sure is still on our side."

CHAPTER 22

I exited the highway and guided the car beneath the glowing streetlights toward the address Adira had given me. We didn't have a map or GPS to guide us, but I was familiar with Fairfax and she'd been to Lassiter's house once before, so between the two of us we deciphered where it would be, now less than two miles away.

I'd spent the drive trying to get more information from her regarding the FOIA request, but she'd been reticent to talk about it. I'd pressed her as much as I felt comfortable doing, but she hadn't been very forthcoming.

Now, as we neared the house, she said, "I need to tell you something."

"Yes?"

"I didn't send in any Freedom of Information Act request."

"It was in your name," I said. "All of the documentation was in order."

"Must have been forged or faked somehow."

"You're serious?"

"Of course I am. How would it possibly benefit me to lie to you?"

That was actually a good question.

If it wasn't her, then who?

Someone else from Homeland?

Lassiter was the only name that came to mind, but why would he have sent it in using her name?

As I turned onto his street, Adira mentioned how odd it was that he hadn't vouched for her and that the number she'd been using to contact him came up as one used by a Russian hacking syndicate.

"Could he have rerouted or spoofed things so the messages sent to him would appear to be for them?" I asked.

"Sure, but why? That doesn't make any sense."

"Unless he was trying to justify having you transferred to that interrogation site."

"Again, why?"

"I don't know," I admitted.

"Well, that's the first thing I'm gonna ask him when we see him."

I shifted the topic to the message I'd gotten earlier in the day from Caruso referring to possible information regarding the date of the fire. "Do you know a Detective Caruso with DC's Metro Police Department?"

She shook her head.

I processed what I knew: the text message from Caruso, the FOIA request, Adira's arrest. All today. And all, apparently, somehow related. "Do you have any idea who those two guys were in the basement at the manufacturing plant?"

"You mean besides being Russians?"

"How do you know they were Russians?"

"Their guns were the first clue. A PSM and a Makarov? Seriously? Then the accent of the guy I knocked out. Also, I saw Russian mafia tattoos on his arms and neck—and I'd say he was pretty well established."

"Um . . ." Even though I was driving, I couldn't help but shoot a glance her way. "How do you know how to decipher Russian criminal underworld tattoos?"

"Has to do with a night in Almaty that I'd rather not get into right now."

"As in Almaty, Kazakhstan?"

"That's right."

"You just made me incredibly curious."

"I have a lot of stories. Don't get me started."

Given her background, I imagined she did have some intriguing stories. I could probe more into all that later. "Okay," I said, "so the two of them are Russians. But why were they after you?"

"Oh, they weren't after me."

"Why do you say that?"

"The guy I fought with, Mr. Mafia, he looked surprised to find me there. He asked who I was—plus, he was ready to kill me. The other guy could've easily taken you out, but he didn't. No, they didn't know me. They came there for you, and they didn't want you dead."

I let that sink in.

Anyone in my position, with my background and clearance level, was a prime target for foreign intelligence agencies. If the two Russians didn't want me dead, it might very well mean they wanted me to help them in ways only a traitor would. I didn't like thinking of myself as an asset, but with what I knew about our DOD programs, I could definitely see why the Russians might view me as one.

I felt a deep and widening sense of unease. From the start, Colonel Clarke and Metro PD had been working from the hypothesis that the fire that killed Sienna was started by someone who knew about my job. Maybe the Russians were involved in that somehow. But—

"There it is." Adira pointed. "Second house up on the left."

I dialed off the headlights and parked across the street from the two-story colonial, its windows black and blank against the night.

But if the Russians want you alive, why would they have tried to kill you in the fire? And why wait this long before coming after you again?

Two good questions I didn't have the answers to.

I could follow up on them both after we met with Lassiter.

With my window down, I heard crickets chittering from the shadows beneath a nearby hedgerow. A few dogs yapped halfheartedly at each other somewhere down the block. The scent of freshly mowed grass lingered in the damp spring air, along with the smell of charcoal and grilled meat from someone cooking out.

Adira opened her door. "Stay here. I'll be right back."

"Wait." I rolled up the window. "I'm coming with you."

"I need to talk to Nathan alone, figure out why no one seems to believe I'm part of his team. Then you and I can—"

"Ms. Halprin, I'm in this now just as much as you are. Whatever he has to say, it's going to be to both of us."

She looked like she might argue, but instead nimbly checked the chamber of the gun she'd obtained from the Russian mafia guy in the interrogation room and slid it under her belt. When I reached over and deposited the gun I'd gotten into the glove box, she said, "Aren't you going to take that with you? It's yours for keeps. We got it fair and square from the bad guys."

"I'm not really a fan of guns."

"Oh? And why is that?"

"Guns kill people," I said.

"So do peanuts."

"Peanuts? Really? You're going to go with that?"

"I'm just saying." She shook her head and exited the car and I joined her in the night. "Oh, and by the way," she added, "ditch the formalities. Call me Adira."

Walking up the driveway past a cobalt blue minivan with a handicapped sticker on the back license plate, we made our way onto the front porch. Adira reached out to knock, then froze, her fist just inches from the wood.

"What is it?" I asked.

Silently, she pointed at the door, which was open slightly, a darkened room just beyond it.

She drew her weapon and signaled for me to open the door. When I did, she crossed quickly past me into the house.

"Nathan?" she called.

A smear of jaundiced light from the sodium vapor streetlamp near the curb made its way through the open doorway, angling across the floor and tracing the shadow of her movements as she stalked, catlike, into the gloom.

"It's Adira," she said. "Are you here?"

No reply.

As I entered the living room, I regretted leaving that gun behind and snatched up a metal poker from beside the fireplace to defend myself with if I needed to.

A wheelchair sat near the couch. An oxygen tank lay beside it.

I didn't recall Lassiter having any health problems, but then a glimpse of a hospital bed in an adjoining room and a catalog on an end table that, even in the dim light, I could see was addressed to Raymond Lassiter, told me that Nathan wasn't living alone.

Adira indicated for me to check down the hallway while she negotiated past a set of matching recliners and headed up the stairs.

—◊—

As Adira ascended the steps, she listened intently for any movement in the house, but heard only the thin creaking of the bare boards beneath her feet.

Nathan's okay. There's no need to rush to conclusions. Maybe he's just not home. He could be out shopping, or—

Yeah, right. With his car in the driveway and the front door hanging open?

She reached the top of the stairs and peered down the shadowy hallway.

No movement.

No sounds.

Two doors stood ajar, and just enough pallid light climbed in for her to make out one additional door, although she already knew the home's layout from the time she'd been here to speak with Nathan about one of her assignments and had used the upstairs washroom.

She checked the first room on the left. A spotless guest bedroom. No sign of her boss.

The bathroom was also empty.

Her worry tightened, stretching the moment taut and thin. Senses dialed in, she crept down the hallway to the main bedroom.

Inside: a packed suitcase lying open on the scrupulously made bed. Evidently, Lassiter was planning on taking a trip somewhere.

A photograph of him beside an elderly man dressed in a colorful shirt and surrounded by four smiling Black men stood propped proudly on the dresser. Adira knew that Nathan's father had been a missionary in Africa for nearly fifty years. The dresser's drawers were still open from what appeared to be a rushed packing job.

She was inspecting the closet when she heard faint footfalls in the hall. In one smooth, practiced motion, she spun, leveling the PSM in front of her, but discovered it was only Travis, standing in the doorway, holding a fireplace poker. Exasperated, she lowered her weapon.

"Adira, you need to come with me." His voice was solemn and strained.

"What is it?"

"I found him. Prepare yourself. It's not something you're going to want to see."

CHAPTER 23

The glowing computer screen and floor lamp in the far corner of the room gave Adira enough light to see around the ground-floor office.

Travis had been right.

Nathan's body sat slouched in the brushed leather swivel chair behind the desk. His eyes were open, as if in surprise, and his mouth hung slack and drooping. He'd been shot in the right temple and a spattering of blood and gruesome gray matter from the cruel exit wound at the other side of his skull was splayed across the wall. A handgun lay on the floor just below his limp right hand.

"Oh, Nathan," Adira said softly.

Travis, whose face was flushed, laid a gentle hand on her shoulder. "I'm sorry."

Though her first instinct was to pull away, she didn't. Instead, she just stood there with the redactor beside her, attempting, in his own, somewhat awkward way, to comfort her as she tried to process things.

Nathan was dead.

Yes.

No! He can't be dead.

But he was.

A note had been typed on the computer:

Sorrow calls to each of us, shouting our name. As we grow older,
our past catches up with us. Peace is an illusion. Pain. Heartache.
I've had enough of them and I can't go on. Regrets overwhelm me.
Ending things this way is the only answer.

"It's a setup," she said. "He didn't kill himself."

"How can you tell?"

She indicated the gun. "It's not his."

"You sure?"

"The Secret Service started switching to Glocks in 2019 but used SIGs
before that. He's very brand-loyal. Stuck with his SIG all these years, even
after moving to TSA. That's a Walther PPQ M2. He doesn't own any Walthers
and he wouldn't use one, especially for . . ."

She couldn't bring herself to finish the sentence. That was when she realized she'd been referring to Nathan in the present tense. It made her throat
tighten.

Travis left her side and examined a cigar stub that was still smoking in an
ashtray on the teakwood executive desk. "Do you have any idea why someone
might've wanted to harm him?" he asked delicately.

He said "harm." He meant "kill."

"No." She still couldn't wrap her mind around the fact that her mentor
was sitting there, dead, in front of her. "But there are a lot of things happening today that I haven't been able to make sense of. Blood takes less than five
minutes to coagulate outside the body, and that cigar hasn't been there for
long. Whoever did this, I think we just missed them. We need to find out
what we can and get out of here."

"Look around," Travis said. "Is there anything you notice? Anything
unusual? Clues about who might've been responsible for this? Could it be
the Russians?"

"I doubt they could've beaten us here, but even if they could have, why
would they shoot Nathan when it's you they're after?" She shook her head.
"No, it wasn't them."

The sound of distant police sirens cut through the night.

"We better get moving," she said.

"Give me one sec."

—⟶—

Turning from the unnerving sight of Nathan's body, I scrutinized the room, committing it to memory, down to the subtlest detail.

She'd lost someone she knew here. For her sake, I tried to remain as composed as possible, but it wasn't easy to keep my shock at what'd happened in check.

As I rotated slowly in a circle, Adira asked, "What are you doing?"

"I have a pretty good memory. I'm trying to take it all in."

In a few moments, I'd memorized the room layout, the twelve brands of liquor on the shelf, and the titles, authors, and order of the one hundred and twenty-two books on the inset shelf near the window. I quickly flipped through and scanned the myriad of papers on the desk, committing them to memory, while Adira, using her fingernails to avoid leaving fingerprints as she typed, pulled up the computer's browser history.

One of the desk's papers was a funeral bulletin from yesterday, commemorating the life of Raymond Lassiter—the same name as the one on the catalog I'd seen earlier in the other room. Eighty-two. Survived by a son: Nathan Lassiter.

If his dad had been staying here, it certainly explained the home health equipment and hospital bed.

"His computer is logged in to his official account," Adira said. "The surfing history's been wiped, but he recently downloaded a PDF about a symposium tomorrow in Oak Ridge, Tennessee: the International Nuclear Association Safety Summit."

"That's it," I muttered.

"That's what?"

"Colonel Clarke mentioned a conference in Oak Ridge when I told him I needed to speak with you." I was distracted, thinking about the suicide note's wording. Something wasn't right. "Apparently it has something to do with Project Symphony."

"What's Project Symphony?"

"It deals with air gap hacking. I can't really say much more than that."

She headed to the printer in the corner of the room, where a single sheet of paper lay facedown in its output tray. Snatching it up, she flipped it over and said, "It's a flight itinerary. He was scheduled to fly down to Knoxville tonight, with a layover in Atlanta."

There was an acrostic in the FOIA request. What about in the suicide note?

"Do you think he was flying down there to Tennessee to meet you?" I asked as I mentally reviewed the suicide note and compared the wording to that of the FOIA request.

"I can't see how," she said, "if he was behind the transfer request to bring me up to that interrogation site. He would've known I'd be up here, not down south."

Timing? Maybe see her first, then fly down?

To confirm my suspicions about the note, I pulled up it up again on the computer.

Yes. The first letter of each sentence's first word held the meaning, just like in the FOIA request: *Sorrow . . . As . . . Peace . . . Pain . . . Heartache . . . I've . . . Regrets . . . Ending.* This time the acrostic spelled out SAPPHIRE.

"An acrostic." I pointed it out to Adira, then directed my focus to the bookshelf again.

"You said earlier there was one in the FOIA request," she noted.

"Yes."

"So he's the one who sent it in."

"That fits." I stepped closer to the books. "It was from Homeland."

"But why in my name?"

"I don't know."

Adira scrolled to the PDF again. "Does Y-12 mean anything to you?"

"It's a Department of Energy security complex in Oak Ridge, Tennessee," I said, sidetracked by the books' order on the shelf. Yeah. That's where I needed to look. "It's where the DOE stores our country's supply of weapons-grade uranium."

"Oh. Brilliant."

The police sirens pulsed outside, coming closer.

You can't let them find you here or you'll never get the answers you're looking for.

"I've never heard of Y-12 before," Adira said.

"Then someone's doing their job. Listen," I exclaimed hurriedly, my eyes on the bookshelf, "most people have an organizing principle that governs how they file things or place their books on a shelf. It might be alphabetical by title or author, or it could be topic or size or usefulness. A lot of people place books of the same color or a similar height beside each other."

"Okay," she said. "And?"

I gestured toward the shelf. "From the looks of it, his organizing principle is size and format rather than author. See the bottom four shelves?"

"What's your point? He likes to organize his books. I don't see what—"

"Yes. But what about the top shelf there? Sizes, topics, titles—they're all over the map."

"It's random."

"Knowing him," I said, "do you think it's random?"

A pause. "No. I don't."

I closed my eyes and tried to concentrate, but the knowledge that the authorities were on their way here, getting closer every second, made it tough.

He likes acrostics.

I sorted through the letters on the spines of the books—the order, the wording, the authors, the spelling—then opened my eyes again. "Wait. Look at the first letters of the authors' last names. Left to right. See?" I pointed as I read off the first word: "SAPPHIRE—the same as the acrostic in the note." I continued, "FLOWER . . . GIRL . . . VENUS . . . TYPHOON . . . BARD . . . Do those words mean anything to you?"

Hurry, Travis. You need to get moving!

"I'm Flower Girl. I'd say those would be the code names of the Red Team members." She stared at me, nonplussed. "How did you even identify that? Who are you?"

"Patterns. Relationships. Latent significance—it's what I do for a living."

Outside, red and blue lights were cycling off the houses down the street. Agitated neighborhood dogs yelped restlessly.

"Let's go." I took Adira's hand to lead her out of the room, but she reached for the papers on Lassiter's desk.

"We should probably leave those here," I said.

"My name's on some of these printouts." She snatched them up. "I want to know why. Besides, this info just might lead us to the killer."

After hastily wiping my prints off the fireplace poker and returning it to where I'd found it earlier, we slipped out the back door, into the night.

Waiting in the bushes for a moment, we watched a patrol car pull up to the house and two officers hop out. They rushed up onto Lassiter's porch, guns drawn.

"Now," Adira whispered to me. "Go."

We kept low and, picking our way through the shadows, quickly crossed the street to the Camry. Just after we ducked inside, one of the neighbor's porch lights came on. I didn't know if someone had seen us, or if they were just curious about the police officers' arrival.

I cranked the engine, praying it would start. After twice failing to turn over, it finally engaged and we rolled forward as the lights of more police cruisers appeared in the rearview mirror and went skidding to a stop in front of Lassiter's house.

"What are you thinking?" Adira asked me.

"I'm thinking I know where we need to go to find our answers."

"Oak Ridge, Tennessee."

"Exactly."

CHAPTER 24

The person who'd hired Sergei and Ilya to speak with Detective Caruso evaluated the progress of all that was in play.

The detective was taken care of—a bit of a messy business, that, but probably the only way things could have gone. In the end, Caruso had confirmed that he'd been looking into both the disappearance of Lena Rhodes, an employee at the State Department's Office of the Legal Advisor, and the fire at the Brock residence. Two cases. Two different sets of circumstances. And yet, related all the same. Despite Ilya's rather earnest attempts at extracting more information, it appeared that Caruso had not shared his hypothesis of a connection with anyone.

That was good. Discovering where Lena currently was would have changed everything.

There were a lot of moving parts here, no question about that, but regarding the conference tomorrow, all of the dominoes were set in place and they would fall in sequence, one by one. Dr. Yong would open the gateway and, when it was all over, the world would be more awake to the apocalyptic power of radioactive isotopes and safer than it had been since the day in 1945 when the atomic age began, even if downtown Knoxville would be uninhabitable for the next few decades.

Yes, a lot of moving parts. But for now at least, that was how things needed to play out. The paperwork for Patmos Financial Consortium's land acquisition in North Dakota had gone through earlier in the day. The final domino placed on the table.

Now, to confirm that the physicist's wife, Su-wei Yong, was secure, and then get some sleep.

Tomorrow promised to be an eventful day, especially with what was going to happen in downtown Knoxville at eleven fifteen, after the children were seated at World's Fair Park directly beneath the bomb.

CHAPTER 25

A s we were merging onto Interstate 66, I kept a close eye out for patrol cars on our tail, but so far we seemed to be in the clear.

Most of my days were uneventful—no one chasing me or aiming guns at me. No danger. Nothing really shocking or exciting or unsettling, a far cry from today. It was hard to move past the brutal images of the three corpses at L & L Manufacturing and the horror of finding Lassiter's body.

Having an eidetic memory doesn't mean you remember everything you encounter at every moment of the day, but it does mean that once images, numbers, and relationships get their hooks into you, it's pretty tough to shake them loose.

Now, in the car, Adira was paging through the dozens of papers she'd taken from Lassiter's desk. "Tell me about Y-12," she said, and I figured that maybe talking about the site would help ease my frayed nerves and maybe assist us in unearthing what the security complex in Oak Ridge had to do with the two of us and Lassiter's murder.

"Y-12 was part of the Manhattan Project back in the forties, which was tasked with producing an atomic bomb to end World War II. Two other locations were also involved in the project, one in Hanford, Washington, and one in Los Alamos, New Mexico. The Y-12 site at Oak Ridge was responsible for finding a way to enrich uranium for the bomb."

"And they managed to do it."

"Yes. They tried a number of different techniques, but the one that worked best—even though it was really slow going—was using something called calutrons to separate uranium-235, which is only .7 percent of the uranium found in nature, from uranium-238."

She looked up from the papers. "What in the world is a calutron?"

"It's a made-up word, actually. Comes from California University cyclotron. They were huge mass spectrometers that were used to separate uranium isotopes. Anyway, eventually, after eighteen months of 24/7 work with tens of thousands of employees using more than eleven hundred calutrons, the site was able to produce enough u-235 to fill a gallon paint can. Enough for one bomb."

"Hiroshima?"

"Yes."

"So, enough uranium to kill what was it, a hundred thirty thousand people?" Her tone bordered on being antagonistic.

"Estimates vary," I said soberly, "but I believe that with the aftereffects it was at least that many."

She was quiet for a moment, then said, "How do you know all this, anyway?"

"Part of my job. Ever since 2020 with the seventy-fifth anniversary of the culmination of the Manhattan Project, there've been an increasing number of FOIA requests regarding Oak Ridge's mission after the war. I've had to read up on it."

I sensed that she was deep in thought, and wondered what was going through her mind.

"What *did* they do after the war?" she said at last. "I mean, did they continue producing more uranium for more bombs?"

"For a while, yes. Officially, Y-12 is responsible for maintaining the safety of the US nuclear stockpile, reducing global radiological threats, and providing enriched uranium—sometimes called feedstock—to the Navy for its nuclear submarines and aircraft carriers."

"And unofficial research too, I presume?"

I hesitated slightly. "Some, yes. I can't tell you everything, but I can say that over the years the Oak Ridge National Laboratory has been repurposed as a research facility for isolating and understanding radioactive isotopes that are currently used in research and nuclear medicine. Oak Ridge was the place where nuclear medicine was first developed."

She flopped the papers to the floor and grumbled in frustration. "I can't make heads or tails of what any of this paperwork has to do with Oak Ridge." She took out the gun I'd gotten from the Russians and, as I drove, she began to fiddle with it, expertly popping it apart and then sliding it back together again as if she were getting ready for a gunfight. "I've heard that was quite an operation back then, during the war. You said tens of thousands of employees?"

"The site was originally designed to house thirteen thousand people, but the population quickly surpassed that—peaking at about seventy-five thousand in 1945, making it, at the time, the fifth-largest city in the state of Tennessee—but also a city that didn't appear on any maps."

She clicked the gun's chamber back into place. I wasn't sure that I loved this new hobby of hers. "A secret city," she said.

"Exactly. And only a handful of people even knew what they were building there. Everyone was told that they were helping with the war effort—they were aware of that much—but it wasn't until after the bomb was dropped that they found out the truth of what they'd done."

"That they were responsible for murdering all those people."

"You mean for ending the war."

She set the gun down and looked directly at me. "Tens of thousands of innocent people died, right? Maybe even hundreds of thousands? Wasn't it Dorothy Day who called it the 'colossal slaughter of the innocents'?" Her voice had taken on a razor's edge.

I didn't want to argue, but I needed to remind her of the broader context. "Upwards of eighty-five million people died all over the world as a result of the war," I said. "That was the greater slaughter. Someone had to stop the madness. The Manhattan Project did that."

"By killing civilians."

"By doing what was necessary."

A touch of silence.

In any discussion about the role of the research done in Oak Ridge and the use of the nuclear bombs, emotions can naturally run high and I prepared myself for a sharp response.

"Why Tennessee?" she asked at last.

"General Groves, who was in charge of the Manhattan Project, chose the site at Oak Ridge because the Tennessee Valley Authority had recently built Norris Dam, which could provide the vast amount of power necessary to run the facility. It was also far enough inland that if enemy bombers identified it, they wouldn't be able to make it there from either coast. The land was cheap and sparsely populated. In fact, in the ninety square miles that were purchased for the project, only three thousand people needed to be relocated. And it was nestled in a valley, so if there was a radiological event, it would've at least to some degree been naturally contained."

"You mentioned the Tennessee Valley Authority. And I recall seeing some Oak Ridge signs when I was in Knoxville earlier. The cities are close, aren't they?"

"Yes. Maybe twenty-five miles apart."

She sighed and shook her head. "Right back to where I started from this morning. How long of a drive are we talking about?"

"I'm guessing seven hours or so. We basically take 81 south, then hop onto 40. A pretty direct route."

"But a lot quicker in an airplane," she muttered. "I'm up for a road trip, but I need some food first. I haven't eaten anything since this morning."

Come to think of it, neither had I.

"I could use a bite," I said.

"We need to find somewhere that doesn't have security cameras. Not a chain restaurant. Not a gas station. Maybe a mom-and-pop place somewhere? That'd probably be our best bet."

"I like how you think, Adira."

"Thank you, Mr. Redactor."

"Let's go with Travis."

"Travis it is. So, just so we're on the same page here: a quick bite to eat, we stretch our legs, use the washroom, and then we're on our way again, pronto."

"Agreed. And, 'pronto'? Really?"

"'Straightaway' just didn't seem to carry the same sense of urgency. And besides, it's a lot more fun to say 'pronto.'"

"It's tough to argue with that."

Without a map, it took a few minutes, but finally we came across Sammy's Burger Pit, an all-night diner that looked like it might fit the bill. I parked in the shadows tucked up on the far edge of the lot. Only two other cars were there.

STEVEN JAMES || 127

"Well?" Adira said. "What do you think?"

"Looks about as mom-and-pop as it gets." I clicked off the sputtering engine.

"Let's eat, let's pee, and let's go." She picked up the papers and we left the car.

Inside the diner, the smell of kitchen grease hung heavy in the air. A dozen empty booths and tables, alternating maroon and eggshell white, were squeezed into the cramped floor-plan.

Adira handed me the papers from Nathan's desk and made a beeline for the restroom. I took a seat in a rear booth with my back to the wall so no one could approach me from behind. From there, I could also keep an eye on the front door.

The flickering fluorescent light above my head buzzed with a constant insect-like whine. Other than that, and the sound of a few clanking dishes in the kitchen, the place was quiet.

It was empty too, and I liked that there weren't any other patrons here to see us, but I *didn't* like that we might end up being all the more memorable to Sammy's staff because of it.

Our server, an enervated woman in her late twenties, had frizzy, burgundy hair and wore an ACE brace supporting her left wrist. She handed me a menu and smiled somewhat wearily at me. "Long day or long night?"

"I'm sorry?"

"You sighed to yourself. Probably didn't even notice." Her name tag read *Sophie*. "I was just wondering: Did you have a long day or is it gonna be a long night?"

I held back a yawn, which was suddenly vying for my attention. "I'd say it's looking like a little of both."

"Well, then you definitely need some coffee." Rather than staring at the scars on my face, she was looking me directly in the eyes, politely and respectfully. I liked it. "How d'ya take it?"

"Black. And bring two, would you?"

"You really do need some coffee," she said lightly. "You know what else you want?"

"Um." I stared distractedly at the menu. "I have someone else with me. She'll be here in a minute. We're in a bit of a hurry . . ."

As if from nowhere, Sophie produced a second menu and placed it across the table from me, then said, "If you're not sure what to get, most people go with the Sammy's Scrumptio-Burger. It's sorta what we're known for. You can get 'em with up to four half-pound patties—those come with coronary bypass surgery coupons for St. Mary's Hospital."

I couldn't help but smile. "A joke, right?"

"Maybe." She leaned close and spoke in a voice hushed enough so that the grill cook wouldn't have been able to hear. "I'd suggest the black bean burger, myself. It's quicker too."

"Gotcha." Not sure if Adira would want to go for a bean burger, I said, "Give me a minute to decide."

"Okay." Sophie knuckle-rapped the table affirmatively. "I'll be back in a sec with two cups o' joe."

As she left, I attempted to trace the clues back to the truth.

Trying to keep from speculating too much, I considered the acrostic messages, Lassiter's murder, and his history with both Adira and me. The evidence pointed toward him being the one to send in the FOIA request in her name. But why? To bring us together? If so, that could explain why he hadn't cleared her name and allowed her to be brought up from Knoxville to L & L.

Not just allowed it, I thought. *Orchestrated it.*

Then there was Colonel Clarke's offhanded mention of the conference in Tennessee, the date of the fire on the FOIA request, and the code names of the five Red Team members: Sapphire—of special significance because she was implicated in the suicide note—Flower Girl, Venus, Typhoon, Bard.

And the Russians. Don't forget the Russians.

Finally, we had the issue of the financial consortium's land purchases nationwide. Could the sites be related somehow to the Oak Ridge National Laboratory? Something to do with Paraden or some sort of nuclear engineering or microprocessor development?

I could sense that there was some deep connection running beneath everything, stretching from the arson all the way to Lassiter's murder, but at the moment, what that might be—or who might be behind it—eluded me. And that frustrated me, because I was the one whose expertise was supposed to be noticing the veiled relationships that most people missed.

CHAPTER 26

Adira left the washroom, located Travis, and plopped down on the slick, plastic-covered seat across the booth from him. As she straightened the facedown stack of papers in front of her, she said, "There was a cockroach as big as a mini-weenie in that bathroom. I'm not even kidding."

"I'm sorry . . ." He seemed deep in thought. "A mini-weenie?"

"Yeah, a cockroach. Scary big." She showed him with her fingers, maybe exaggerating just a shade for effect. "You ever wonder why we only do that with little weenies?"

"Why we . . . ?"

"Stick 'mini' in front of them if they're small. We don't have mini-burgies, mini-bratties, or mini-wingies."

"Wingies?"

"Chicken wings."

"Oh."

"Nope. Just mini-weenies."

"Yeah. Okay . . . gotcha. Oh, I ordered you a coffee."

"Only way I can drink that stuff is if I kill the taste with sugar." Nathan's murder weighed heavily on her, but she did her best to pretend that it wasn't troubling her. She had to or she might lose it. She began collecting a pile of sugar packets from the bowl on the table, then scanned the menu. "What are we ordering?"

"Most people get the Sammy's Scrumptio-Burger," Travis answered. "But I have it on good authority that the bean burger is worth a try. And it's quick."

"Whose authority?"

"Sophie's."

She eyed him.

"What?"

"You're on a first-name basis with the server already?"

"She was wearing a name tag. That's what they're there for, so you can get to know your server's name."

"Uh-huh." She smirked.

"I'm not sure what you're—"

"You were flirting with her, weren't you?"

"No. Of course not. She's too young for me."

"Ah. I see. And how old are you?"

"Thirty-seven."

"How old do they need to be?"

He blinked. "Do who need to be?"

"Women. For you to flirt with them?"

"Um . . ."

"Do you know how old I am? Oh wait, you read my file, didn't you? So, yeah, you know. Thirty-four. Do I make the cut?"

"The cut . . . ?"

"Yeah. Would you flirt with me?"

"I mean . . . I . . ."

"You're not very good at this are you?"

"At what?"

"Witty banter."

"It might not be my specialty. No."

"Hmm. Well, that's something for us to work on then, isn't it?"

He opened his mouth as if he was going to reply, then closed it again without saying anything.

Sophie returned carrying two cups of coffee and Adira greeted her. "Hi, Sophie." She tapped the menu. "We'll have two of the bean burgers. I hear they're to die for."

"Um. They're good. Yeah."

"Alright. Load 'em up. The works." She glanced at Travis. "The works work for you, dear?"

"Sure."

"And do they come with fries?" Adira asked. "We love french fries."

"They come with fries," Sophie said.

"Perfect."

"Okay." Sophie gave Travis a brief, quizzical look, then retrieved the menus and headed toward the kitchen.

Adira smiled. "She seems sweet."

"Dear?"

"Yes?"

"No, I mean why'd you call me 'Dear'?"

She reached over and tenderly took his hand. "It's part of our legend. We're a happily married couple." She let go. "A legend is a fake identity."

"I know that."

"Good."

She let go of his hand and turned to the sugar packets. After ripping open seven of them, she poured their contents into her steaming coffee, swirled them around with the overturned handle of her spoon, took a sip, frowned, and then added three more packets.

Travis tried his coffee. He went with it black and it didn't seem to bother him. "You okay?" he asked.

"Yeah." She studied him. "Why wouldn't I be okay?"

"Well, there were those guards who were shot at the manufacturing plant, and then Nathan . . . It's . . ."

"A lot to take in in one day," she said, anticipating where he was going.

"Yes."

"A lot of death."

"Yes," he said. "It is. It is a lot of death."

"Are *you* okay?"

"I'm working through it, but I didn't know Nathan. Losing someone you know is a lot different than just coming upon . . . well . . ."

"Yep. I'm fine."

"Because if you need to talk or—"

"I said I'm fine."

"Okay." After a brief pause, he asked, "How long did you know him?"

She was tempted to evade the topic, but then Travis might think it really *was* upsetting her, which she told herself wasn't the case.

"Ten years. But you read my file. You probably already knew that."

"Not everything is in your file."

"Like?"

"How you feel. Who you care about. Where you hurt."

"You're getting better."

"At what?"

"Saying the right things." She gulped down some coffee. "I first met Nathan when I was in the Secret Service. That's how he knew about me. Later on, when he transferred to the TSA to oversee the Red Team, he started recruiting people and called me in. At the time, I was going through a bit of a rough patch in my life and he was there for me."

"He was more than your boss," Travis concluded softly. "He was your friend."

"I thought I knew everything back at the Secret Service, you know? I was so sure of myself. Then, when I was finishing my training, Nathan asked me if I was ready to do what needed to be done to carry out my job. I said, 'Yes, of course.' Then he asked me, 'What if you found out I was a double agent? Would you do your job then?'"

"Your job?" Travis said. "You mean arrest him?"

"Not quite arrest."

"Oh."

"Yeah. And I said, 'I would have to confirm it first, sir. To know for certain.' And that's when he shook his head and said, 'Adira, in this line of work, certainty is a luxury you will rarely have. Go where the evidence takes you. Do what has to be done, even if you're not *sure*.'"

Travis waited and finally, she went on. "I never forgot that: certainty is a luxury I'll rarely have. That's how I've tried to live since then, trusting my instincts and moving forward even when I'm not certain about things. And now, he's gone."

"I'm sorry," Travis said, and it sounded like he really meant it. "I wasn't trying to pry. I—"

"It's alright." She put on a smile and brushed away a stupid tear that was leaking for no reason from her right eye. Going for her coffee again, she downed the rest of it. "Now what? Where are we at?"

He must have realized that she wasn't ready to discuss her grief any further because he let it be and moved on. "I've been thinking," he said reflectively. "Maybe we should just turn ourselves in and tell the authorities the truth."

"Not on your nelly."

"Wait—on my nelly?"

"It's an old saying my Gramma used to use. I just mean you need to erase that option from your bright ideas list. You might have amazing observational skills, but right now you're not thinking clearly."

"Why do you say that?"

"Because I told the truth and look where it got us—I ended up arrested, Nathan ended up dead, and you ended up on the lam with a wanted terrorist."

She was reminded again of the stakes of getting caught—unless they found some answers now, she might not be able to clear her name, especially with Nathan dead. But if she could figure out who killed him, she might be able to exonerate herself.

"Do you have any idea who might be behind this?" Travis asked. "Could it be someone else on your team?"

She sensed movement behind her, turned, and saw Sophie striding their way with a coffee pot in hand.

"I'm good," Adira told her.

Sophie looked at Travis, questioningly, one eyebrow raised.

He placed his hand over his cup.

"Okie dokie," she said. "Your food should be out in a minute."

Adira waited until Sophie had returned to the kitchen, then said to Travis, "It *could* be someone on the team. I mean, let's say the killer had a gun on Nathan and made him write a suicide note and he takes the opportunity and leaves the acrostic SAPPHIRE. I think we can assume he was at least *potentially* leaving the name of his killer."

"It's a place to start."

"Yes. However, I don't even know who the team members are, and with Nathan dead, I'm not sure how we're going to find out their real identities. I mean, we might have their code names now, but I don't know how much good that's going to do us. How did the Russians know where you were, by the way? Back at that interrogation site?"

Travis shook his head. "I'm not sure. Followed me from the Pentagon, I guess."

"On the flight up to DC, the guy who was questioning me told me that the phone number I'd been using to contact Nathan was a number that'd been associated with a Russian hacking syndicate."

"Russians again. Do you think Nathan was compromised?"

"I hope not, but I think all of this is somehow tied together—the Russians targeting you and someone setting me up with a Russian hacker group." She paused and considered the implications of what she'd just said.

"What is it?" he asked.

"If we only had a computer, you could use your clearance to maybe find out who the other Red Team members are—their real names, that is. That might help us figure out how Nathan was involved, or why he was targeted."

"True," Travis acknowledged.

"And if he was a part of Project Symphony—the air gapping research you mentioned earlier."

"Yes."

"You going to tell me any more about that now that we're married?"

"Can't. Nice try, though."

"Uh-huh." She gave him half of the stack of papers from Nathan's desk. "I don't know if any of this is relevant, but let's see if we can figure out what he was working on when he was killed."

CHAPTER 27

Brock must not have identified the tracker on his computer bag yet because Sergei Sokolov was able to follow the Camry to a diner. Parking the van fifty meters down the street from the restaurant, he asked Ilya, "Are you finding anything on her? What do you have?"

Ilya whipped through a quick background on the woman: Her name was Adira Halprin, she'd spent a couple of years with the Secret Service, then started working as a bodyguard and, most recently, took a part-time job with DHS, although her role there was a bit unclear. "Was not easy to uncover any of that. Someone went through a lot of trouble to bury her past."

"But if she's working for Homeland, why would they arrest her and then take her away to interrogate her?"

Ilya shook his head. "Don't know. We take them now?"

After a brief deliberation, Sergei said, "Maybe. Keep searching. Let's see what else you can find out about her Homeland Security work before we contact our employer to figure out the next appropriate step."

—ᴠᴠ—

As we waited for our food to come, I perused the papers and kept one eye on the door while Adira carefully reviewed the printouts, studying them for anything that might shed more light on what was going on.

She noted that a number of the pages mentioned studies done by the Nobel Prize-winning physicist Dr. Chia-hao Yong. Apparently, Nathan was quite interested in his research. One of the printed pages from Yong's website included his speaking schedule—and he was going to appear at the International Nuclear Association Safety Summit in Oak Ridge in the morning—another confirmation that, by driving to Tennessee, we were heading in the right direction.

I pointed to a symbol that'd been drawn on the edge of a couple of the sheets. "Do you know what this might mean?"

Adira shook her head. "A fishhook? A shepherd's staff? A meaningless squiggle? Could be anything." One stapled printout included a list of her executive protection detail gigs from the last three years. She studied them carefully, then turned to the fourth page and showed it to me. "These are from the jobs I worked when I wasn't doing Red Team assignments. It's all off my personal calendar. Obviously, I don't publicize that or post it anywhere. He would've had to do some real digging to pull this stuff up."

One of the assignments in Belgium was highlighted. I indicated it. "Why draw attention to that one?"

"No idea. It was an environmental conference. Had nothing to do with nukes."

"Let's piece together what we know." I held up the funeral bulletin. "Yesterday was Nathan's dad's funeral. And based on the hospital equipment at the house, he was clearly taking care of him."

"And he was packing for a flight down to Knoxville. But he just booked the flight this morning." She consulted the printouts. "Just before nine o'clock."

"Two hours after the FOIA request came in. What do you know about his dad?"

"Not much," she replied. "He was a missionary in Africa for most of his life—Nathan mentioned that to me once. He was proud of him, of his values. Dedication to what he believed in and to social change. It meant a lot to him."

I thought of the contrast between how Nathan had seen his father and how I saw mine—polar opposites, from the sound of it. One man placed the needs of others first; the other thought only of himself. One man reached out to help others with an open hand; the other beat his wife with a closed fist.

"And Nathan's mother?" I said.

"Never mentioned her. I don't know how much she was ever in the picture." Adira thought for a moment. "Nathan could have easily cleared my name, but instead he had me flown back to DC to be interrogated."

"And he put your name on the FOIA request that he sent to me."

"He was trying to get us together," she muttered. "But why . . . ? Earlier you said he knew you, knew what you did. Maybe he needed information from both of us, but couldn't come right out and say it."

"Because he was afraid?" I suggested. "His life was threatened?"

"And then it was taken from him," she said somberly.

I failed to come up with anything to say that might have helped. Instead of trying to fill the silence with words that wouldn't have been enough, I laid my hand on hers.

After a moment, she nodded, then pulled her hand away.

Sophie appeared, skillfully balancing a serving platter with our plates of bean burgers and fries, as well as two topped-off glasses of ice water. She left the kitchen and headed toward us.

Even though we were the only patrons at the restaurant, I felt exposed being here and I was becoming more and more anxious to get back on the road. "Let's get moving," I said to Adira. "We can eat just as well in the car as we can in here. And we run less of a risk of being seen by someone. More time here means more exposure."

"Great minds." Adira collected the papers. "The sooner we get to Oak Ridge, the sooner we get some answers."

As Sophie approached our table, I told her, "Listen, could we have some boxes to go?"

"Oh. Sure." For some reason she sounded disappointed. "I'll be right back." She set everything down and then left to find boxes for us.

Without waiting for them, Adira slathered a huge dollop of ketchup across her fries. "Thanks for treating, dear. Next time, I'll pay. By the way, do you have anything other than hundreds?"

"No."

"Why all the Benjamins?"

I shrugged. "No reason. Just the way it turned out. I'd take money out of the bank, stick it in my car for when I might need it. I guess it was just easier to save it by getting hundreds."

"For when you might need it?" A touch of suspicion in her voice. "You mean in case you needed to disappear, like you said earlier?"

I didn't want to get into explaining that I'd wanted to be prepared if I needed to go off the grid someday in my search for Sienna's murderer, so I just nodded.

"Well, then," Adira said, evidently deciding not to probe, "the tip will be your good deed for the day."

"What are you saying? Leave a hundred?"

"Why not? You're made of money. Actually, give her an extra one too."

"Why?"

"She's a waitress with a brace on her wrist, for goodness' sake. Probably makes less than minimum wage."

"Don't you think that'll make us more memorable?"

"Really?" She eyed me. "I mean, no disrespect—seriously—but she's seen the scars on your face. They're not easy to miss. You're a memorable guy, Travis Brock, regardless of how big or small of a tip you might leave."

I wasn't sure how to reply to that. She actually had a pretty good point.

When Sophie returned with the takeout boxes, I handed her the bills and Adira said, "Get that wrist taken care of."

While Sophie stood there dumbstruck, I deposited the food into the boxes, Adira collected the papers, and then the two of us left for the car.

"I'll take the first shift," I offered as I pressed the diner's door open.

"Good. I get ketchup all over myself when I try to drive and eat fries at the same time. I'll feed you yours, though. No problemo."

"Thanks, dear."

We walked out into the night.

"Don't mention it."

CHAPTER 28

9:58 P.M.

Dr. Chia-hao Yong stared at his drink in the crowded sports bar inside the lavish hotel attached to the Oak Ridge Tech Corridor Conference Center. A bead of sweat formed on his forehead. All he could think about was his wife's severed finger and her abductors' demands.

Was Su-wei even alive? Where had they taken her? Who was responsible for this? What would happen if he mounted the USB drive during his presentation in the morning? Did the people who had her know that he would be meeting with Senator Richardson tonight? Were they watching him even now?

Chia-hao nervously looked around the bar to see if anyone was staring at him. The place was busy, but it didn't appear that anyone was paying him any particular attention.

Based on his consulting work with the United States government, he knew that USB drives weren't allowed on military bases or in secure federal facilities. This conference, though run by a civilian organization, dealt with matters of security and sort of blurred that line, so even though he might get into trouble for mounting the flash drive, he could probably get away with it.

The senator's flight had been delayed and he'd texted a change of time to ten o'clock. Although it was later than Chia-hao would have liked, he'd felt obligated and agreed to still meet.

He lifted the whiskey to his lips, thinking that he would only take a sip, but then swallowed the whole drink and held the glass out to the bartender for a refill.

He thought of Su-wei and their life together and the grave danger she was in.

Senator Richardson might be able to help. He has contacts. He has resources at his disposal. Maybe he's on some committee in Congress that would be able to work with the FBI or the CIA to find Su-wei.

But of course there was that warning not to tell anyone what was happening or else the captors would kill her.

Honestly, Chia-hao had no idea what steps to take.

If he followed the instructions from the USB drive, it would most likely infect the network with malicious software that might find its way into Y-12's system files. With the right kind of coding, it was certainly possible. It could undermine everything he'd dedicated his life to accomplishing. But with Su-wei's life at stake, what choice did he have?

One final, unsettling question scratched away at the back of his mind: How had they gotten her finger here so quickly?

He felt a chill as he realized that it had most likely been on the same flight as him. He'd checked his bag and consequently had to wait for it to come through at the baggage claim, so it was certainly possible that someone could have simply carried the finger onto the flight and then delivered it directly here to the hotel.

Which would mean there was someone working with her abductors here, in the area.

Chia-hao found himself peering around the bar again.

Nothing unusual. No one he recognized.

Earlier, he'd looked up Senator Richardson's photo online, but that was an official picture, and he wasn't sure he would recognize him in person when the time came. The senator had promised to text him when he arrived. Chia-hao checked his phone but found no new messages.

Anxiously, he rolled the whiskey glass between his fingers and thought about how he'd gotten here, into this predicament in the first place.

Everything had changed for him when he won the Nobel Prize in Physics. Until then he'd worked, and lived, in relative obscurity. Certainly, his research was known to a small group of scientists, but beyond that, he didn't imagine that many people in the general public would have recognized his face or even heard of his name.

Then, two years ago: the prize.

Yes, the money that went with it was nice, although he'd poured most of it into his research and philanthropy. His lifestyle hadn't changed much, but his sphere of influence had expanded exponentially. There were the seemingly endless interviews on news networks and for leading media outlets and podcasts—all of which allowed him to get his message out.

Admittedly, though, it wasn't a very cheerful one.

Chia-hao didn't want to be the harbinger of bad news or a naysayer to progress—but in light of the impact humans were having on the planet, the entire concept of "progress" needed to be redefined. Success could no longer mean simply material acquisition. It needed to take into account the well-being of other humans, as well as the other inhabitants of our fragile biosphere.

When managed properly, nuclear, along with solar, wind, geothermal, and wave capture technology could provide all of humanity's current energy needs and enough for perhaps another four or five billion people on the planet.

The key to employing nuclear energy was the proper—and safe— utilization of radioactive isotopes. But in today's world of cyber threats to nuclear systems, it was becoming harder and harder to ensure that the necessary safety measures were in place. So his research had shifted toward safeguarding against targeted attacks on closed systems.

That's what he was planning to address in his opening keynote tomorrow morning at the summit—at least, as much as possible without revealing any of the classified information he was privy to because of his consulting work with the Pentagon's research arm, DARPA.

He checked his phone again, and this time found a text: **I'm here, Doctor. Sorry I'm late. I see you at the bar. I'll be right there.**

Chia-hao looked up from his refilled drink and noticed a lanky, distinguished gentleman making his way through the packed bar. The man appeared to be in his early fifties, had light-brown hair, and was dressed stylishly with a loosened tie. He smiled amiably as he approached.

"Senator Richardson?" Chia-hao asked, bowing slightly as a means of greeting.

"Dr. Yong. It's a pleasure to meet you."

Only after the man took a seat on the barstool beside him did it occur to Chia-hao that he had no way of confirming if this really was the senator. It looked like him, yes, but Chia-hao wasn't certain, and he was so nervous that, at the moment, he didn't trust himself to get anything right.

"Once again, I'm sorry I'm late," the man said.

"It is alright."

He indicated Chia-hao's glass. "What are you drinking?"

"George Dickel. Tennessee whiskey."

"Sounds agreeable to me. When in Rome." He placed his drink order and slid closer to the bar.

"Please forgive me," Chia-hao said, suddenly more wary than he had been all night. "How can I be sure that you are who you say you are?"

The man nodded. "Prudent. Yes. That's smart." He produced his congressional badge and driver's license. "Beyond these, I'm not sure what you would want from me."

"Tell me when you first contacted me to set up this meeting."

"Three days ago, via an email from my official account."

"And the name of my wife is . . . ?"

"I'm sorry." He shook his head. "I'm afraid I don't know that."

There was no hint in his tone or demeanor that he was hiding anything about Su-wei or her kidnapping.

After a short internal debate, Chia-hao decided to trust him, but wondered again what to say—if he should bring up anything regarding the grisly package that'd been delivered to him or the demand that went with it.

"To what do I owe the honor of this meeting?" he inquired as calmly and pleasantly as he could. "I should tell you first, though, that I cannot stay long. I must review my notes for the morning."

"Of course, and I don't want to keep you. Listen—I know how important security within the nuclear industry is to you. From the legislation I've championed since being elected to Congress, I'm sure you can understand that we are on the same page here. I have a request to make of you."

"And that is?"

"I'm hoping you'll agree to postpone your talk tomorrow morning and let me take the podium instead."

"What?" Chia-hao found himself staring at the senator's face, trying to discern what was behind this request. "Why would you ask that?"

"I need to make some opening comments myself. Additionally, leaked information regarding your involvement in Project Symphony has made its way onto the dark web. Colonel Clarke is concerned about you revealing too much."

"Colonel Clarke?"

"Yes."

Chia-hao processed that, thinking of the kidnappers' demands. He knew the colonel through his work on the project. In the past, he'd never gone against Clarke's directives or wishes, but in this case he had Su-wei's life to think about.

"No," he told Senator Richardson firmly. "My lecture is vital."

"I understand your reticence. Really, I do. However, I can assure you that the announcement I need to make is just as important as your lecture. If you wish, I can say that you weren't feeling well and asked me to fill in for you. I'll focus on cybersecurity. It's close enough to your talk that the attendees will be satisfied."

"I am afraid that is quite impossible. I need to do my presentation."

"Please, Doctor, consider—"

"I am sorry." Chia-hao stood, unpocketed some bills to pay for his drinks, and placed them on the bar. "I will be giving my speech. I must. Innocent lives depend on it."

CHAPTER 29

Gunnar Bane handed his credentials to the austere Fairfax Police officer standing sentry beside the line of police tape surrounding Nathan Lassiter's home. She held a disposable cup of truck stop coffee and sipped it methodically as she studied his ID.

"Colonel Clarke sent me," he said. Then, anticipating that she might balk at the authorization because of jurisdiction issues, he added, "It's a matter of national security."

"Yeah, yeah, I got a call you'd be coming." She returned the ID to him. "You know the routine?"

"I do. Has the scene been processed?"

"CSI just left, maybe ten minutes ago. Still, they're requiring gloves and booties." She gestured toward a plastic bin nearby on the ground. "For some reason. Why? I don't know. I'll never get those guys."

"Right." Gunnar donned the gloves, slipped the booties on over his shoes, then ducked under the yellow caution tape and entered the house.

He wrote the scene even as he lived it: *Bane hadn't known Nathan Lassiter well, but the TSA's Deputy Director in Charge of Special Projects had seemed like an honest and dedicated man, and that mattered. It also made it all that much tougher to enter his home, knowing that he was gone. To lose a patriot was to lose a brother.*

According to what Gunnar had been told by Clarke, one of Lassiter's neighbors had seen a sedan matching the color of the Camry that Brock and Halprin were driving pull down the street as the patrol cars were arriving here on the scene. Motive was unclear at the moment, but the two of them certainly had means, opportunity, and access. So, at least three out of four. They could certainly be responsible—if it wasn't a suicide, and Gunnar had his doubts that it was.

He angled through the living room, taking note of the in-home health care equipment that Lassiter had for his father, Raymond, who'd been living with him. Alzheimer's. Must have been tough. A bedroom suite on the first floor contained a hospital bed and an end table covered with half-empty prescription bottles.

In Clarke's briefing, the colonel had mentioned to Gunnar that Raymond had no insurance and Nathan had tapped himself dry paying for his care. Okay, but then why take your own life after he was dead? Grief? That seemed like a stretch.

If Nathan was financially strapped, it could have made him vulnerable to being bribed or compromised. He wouldn't have been the first Homeland employee to be targeted in a situation like that. Something to look into.

Clarke had sent along a text containing the contents of the cryptic suicide note that was found on Lassiter's computer, but for Gunnar it only raised more questions. A suicide was too convenient. Lassiter had signed up at the last minute for a summit in Oak Ridge, Tennessee, and the most recent purchase on his credit card was a flight to Knoxville. Also, according to the case files, Lassiter had a suitcase packed upstairs and the last email to his account was from Delta confirming his upcoming flight.

Do you really book a flight, sign up to attend a conference, pack for a trip, and then commit suicide? It didn't jibe. This guy wasn't planning to kill himself; he was planning for the future. And that'd been stolen from him by someone. Maybe Halprin and Brock.

Gunnar noted that, apart from a sympathy card near the ashtray, Lassiter's desk was completely devoid of papers and his inbox stood empty. Either Lassiter was a neat freak, never brought work home, or whoever killed him took the time to remove anything that might point to something other than a suicide.

The voice in his head narrated the scene: *Bane studied the card and saw that it'd been signed by someone named Sean. No last name—which told him that whoever Sean was, he was close to Nathan and didn't need to include a surname. It was also the only card on the desk—though he must certainly have received more at the funeral. A relative? A work associate? A close friend? Something more than that? All worth a look.*

Lassiter's computer had been logged in to his official account and Clarke didn't want any Homeland Security files to be accessed by any unauthorized people—even if they were cops, so, at his request, the computer had been taken in as evidence.

Lassiter's body had also been removed, but the blood spatter on the wall gave grim evidence to the tragedy that'd occurred in this room just a few hours earlier.

Gunnar investigated the back door. No forced entry there or at the front of the house. No broken windows. No sign of a struggle—all strong indications that Lassiter had known his assailant, if there indeed was one.

Gunnar was heading for the stairs to view the suitcase in the main bedroom when a call came through from Colonel Clarke.

"I'm at Lassiter's house," Gunnar informed him. "Having a look around."

"Good. Listen, the body of an MPD detective was found in his car in front of police headquarters earlier tonight. They're trying to keep it quiet, but Detective Caruso was tortured before he was killed. Preliminary findings tie the nature of his wounds to the signature of a Russian mercenary named Ilya Vasiliev. You've run into him before, I believe."

"A couple of years ago on an assignment in Quito, Ecuador. Vasiliev is as cold and ruthless as they come." He had a few more vivid terms in mind to describe the man, but kept them to himself. "Bites off the left ears of the people he kills and leaves them jammed down the victim's throat. That what happened to Caruso?"

A brief pause. "Yes."

"Vasiliev rarely works alone," Gunnar noted.

"Which gives us a team of Russian assassins. And here's why I'm calling: Caruso had a full caseload, so his death might be associated with any one of a dozen different investigations, but one of those cases was the arson that killed Travis's wife a year and a half ago. And the last outgoing text from his phone was to Travis. Sent this morning."

Gunnar started up the stairs to the second floor. "Do we know what it said?"

"Caruso indicated that he might have some new information about the timing of the fire. CCTV cameras at the funeral home show him attending Raymond Lassiter's funeral yesterday."

"He knew Nathan." Gunnar reached the top of the steps.

"Yes. And texts from Lassiter to Caruso earlier today confirm it."

"And now they're both dead."

"Yes," Clarke said solemnly.

Gunnar crossed the hallway and found the main bedroom, where the packed suitcase still sat on the bed. "Caruso's first name wouldn't happen to be Sean, by any chance?"

"It was. How did you know?"

"A card here at the house. Were they close?"

"I'm not sure. I'll see if I can find out anything along that front." There was a short pause before Clarke continued. "By the way, I checked, and Vasiliev has connections to the same hacking group that Adira Halprin's text messages were linked to."

And now she's on the run with Brock.

"Could Lassiter have faked that? After all, he was apparently still alive when she was transferred up from Knoxville and he wasn't answering his calls."

"Perhaps. But why?"

"No idea. Just covering the bases." Then Gunnar probed deeper: "Do you think your redactor has turned? That he's working with the Russians?"

"It's possible," Colonel Clarke said carefully. "I've known him for fifteen years, but in this business, as well as you think you know someone, there are always surprises."

True, that.

Gunnar flipped through the clothes in the suitcase. Just two outfits. Nathan did not have a very long trip in mind.

As he studied the bedroom, trying to discern if the CSI team had missed anything, Gunnar said to Clarke, "Vasiliev has a specialty of getting people to talk." He saw nothing in the room that he hadn't already read about in the initial report, and returned to the stairway. "And from what you've told me, the last person we need to be giving up secrets to the Russians is Travis Brock."

"If Russian mafia members, or even Russian intelligence services' operatives—I mean, if Vasiliev is coordinating with his government—if they're here stateside torturing people to get information, well . . ."

"We definitely need to find Brock before they do," Gunnar finished the colonel's sentence for him as he jogged down the stairs.

"Yes, we do. I'll keep you updated on what I find out."

"I'll do the same."

End call.

Outside the house, Gunnar nodded his thanks to the officer, who drained the last glug of her coffee and crumpled up the cup while he bent to tug off the booties.

"Find any answers in there?" she asked him.

"Just a surfeit of more questions."

She scrunched up her face. "A surfeit? What's that?"

"In this case, it means a bunch more than I'd anticipated."

All the way home, Gunnar mentally replayed the colonel's words, evaluating the ties between the two dead men and the two people he was looking for: Caruso had been investigating the arson at Brock's house; Lassiter served as Halprin's supervisor.

But what could have provoked either Halprin or Brock to kill Lassiter? How would they benefit from his death? The more he thought about it, the less it fit. And neither did the idea that they were responsible for the three bodies at L & L.

From all appearances, a day after Raymond's funeral, his son had been forced to write a suicide note and was then murdered, after a police detective who was close to Nathan was tortured to death.

Did someone see them together at the funeral? Could that be what initiated all of this?

A case like this could go in any number of directions. Best not to get too far ahead of yourself. Best to wait for more intel. Assess it. Look into the context, form a hypothesis, and move on from there.

At his house, Gunnar tried to unwind and get some sleep, but when he closed his eyes, his thoughts of the case kept him awake. Finally, he turned to the novel he was writing and dictated a few ideas into his phone.

Currently, he was working on the first draft of a love scene, and it was tougher than he thought it would be. Finding his narrative voice was still something he was working on.

"Jessie stared at Donovan with her soft and alluring orbs," Gunnar said into his phone, "inviting him closer. He moved toward her. Closer. Closer! She leaned in breathlessly, her hungry eyes searching his, her bosom undulating beneath her billowing blouse."

Gunnar paused.

Good alliteration there, but maybe he should say her heart was undulating instead? Would that be better? There was a subtlety to that word, *undulating*, that he wasn't quite sure he was tapping into. Do hearts *gyrate*? Would that be better? Or maybe *palpitate*? No, that sounded more like a villain in a Star Wars movie than what Jessie's bosom or heart would be doing.

Give it a bit more thought.

In the end, he decided that first thing in the morning he was going to get permission from Clarke to search through Lassiter's and Caruso's financials to see if someone might've been paying off either of the men, and if so, who that someone might be.

CHAPTER 30

As I drove southbound on Interstate 81 toward Oak Ridge, I caught myself glancing in Adira's direction.

She must have been exhausted from everything she'd been through during the day, because ever since we'd finished eating several hours ago, she'd been dozing.

She'd nestled her head up against the inside of the door. For a pillow, she was using a rolled-up wool blanket that the young woman we'd rented the Camry from had left behind.

In the soft passing light of oncoming traffic, I was struck by how lovely Adira looked. She wasn't gorgeous in a glamour magazine sort of way. *Cute* was a better word to describe her. She could look good with makeup and just as good without it.

With a slight touch of nervousness, I redirected my gaze to the road.

Noticing how attractive she was reminded me of the few dates I'd been on over the last couple of months. I hadn't felt entirely comfortable going out, and none of the first dates had led to second ones. On the one hand, I believed I was ready to start a relationship again. On the other, it seemed like I needed closure on who'd set the fire that killed Sienna before I would be ready to move on with anyone, whoever she might be.

But that might never happen, I thought. *You might never find the answers you're looking for.*

I quieted that voice, just as I'd had to do so many times since the fire. Instead, I assured myself that closure *would* come, that I *would* be able to move forward, that justice would, in the end, be carried out.

If I told myself that enough, it just might come true.

My thoughts turned to the Patmos Financial Consortium, the equity firm purchasing land countrywide. Sometimes the sites were in rural areas, sometimes in urban ones.

Based on what I'd seen earlier, there was no obvious connection between the locations.

Investment properties? A hotel chain? I began to wonder if the firm might be involved in some way with the distribution of raw materials related to the research done at the Oak Ridge National Laboratory, the Department of Energy's research facility just down the road from Y-12.

"How are you doing over there?" Adira's voice drew me back to the moment.

"I thought you were asleep."

"In and out." She stirred and turned my way. "You need a break?"

"I should be alright, but we do need some gas."

"When you stop, get some bubble gum."

"Bubble gum?"

Out of the corner of my eye, I saw her arch her head and knead the back of her neck. She yawned, then rubbed her eyes, presumably in an effort to wake up. "Mm-hmm."

"You like gum, huh?"

Oh, genius question there, Travis.

"Who doesn't like bubble gum?" She turned on the radio and found a country tune being sung by someone who sounded like he had a mouthful of gravel. "*She's got a master's degree in how to be a woman,*" he crooned. "*Got a PhD in how to love a man. And when she looks in your eyes, boys, class is in session. So sit down, son, and take your exam.*"

Adira scoffed at that, dialed past an irritating, shout-your-way-into-someone's-wallet car dealership commercial, and landed on a hip-hop song. After about twenty seconds of listening to misogynistic profanity, she shook her head, sighed, and clicked the radio off again.

Then, it was almost like she could read my mind and knew what I'd been thinking about while she was sleeping. "Earlier, you mentioned that a fire killed your wife," she said. "Arson."

"Yes."

"And you don't know who did it?"

"No." I tightened my grip on the steering wheel. "But I'm going to find out."

"And then what?"

"What do you mean?"

"Justice or revenge?"

I looked her way. "What are you talking about?"

"When you find out who started the fire that killed her, are you going to seek justice or are you after revenge?"

"Um . . ."

"Are you going to kill them?" she asked bluntly. "An eye for an eye, a life for a life, a punishment-fits-the-crime sort of thing?"

"Why are you asking me this?"

"Because I want to know what kind of person I'm stuck in this car with." There it was again: blunt honesty. Total openness. No beating around the bush. No fear of offending me. "And," she added, "you said earlier that you might need to drop off the radar. I'm just connecting the dots."

"I'm someone who feels that justice needs to be served," I told her vaguely, skirting around her question about whether I was planning to kill anyone.

"Uh-huh," she said. "But the revenge part—it's there too, isn't it?"

With my memory what it was, details tended to stick with me even when I didn't want them to, remaining so vivid that I couldn't help but relive the past in full color, even years later. And the painful recollections of the night of the fire still troubled me like an infected wound.

The pain hadn't faded with time but remained tender to the touch, to the thought. Other people might be able to forgive and forget, but how do you do the first when you can't do the second? Sometimes I wished it was possible to forget more, that the passage of time would give me that gift, but so far time had been my enemy, not my ally. And now, with Adira's questions pressing in on me, my painful past was staring me directly in the face once again.

Revenge? Did I really desire that along with justice?

Well . . .

I was quiet for a moment, then said, "A mile or so back, I saw a sign for a gas station. I think the exit is just up ahead."

"Don't think I haven't noticed that you didn't answer my question."

"I'm still formulating a reply," I said judiciously.

"Well, you better have your answer ready before we meet up with the people you're looking for. You don't seem like a killer to me, but hey, I'm not exactly the best judge of character. You can just look at any of my ex-boyfriends to figure that much out."

I drove in silence.

"You told me earlier that you got your law degree," she said.

"Yes."

"So you studied justice. The legal definitions of it."

"I did."

"Well, how do you define it?"

"The classic answer is that there are four principles that the justice system is designed to serve. Goals, I guess you could say: rehabilitation, retribution, general and specific deterrence."

"Uh-huh," she said. "That first one is easy enough to understand, and so are the last two."

"Yes."

"But it's that second one—retribution—that can get a little thorny."

"It can," I admitted.

"And theories about justifying punishment?"

"Well, there are two prevailing schools of thought regarding punishment— the retributive and the utilitarian perspectives. The retributive argues that wrongs committed deserve some sort of punishment—that is, suffering or some type of deprivation."

"Of freedom," she inserted. "Or, maybe, of life."

"Yes. The utilitarian perspective argues that punishment is justifiable only if it benefits society. So, retributive focuses on actual wrongs that have been done in the past; utilitarian on potential wrongs that might be done in the future."

"And injustice? How do you define that?"

"Why all the questions?"

"Stick with me. There's a point to it all. Trust me."

"Most of the time, you can substitute the word *oppression* for *injustice* and you'll be on the right track. Maybe the best answer I've heard is in Ecclesiastes 4:1: 'So I returned, and considered all the oppressions that are done under the sun: and behold the tears of such as were oppressed, and they had no comforter; and on the side of their oppressors there was power; but they had no comforter.' That's injustice in a nutshell—oppression by those who have more power over those who have less, the forcing of one's will upon another to his or her detriment."

"Looks like you've got your definitions down pat."

I couldn't tell yet where she was going with this. "I guess so."

"But how they all play out in the real world, that's the kicker."

"Yes. It is."

I took the exit and turned right, heading toward the gas station a quarter of a mile away on an access road.

"Okay," she said, "so when I was a girl, maybe ten or so, I was bullied by some older girls who made fun of how slim I was—well, scrawny. Anyway, at the time, I didn't know how to take care of myself all that well in situations like that. I didn't know what to do."

"So," I said, anticipating where this was going, "you turned to retribution?"

"Not quite. I asked my grandma why life wasn't fair. She was the oldest person I knew at the time. I thought she was as smart as God. I thought she might know."

Adira paused.

"What did she say?"

"She said, 'You're right. Life isn't fair, and truthfully, I don't know why. But we don't have to know why it's unfair to do something about it.'"

Aha, so here was where we'd get to retributive action, from her grandmother's perspective.

"I asked her what she meant," Adira went on, "and I don't remember precisely, not her exact words, but she said we needed to care for others even when we had no answers. To speak up for those who had no voice. To stand up for the less fortunate. To share our food with the hungry. To visit those in the hospital and invite strangers in. To protect the helpless, the forgotten, the frightened, the lonely. Basically, fighting against the oppression you just spoke about, that was referenced in what you quoted from the Bible."

She waited for a moment before going on, but finally concluded, "This part I do remember word for word. Gramma said, 'The question isn't so much why life isn't fair, but what we're going to do about it in the meantime, while we search for answers.'"

"Sounds like your grandmother was quite a woman," I said, thinking of another Bible verse, this one from Romans 12:21, where Paul says we should not be overcome by evil, but should "overcome evil with good."

"She was," Adira told me. "And?"

"And?"

"The takeaway."

"I'd say, justice isn't so much a concept to be defined as a decision to be made in the face of injustice."

"Well put."

But what was the decision asking of me? What does it ask of any of us? That was where the rubber met the road.

And what about retribution? If we are, each of us, responsible for seeing justice done, then what role do we each have to play in that second, thorny, morally challenging aspect of seeing justice played out? What role, individually, should we play in pursuing or facilitating retributive action? Or should we passively sit by and let injustice go unchecked?

Even though I wasn't thrilled about showing up on some gas station's CCTV camera, I figured that it would be better if it was me rather than Adira, so I parked at a pump, went inside to pre-pay with cash, and was about to leave when I remembered the bubble gum. Unsure which flavor she might prefer, I grabbed three packs, each a different brand, and set them on the counter.

"You must like bubble gum," the greasy-haired gas station attendant said.

"Who doesn't like bubble gum?"

There was also a special on a soft drink called Dr. Enuf that the man promised me was worth trying. "It's from East Tennessee. Johnson City," he said with a touch of pride. "Only place on earth it's made. It's sweet. The taste of the mountains. The taste of the South."

As I returned to the Camry with the gum and two bottles of soda, I thought about Adira's questions regarding justice and revenge. Were the two of them really so different? Where did one end and the other begin?

When I was in law school, my professors had taught us that no one should take the law into his or her own hands, that meting out justice was society's role, not the job of any sole individual.

But what if society failed to carry it out? What if the authorities weren't able to, or chose not to, see justice done? Wasn't justice a worthy enough goal to pursue, regardless of whose hands it ended up being in? And besides, society is made up of individuals, each with a moral responsibility to see justice carried out, no matter what it might cost them. If we're responsible as a society to do what's right, aren't we just as obligated as individuals to do so?

You're not above the law, I thought.

Then another voice replied, *No. But I'm willing to work beside it and take over if it's too afraid to do its job or get its hands dirty.*

I'd never quite thought of my search for answers—for justice—in those terms before and I sorted through the implications and what it might ultimately mean to "get my hands dirty."

The law may not be perfect, Travis, but it's all we have.

No. No, it's not. We have our own choices. Our own actions. We have our own opportunities for effecting positive change.

If it was true that justice isn't so much a concept to be defined as a decision to be made in the face of injustice, then what was my decision going to be?

Back at the car, as I started filling up, I noticed that Adira had shifted to the driver's seat. She'd rolled her window down and was holding her hand out and wavering it through the air as if she were feeling the wind pass across her fingers while racing down the highway. Given all that was going on, I wondered how she could exhibit such a calm and carefree attitude. She seemed to go with the flow and embrace life, no matter what curveballs it was throwing her way. I couldn't help but admire that.

"I'm okay to drive," I assured her.

"It's cool. I'm rested."

While I waited for the pump to click off, I handed her the gum and a Dr. Enuf.

"What's this?" she asked, studying the green glass bottle.

"The guy inside told me it's good. It's an East Tennessee thing."

"We're getting closer, huh?"

"Little by little."

She chugged some of the soda. "Crazy fizzy." She smacked her lips. "It's got attitude. I like it."

She unwrapped two chunks of cotton candy-flavored bubble gum, popped them both into her mouth, and then switched topics entirely, as I was noticing she was apt to do. "Why do you think the arson is connected to everything else that's going on?"

"That date on the FOIA request. Though it just came in, it was backdated to the day of the fire. That can't just be a coincidence."

"I mean, it *could* be," she countered. "Coincidences *do* happen, but I hear what you're saying. Lassiter knew us both. If he sent it in and put that date on it, I'd say he was definitely trying to get your attention. He's the fulcrum here."

"But he's not the only person involved. There's more to all of this."

"The person who killed him," she said.

"Yes."

"Sapphire."

"Possibly." I said, trying to be careful not to presume too much.

Adira looked my way thoughtfully. "I suppose if we can figure out the why behind the when, we might just be able to figure out the who behind the why."

"I like the way you put that."

She blew a bubble. "Thanks."

I finished refueling, climbed into the passenger seat, and Adira keyed the ignition. The car started immediately without sputtering or backfiring.

"How did you do that?" I asked.

She patted the dashboard. "This baby just needed a woman's touch."

As she guided the Camry out of the parking lot and back onto I-81 South, I put thoughts of justice and revenge aside for the moment and took the discussion in a different direction. "I've been wondering something."

"What's that?"

"Back in the interrogation room, how did you knock that guy out while your hands were cuffed?"

"I kicked him in the head. I got lucky."

"I'm guessing it wasn't just luck, was it?"

She shrugged.

"You have skills," I observed.

"I have training. You?"

"What—skills or training?"

"Either."

"More like neither. I took karate classes for a couple of years in elementary school, but that's about it. I mostly remember bowing a lot and kicking and punching the air. We never actually got to spar with other people. I guess I was too young, or just not good enough for them to chance me getting hurt."

"The air doesn't fight back."

"No. It doesn't."

"I'll have to teach you sometime—how to fight against someone who does fight back."

With things going the way they were today, I might need that lesson sooner rather than later. "I'd be up for that."

"We'll need a pair of handcuffs, though. To make it authentic."

"Authentic works for me."

"By the way." She tapped her finger thoughtfully against the steering wheel. "As far as I know, my SUV should still be there in the parking garage at the Knoxville airport. I have a DHS encrypted tablet in there. You said that Oak Ridge is near Knoxville. By now law enforcement will be looking for this car. I think we should swing by and switch vehicles. Also, it'll give us access to that tablet. It's possible that with that computer and your level of access, we'll be able to figure out the real identities of the other Red Team members—wouldn't you say?"

"It's possible. But wait—you left your tablet behind?"

"I don't take it with me through security checkpoints and, as you mentioned earlier, I've never been caught before. I wasn't expecting all this mess, but at least it's encrypted. Enter the wrong password and that puppy will flatline for good."

"Gotcha."

"So," she went on, "I'm thinking that, with the tablet, maybe we can sort out who betrayed me. Find the who behind the why, like we were saying. Plus, I have some other stuff in the car that might come in handy."

"Other stuff?"

"I'll let that be a surprise."

"Wouldn't they have searched your vehicle after they arrested you?"

"Maybe, but I was pretty careful about checking for CCTV cameras when I scouted the place out. I don't think I appeared on any footage until I entered the building. The CR-V isn't registered under my real name, so I'm not sure how they would connect it to me. It's just another vehicle in a parking garage. There's always a risk, of course, but in this case I think it's one worth taking."

"Hmm. Let me think about it."

"Get some sleep," she said. "You should be able to think more clearly when you wake up."

"You mean agree with you more readily?"

Another bubble. "Now you're catching on."

CHAPTER 31

THREE MONTHS AGO

HYDERABAD, INDIA

Rakesh felt the acrid air rush past him as he wove his motorcycle through the chaotic city traffic on the way to his apartment. Skirting in and out of the melee of cars, motorbikes, and rickshaws, he thought about what he'd put into play.

Inserting the code onto the microchips being shipped to the Oak Ridge site hadn't been easy, but he'd managed.

And now, because of his actions, his family would be taken care of. The amount of money he'd made with that one simple act would assure that he could pay for his son's education all the way through secondary school.

Most of the United States' microelectronics were produced in Taiwan and South Korea, but that was slowly changing as India continued to rise as one of the leading technology exporters in the world. And since Hyderabad had emerged as a major Indian tech hub, over the last five years the US had been buying more and more electronics from the plants there—especially Andhra Pradesh Microelectronics Corporation, the company where Rakesh had been working for the last nine years as a computer technician, making just enough money to get by, but not enough to get ahead.

He swerved around a massive truck rumbling out to deliver water to one of the cobra-infested villages north of the city. The way most drivers signal in

India is with the heel of their hand on their vehicle's horn, and a cacophony of horns echoed all around him from people jockeying for position on a road that might have safely held four lanes of traffic, but now contained a crammed seven.

As he rounded the corner near his apartment, he swung past a pedestrian, missing her by mere centimeters. But the people crossing the streets here were used to this kind of turbulent traffic and she didn't even flinch.

Rakesh parked outside the building and parked his motorcycle next to his friend's clothing shop. His neighbor specialized in providing tailored clothes and Punjabi suits for the Americans working in the tech industry who wanted to dress fusion or look Indian. After waving to him through the window, Rakesh walked up the uneven stone path toward his home.

The varied scents of the city curled around him: tendrils of exhaust and incense and simmering vegetables from roadside vendors, all intermingling in the dusty air.

A clutch of women in colorful sarees passed him on the way to finishing their shopping. Two older men sat on rickety wooden stools near the street corner, deep in thought, taking tired drags from their cigarettes as they silently watched the world pass by.

A blind beggar with cloudy eyes sat on the walkway with his hand outstretched. Nothing unusual about that—there were beggars all throughout the city. Everyone was hustling past this man without giving him so much as a second glance.

Nothing unusual about that either.

You get used to the beggars on the streets of Hyderabad.

Or you don't.

Growing up, Rakesh had been a rag picker, one of the poor, often orphaned, children who scrounged whatever they could find—rags, bits of paper, cigarette stubs, anything—and tried to sell them for a few rupees. He knew what it was like to be poor, to be an outcast, and so, though he didn't have much money with him, he dug out the coins that he did have and gently laid them in the blind man's hand. The beggar responded by placing his palms together as if in prayer and bowing his head in thanks.

Rakesh assured himself that now that he'd finished the work for the American who'd contacted him, money would no longer be an issue. He would be able to help many beggars, just as he would be able to better provide for his family's financial needs for years to come.

Until today he'd kept the news to himself, but now that the chips had been delivered, he could finally tell his wife that their financial problems were over.

Smiling and excited, Rakesh opened the door and called her name. "Bhavini!"

No response, but maybe she was out. It wasn't unusual for her to shop at this time of day, taking their ten-year-old son, Jairaj, with her.

Rakesh entered the apartment and shut the door behind him. He tried turning on the light, but it didn't come on. Somewhat annoyed, he tried clicking it several more times, with the same result.

Maybe a burned-out bulb, but electrical shortages weren't that unusual in his neighborhood, either, so maybe it was just—

"Hello, Rakesh."

The man's voice came from the shadows layered across the far side of the room. In the faint light that seeped in beneath the shade-drawn windows, Rakesh could just barely make out the shape of someone sitting in the chair facing him.

"Who are you?" Rakesh asked, a mixture of confusion and fear in his voice. "What are you doing here?"

"I'm the one who hired you. The one who provided you with the code to put in the Y-12 chips."

Rakesh caught himself swallowing. "I placed them in the shipment for you. It's done."

"Good."

"I don't understand why you're here."

Now that his eyes were becoming accustomed to the dim light, Rakesh saw what appeared to be petrol cans at the man's feet.

"I have word you've been poking around in files you have no business looking into."

"No, of course not, sir." Rakesh's voice faltered. All he could think of was his family. "Bhavini?" he called again. "Are you here?" When no one responded, he cried out for his son. "Jairaj!"

"They're in the other room."

An initial surge of relief quickly turned to unease since he still hadn't heard a reply from either of them—or any sounds at all from the adjoining room.

And with that realization, the unease shifted to terror.

He started toward the doorway, but the man commanded him to stay where he was. "You'll be reunited with them in a moment. For now, give me the product numbers."

"I have sent the SMS. I confirmed it. I swear."

"Confirm it with me."

"Chips GA492 through GA500. You should already have all of that. What do you want from me?"

"Assurance that our business dealings remain discreet."

"Yes, I assure you! I promise!"

"Not that kind of assurance."

───❦───

The intruder squeezed the trigger of his Walther PPQ M2 twice and Rakesh's chest flashed crimson as his body tumbled backward and dropped clumsily to the floor.

As the man watched the blood spread out, soaking through the front of Rakesh's shirt while also pooling out from beneath him in a shiny dark puddle, he called his employer and explained that things in Hyderabad were taken care of.

"Will there be any repercussions?" the electronically masked voice asked.

"No." He eyed Rakesh's motionless form. The bleeding was slowing now because his heart was no longer beating. "All the repercussions appear to have been dealt with."

After his employer ended the call, the man took the gasoline into the other room and splashed it across the bodies of the woman and her boy, then lit the match and tossed it onto Bhavini's gas-soaked clothes. Flames shot out in all directions—swift, living slithers of fire, engulfing her and her son in a matter of seconds.

Before leaving the apartment, the man placed the gas cans near Rakesh's body and then, as black wisps of smoke began leaking out of the cracks around the windows of the dead family's home, he disappeared into the busy, teeming streets of Hyderabad, dropping a coin into the hand of a blind beggar as he did.

—∿—

In the spare bedroom that he'd turned into a home office, Metro Police Department Detective Sean Caruso opened up the worn and creased manila file folder with Travis Brock's name on it, his heart racing with the discovery he'd just made. Finally, after all this time, he might have uncovered something solid regarding the arson at Brock's house.

At yesterday's funeral for his friend Nathan Lassiter's elderly father, Nathan had made some puzzling comments that got Sean refocused on the Brock fire.

Sean had been a friend of Nathan's ever since the days when Nathan still worked with the Secret Service and they'd both shot competitively at the same gun range just outside of DC. Since then, they'd gone their separate ways, as people do, but they'd stayed in touch online. So, when Nathan's father passed away last week, Sean had wanted to attend the funeral to encourage his friend and share his condolences.

Rather than holding a separate visitation and funeral, Nathan had chosen to have a single memorial service for close friends and family. Sean had never been to that particular funeral home before, and from the moment he first walked in, he noted that it seemed even more somber than most—dark hues, subdued lights, languid music, and imposing drapes drawn together to cover the infrequent windows, smothering out all but the most persistent rays of sunlight from sneaking in around the edges. Very *Addams Family* all the way around.

After the service, as the final two people who'd come to pay their last respects were filing out the door, Nathan held up a finger as if he were indicating for Sean to wait. He took out his cell phone, pointed at the screen, and set it softly on one of the back row's padded pews.

Then, he gestured for Sean to follow him to the front where the casket sat. As they came to the old, dusty piano in the west corner of the room, the faint smell of mildew and some type of embalming chemicals tainted the air, adding to the morbid atmosphere. Nathan kept his voice low and said, "I think they're watching me."

"What are you talking about? Who?"

He led Sean closer to the casket, which was still open, revealing Raymond Lassiter's powdered, death-still face.

Sean found it slightly macabre and unsettling to have the conversation there beside the body, but the fact that Nathan had purposely left his phone at the far end of the room made him more than a little bit curious about what his friend had to say.

"The Pruninghooks Collective," Nathan said softly.

"That antinuke group? Why would they be watching you?"

"I'm not sure. It might not be them, but . . . I can't do it anymore."

"Nathan, what's going on? What can't you do?"

"Pretend." Nathan placed a hand on the casket's silver handle and stared at his father's face for a long moment, then turned at last to Sean. "I did it for him, you know. That's the only reason."

Sean waited for him to go on, to clarify; when he didn't, he said, "I know you've been through a lot here, buddy, but—"

"You know Travis Brock, right?" Nathan had a fierce yet distant look in his eyes. "At the Pentagon? Are you still working the arson at his house?"

"Yes. The case is still open."

"Take a careful look at his wife's job. Her last assignment with the State Department. If I'm right, the fire wasn't started to kill Travis."

"Then why? To kill her? Both of them?" Sean cocked his head curiously. "What do you know about this?"

"I'm . . . I never should have spoken to her." Nathan took a deep breath, then rubbed his forehead. "I never should have helped them."

"If you know something about the fire or about—"

"I need to go," Nathan cut him off. He was looking around, nervy and anxious. "We'll talk about this tomorrow. Lunch? Maxine's Sub Shop?"

"Sure." Maxine's was a local cop hangout in Springfield, Virginia, not far from where Nathan worked. A good place to talk. "You okay?"

Nathan placed a hand on Sean's shoulder. "Thanks for being here."

"Of course."

"One, then," Nathan said. "For a late lunch."

"Yeah," Sean replied, slightly bewildered by his friend's odd behavior. "One o'clock. I'll see you at Maxine's."

A single nod, and then Nathan had hastened quickly back down the center aisle between the pews, collected his cell phone and, without another word—and only a brief backward glance—hurried out the door.

After returning home, Sean had done as Nathan had directed him and looked into Sienna Brock's work assignments. It'd required calling in a few favors on a Sunday afternoon, but eventually he'd gotten access to the State Department files he needed.

Though he hadn't uncovered anything solid yesterday, this morning he'd gotten up early and, after two hours of work, found that indeed Sienna had completed a translation project for the State Department the week of the fire. A Russian treaty. She'd been working with a legal advisor there named Lena Rhodes.

And that was the catch—Rhodes disappeared after leaving work two days before the fire. She'd filed a complaint to her supervisor about some supposed discrepancies in Sienna's work, asking for further scrutiny into the project. Evidently, Lena took a number of sensitive files with her when she left, and suspicion had shifted toward her and why she'd cleared out her bank accounts and then dropped off the grid. In the end, the grievance regarding Sienna's translation project hadn't led anywhere, but it was a point of convergence between Lena's disappearance and the fire at the Brocks' residence.

Could Rhodes have found out what Travis did for a living? Was she behind the fire? Did she go after Sienna? Is it possible? Is there a motive couched in there somewhere that you're missing?

It wasn't an answer, but it was a connection. That's how cases like this went: You dig, you take what you uncover, and you dig further until you find the truth begin to emerge—and then you keep going no matter how deeply it's buried, until you find enough of it to see your way forward. And, given Nathan's strange behavior yesterday, Sean thought it was worth exploring this connection with Rhodes more in-depth when they met at Maxine's for lunch.

He consulted his notes in his field interview notebook, then located a photo of Brock's burned home and scribbled down the initials *L.R.* and two questions: *Were you there? Were you watching?*

Then he slid the sheet into the folder and texted Travis, who he was guessing would already be at work at the Pentagon: **Call me as soon as you get a chance. I might have something regarding the timing of the fire.**

He was gathering his things to leave for Metro HQ when he heard a knock at the front door, which was surprising. There was no way he was expecting anyone at this time of day.

Another knock.

Yesterday Nathan was worried he was being watched. Are you being watched as well?

Sean unholstered his Glock 19 and cautiously approached the door.

But as it turned out, not cautiously enough, because someone brutally kicked the door in and rushed him as he edged it open. He managed to get one awkward shot off, but it missed the man wildly, and then he was being tackled and held down as a second man appeared and jammed a cloth firmly and securely over his mouth and nose.

Sean tried to hold out, tried not to breathe in the sweet-smelling chloroform, but in the end, as the men spoke something undecipherable to each other in Russian, he couldn't help but give in and was overwhelmed by the thick grip of an inescapable and all-consuming darkness.

IIAJWEOPFIJAWEPE

NE
VP
PO
JV
EG
JE
PIAW
HWEE
S;FO
OOSJFPOWEIRPOW
IUUAWPOFIIJAS;OOJFPAWOE
FOIJAWPOEIFJAPWOIE
JDFOIJERPFJR3POIA
IIAJWEOPFI
WEEFPOIIAJWEPEOFIJA
PFOFJV;L
GFFP'AOM
NIFUHVV;NAVPOAWEE
OAEHRFPIGUHERE;FN
PAOKKBOOKBJPOKBJAP
JNVPIOIOWERHRE
HFPOAHC;OA
REYVHUNFDEIOJOI
SHVBVAIUUHVHNAO
UERHVUHERVUNEV;O
VOPIAWJVPOOEARJHVV
PIAWJVPOOEARJHVV
HWEEHEPORIIHQWPO
S;FOIJAW;OFIJAW
OOSJFPOWEIRPOWIUR
IUUAWPOFIIJAS;OOJF
FOIJAWPOEIFJAPWOIE
JDFOIJERPFJR3POIAP
IIAJWEOPFI   EOO
WEEFPOIIAJ
PFOFJV;LKME;IFIJ;OI
GFFP'AOMW;GFPOOAWGPO
NIFUHVV;NAVPOAWEEH
OAEHRFPIGUHERF;FNSI;OM
PAOKKBOOKE
JNVPIOIO
HFPOAHC;OAJ
REYVHUNFDEIOJOI
SHVBVAIUUHVHNA
UERHVUHERVUNE
VOPIAWJVPOOEARJH
POAIJERV;AK;ERVPOAI;REV
JVBAPO
EGFPOA
JEOAIJERV;BEV;W;E;EGLV
PIAWJVPOOEARJHVVOAEIE
HWEEHEPORIIHQWP
S;FOIJAW;OFIJAW;OFIJAWA
OOSJFPOWEIRPOWIURTRI
IUUAWPOFIIJAS;O
FOIJAWPOEIEJAPWOIFF;INW
JDFOIJ
IIAJW
WEEF
IIAJ
WEEF
PFOF
GFF
NV
HF
J

PART III

The Deep End

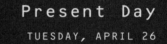

Present Day

TUESDAY, APRIL 26

I was both aware and unaware that I was dreaming, held captive somewhere in that flickering twilight region between waking and sleeping where you're not sure whether or not you're asleep, but you sense that you are.

And now, I could only hope that I was.

And so.

My dream.

In the shadows of a formless expanse, a cemetery appears before me, illuminated by a flashlight in my hand. Scraggly, weathered trees bow somberly over graves as if they're weeping over the dead. Tombstones tilt at skewed angles in the rough dirt.

I proceed forward, picking my way past the graves, seeing names that I recognize.

Or maybe I don't. Because this is a dream, and dreams can't be trusted to offer you the truth. Just the subconscious's perception of it, mirrored back to you through images you can't control. Blurred memories merged with imagination. You can't reward nightmares with certainty.

I come to a freshly dug, open grave. Approach the edge of it.

Peer inside.

And find a corpse, cold and gray, lying on its back.

It opens its eyes, ghost-white, and directs them toward me. "You're the one." The words are juicy and wet. Foul liquid seeps from the lipless mouth.

"No," I stammer.

"The one," the corpse repeats and then grabs at the bulging roots that snake down into the grave, and somehow hoists itself up until it's standing.

I stumble backward and watch as the corpse climbs out of the ground, and then rises to its feet before me. Now I can see that it's a woman.

"You're the one," she rasps.

"I didn't do anything," I object. "Who are—?"

She laughs, a yellow-toothed cackle that ends with a gaping grin much larger than a human mouth should be. A viper's unlocked jaw opening in the weary light. "Next." The word is almost a hiss. "You're nexxxxxt."

A dream.

And now she's reaching out to me with a tendony arm and an accusing, bony finger. Another laugh. "You can't stop it."

In desperation, I swipe the flashlight forward and the light's beam slices into her like a blade. She screams. As I swing the light, it tears her apart at the waist, smoke rising from the searing wounds. But even that doesn't stop her. Now just a torso with a head and two arms, she claws her way forward across the ground.

In my dream.

She twists her neck and then swivels her head to peer up at me. Her face has morphed from something indistinguishable to something all too familiar, and in a plummet of terror I recognize who she is.

My wife.

Sienna.

With a reeling surge of horror, I awaken.

My hands shake and my wretched heart is racing.

No, no, no. It's not true, I tell myself. *It's not real. It was only a dream. Just a dream.*

I glance at the time.

3:43 a.m.

Even if I would've wanted to, there was no going back to sleep after a nightmare like that.

"You okay?" Adira asked me concernedly from where she sat driving the Camry down the highway.

"Yeah. Just a little rattled. Bad dreams."

"You were crying out in your sleep."

I tightened and then relaxed my fists, trying to overcome the tension that'd gripped me. "What was I saying?"

"It sounded like you were repeating the same thing over and over: 'You're next. Next. Next.'"

Taking that in, I stared out the window.

A road sign told me that we were on I-40, which meant we had to be closing in on Knoxville. This road was a major artery up to DC and New York City. The traffic on it rarely slowed down, so despite the late hour, it was still busy—mostly truckers making their deliveries through the night.

When I offered to take over driving for the final leg of the trip, I suspected Adira would tell me she was fine, but she must have been more tired than I'd guessed because she immediately agreed, signaled, and pulled onto the gravel-strewn shoulder, sending a spray of rocks spitting up against the car's undercarriage.

We switched places. She buckled up and said, "Tell me about your job. As a redactor."

Honestly, I had a tough time focusing on her question. I was still so troubled by the dream, still caught up in the nightmare world of rotting corpses and death and harsh, burbling laughter.

In an attempt to escape those thoughts, I answered Adira, "It's not really all that interesting."

I set about readjusting the seat and mirrors. When I looked in the rear-view mirror to make sure there was no traffic, I noticed Adira turning back to stare behind us as well. "What is it?" I asked.

"Just checking."

Then it struck me. "You think we're being followed?"

"Force of habit. But no other cars have stopped or pulled over. I think we're alright."

With the coast clear, I merged onto the Interstate again.

"So." She blew a bubble. "Your job. It's not interesting. Got it. Tell me anyway."

"Basically, I scour through hundreds of pages of documents every day, analyzing what material we can safely release to the public. I scrutinize different DOD programs and the interactions between them, then consider potential negative consequences to the public or to those initiatives if the information were to be released. Finally, I break out a black marker and block stuff out. That's about it."

"How do you decide what's redacted and what isn't?"

"There are nine exemptions that apply to what's required to be released to the public. We withhold information when we—quote—reasonably foresee that disclosure would harm an interest protected by one of these nine exemptions—unquote."

"What are they? The exemptions?"

"The first is the main one I deal with: information that's classified to protect national security. The other ones pertain to internal personnel rules of government agencies, trade secrets, privileged financial information or communication, personal privacy, and law enforcement rules and regs."

As I spoke to her, I tried to shake the alarming impressions left by that dream, but it wasn't working. Even as the specific images faded, its terrible culmination drilled itself deeper into my memory.

The vision of death.

Of Sienna's stalking corpse.

"And computers can't do that?" Adira said. "I mean, no offense, but AI does just about everything else these days."

"Maybe someday AI will take over. For now, though, redactions are still done by actual people."

"You're not expendable quite yet."

"Not quite yet."

"It's good to know that my husband has at least a modicum of job security."

"A modicum is better than nothing."

"Yes," she said. Then, "Is it hard?"

"Doing what I do?"

"Knowing what you know."

"It can be," I acknowledged, thankful that the conversation was taking my attention in a new direction, away from the nightmare. "There's a lot at stake. Covers of operatives have been blown, lives have been lost, vital programs have had to be shut down, all because redactors didn't do their job right or well."

"What do you do when something that shouldn't be out there gets

STEVEN JAMES || 177

released? It must happen sometimes, right? Do you try to rein it back in—which would, I imagine, risk drawing attention to it? The Streisand Effect, you know? Or do you let it be and hope no one notices that it should've been redacted in the first place?"

"Those are very astute questions," I said, which I was well aware wasn't an answer.

"That ever happen to you? Where you failed to redact something and later regretted it?"

I didn't reply but rather drove in silence, because one instance did come to mind. One time when I'd made a judgment call that'd come back to haunt me—though I wasn't sure I was comfortable bringing it up with Adira right now.

However, my silence betrayed me.

"Something happened, didn't it?" she said. "Something bad?"

"Once. Yes."

"Well?" she pressed me. "Go on. What was it?"

I debated whether or not to say anything, but finally decided I could trust her. And, if I was being completely honest with myself, I wanted to let her in on more of my past.

"A little over four years ago, someone sent in a FOIA request regarding a DOD program that I really can't say much about, except that it has to do with nonlethal means of crowd control. Anyway, based on clues from what wasn't redacted, a journalist identified the researcher behind it and his cover was blown."

"What'd you do?"

"There wasn't any viable way to walk it back, so we left it out there."

"And?"

I said nothing.

"C'mon, that's not the end of the story. How did it end?"

"The man was mugged the next night. Killed. No one knows if it was connected. Nothing was ever proven, but I've always blamed myself for it."

She was quick with her reply. "It could have been a coincidence."

I wasn't so quick with mine. "Maybe."

"We talked about coincidences earlier."

"Yes. We did."

"Well, did someone else have to sign off on it? On the release of the information?"

"In that case, yes. My supervisor at work. Colonel Clarke."

"And I'm assuming he had more intel at his disposal than you did?"

"Administratively, yes, but—"

"There you go," she said with finality. She readjusted the vent to square the cool airflow on to her face. "It's not your fault. It's this colonel guy's—if it's anyone's fault at all. It sounds like you did the best you could and things turned out badly. That happens sometimes. It happens to everyone."

Maybe. But that doesn't mean people end up dead because of it.

Though only a few moments ago I'd been thankful for this discussion, now it was serving to bring back a snarl of harsh memories I didn't want to think about.

Turns out there were a lot of things right now that I didn't want to think about.

Time to change the subject.

"When we get to the airport," I said, then caught myself. "Wait. Do you even have your car keys with you?"

"There's one in a hide-a-key thingy under the car, near the left rear tire. We're good."

I thought through our situation, tried to anticipate problems with this plan. "You remember all the security camera locations in the parking garage?"

"Sure."

"Sure?" Skepticism had crept into my voice.

"Yes. I do. Seriously, we can pull this off."

"And there's a route in that won't get us seen?"

"There are cameras monitoring which vehicles enter and exit the garage, of course." She considered that. "How about we leave this car in long-term parking and walk to the SUV? That way we don't enter the garage in one car and leave it in another. It'll be less conspicuous."

I evaluated her suggestion, trying not to think only about what would be the best choice for me, but also for her. "It's not worth it for both of us to chance getting caught. Tell me where the cameras are. I'll drop you off somewhere near the airport, go in like you said, switch cars, and then come back around in the SUV and pick you up."

"No. You'd never make it past all the CCTV sight lines. If it's going to be only one of us, it needs to be me. You know that. I'll go."

I still wasn't completely convinced that retrieving the car from the garage was the best move. "Is it really worth it?" I said. "Chancing showing up on surveillance cameras? Switching vehicles? Any of it?"

"I'm sure that by now they know we have this car. There's got to be a BOLO out for it. For us. Switching to the CR-V will give us a different vehicle that can't be traced, a tablet for research—also untraceable—and with your clearance level, it might actually lead us to some answers. It'll also give me clothes, wigs, IDs. I have everything I need for three different identities in that car."

"And what about me?"

"You'd look good in a wig."

"A *woman's* wig?"

"I'm not one to judge."

"Uh-huh. But with the scars on my face . . . well, they're hard to miss." I hadn't intended to bring them up and immediately regretted doing so.

After a pause, she said, "Did you get those in the fire? The one that killed your wife?"

There was that unapologetically forthright manner of hers again. From her, the questions didn't seem impolite or inappropriate. They had a certain quality of childlike innocence. I found that I didn't mind addressing them.

"Yes," I said.

"You can tell me about it—if you want to, I mean. No pressure. But it is possible that it might help us figure out what my connection to all of this is. How our stories might connect."

"I was asleep," I said, haltingly at first. "I woke up in bed, alone, smoke in the air. Because of the flames, I couldn't get down the stairs, so I had to jump off the balcony to escape the house. I thought I'd seen Sienna outside, but I was wrong." I found my knuckles tightening. "It wasn't her. So I went back in to look for her."

"You went back into the house?"

"Yes. But I couldn't save her."

"I doubt that most people would have gone back in like that."

It didn't help, I thought grimly, but said nothing.

"It shows what kind of person you are," Adira said. "You have a very rare trait."

"What's that?"

I wondered if she might jokingly remark something along the lines of *stupidity*, but instead, she said, "A combination of both guts and heart. Some people are brave but think only of themselves. Other people might be in love with someone, but they don't know how to sacrifice for them. To find someone who's brave for the right reasons and when it matters most . . . well, that's tough to find. Believe me. I've been around. I know."

I wasn't sure how to respond; instead, I found myself caught up remembering the fire and how the firefighter carried me out of the house and refused to go back in for Sienna when I begged him to.

I asked Adira to unscrew the cap of the bottle of Dr. Enuf I'd been saving, and after she passed the soda to me, I took a sip of the sugary-sweet drink. "The taste of the South" the gas station attendant had called it. In that case, I liked how the South tasted.

As I drove, I thought of Sienna and found myself mentally sorting through what I did know and what I didn't know about the fire, trying, but failing, to think about it all objectively. With her work as a linguist in the intelligence community, I'd wondered at times if whoever started the fire might have wanted her dead as well as me. The arson could've been intended to be a double homicide.

I'd had nearly a year and a half to process the loss of my wife, and while I'd made some progress, I was still looking for closure, for that elusive administration of justice. I'd given myself permission to grieve, but not permission to move on.

The fire, my loss, my search for answers, and the scars that need more than simply time to heal—I got caught up turning all of that over in my mind. Distracted, I kept driving and it wasn't until five miles or so down the road that I realized Adira had placed her hand softly and reassuringly on my knee.

And as I passed a semi on the right and directed the car into the darkness before us, I didn't pull away.

CHAPTER 33

The ringing phone startled Gunnar Bane out of a fitful sleep. Immediately alert, he snatched it up, and only then realized that instinct had taken over and he'd grabbed something in his other hand as well—his Heckler & Koch VP9.

After assessing the room and finding no threat, he returned the gun to the nightstand, next to his journal.

"Bane here," he said into the phone.

"Excuse me, sir. It's Major Díaz. Sorry to call at this time, but earlier tonight a waitress in Virginia posted a picture of two bills—both hundreds, the same denomination Brock used for the Camry rental. A couple left the bills as a tip to help her with an injured wrist. The photo went viral."

If Gunnar hadn't been completely awake before, he was now. "Did you talk to her?"

"Yes. She described the man and the woman to me. The scars the guy had . . . Well, it's Brock and Halprin."

In one motion, Gunnar sat up and swung his legs to the floor. "When were they there?"

"They left just after nine o'clock."

His phone told him it was now nearly five.

"And did she give you any indication of where they might've been heading?"

"She said she was so shocked by the tip that she watched them drive away. Couldn't help it. They hopped onto 81 South."

"Put the word out there to all highway patrols along I-81. Anything unusual, anyone spending hundred-dollar bills, or anyone with Brock's distinctive scars. And let's find that Camry."

"Yes, sir."

Halprin, with her background, should have sensed that leaving such an extravagant tip behind might attract attention—and she was an expert at disappearing. What was going on? Did she want to get caught? And if so, why?

After the call, Gunnar was too jacked up to even think about going back to sleep.

It was too early to call Clarke and request permission to go through Lassiter's and Caruso's financial records to see if either of them had been receiving unwarranted payments.

Instead, Gunnar cranked some vinyl Led Zeppelin IV on his old-school stereo, and put on a pot of Black Rifle coffee, his favorite brand. Not only was the java legit, but the company was veteran-owned and donated a portion of its proceeds to support law enforcement and first responders, something he was totally on board with.

While he waited for the coffee to brew, he typed in a few thoughts for his novel.

The story had started off as a military thriller, but then morphed into another type of story altogether—one he never would've guessed he would write, until he found out how many books sold every year in that genre.

Romance.

His sister's family had never had a ton of money and he'd never been able to help all that much. This writing gig, though, would change all that. After he landed this puppy at a publisher, his niece, Skye, would be able to attend college.

He wrote, *Donovan's eyes bounced around the room and landed on the gentle slope of Jessie's face, which held—encased in her ivory skin—high, regal cheekbones as well as the rest of the bones of her shapely skull. He let his gaze probe hers, and then travel down her face toward the top of her recherché neck that sloped down even further to where it met the top of her body's torso with grace and elegance.*

Yeah. He liked that. A touch of allure without giving everything away.

High cheekbones were vital. In fiction, women always had high cheek-bones. You'll never meet a woman in a romance novel who was described as having "lovely low cheekbones." For men, it was jaws: square jaws, strong jaws, lantern jaws—whatever that was. Maybe the guy had a goatee and he lit it on fire, who knows. Jaws for guys and cheekbones for ladies. The secret to great character descriptions. Simple as that.

The coffee maker beeped, letting him know that the Black Rifle was ready.

He closed the word processor and, cup in hand, turned his attention to an online search for known relatives or friends of Halprin and Brock, especially along Interstate 81 South. Time to figure out where the two of them might be heading.

CHAPTER 34

As she and Travis reached Knoxville, Adira found herself wondering once again why Nathan had submitted that FOIA request in her name. She decided it must have been his way of trying to lead Travis to her.

Now, they turned south for the fifteen-minute drive through the city to the McGhee Tyson Airport. When they were about two miles away from it, Travis swung into the parking lot of a small Baptist church on the Alcoa Highway, climbed out, and Adira took his place in the driver's seat.

"See you in a bit," she told him.

"Be careful."

"Which reminds me." She clicked open the glove box and handed him the Makarov. "Just in case."

He hesitated, but accepted it, sliding it beneath the back of his belt.

"You know how to use that, right?" she asked.

"I saw you putting it together and taking it apart in the car earlier."

"Show me."

He did so, exactly as she'd been doing while he was driving. He looked like he'd done it a thousand times before.

"Huh," she acknowledged. "You do remember things pretty well. So just point and shoot if you need to."

"Got it."

—∽∿∽—

Adira hopped back onto the highway and followed the signs to the airport's long-term parking, where she pulled to a stop and, redirecting her thoughts away from her murdered friend, took in her surroundings.

Not much happening. An older couple in the next row of cars over was wrestling an overstuffed bag out of the trunk of their Audi. Under different circumstances, she might have offered to help, but today she needed to keep as low a profile as possible.

She waited until they were on their way to the terminal before she left the old Camry and stuck a small piece of gravel in her left shoe. It would alter her gait so that in case, somewhere along the line, the authorities had analyzed her stride and were using gait-recognition software, it wouldn't peg her. The stone in the shoe bit was a tried-and-true spy trick used when developing disguises and false identities. An oldie but a goodie. You gotta love the classics.

Warily, she made her way toward the parking garage.

The sky held only the faintest hint of dawn, and darkness still lurked along the edge of the lot, but the towering lights stationed throughout it left few shadows for her to capitalize on, even if she had been wanting to move in a stealthier fashion to the garage. Instead, she simply walked nonchalantly beneath the blaring lights, directly toward it.

As she neared the concrete structure, she began to wonder if this might be her chance to protect Travis from the consequences of being caught with her.

She could simply pick up her CR-V and take off. She was good at disappearing, and the vehicle held everything that she needed to do so. By using the different identities she'd developed over the years to get through airport security without detection, she could even fly out of the country if she needed to and go to a place without an extradition agreement with the United States.

There you had it. One and done.

The idea of leaving, of bailing on her life like that—while not something she would have ever expected herself to contemplate—did have its allure. She'd be free to be whoever she wanted to be in that moment and to move around as she pleased. No personal ties. No daily obligations.

But where would that leave Travis?

He'd helped her so far. And unless they could resolve things, he might be facing some serious consequences.

Of course, he could just claim that she'd forced him to come with her. That might take care of everything.

Or it might not.

He intrigued her and she wouldn't want to leave him high and dry. Wouldn't be fair.

Debating what to do, she entered the parking garage. She located the two cameras that she would need to hide her face from and made sure she was turned away as she entered the stairwell to the second level.

What if the authorities somehow identified the CR-V as yours? What if they're surveilling it now?

Well, she was here. That ship had sailed. She would just need to deal with whatever the consequences might be.

As she left the stairwell and entered the level where her car was, she saw a woman with a toddler beside her getting her things out of a minivan just two vehicles down from her Honda.

Four years ago, Adira had spent a couple of weeks dating a hot but somewhat unstable Marine. Now their unofficial motto—which he'd liked to quote to her at the most inopportune moments—came to mind: improvise, adapt, and overcome.

Not bad advice.

So now, pause or continue?

Improvise.

Adapt.

Overcome.

She realized that it would attract more attention if she loitered here, especially if the woman saw her fiddling around, pretending to open another car's door. Instead, she casually walked forward, tilting her face away from the sight line of the camera west of her, and approached her SUV.

To get in, she first needed to retrieve the key from where it was hidden beneath the car.

Do it discreetly. Don't attract any undue attention.

However, as she neared her vehicle, an iconic silver Mustang came barreling up the ramp, going way too fast.

And then it happened—a cycle of events that should never have taken place, unraveling like a ball of yarn rolling away from her and out of reach in the wrong direction.

The toddler waddled away from his mother and toward the center of the garage, right in the path of the oncoming car. Adira's heart nearly stopped.

That driver was never going to be able to brake in time, if he even saw the child at all.

The boy's mother was bent over, grabbing her purse. Only when she straightened up and turned did she see what was happening.

But it was too late.

Time shrank and then expanded. Everything began to play out in slow motion.

As Adira sprinted toward the toddler, she heard the long, strangled cry of his mother echo off the constricting walls of the garage: "Noooo!"

The Mustang's driver slammed on his brakes, but at the speed he was traveling, it was too little, too late.

Adira swept the boy up in her arms and spun sideways to avoid the car, but the driver had swerved to the side as well and as the car skidded to a stop, it slammed into her left leg.

The impact sent her careening sideways over the hood, but miraculously, she managed to hold on to the toddler and protect him with her body while throwing out her other leg to arrest her forward movement as she slid off the car.

The angle was awkward and ended up tweaking her ankle, but she kept the kid off the ground. With pain throbbing up her whammed leg and fire in the other ankle, she hobbled away from the Mustang. In her arms, the startled child stared wide-eyed around him. It looked like he was on the verge of erupting into tears.

She felt seriously sorry for the kid. Screw the cameras. She was just glad she'd been in the right place at the right time. A fraction of a second later or another few feet to the side, and she wouldn't have been able to save him.

Frantic and desperate to get to her boy, his mother rushed forward, arms outstretched, and Adira handed the toddler over. The woman gushed her thanks and set about calming her rattled child, drawing him to her chest.

The ashen driver had gotten out of his car and now exclaimed defensively that he hadn't seen the boy and that it wasn't his fault and that the kid shouldn't have been out there in the first place. Adira was tempted to walk over and punch the guy in the face, but that wouldn't have served her very well in keeping a low profile—as if that was even possible at this point, anyway.

"Are you okay?" he asked her. The concern in his voice might have been for her; might have been from fear of getting in trouble.

"Yeah. I'm fine."

The mother glared at the driver, her eyes icicles. Adira was afraid of what she might do, but she simply shook her head, spun on her heels, and, with her boy cradled in her arms, left for her minivan, pausing only long enough to glance at Adira and mouth the words, *"Thank you."*

Adira gathered herself. The driver was staring at her nervously. "You sure you're—"

"Just go." She held herself back from calling him the names she was thinking, which took considerably more self-control than she would have thought she'd have in a situation like this. "Watch out and slow the hell down!"

"Yeah." He sounded like a rebuked child. "I will."

By the time Adira reached her SUV, she realized that there was no way the incident would have escaped the watchful eye of the CCTV cameras. It was quite possible, in fact, that security personnel were already headed her way.

Just get in and get moving.

It took her only a few seconds to locate the car key. Once inside the CR-V, she removed the stone from her shoe, verified that her tablet and her wigs and outfits were in the back, and considered carefully what'd just happened and how best to move forward.

Then, she made her decision regarding whether or not to pick Travis up and guided the SUV out of the garage, paid cash for the parking stub, and headed for the highway.

CHAPTER 35

Dawn was starting to etch its way across the sky as I waited for Adira to return to the empty parking lot of Alcoa Baptist Church.

The classic sloped roof and traditional steeple reminded me of growing up attending services at a small Presbyterian church with my mother. Over the years I'd wavered in my commitment to the lessons I'd learned in church—never quite abandoning them, but never quite applying them like I might have either.

Now, it occurred to me that I hadn't entered a church since Sienna's funeral. Before that, we'd attended nondenominational services together every month or so. In truth, I wasn't certain what I believed about God and Jesus and miracles, but any way you looked at it, Jesus was one of the most influential people in history—probably *the* most influential person to ever walk the earth. His birth split the world's calendar in two; even today, over half of the world's population believed he was at least a prophet, if not the Son of God. I'd always felt that, regardless of a person's background or religious heritage, it was worth learning what someone with that kind of impact believed.

And so, during law school when we were examining definitions of justice, I'd scanned the Scriptures, both the Old and New Testaments, and studied both the prophecies regarding a coming Messiah and the ways the Nazarene fulfilled them.

As far as justice and injustice, in addition to the Ecclesiastes verse I'd quoted to Adira earlier, there were literally hundreds of biblical verses that dealt with different aspects of the topics—who to extend justice to, how it should be administered, how to respond when it's not carried out, and more. The list went on and on. Yet I'd noticed that, for some reason, the topic of justice wasn't typical fare for Sunday sermons. Instead, the messages tended more along the lines of "Feel good about yourself. Forgive yourself. Accept yourself. Follow your heart. Believe in yourself. Be true to yourself. Follow your dreams." Those admonitions were a lot more common in the sermons I'd heard in recent years, even though the Bible didn't teach any of them. Not a one.

So, yeah, a bit of a disconnect there. But references to justice—they appeared everywhere. You couldn't objectively read the Bible and not come away with the idea that God hates injustice and the oppression of the weak by the strong. In fact, Luke recorded Jesus using a verse from Isaiah about setting the oppressed free as a way of proclaiming that he was the one who had come to fulfill God's promises.

So that's what I thought of now, here in this parking lot: a God who proclaims and promises justice, and yet, for some reason, all around us, we see injustice spreading its dark wings across the world in ways that seem to go utterly unchecked.

Another disconnect.

Is God too impotent to take a stand against it? Or, maybe, has he simply given up on us?

Or, does he empower us to fight injustice on his behalf?

If so, what did that actually require of us? What did justice, true justice, look like?

My discussion with Adira regarding injustice came to mind again, and as I considered the idea of standing up against oppressors, I started thinking about what was going on here, this week.

Nathan Lassiter's murder. The loss of life at L & L Manufacturing. The connection to Sienna's death.

I found myself considering the papers we'd found on Nathan's desk: the funeral bulletin, the printout detailing Adira's executive protection work, Dr. Yong's bio and speaking schedule. Though the FOIA request had been sent in Adira's name, Nathan had apparently used it to draw us together. I still didn't know why, but everything from the FOIA request to Colonel Clarke's comments to Nathan's conference registration seemed to point to Oak Ridge.

I processed the implications. At the moment, I couldn't poke around online to see what the relationship between Oak Ridge and Nathan Lassiter might be, but one name had been prominent in his paperwork: Dr. Chia-hao Yong.

As the Nobel-winning physicist's calendar indicated, he was scheduled to present the opening keynote at the symposium in Oak Ridge in just a few hours.

Could he be involved in Project Symphony?

As I was considering how his work might be related to Paraden or even to the antinuke Pruninghooks Collective activists, a police cruiser came crawling into the parking lot and rolled toward me.

Oh.

This was not at all what I needed right now.

Okay, just talk your way out of it; just convince him that you're supposed to be here in this empty lot this early in the day.

Yeah, good luck with that.

Getting identified would be disastrous. So, I turned my face to obscure my scars as much as possible in the shadows cast from the sun rising in the east.

The officer blinked on his cruiser's blues to make it clear that he wanted to have a conversation. When he was about ten feet from me, he lowered his window. He was a hefty fellow—so thick and wide that he barely fit in his seat.

"Lost?" he asked.

I smiled, trying to play off his question as no big deal. "I'm just waiting for someone."

He sank his gaze into me. "At this time of day?"

As I thought about how to respond, I realized that I still had the gun from the Russian with me, tucked behind the back of my belt. If this officer found that on me, it would create all sorts of unwelcome questions. Turning around would definitely not be a good idea.

"Yes," I said simply, "I know it's early, but—"

"Who is it?" he said. "This person you're meeting?"

"A . . ." Thinking of our legend, I blurted out, "My wife."

He studied me coolly. "Y'all members of this here church?"

I wasn't sure why he was being so inquisitive, but as Adira had pointed out earlier, there was certainly a BOLO for us by now, so it was possible he was searching for a couple fitting our description. I doubted that an order would've spread to look for us this far south, but it was possible.

"Well, we . . ." While I was formulating my reply, a white Honda CR-V exited toward us and entered the lot. I figured that it had to be Adira, and although I was glad she was here, I didn't want the officer to question her as well. If he identified her, we could both be arrested before we had any answers, or any justice. I hadn't come this far to have things end like that. "We're new to the area," I said truthfully. "Not members of any church yet. Is this a good one?"

"Huh." He shifted his attention to the SUV, then opened his door and unwedged himself from the driver's seat, emerging stiffly from the cruiser that he'd somehow crammed himself into. The car creaked and seemed to heave a sigh of relief as he exited it.

I felt a prick of fear as I made sure I was positioned so he wouldn't see the gun.

"You have any ID with you?" he asked.

I did, but I couldn't imagine that showing him my Pentagon creds was going to help us keep a low profile here. On the other hand, if I failed to produce any identification, he might become even more suspicious.

Sweating, I searched for the right direction to take things as Adira parked, rolled down her window, and called to me, "There you are, honey."

"Yes, dear," I replied.

"This man with you?" the officer asked her gruffly.

"Oh, yes," she said, "he's a little, well, you know." She tapped her head and whispered, just loud enough for him to hear, "He gets confused sometimes."

"You mean . . . ?"

"Yeah. He's not all there. Not all the time."

"Oh . . ."

"Plus, he was just diagnosed with . . . well . . ." Her voice caught. "It's going to be a long road ahead."

"I'm so sorry, ma'am. I had no idea."

"It's okay. I appreciate that." She dabbed at a tear that had magically appeared just beneath her left eye, then turned to me. "Come on, sweetheart. Climb in. We need to get home. It's time for your medication."

Hastily, and before the officer decided to probe any deeper into the situation, I joined Adira in the SUV, keeping the gun shielded with my body, but trying not to walk too much sideways to alert him that I had anything to hide. In order to sit down I needed to surreptitiously remove the handgun, but I trusted that the door hid my movement.

The guy probably has a dashcam or a body cam. Probably both. He might've recorded all of this.

While that was certainly possible, we hadn't done anything to cause alarm, so I figured that the footage wouldn't pop up on anyone's radar screen and I told myself that we would be in the clear. Adira smiled at the officer and gave him an affable wave, but before we could leave, he started our way. "Hang on a moment. One more thing."

I glanced at Adira and saw that she was looking my way as well.

"Just be cool," she whispered.

I quickly hid the gun beside my seat.

The officer lumbered to the driver's side window, leaned toward it, and peered into the vehicle, first at Adira, then at me. Even from the far side of the car I could smell the minty mouthwash on his breath.

"Yes?" Adira said to him calmly. I looked their direction, unsure how to respond if he asked us to get out of the car.

He looked quizzically at me, momentarily studying the scars now clearly visible on my face, and then directed his attention to her. "Y'all drive safe now."

"We will," she said.

He gave her a final, congenial nod, then rapped the side of the SUV, swiveled around, and stalked off toward his cruiser.

Adira didn't wait around any longer than she needed to before leaving the parking lot.

As we drove off, I let out a breath of relief, and faced her. "It's good to see you."

"Good to see you too, honey."

I slid the gun into the glove box. "I get confused, huh?"

"Mm-hm."

"And I'm not all there? Not all the time?"

"It worked, didn't it?"

"I'm just glad you showed up when you did. I was running out of witty things to say to stall him."

"I can only imagine."

"What did you make of Officer Friendly coming over to the car like that right before we left?"

"Dunno," she said. "But what's done is done. I think if he was suspicious of us at all he wouldn't have let us drive away."

"So it went alright, though, at the parking garage?" I patted the dashboard. "No glitches picking this thing up?"

"Mm . . . Well, there might've been one tiny, *minuscule* glitch."

"And that was . . . ?"

"I'm not one hundred percent *certain* I made it out of the garage without getting caught on camera. But let's not dwell on that. Even if I did appear, no one would know we're going to Oak Ridge."

She shifted slightly in her seat and winced.

"You okay?" I asked.

"It's just my leg. I sorta bumped it."

"Are you good to drive?"

"Yeah." Then, "By the way, in case we need to be in touch but can't call each other by our actual names or terms of endearment, we'll use code names."

"That sounds appropriately spy-ish. What did you have in mind?"

"On the Red Team I was Flower Girl."

"You mentioned that earlier. How'd you get that name?"

"It's because of my middle name. My mom named me after her favorite flower."

Though I'd read her files yesterday, surprisingly, her middle name hadn't been listed. "Let me guess—Rose."

"Nope."

"Lily."

"Uh-uh."

"Hmm . . . Daisy?"

"Not Daisy. Give up?"

"No. Violet?"

She shook her head. "This could take a while."

"Amaryllis?"

"That's a good guess, but that's not it."

"Ah! Iris."

"It's not Iris either."

"Okay, hmm . . . I guess I do. I give up."

"Chrysanthemum."

"Yeah, I don't think I would've gotten to that one until next week sometime. It's pretty. I like it."

"Thanks. So what about you? What's your middle name?"

"Nothing all that special. I'm just named after my grandpa—Donald."

"Donald, huh?" She smiled. "Then you get to be Duck Boy."

"You've gotta be kidding. As in Donald Duck?"

A nod. "It's perfect. Not only is it your code name, it's also your superhero name."

"Wonderful."

"Flower Girl and Duck Boy. Watch out, world; we have arrived."

I wasn't certain how to move gracefully into the next subject, so I just went ahead and said what was on my mind. "I wasn't entirely sure you were going to pick me up again."

"What?" she said in mock surprise. "You thought I might leave you behind?"

"The possibility did cross my mind."

A slight pause. "It crossed mine as well."

"What brought you back?"

"I think, at least for the time being, we're better off together than apart. You're my best bet for getting out of all this, and since I have the encrypted tablet here with me, I'm yours."

"Looks like we're stuck together, then."

"There could be worse things."

Yes, I thought. *That is true.*

"You do know," she said, "that you're going to get into a lot of trouble for all this, for helping me."

"Yeah. Probably."

"Then why?" We came to a sign for Interstate 140 leading to Oak Ridge, and she slowed for the exit. "Why would you risk so much to help someone you never even met before? Someone who, for all you know, is a potential terrorist?"

"Like I told you yesterday, I'm doing this for the truth."

"And for justice."

"Well . . ."

"That's worth prison?"

"It's worth everything."

"Well put, Duck Boy."

"Yeah, we're going to have to rethink that name."

She exited the Alcoa Highway. "Have you been considering our next step?"

"The FOIA request's acrostic was PATMOS LAND. I believe whatever's going on has something to do with Patmos Financial Consortium's land purchases. There's also a presentation today at the conference, by that physicist, Dr. Chia-hao Yong. We need to look into that. They might be related. I don't know."

"Valid. And the Red Team members," she said. "We need to figure out their real names and see if we can confirm if Sapphire was responsible for Nathan's murder."

"Yes," I said. "And you're sure you don't know anything about this Patmos firm or their investments?"

"Positive. What do *you* know?"

"It's an equity firm," I explained. "They've invested in more than fifty tracts of land all over the country. I haven't been able to figure out the significance of that—or how it connects to anything else that's going on."

"Like this mysterious Project Symphony that you referred to earlier?"

"Right," I said. "Do you have those papers from Nathan's desk?"

"Oh." She cursed under her breath. "I left them in the Camry. I was so focused on switching vehicles—I wasn't thinking. But you can remember what was on them, can't you?"

That seemed out of character for her. She must have *really* been distracted.

For just a glimmer of a second I wondered if she might've left them there on purpose, but I immediately dismissed the idea as being ludicrous. What could she possibly have hoped to accomplish by doing that?

"I should be able to remember them alright," I told her.

"Good. Still, it looks like we've got our work cut out for us."

"At least we've got a plan."

She nodded. "Oak Ridge, here we come."

CHAPTER 36

OAK RIDGE TECH CORRIDOR CONFERENCE CENTER

The inviting scent of sizzling bacon intermingling with the smell of fresh coffee permeated the air as Senator Cliff Richardson worked his way through his breakfast at the hotel's posh ground-floor restaurant.

He was taking a final bite of his eggs Benedict when the text came through conveying the tragic news about Senator Bill Presnell's fatal heart attack at dinnertime last night.

Immediately, Cliff felt a surge of grief and sympathy for Presnell's family, for their loss, but he also felt a debilitating wave of guilt, because he didn't believe for one minute that the heart attack had been natural. He suspected— no, he *knew*—Joshua had been behind it.

Things weren't supposed to go like this.

People weren't supposed to die. That was why he was doing all of this in the first place—to protect innocent lives, not to have some psychopath take them.

And in that moment, it struck him that Joshua was indeed a psychopath. Not the out-of-control-chortling-madman type, but the cold and heartless man-without-a-conscience kind.

Finding him six months ago hadn't been as much of a challenge as Cliff would've guessed. Hiring him using an untraceable cryptocurrency hadn't been prohibitively difficult either.

Now, as he stared at his plate and picked halfheartedly at his hash browns, all of that got Cliff thinking.

His experience in the tech world in Silicon Valley spanned nearly three decades. He'd watched the meteoric rise and fall of dozens of startups. It'd given him more than just knowledge of the business; it'd given him perspective.

With his background in programming, he knew ways to search beyond the search engines, both on the surface web and the deep web, so he had extensive experience finding information that was difficult for the uninitiated to obtain.

In fact, if things had turned out differently for him, rather than founding TalynTek, he might very well have taken another path that would've led him to become a white hat hacker instead of a senator. But then, when his brother, Keith, was killed in combat, everything had changed.

Late last year, when he began tooling around the dark web, he told himself that he was simply curious. And that might have been the case, at first. But in light of what he'd learned regarding the vulnerabilities of the United States' nuclear infrastructure, he had formed a plan.

Or hatched one, as they say.

But no, that's how they phrased it when the villain of a story came up with his scheme. Semantics. Like when you referred to one country's government officials as an "administration" and another country's—one you didn't like—as a "regime."

No, his plan hadn't been "hatched." He wasn't a villain by any stretch of the imagination. He was the person responsible for stopping the true villains from attacking the infrastructure of the country he loved, the one that'd provided him with the opportunity to grow a business, to become rich beyond his wildest dreams, and now to serve his constituents as a senator. In putting them first, he'd had to put his own interests second.

With that, his thoughts circled back to Joshua.

Yes, it had been relatively easy to find him.

Then, a realization came to him unbidden, one that should've occurred to him earlier: *Maybe it was too easy. Maybe he was searching for you. Maybe the hunter is really the hunted.*

Was it possible Joshua had targeted him instead of the other way around?

Well, no matter what their history was or who had found whom, Cliff reminded himself that now, here, at the conference center, he needed to stay wary. When all of this was over, he would accept responsibility for what'd happened and turn himself in. He'd give the authorities the truth, but until then he needed to keep his head down and his attention on what lay before him.

Focus on finding the most opportune moment to reveal the details about the microchips.

Yes, but in the meantime, he needed to share his sympathies and send his condolences to Senator Presnell's surviving family members.

As he was finishing up sending a message doing so, a text came through from the very person he'd been thinking of only moments earlier. Joshua wrote that he wanted to speak before the presentation. **I might be able to get us into Y-12,** he texted. **Meet me in the hotel lobby at nine.**

Less than two hours away.

Cliff put the breakfast charge on his room, then rose and went outside for a quick walk and to get some fresh air, realizing soberly that, if things went sideways, it might be his last chance to do so in a very long time.

—✺—

MCGHEE TYSON AIRPORT

TWELVE MILES SOUTH OF KNOXVILLE, TENNESSEE

The GPS tracker that Sergei and Ilya had been following had stopped moving at the Knoxville airport, and Sergei wasn't certain what to make of that.

It was possible that Brock and Halprin had found a flight and were in the air already—or they might still be here.

Ilya hadn't discovered anything more about Halprin's DHS work, which told Sergei that someone didn't want those details out there—and they were serious about keeping her work responsibilities confidential.

While he swung the van into the airport's long-term parking lot where the tracker was currently located, he had Ilya research which flights had departed during the last hour and which ones were upcoming. Then he parked, exited the van, investigated the Camry, and identified Brock's computer bag in the backseat.

Maybe he and Halprin had discovered the GPS patch and left the bag there on purpose. Or maybe they'd just chosen not to bring it with them and had no idea there was a tracker patch on it at all.

No way to tell.

"Got the flights," Ilya announced.

"Go on."

"Houston flight and one to Dallas already left. Flight to Charlotte leaves in an hour. Later this morning there are departures to DC, Atlanta, Detroit, and Orlando."

Sergei debated where to take things. "Let's see if Brock and Halprin are in the terminal."

A brief pause. "You sure?"

"Yes. Let's go."

He led Ilya across the street and into the building, where it didn't take them long to look around baggage claim and the airline counter areas.

No sign of Halprin and Brock. If the two of them were in the airport, they must have passed through security already.

"What now?" Ilya asked him quietly.

Sergei kept his voice low as well. "Can you hack into the flight manifests and see if Brock's name pops up on any of them?"

"That would take time."

The one thing they didn't have.

"Alright, let's see if they boarded a flight." He told Ilya what to say at the check-in counters. "I'll take left; you take right."

He found the American Airlines counter and approached the young gate agent who looked like she'd already worked an eight-hour shift.

Sergei offered her a cordial smile. "Excuse me. I'm supposed to be meeting my party here and I can't seem to find them. Can you tell me if they've already checked in?"

"Last names?"

There was no way to know if they'd used their real names, but at this point he had to assume they had.

"Halprin and Brock."

She busied herself at the keyboard, then scrunched her face up in obvious confusion. "I'm afraid I don't have any record of them being on any of our flights today."

"What? Okay. We must have gotten our signals crossed."

He shifted his attention to his phone so she wouldn't ask him any follow-up questions, waved his thanks to her, and left for another airline's counter.

When he'd finished with his airlines, Sergei met up with Ilya, who shook his head.

"Nothing," Ilya muttered. "You?"

"No. Let's head back to the van and get out of here."

He still had one card up his sleeve, as it were, but he wasn't convinced that he needed to play it quite yet.

On the way through the parking lot, he took a moment to stop by the Camry again. Using his shirt to glove his hand so he wouldn't leave any prints, he tried the doors.

Locked.

He studied the inside of the car. Empty soda bottles, bubble gum wrappers, two restaurant to-go boxes, a pile of overturned papers in the backseat with a funeral bulletin on top, but nothing that told him anything useful about where Brock and Halprin might have gone. Breaking into the car was an option, but not ideal.

"What you thinking?" Ilya asked him.

"If they didn't fly out, it's likely they drove out of here. Let's see if there are any vehicles registered in either of their names. Maybe we can get lucky and find one that has GPS we can track. Also, with the three casualties back at the manufacturing plant, we won't be the only ones looking for them. We should start monitoring law enforcement channels. Beyond that, though, I think it might be time to contact our employer and explain what's happened."

"Are you certain?"

No, he thought. *I'm not.*

Sergei didn't know the identity of the person who'd hired them to bring in Travis Brock. All of the communication so far had been through encrypted messages, dead drops, and electronically altered voice calls. He didn't even know if it was a man or a woman.

He had his suspicions that it was someone in the Russian government—and there wouldn't have been too many entities as interested in what Brock knew as the Foreign Intelligence Service or its military counterpart, most commonly known here in the States as GRU—in particular, its enigmatic Unit 29155. The two agencies often competed for confidential sources and didn't always communicate well with each other. Either might be involved, and if that was the case, it would've been unlikely that they would have informed the other agency of their interest in an asset as valuable as Brock.

If either was the responsible party, then Sergei's ideology was aligned with that of his employer. If not, when he found out the person's true identity, he would take whatever steps ended up being necessary for the well-being of his motherland.

It was also possible that their employer was a member of the United States government. Perhaps someone who might benefit from the information Brock could provide? Or a group involved with defense programs or private military contractors? All very real possibilities.

Ilya interrupted his thoughts. "I will search vehicle registrations and law enforcement notices for them before you make call."

"Yes. Alright."

Sergei directed Ilya back to the van, which was lined with plastic sheeting and the restraints that would serve the purpose of keeping Travis Brock and, if necessary, Adira Halprin secure during transport.

CHAPTER 37

Gunnar Bane finished his research into the known associates of Halprin and Brock without learning anything particularly helpful—except that both the redactor and the Red Team member kept off social media and were veritable ghosts online.

Nothing about this assignment really made sense to him. There were hints of a relationship between the Russians and the two of them, but he couldn't nail down anything solid.

He tried calling Clarke to get permission to investigate Lassiter's and Caruso's relationship and finances, but when the colonel didn't answer, Gunnar decided to deal with his frustration with a workout in the garage. Maybe it'd help clear his head.

He started with pull-ups on the hangboard, taking time between sets to record lines for his novel.

Recently, the story had moved from being about an elite military force in South America fighting a Colombian drug cartel—something that was a little bit too close to home for him, but a plotline he actually knew something about—to a more domestic location.

And a slightly different plot.

Just slightly.

His current pitch: After her idyllic marriage crumbles, Jessie, a caring and big-hearted veterinarian, moves from the big city back to her hometown in Montana to start over. There, while treating one of the horses at the local rodeo, she runs into Donovan, a local cowboy and old flame from high school who is looking for a fresh start of his own.

So, yeah, slightly removed from the drug cartels in Colombia storyline.

As he counted off reps of pull-ups, he found himself thinking of the scene he was working on: *As Donovan reached for the door, his hand brushed across Jessie's fingers and he felt a surge of fire in his . . .*

And see now, this was tricky territory. He didn't want to be too graphic or suggestive, but he also needed to be honest to the story. There weren't really a whole lot of subtle ways to refer to what was happening, not without being too crude or too clinical about it all. Nothing vague, but also nothing vulgar. That was his goal. Family friendly content for his more conservative readers.

What about loins? A fire in his loins?

Huh, that was a possibility. It kind of walked that fine line. Not too many people used the word *loins* anymore. A shame, really. Maybe Donovan could gird up his loins? Loin girding was actually a thing. Maybe Jessie could? Even women can gird up their loins, although Gunnar didn't believe it was quite so common. More of a guy thing.

No, come to think of it, he wasn't aware of much female loin girding in contemporary fiction at all. So, if he could figure out a way for Jessie to do so, it might be memorable. Maybe even trend-setting.

Hmm. Figure that out later.

He paused his workout and dictated: "Her trembling lips opened longingly as she leaned into Donovan's waiting embrace. His arms enfolded around her. He drew her to his face and pressed his lips up against hers, their mouths kissing each other passionately."

Not bad. Why hadn't he started this project earlier? He could have been writing these babies for years.

In between sets, he recorded more lines into his cell phone, then moved on to alternating between push-ups and lunges—which he was definitely not a fan of. As he was finishing up a second set of sixty push-ups, the phone rang, giving him a chance to at least momentarily put off more lunges.

Toweling off his face, he tapped the screen. A video call.

Major Díaz: "We have a hit, sir. It's Halprin."

"Tell me."

"The Knoxville airport. There's footage of a woman saving a toddler from getting hit by a car in the parking garage less than an hour ago. Facial rec gives us an 83 percent probability that it's her."

"Send me the footage."

"Yes, sir. Give me just a moment."

While Gunnar waited for Díaz to send the file, he caught his breath and then downed some water from a well-loved Nalgene bottle plastered with stickers of his favorite mountaineering equipment and surfboard companies.

It gave him a moment to mentally shift from focusing on the workout and the love scene to the search for Brock and Halprin: Here was Halprin, at the Knoxville airport. Also, that waitress who'd gotten the hefty tip had said that Brock and Halprin headed south on I-81. A quick calculation told him the timing fit.

You're going to that conference Lassiter registered for, aren't you? he thought. *The one in Oak Ridge?*

But why? That was still the big unknown.

When the video of the parking garage incident came through, Gunnar studied the footage carefully. He could clearly observe that Halprin had been standing well clear of the speeding Mustang. She hadn't needed to risk her personal safety to save the toddler, but she'd done so anyway.

He evaluated that, then scrubbed the video back and watched it again.

Yeah, it was her, and she'd been hit pretty hard by that car before returning the kid to his mom and driving off in a white CR-V.

Unless Halprin and Brock switched vehicles again somewhere along the line, that car they rented from the college student should still be at the airport.

"Get Knoxville PD on this," he said to Díaz. "Find that Camry they were driving. If it's not at the airport, have them look in nearby hotel lots, restaurants, ride-share businesses. Anything. When they locate it, have them check for prints, DNA. Whatever we can get—let's see if anyone else was with them."

"On it."

He doubted that Halprin would go to a hospital, but that Mustang had given her more than just a gentle nudge, so he advised Díaz to check the ones in the area just in case.

"Yes, sir," the major told him.

What was so important in that SUV at the airport that Halprin would risk getting caught on video to go back for it? Just to switch vehicles? Really? Was that enough of a reason?

"What about Brock?" Gunnar asked Díaz.

"No sign of him."

"Thanks, Major," Gunnar said, closing up the call. "I'll pass this information along to the colonel."

After ending the video chat, Gunnar promptly called Colonel Clarke, who picked up on the second ring this time. "Sorry to disturb you so early, Colonel, but we have something." Gunnar filled him in on what they knew about Halprin and sent him the video of her stepping in and getting to the child just in time to rescue him. "I think they might be on their way to Oak Ridge."

"Project Symphony," Clarke muttered.

"Sir?"

"Sorry. Yes, Oak Ridge. The International Nuclear Association Safety Summit today. Travis knows about it. That makes sense."

"What's Project Symphony?"

"It's classified. It has to do with a DARPA research program working in conjunction with the private sector. And a scientist who's down there in Tennessee this week—Dr. Yong. That's about all I can say."

That was enough.

"Can you get me access to Lassiter's and Caruso's financial records?" Gunnar asked. "I want to look for anomalies. See if there've been any payoffs."

"I'll put the request through. Oh, I did some checking. Lassiter and Caruso were close friends, had been for years. Met competition shooting." Then he added grimly, "I knew 'em both. Now they're both gone."

Gunnar considered the next step. "From what we know, Ilya Vasiliev is involved with this. The guy's got a special talent for getting people to give up their secrets. And as we spoke about earlier, he doesn't typically work alone. No matter how tough Brock is, if they find him . . ."

"Everyone breaks."

"Yeah." Then Gunnar again raised the question he'd floated the day before. "Do you believe he's been compromised?"

"I don't know," Colonel Clarke admitted. "And not knowing isn't good enough. We need to find him before the Russians do. And we need to make sure the secrets he knows remain secret."

"At this point, you could go with local law enforcement or the FBI. Major Díaz and his men are up to speed on what's happening. You could send them down if you prefer. Or . . ."

"I could send you."

"Yes."

"Go on. I'm listening."

"I work discreetly. I can move under the radar. Nothing from your end needs to be officially sanctioned. No paperwork. No trail. Travis doesn't know me. I can get close, and I'm good at what I do. Besides, there'll be security at Oak Ridge, right? I can call them in if necessary."

"I want you there," the colonel said, and Gunnar had the sense that Clarke had already made up his mind to send him down even before inviting him to make his case.

Gunnar glanced at the Heckler & Koch VP9 that he'd brought into the garage with him. Force of habit. "In this task of making certain that Brock's knowledge doesn't fall into the wrong hands, how much discretion do I have?"

"We can't afford anything less than full containment. Use extreme prejudice."

"And the woman?" he asked. "Halprin?"

"Bring her in—unless you're required to stop both her and Brock at the same time. Then do so by whatever means necessary."

"I understand."

"I can get you a flight out of Dulles. I'll make the arrangements. You'll be in Knoxville by eight fifty. There'll be a car waiting for you when you arrive. Keep me updated."

"Yes, sir. I will."

"I'm giving you four hours from the time you land before I call in the cavalry."

Why four? Gunnar wondered. *Why would that time frame even come up? Why does that matter? Maybe something to do with this Project Symphony?*

Despite his curiosity, he accepted the deadline without questioning it. "Four hours. Got it."

End call.

Taking his weapon with him, he headed into the house for a shower.

Game on.

CHAPTER 38

I looked around as Adira parked in the Oak Ridge Tech Corridor Conference Center's sprawling, packed lot.

Above us, mountains of leaden clouds towered high into the heavens, but there weren't enough of them to keep all of the eager April sunlight at bay.

"We're here," Adira announced unnecessarily as she turned off the ignition.

As I was considering how we were going to find Dr. Yong and speak to him without raising suspicion, I studied the lot.

Already, protestors were lining the street and jostling for position, brandishing placards decrying nuclear weapons. The obvious: "Nukes kill!" The alliterative: "Banish bombs!" And the classics: "Make love not war," and "Give peace a chance!"

A few people carried signs bearing a curved symbol reminiscent of a question mark—the same symbol that we'd seen squiggled on the papers on Nathan Lassiter's desk. So, that established a connection to what was happening here and confirmed to me that we were in the right place—though I still wanted to know what the symbol stood for.

A dozen news vans lined the northwest side of the parking lot. Although there weren't any reporters out yet, I suspected that it wouldn't be long before they emerged and started their live feeds.

Adira pointed toward the assemblage of protestors. "This isn't even the place where they store nuclear isotopes, is it?"

"No. Y-12 is down the road, but in the eyes of these protestors, this is probably close enough." A trio of turkey vultures circled purposefully over the forest nearby. "Besides," I said, distracted by the birds and by thoughts of the dead, "they get more exposure waving their placards around here at an international nuke conference than they would at some obscure Y-12 security gate."

The presence of the vultures and the protestors made me think of an arcane text from the Bible, one of Jesus' sayings from the twenty-fourth chapter of Matthew: "Wherever the carcass is, there the vultures will gather." His words came in the context of a message about the end times. From my limited understanding of theology, I knew there were a variety of interpretations about what specific point the Galilean carpenter was trying to make, but right now with these activists here clamoring for peace, the vultures overhead, and with the lethal power of Y-12 so close by, I couldn't shake the image.

Vultures gathering around the dead.

My nightmare came back to me: the living corpse, the cemetery, the sizzling wounds made by the flashlight's beam.

Death and decay—I just couldn't seem to escape thoughts of them this morning.

Hoisting their placards, the protestors started chanting, "The fruit of justice is peace!"—the same words that Sister Megan Rice and her two friends had spray-painted on the side of the Highly Enriched Uranium Materials Facility back in 2012 after cutting through four of Y-12's security fences.

But does justice really lead to peace? Maybe to a certain degree. However, they were distinctly different concepts, and making justice into a slogan seemed to, in my mind, diminish its importance. It was something worth living for, worth dying for. Much more than just a bumper sticker saying or catchphrase.

I directed my attention back to the parking lot and, noting the number of cars, reasoned that the chances of finding a room at the hotel were pretty slim. It might not be necessary, however—except as a place to covertly set up shop and avoid attracting attention while we searched for the physicist.

I gestured toward the back of the vehicle and asked Adira, "Do you have anything in here that we'll be able to use besides your tablet computer?"

"A couple things. I'll show you once we're in our room."

"I'm guessing there won't be any available—also, it's awfully early to check in, anyway."

"Leave that to me."

She popped the rear hatch, rummaged around in her suitcase, stuffed a few things into an oversize purse, and then pulled out a brunette wig and put it on.

"Women are a lot better at identifying women by their faces," she explained. "Men tend to look at hair first. Change your hair and, to most guys, you look like an entirely different person." Then, as if to fend off any objections I might have had, she added, "It's psychology, not sexism."

"Okay. But that's your plan? Wear a wig while you talk to the scientist? I don't get it."

"Trust me. I'll be back in five minutes with a room key." She flashed me a smile and left for the front doors of the ultramodern hotel.

⸺·⸺

Adira hadn't told Travis this, but when she'd driven up, she'd observed a man through the hotel's window working behind the front desk. The guy might be an outlier, of course, but in her line of work she'd learned to play the odds.

Understanding human nature, body language cues, and people's typical mannerisms and preferences had always been a crucial aspect of her career. Reading people was part and parcel of what she did. And, as she'd mentioned to Travis at the diner last night, life was about evidence, not certainty. Sometimes you just had to go with your gut.

Toting her purse, she strode confidently through the lobby. Without making eye contact with the front desk worker, she headed directly down the hallway toward the conference center.

There would be a set of restrooms there.

She found the women's, entered a stall, and began to undress. After debating about taking her bra off or keeping it on, she decided that for her disguise it would be best—or most believable—if she wasn't wearing it.

She unsnapped it and shrugged it off. Opening her purse, she pulled out the set of pink pajama bottoms and the Taylor Swift T-shirt she'd stuffed into it back in the parking lot, and put them on.

As she changed, she examined the grayish-purple bruise on her left thigh. She didn't bruise easily, and this one was tender to the touch. It didn't hurt enough to make her think she had a broken bone—if that was the case, she wouldn't have been able to stand up, let alone walk—but still, it bugged her. In addition, her right ankle felt tight from when she'd planted her foot to stop her momentum when she was sliding off the hood of the car.

Good thing she'd been there when she was, though.

Idiot racing through that garage.

At least that little kid was okay.

She took off the brunette wig and mussed up her pixie cut blonde hair. Bed head. She stuffed her clothes, shoes, and purse into the garbage can near the door where she could retrieve them later.

When she studied herself in the mirror, she saw that her eyes were puffy and red from being up so much of the night. Bags under them. Perfect.

Wearing fuzzy penguin socks, the T-shirt, and pajama pants, she padded down the hall, cut through the restaurant and walked to the front desk. The guy working there looked up as she approached. She yawned to see if she could get him to yawn as well.

He did. The power of suggestion. Just seeing someone yawn or even talking about yawns was enough to get most people to follow suit.

Human nature.

You learn to play the odds.

Who would wear pj's and socks to a hotel restaurant? Only someone who was a guest there—at least that's what she was counting on him thinking.

"I came down for breakfast and left my key in my room," she explained, then bit her lower lip in feigned embarrassment. "I feel like an idiot. Can I get another one?"

"Certainly. What room was it?"

"513," she said, choosing a number at random.

He tapped at his keyboard, then looked at her curiously. "Mr. Alvarez?"

"Ah." She winked at him. "So that's his last name. We just met the other night. We're gonna get married."

"Oh. Uh-huh."

"He's still in bed. It was a bit of a late night. I don't wanna wake him up."

And now, for the moment of truth. He would either go by the book and perhaps send a security guard up with her to the room, or accept her story and pass her the key.

He studied her for a moment, she gave him an innocent, shy smile and, with a light sigh, he keyed a card for her.

She accepted it and blew him a kiss. "Thank you."

Assuming that he would watch her walk away, she sashayed a bit as she headed to the elevators, giving him something to look at, then took an elevator up one floor before descending the stairs to the ground level again and circling back to the bathroom.

Finally, wig and street clothes on again, pajamas and penguin socks back in her purse, she walked casually past the front desk—where the guy she'd spoken to didn't even give her a second look—and out the door to the CR-V, where she showed Travis the room key.

"How did you get that?"

"How does being a Mr. Alvarez sound to you?"

"Mr. Alvarez?"

"Follow me."

—m—

Avoiding the front desk, Adira and I entered the hotel via a side door that led through the attached conference center. We rode up the glass-enclosed elevator, whose walls afforded an unrestricted view of a verdant valley and the wooded hills that swept back grandly toward the distant ridgeline of the Great Smoky Mountains.

Though it hadn't yet started to rain on the secret city, those ominous clouds had continued to mount in the western sky. I knew from my research that Chestnut Ridge rose above the Y-12 Protected Area, and now I wondered which of the nearby hills hid the valley containing the infamous site.

I carried the tablet. Adira held her purse in one hand and rolled her suitcase behind her with the other.

"I've been wondering about something," I said, as we exited onto the fifth floor.

"What's that?"

"Why do you think Nathan turned to me in the first place?"

"He trusted you. He knew there was no one else at the Pentagon with your memory, your access, and your ability to weave things together. Seems pretty clear to me."

"But what was it exactly that he wanted me to uncover?"

"The connections between everything. The thread that ties all these facets together—Paraden, Patmos, and Y-12."

"But I didn't find it."

"Maybe you did and you didn't realize it. After all, we're here."

We took a right at the T that split the hallway in two. I couldn't help but notice that Adira was favoring her left leg. "You're limping. Is that from when you bumped your leg?"

"I'm alright."

"You didn't just bump it a little bit, did you?"

"Technically, something bumped me."

"What was that?"

"A car."

"What? You were *hit by a car*?"

"It's nothing."

"Adira, you're—"

"Trust me. It's fine. I'm fine." Now it looked like she was trying to hide the limp, but without much effect.

I wanted to protect her, to make sure she was safe and taken care of, but I wasn't sure how to do that. That protective urge wasn't something I'd felt this strongly in a long time, not since I'd been with Sienna. "I wish you'd told me earlier. I would've—"

"I didn't want you to worry about me."

Referring back to our legend, I said, "You're my wife. I'm supposed to worry about you."

She was quiet, but hoisted her purse strap up onto her shoulder and took my hand.

We passed room 509.

Whether it was part of our legend or not, holding her hand felt surprisingly natural and I didn't let go.

Leaving the subject of her limp behind for the moment, I said, "We need to see if I can access my work account from your tablet."

"Yes, but there's something we need to take care of first."

"What's that?"

She paused and nodded toward the door to 513. "See if the real Mr. Alvarez is in his room. Oh, and have your Pentagon creds ready. You never know how this might go."

"There's someone in the room right now?"

"There might be. Let's find out."

CHAPTER 39

Wondering what I'd gotten myself into, I placed the key card against the reader and gave Adira an *Okay, here we go* look.

The indicator light on the sensor blinked red at first. I repositioned the card, and the green light came on.

I pressed the door open. "Mr. Alvarez?"

A well-dressed Hispanic man in his late fifties was tightening his tie in front of the full-length mirror on the door to the bathroom. Across the room on the television screen facing us, two morning news anchors bantered pleasantly about a spring dog show.

"Excuse me?" the man exclaimed. "What are you doing here? How the hell did you get a key to my room?"

"There's a security matter we need to discuss with you," I said diplomatically. "We're going to need your room for a couple of hours."

Figuring it would be best not to try negotiating this while standing in the hallway, I eased into the room. Adira followed suit, then closed the door.

"A security matter?" Mr. Alvarez looked at us dubiously. "What are you talking about? You're with the hotel?"

"Not exactly," Adira said.

"I'm calling the front desk." He took a somewhat threatening step toward the phone.

"And see"—she raised an authoritative finger—"this is your chance to make a very important decision."

"Oh, yeah? And what decision is that?"

I spoke up. "Rent us your room."

"Rent you my—"

"We'll make it worth your time." Adira interrupted him. "We just need three hours."

"This is not *that* kind of hotel," Alvarez said indignantly.

"And this isn't that kind of offer," she replied. "We're just looking for a place to regroup during an ongoing investigation." She glanced at me. "Show him."

I unpocketed my Pentagon creds. "We work for the government. We're looking into a matter of national security."

Alvarez studied the ID carefully, then as I put it away, he said, "The government is actually willing to pay *me* for something?"

"That's right," Adira said, ignoring the fact that it was technically my money and not the government's.

"Huh," Alvarez sniffed. "Now, there's a switch."

"Two hundred dollars an hour," she told him. "Cash. Go buy yourself a cup of coffee. Or a couple hundred of them."

"Six hundred bucks?" His eyes widened. "I've gotta grab breakfast and then I have a pre-conference panel to attend anyway. It's free money."

She held up her palms. "Works out perfectly, then."

I peeled off six bills and handed them over. "In three hours, go to the front desk, show them your ID to prove that you are who you claim to be, and have them rekey your card. When you come back up, we won't be here, and you won't see us again."

"Don't touch any of my things."

"Trust me," Adira said impatiently. "That's not what we're here for."

"Take anything with you that you like," I suggested.

"I think I will." He scanned the room distractedly, then collected his wallet, computer bag, and, somewhat inexplicably, his toothbrush.

"We'll throw in another hundred to cover room service," Adira said.

"Have at it."

I gave him the money. "The federal government thanks you," I told him.

"Right."

After he left, Adira looked at me with one eyebrow lifted. "The federal government thanks you?"

I shrugged. "Seemed like the right thing to say at the time."

She trailed her finger along the glass countertop. "We could have just tied him up, you know. Saved you some money."

She might have been serious. I couldn't tell. "That probably wouldn't have been the smartest thing to do."

Now it was her turn to shrug. "How's the cash holding up?"

I studied our reserves. "We should be alright as long as we don't need another car or room for too long. By the way, two hundred dollars an hour? That was generous."

"What can I say?" She clicked off the TV. "We're a generous couple."

I held up the tablet. "I guess we should get started on that research."

She went for the room phone. "First, let me order some food. I'm starving."

She placed a room service breakfast order—two glasses of orange juice, two bowls of oatmeal, and a fruit plate for us to share. A meal that wouldn't take much time to prepare and that they could bring up right away. "Just leave it outside the door," she told them. "Thanks."

When she hung up, I said, "What do you think? Look into the Red Team first or search for the physicist?"

"Before we do either of those, show and tell." She flopped the suitcase onto the bed. "Assess our resources. Should only take a minute."

After indicating for me to take a seat on the bed across from her, she tipped open her suitcase with a flourish, using the lid to hide the contents, like a stage magician—*Watch and be amazed!*

The first item she pulled out was a bracelet made of some type of inter-laced, interwoven rope.

"Parachute cord," she told me as she slipped the bracelet onto my left wrist. "It can be used for sawing through plastic restraints—just work it back and forth quickly, with pressure. It's not nearly as hard as you might imagine. Also good for strangling someone, if it were ever to come to that. You can even use it to create prusiks to ascend rock climbing ropes."

"Handy."

"Very." She reached into the bag and produced an industrial-size tube of super glue. "This is also great to have on hand."

"On hand?" I said lightly. "Isn't that something you'd want to avoid?"

"Ha-ha. No, I mean *available.* You can glue someone's lips shut, glue their fingers together, or secure the person to a chair if you find yourself out of rope."

"I have to say, I'm glad you're on our side."

She pulled out a plaster forearm cast. "Wearing a cast makes you seem less intimidating and more vulnerable. It can help you get close to people without being seen as a threat. Also, it provides an opportunity for weapons concealment." She abracadabraed out a small metal shiv that'd been hidden inside the cast. "Nice, huh?"

"You remind me of Q arming Bond for his next mission."

"One of my heroes. Just about anything can be used as a weapon. Watch any Jackie Chan movie, you'll see what I'm talking about." She held up a light-blue wind jacket. "And finally."

"In case it rains? Gets windy?"

She pointed. "The zipper. It's special." She zipped it up and down a few times, then handed the jacket to me. "Here, feel it, but be careful."

Hesitantly, I touched the zipper. "That is *surprisingly* sharp."

"Zippers almost never draw attention. The two sides can be redesigned, sharpened, and used like chainsaw blades to saw through a myriad of things. Warp. Tighten. Tug."

"I've never heard of that before."

"I came up with the design myself last year." She offered me a pleased smile. "I have an assortment of outfits, IDs, and wigs here too, but I don't need to show you all of those. I think it's time to find this physicist."

"Agreed," I said. "He's scheduled to present in the ballroom for the opening keynote at ten, so I'm guessing he's probably staying here at the hotel. Which means we just might be in luck."

"How do you propose we track him down?"

I pointed to the room phone near her. "We call him."

"But we don't know what room he's . . ." Then she caught on. "Ah. That shouldn't matter, right?"

"Right. For security reasons they probably won't tell us his room number, but the front desk should be able to route a call to it. And who knows? He just might pick up."

"Never underestimate what the obvious affords you," she said. "Sometimes the toughest thing to notice is the significance of what's right there in front of you."

By the shy and slightly coquettish look on her face, I realized she wasn't just talking about the phone call to the physicist.

Believe me, I thought, *I notice you.*

"Yes," I said judiciously. "It can be easy to take what is right in front of you for granted."

She handed me the phone's receiver. "You can have the honors. The guy at the front desk might recognize my voice from when I got the room key."

I tapped the button for the front desk and, when the receptionist picked up, I said, "I'm with the conference. We need to do a sound check with Dr. Yong. Can you connect me with his room, please?"

"Certainly," the man replied. "Just one moment."

I waited for the call to go through, waited while it rang, waited while it went to voicemail: *"The guest you are trying to reach is unavailable at this time. Please leave a message at the beep."*

After the tone, I said, "Dr. Yong, my name is Travis Brock. I work for the Pentagon. I have some questions for you regarding your research and your speech this morning. If at all possible, I'd like to speak with you before your presentation. Please call room 513 as soon as you receive this message."

I hung up and said to Adira, "Let's give him until nine fifteen. If we don't hear from him by then, we turn to plan B."

"Which is?"

"Actually, I'm still working on plan A."

"Aha," she said. "So, that gives us just under thirty minutes. What next?"

"One more call. While I put this through, see if you can do an image search on your tablet for that symbol Nathan drew. The protestors outside were carrying signs with it." I dialed Detective Caruso's number, but he didn't pick up. I left a voicemail for him that I'd do my best to contact him later today.

"What was that about?" Adira asked. She'd drawn a copy of the symbol, taken a picture of it with the tablet, and was busy searching for it online.

"He's the detective looking into the arson at my house. He left me a message yesterday morning that he might have a clue about the timing of the fire.

Since that's also the date that was listed on the FOIA request, I wondered if it might be related to everything else that's going on." I set down the receiver. "We'll figure that out later."

"It's the Pruninghooks Collective," Adira declared, tilting the tablet's screen toward me. "That symbol is a pruninghook—bladed tip, wooden handle. They're an antinuke activist group."

"I'm familiar with them," I said.

"And since Nathan drew that symbol on his papers, so was he, apparently."

"It fits. Over the years they've sent FOIA requests in regarding Y-12, Project Symphony, and Paraden. All three."

"Hmm." She processed that. "Now what?"

"Red Team research."

"Only one of us can use the tablet at a time, and you have a higher clearance level than I do, so I'll let you handle that. Besides"—she dramatically sniffed her armpit, then grimaced—"I need a shower—and you don't have to agree with me about that."

"Fair enough."

After typing in the password, she handed the tablet to me and immediately started taking off her shirt.

Quickly, I turned my back to her. Before I could offer any sort of an explanation for my reserve, she said, "Modesty. Right. Gotcha. I can respect that." I heard her walking toward the bathroom. "I'll be back in a jiff."

"I haven't heard that phrase in years."

"I'm hoping to bring it back into the lexicon."

CHAPTER 40

Gunnar Bane landed in Knoxville and found the car that Colonel Clarke had promised would be waiting for him. Before leaving for Oak Ridge, he checked his messages.

Just one: a text from Clarke letting him know that they didn't have the satellite images he'd requested.

Gunnar had been hoping for photos that would show where Halprin had driven after leaving the airport, but nothing helpful came up. Despite recent advances in satellite imaging technology, moving from optical imaging sensors to synthetic aperture radar, the images they had still weren't giving him what he needed.

He sent a message requesting Clarke's people to use the sats to scan the cars in Oak Ridge to search for the CR-V that Halprin had driven out of that parking garage.

A long shot maybe, but it was worth a try.

During the flight, Gunnar had gone through Lassiter's and Caruso's financial records looking for any anomalies. Nothing came up with Caruso, but Lassiter had an obscure bank account buried in an investment portfolio that'd been kept in his father's name. It contained five $100,000 cash deposits made around the first of the year. That much cash with no paper trail meant that Lassiter had sold something valuable to someone who did not want to be tracked down or identified.

Also, someone making a payoff like that might not take kindly to being turned in, and that added up to a motive for murder.

Gunnar retrieved his Heckler & Koch VP9 from his suitcase, slid it under the driver's seat, and took off for Oak Ridge.

—⁓—

While Adira showered, I took the tablet to the desk.

Since I was on the run, I expected that my federal account would be frozen, which it was. However, I'd spent nearly fifteen years studying and remembering the Department of Defense's most closely guarded secrets, and I knew enough about the inner workings of Pegasus, an encryption-breaking software program, to get around the firewall to my account.

It wasn't easy, but—honestly—it should have been harder.

Once in the system, I began to search for the actual names of the other four Red Team members.

I soon discovered that someone had corrupted the DHS personnel files I'd accessed when I was probing into Adira's background less than twenty-four hours ago. Rather than locate what I was looking for, I found myself trying to navigate through a frustrating labyrinth of missing file links and dead ends.

Who would have altered these files since yesterday? Nathan Lassiter? But why? His computer had been logged in to his official account, so maybe the person who killed him—Sapphire, whoever she was? It was possible.

As the water ran in the shower, Adira began singing "Bohemian Rhapsody." Not a bad rendition, either.

I'd always wondered about the whole singing in the shower thing—what makes people do it? Is it just the solitude of being in there alone, knowing that no one is going to judge you? Maybe it was a chance to finally take off all your masks and just be comfortable being yourself—although that didn't seem to be a problem for Adira. I found her simple, forthright honesty refreshing and endearing. Captivating, even.

I went back to my research and my question about who might have deleted the files. And then, out of nowhere, a name came to mind: Colonel Clarke.

Was that even possible? He would have known about Lassiter, as well as the Red Team, and could have easily discovered my research into Adira's background. But why would he have corrupted or erased the files? For what possible reason?

Even *considering* that Clarke might be involved in this didn't sit right with me and felt like a betrayal to our friendship. I couldn't bear to entertain the notion that he was working against us, though I reminded myself not to overlook any possibility.

It was all about trust again—that fragile dynamic in every friendship. You had to have it; you couldn't live without it, but people are imperfect and they will always—eventually—let you down.

Who can you trust? *Really* trust?

You can never really know someone else, but if you know yourself, then you know enough about human nature to realize what people are capable of, to recognize that no one can be fully trusted to do what's right.

For now, I decided to table the prospect that Colonel Clarke might've been involved in some way.

Since I wasn't able to figure out the Red Team members' names, I turned my attention to the locations of the Patmos Financial Consortium's land purchases, trying to discern what the sites might have in common or how they might relate to Paraden or the Pruninghooks Collective. I overlaid a satellite map of the United States with the locations highlighted to see if that would shed any light on things.

Commerce maybe? If there were exit ramps or intersections near the sites, I might be looking at a map of potential restaurant or gas station sites. However, when I identified the locations, I found that most of the tracts of land were in rural areas, away from roads. In fact, some were veritably in the middle of nowhere.

I racked my brain, but couldn't come up with how the locations might be associated with each other, let alone how they connected to everything else that was going on, unless this was somehow related to the air gap hacking research and Project Symphony—but what that might mean for us remained a mystery. None of the sites contained offices or branches of either organization.

Stymied, I set aside the tablet, paged through the conference booklet that Mr. Alvarez had left behind, and took a moment to familiarize myself with the schedule. The workshop descriptions detailed what each of the presenters was speaking about—everything from isotope research to containing radiological events to lessons we can learn from Chernobyl. There was even a safety training exercise, sponsored by the Department of Energy's Office of Radiological Security in Y-12's building 9109, that reenacted an intrusion into the Protected Area and detailed how to respond to contain it.

Overall, although the conference planners had tried to put a positive spin on everything, it looked like it would be a bit of a downer to attend: *Here are the things you need to do in order to avoid being vaporized or radiated. Cheerio, mate! Have a jolly good day!*

There was nothing in Dr. Yong's bio about Project Symphony, which— since it was a top secret research program—wasn't exactly a surprise.

The water in the bathroom turned off, but Adira's singing continued: "Oh, mama mia . . . mama mia . . . mama mia, let me go!"

Though I hadn't been the most scintillating conversationalist with her, I felt like she gave me permission to be myself around her, just as Sienna had. The personalities of the two women were miles apart—Sienna was much quieter and more bookwormish, while Adira was spunkier and more spontaneous— but they had a similar effect on me: They both invited me out of my self-enclosed life while also letting me feel comfortable with the fact that I had one.

Adira emerged from the bathroom wearing, as far as I could tell, only a towel wrapped around her, covering her legs from the middle of her thighs up past her torso and to her armpits. She'd done an expert job of tucking the towel's top edge over itself to keep it in place.

I tried not to stare, but the outfit was, admittedly, distracting. So much so, in fact, that when she asked, "Did you find anything interesting?" I almost said, "Yes." And my answer wouldn't have been related in any way to the investigation.

When I was slow to reply, she said, "The Red Team?" She dabbed water out of her short hair with a hand towel. "Anything on the other members' identities?"

"Right. Yes. Actually, the files I was looking into yesterday have been either deleted or they're corrupted," I informed her. "I kept getting a '404 page not found' error on the links I tried."

"Weird. You think it was Nathan?"

"Maybe. Or it could've been the person who killed him."

"So we're back where we started."

"More or less." The deep bruise on her leg just beneath the towel's edge gave evidence to her being "bumped" by that car. No wonder she was limping. "You sure your leg is okay?"

She flexed it back and forth a couple of times. "It could have been a lot worse." Then she tilted it in my direction. "How does it look to you?"

"Your leg?"

"Yeah."

Sleek and toned, I thought.

"Like it hurts," I said.

She shrugged. "So, if the links didn't lead anywhere, at least we know one thing we didn't know before."

"That someone doesn't want that information about the other Red Team members found," I concluded.

"Right. Nathan's computer was logged in to his account. So Sapphire, if she really was the killer, could've changed them to cover her tracks or hide her identity. Otherwise, it'd need to be someone with your level of clearance."

"Looks like it. Yes."

Colonel Clarke came to mind again, but I shoved those thoughts aside.

Adira tipped her head to the left and shook it slightly, ostensibly to get water out of her ear, then gestured toward the bathroom. "Your turn, dear."

I was about to tell her that we didn't need to carry on our legend while we were alone in here, but held back. "Okay. I'll be out in a couple minutes."

She reached up to the folded-over towel as if she were going to untuck it and said innocently, "Need a towel?"

I couldn't tell if she was joking or not. "I'll find my own. Thanks."

When she replied, I wasn't sure if she said, "You're the boss," or "Your loss," and I didn't ask her to repeat herself.

CHAPTER 41

In downtown Knoxville, Tennessee, the man dressed in a custodial worker's uniform set down the duffel bag he was carrying and propped up a sign in front of the pair of public elevator doors that led up to the city's iconic Sunsphere: *Excuse the inconvenience. Maintenance in progress.*

Then, taking the duffel with him, he entered the service elevator and rode it up to the observation deck more than two hundred and fifty feet above the city.

On a strap around his forehead, he wore a camera, which was transmitting live footage of his actions to the donor who'd paid for the day's anti-bullying rally for middle-school children. The program would begin at eleven at the outdoor amphitheater just below the tower.

The Sunsphere, constructed for the 1982 World's Fair, was a quintessential part of Knoxville's downtown scene and a distinctive feature of its skyline. Rising twenty-six stories above the city, the sleek, steel truss tower served as a constant reminder to everyone who lived in the region of the last successful World's Fair held in the United States. The Cold War fair had focused on energy and the future. A fitting place for what was going to happen here later this morning.

The seventy-five-foot-tall observation sphere on top of the tower provided a stunning 360-degree view of the nearby University of Tennessee campus, the city of Knoxville, and beyond. The sphere was constructed with hundreds of window panels, each infused with 24-carat gold dust so that they would shine golden in the sunlight.

After reaching the sphere's enclosed, circular deck, the man exited the elevator and jammed a steel bar in between each of the three elevators' doors so they couldn't close and the elevators wouldn't be able to descend until he was done with his job. An exterior stairwell led down to the street level, but he wasn't too worried about someone ascending twenty-six stories' worth of stairs and interrupting him.

A voice came through in his earpiece from the person watching the feed. "Turn left. I'd like to see the hospital."

The man obeyed, walking to the window overlooking the city and facing Knoxville's Advent Regional Medical Center. Just two blocks away, the hospital was within easy walking distance of the Sunsphere.

Which made it the ideal location for what they had planned.

"Okay," the voice said. "And walk right. Let's have a look at the amphitheater."

World's Fair Park lay beneath the Sunsphere and contained the one-thousand-seat, open-air amphitheater that would soon be packed with nearly that many students.

—⁂—

The person who'd orchestrated the abduction and transport of Dr. Yong's wife to the States stared at the footage of the arching canvas covering that was intended to keep those in the amphitheater's seats dry in case of inclement weather.

The canvas would provide some protection from the blast, but any radioactive particles would still be inhaled, and dust under five microns tends to make it to the alveoli. From there, the stochastic effects would be terrifying. For this reason, the RDD was seeded with a jacket of fine powder that would spread throughout several city blocks.

Here is where it would happen. Here, at eleven fifteen, after the children were seated. Here, the message to the world would be sent.

Making an RDD—that is, a radiological dispersal device, or a dirty bomb, as it was more commonly known—wasn't prohibitively difficult with the right training and tools. Constructing it didn't take extraordinary technical skills, just sufficient conventional explosives and enough proportional radioactive isotopes to adequately disperse when the detonation occurred.

The design for their device today came from plans of a prototype that'd been developed at Paraden Defense Systems. A Department of Homeland Security employee had given them the security codes to get into the plant where they'd stolen the schematics. It'd only cost half a million dollars—nothing compared to what the plans would be worth in the long run.

Of course, the type of isotope in an RDD mattered. And even though some experts would've recommended a lighter one—perhaps a gamma emitter like cesium-137 or cobalt-60, for instance—in this case, with the type of third-generation VTU detonator and the explosives being used, u-235 was the right choice. Additionally, uranium was more well-known and more feared than the other isotopes, so the impact and the impression on the public would be more efficacious.

After all, the goal wasn't by any means an indiscriminate slaughter of hundreds of thousands of people—that wouldn't have been a desirable outcome in this instance, anyway. The objective was simply precipitating a contained radioactive dispersal event that would result in sufficient casualties. A statement. A way to awaken the world's consciousness. And what better way to do that than with enriched uranium obtained from Cold War nukes in a tower dedicated to the prospect of future energy use?

There were always growing pains during the evolution of a civilization. Collateral damage in the name of progress is often an unfortunate necessity.

The RDD would, of course, be fatal for those close enough to the explosion and cause contamination and severe health issues for anyone nearby. Additionally, it would cost billions of dollars to clean up the city. The response would require demolishing and removing dozens of buildings. For all intents and purposes, Knoxville's downtown would cease to exist.

The benefactor watched through the feed as the man posing as a custodian carefully removed the high-end explosives from his duffel bag and set to work. It hadn't been easy getting the RDX, but in this case, it was the ideal alternative to C-4 and the donor's British military contacts had come in quite handy in helping them acquire it.

"How much do you want me to set?" the man on the observation deck asked.

"All of it."

A pause. "You sure about that?"

"Yes."

"You're not gonna want to be anywhere near downtown when this thing goes off."

"Noted."

"And the timer?"

"Set it for eleven fifteen. The rally should be well underway by then."

CHAPTER 42

Sergei evaluated things.

Ilya hadn't found anything of consequence in his search for vehicles that Brock or Halprin might have been driving. And though he'd picked up some law enforcement chatter regarding a search for two fugitives who might be driving an SUV somewhere in the area, it hadn't led to anything substantive.

So now, using his encrypted cell, Sergei put a call through to the person who'd hired him.

An electronically altered voice answered. "Have you located him?"

"We ran into a bit of a hiccup." Since Adira Halprin hadn't come up in their communications with each other earlier, Sergei explained the situation and what they knew about her, then finished by asking, "Can you locate them?"

"If they're on the grid, yes. I have an idea of where they might be. For now, drive to Oak Ridge. I'll contact you. Halprin might be useful, so if you have the opportunity to bring them both in, take it. If not, Brock remains your first priority. If she gets in the way, remove her from the equation."

"Understood."

After the call ended, Ilya asked, "Any instructions regarding the woman?"

"If possible, bring her in. If necessary, take her out."

He cracked his knuckles. "Gladly."

—〰—

As I showered, I considered the observation Adira had made last night that the Russians hadn't been the ones to kill Nathan Lassiter. Someone else had targeted him—but why?

If she was right, we were dealing with at least two different groups here. And, whatever they wanted, Adira and I seemed to be in the crosshairs of each of them.

After getting dressed in the bathroom, I returned to the hotel room itself, somewhat apprehensively, since, in truth, I wasn't sure whether or not Adira would be clothed when I walked in.

She was.

Now she had red hair, but it looked so natural that if I hadn't seen her blonde pixie cut earlier, I never would've suspected that she was wearing a wig. She also had on a fresh outfit from her suitcase: a green untucked blouse, black skinny jeans, black wedges.

As I walked in, she slipped on a slimming leather jacket, also black, and posed, slinging one hand to her hip. "How do I look?"

"Who are you and what've you done with my wife?"

"That good, huh?"

"The true you is nearly invisible."

"What makes you think you've even met the true me?" She slid on a pair of trendy glasses. "For all you know, I might not be who you think I am at all."

"You might be leading a double life?"

"You never know."

"Sometimes I think we all are," I said.

She regarded me slyly. "Are you saying we all have secrets?"

"Yes. And we all wear masks."

As she readjusted her glasses, I had the sense that if we were in a movie, this would've been the moment of the big reveal. The killer twist. That plot pivot when everything the audience thinks is real is turned on its head and they find out that the characters aren't really who they thought they were at all.

The good guy is really the bad guy.

The bad guy isn't so bad after all.

I went on. "And some people wear their masks for so long that they have a hard time taking them off—or even realizing the mask is there."

"Intimacy is when people take off all of their masks," she said philosophically, a knowing finger in the air, "and not necessarily all of their clothes."

I didn't quite know how to respond to that. "I suppose it is."

Our breakfast had arrived while I was showering. She'd placed the food on the room's desk, and now we took seats on both sides of it. As we ate, I said, "While I was in the shower, I realized that I've been overlooking something obvious."

"What's that?"

"Paraden Defense Systems." I took a sip of orange juice. "A few months ago there were reports that some of their files might have been compromised. Nothing solid, but Nathan mentioned that contractor in his FOIA request, so . . ."

"You're thinking that might be his fault?"

"There's a whistleblower or a leak somewhere."

She reflected on that. "The last text that Nathan sent to me while I was still in Knoxville—if it was actually from him—was '11 am tomorrow. Be aware.'"

"Do you know what it was referring to?"

She shook her head, then bit into one of the strawberries in the bowl. She wiped some of the juice off her lips with the tip of her index finger and said, "But I'm guessing it's related to everything else that's going on. And that gives us less than two hours to figure out how all of this is connected."

I felt a renewed sense of urgency from the time crunch. "You missed some."

"I missed some?"

I pointed to the corner of her mouth. She slipped her tongue out and slowly licked across her lip, perhaps letting her tongue linger there for a fraction of a second longer than necessary.

"Thanks." She reached for another strawberry.

"Sure."

"So, I've been thinking that, based on everything you've told me, it seems that we might be dealing with an insider with top secret clearance."

"Yes."

"Like you."

"Yes," I said. "Like me."

She studied my face. "Are you behind all of this, Mr. Brock? Was it all some elaborate ploy to get me alone in a hotel room with you?"

"I'd never be able to pull off something *that* elaborate."

"Hmm." Adira tilted her glasses down and eyed me over the top of them. "Are you sure you are who *you're* claiming to be?"

"Pretty sure."

"Are there any other redactors who have the same clearance level as you?"

"Some of the ones in the Departments of Energy and Justice do, but for the DOD, I'm the guy."

"What about that colonel you were telling me about earlier?"

"Clarke? Sure. But there's no way he's involved."

"Let's be careful not to assume too much about anyone," she said, "either regarding their guilt *or* their innocence."

We both deliberated on that for a moment as we finished our breakfast. Then she checked the time. "We agreed to give Dr. Yong until nine fifteen and it's five after," she observed. "We need to find something to occupy us for ten minutes."

"What were you thinking?"

"I have a few ideas."

"That's not a lot of time," I pointed out.

"Depends on the activity."

"True. Last night you promised to teach me some fighting moves."

"Hmm . . . ," she said. "Unfortunately, I don't have any handcuffs with me."

"We'll save that part for later." I stood up to get ready for the lesson. "For now, just talk me through some of the basics, what I need to know in case things go sideways. Street fighting 101."

"Alright." She set her glasses on the desk and rose to face me. "Let's see . . . where to start . . . Well, first you need to practice situational awareness. Close your eyes."

I closed them.

"No peeking."

"Okay."

With my eyes closed, my other senses became more acute. I tasted the lingering tang of orange juice on my tongue, heard the faint warble of a television that must have been on in a nearby room, and smelled the vanilla-scented bath soap I'd used on my face in the shower.

"Now . . ." It sounded like Adira had moved closer to me. "How many lamps are in this room?"

"Three. One on either side of the bed and one in the southeast corner near the window."

"How many people did we pass in the hallway on our way up here?"

"Four."

"Specifics?"

"A Caucasian octogenarian, a Black couple in their midthirties, and their son, who was maybe ten or eleven. Do you want to know what they were wearing?"

She evaluated that. "I think you've got situational awareness covered. What color eyes do I have?"

"Stormy seas."

"Stormy seas?" Her voice was closer still. Now, I noticed the floral scent of lavender shampoo. Clean. Fresh. From her shower.

"Restless waves on the ocean," I said, "reflecting back dark clouds edging in over the horizon."

"That's very specific."

"Yes. It is." And then, "Can I open my eyes now?"

"Yes."

I did. She stood directly in front of me, looking at me intently with those entrancing eyes. She'd taken off the black jacket. She reached over, removed my glasses, and placed them beside hers on the desk.

"For a fight," she said, her voice soft, almost demure, "you'll want to determine what other threats are present, what other attackers are likely to engage you, and what other potential victims you might need to protect. All of that will affect how you deal with the current threat."

"Right now, it looks like it's just the two of us."

"Yes, it does."

"And besides the glue, the rope, the zipper, and the shiv, I don't appear to be in any danger."

"Appearances can be deceiving."

"Yes, they can."

She cleared her throat lightly. "So. Fighting on the street. Let's start with the basics: When my attacker is taller than me, which is almost always the case, one technique is to grab him by the shoulders."

She put her hands on my shoulders, looked up into my eyes, and held my gaze. "Headbutt him with the top of your head," she said, "not your forehead like they do in the movies. Hit him with your dome and he's going home. Go for the nose, break it. His eyes will water, obscuring his vision. Gives you the chance to end things quickly."

She was still holding my shoulders and looking into my eyes.

Stormy seas.

Peering intently at me.

Her eyes had a language all their own, daring mine to reply.

"Most fights in real life are extremely brief and over after only one or two punches," she explained. "They involve unarmed, untrained aggressors, and their outcome is typically determined more by motivation than by experience. People most often swing for the head with their dominant hand while grasping the clothing of the potential victim with their non-dominant one. So, keep an eye on which hand he uses to grab your clothes. Which of my hands is dominant?"

"Left."

"You've been watching me," she said.

"Situational awareness."

"And what else are you aware of right now?"

"You're not going to headbutt me, are you?"

"I was thinking of doing something else, actually."

Gently but firmly, she shoved me backward onto the bed. "In a fight, you'll want to stay on your feet but get your opponent to the ground," she said. "Go for the groin, the neck, the eyes, the ears. You're not in a dojo practicing your form. You're on a street, fighting for your life. So grab clothes—or whatever else you can—and throw him to the floor."

Or the bed, I thought.

She stepped closer to me. "Get him beneath you. Assume your opponent is armed. Assume he's not alone. Assume he's stronger than you and has out-trained you. Assume he means to do you irreparable harm. It's your job to outsmart him, not outfight him."

"And if you have to fight?"

"Stay low. Be scrappy. Don't unnecessarily expose your neck. Protect your personal space. Stay attentive. Give nothing about your intentions away."

"And what are your intentions?"

"About?" She raised an eyebrow.

"The fight," I said.

"Ah. Well, I have a three-step theory when it comes to fights: Act preemptively. End them definitively. Get to safe ground."

"And how have you acted preemptively so far?"

"I've got you right where I want you."

"Is that so?"

She leaned toward me. "It sure looks like it."

"How do I escape?" I said.

"Is that what you want?"

The heartbeat of the moment was rich and alive, bringing with it a tangle of emotions and desires that I hadn't felt since I'd been alone with Sienna all those months ago.

I was about to give Adira an all-too-honest reply when the phone rang. "That might be Dr. Yong," I said carefully. "I should answer that."

Ring.

"Oh." She sighed and stepped away. "We're definitely going to have to work on our timing."

Ring.

Sitting up, I snatched up the phone. "Hello? Yes?"

"I had a message to call this number." The man had an East Asian accent. "You said you are from the Pentagon?"

"Dr. Yong, yes, this is Travis Brock. It's very important that I speak with you about—"

"Does this have to do with my wife?" he asked urgently.

"Your wife?"

"Yes, yes, Su-wei. If you know who took her . . . Or, if you are really one of the people who . . . Please, please do not hurt her. I will do whatever you ask."

"Dr. Yong, I don't know what happened to your wife. I don't know anything about that." I tried to sort out what to say next.

He said she was taken. Everything's connected here. You're a part of all this. Figure out that connection and you might be able to find her.

"We'll help you," I offered. "Come up to room 513 and—"

"No." I could almost hear a headshake in his voice. "Meet me in 408. There is something I must show you. Come quickly. And come alone."

Then, only silence.

"Hello? Dr. Yong?"

A dial tone confirmed that he'd hung up. I did the same.

Adira was waiting expectantly beside the bed. Her fighting lesson didn't seem like something that'd ended just a few moments earlier, but rather hours ago. And when she asked, "What do we know?" her tone was entirely professional.

"He wants me to come see him in room 408," I told her as I retrieved my glasses. "Someone abducted his wife, Su-wei. He says there's something he needs to show me."

"Well, let's go."

"He wants me to come alone."

"Travis, if it's just going to be one of us, it needs to be me."

"Why's that?"

"Years of tactical training. Experience in hostage negotiation and abductee retrieval." Her voice had turned steely. "I've worked four kidnappings before. Do I need to go on?"

"Listen, I get it. Yes, you've got all that on your side, but right now, he's scared. Something terrible has happened. If you show up instead of me, who knows how he might respond? I need to go alone."

She processed that. "I'm not good with sitting on the bench."

"Why don't you take a look at the info I pulled up on the Red Team and see if you can figure out their true identities? It'd be good to get your eyes on it."

"I thought you ran into dead ends?"

"They were to me, but as a Red Team member yourself maybe you'll be able to make sense of the links. I left one about their job responsibilities open. If you analyze the location of enough dead ends—"

"You can find your way through a city."

"Well put." I stood. "My research into Patmos Financial Consortium is on the tablet too. See if the locations bring anything to mind."

"You sure it's connected?"

"Right now I'm not really sure about anything, but based on the content of that FOIA request and the acrostics, it certainly appears so."

She stared past me for a moment, collecting her thoughts. "Once you get to Dr. Yong's room and find out what he has to tell you, call me," she said. "If I don't hear from you in, let's say ten minutes, I'm coming down."

"Give me a little more time. Twenty minutes."

After a short internal debate she said, "We'll go with fifteen. You have the gun from the Russians?"

"Um . . ."

"Take it with you."

"I told you, I'm not a big fan of guns."

"Yeah, well, the people we're dealing with obviously are. You've just been thrown into the deep end, Travis. It's time to swim."

After a slight hesitation, I retrieved the gun from the bathroom counter, where I'd left it when I undressed for my shower. When I returned to the room, she was holding out the wind jacket and the tube of super glue, offering them to me. "Just in case," she said.

I had no idea what good they were going to do, but I accepted them. "Thanks." I pocketed the glue. Since the jacket wasn't my size, I wrapped it around my waist and tied off the arms in front of me.

"Be careful," she said.

"I will."

"And don't be afraid to act preemptively."

"Preemptive it is."

PART IV

The Children Arrive

CHAPTER 43

Senator Cliff Richardson waited in the hotel's luxurious lobby for Joshua to arrive. He checked his watch.

9:11 a.m.

His associate was late, which never happened. Something was off.

Cliff glanced around again, but saw no sign of the man he'd hired to implement their plan.

Dr. Yong's speech started in less than an hour. Cliff thought that maybe if he could track him down beforehand, he could try one last time to convince him to relinquish his time at the podium.

With that in mind, Cliff started down the east hallway and was on his way to the main conference hall to find Dr. Yong when someone behind him called his name. "Senator Richardson?"

He turned. "Yes?"

An impossibly beautiful dark-eyed woman of Middle Eastern descent smiled politely at him. "I'm Haniya Nishapuri with Cable Broadcast News." She hastened his way. "May I ask you a few questions?"

She had no videographer with her and didn't appear to be carrying or wearing a mic, but as easily concealed as microphones were these days, Cliff didn't want to assume anything.

"What is this concerning?" he asked.

"I know our viewers would love to hear your perspective on this convention."

She was slightly out of breath from hustling to catch up with him. "If I get my cameraman, would you be able to speak with me in five minutes or so?"

Cliff evaluated his situation. Ideally, he would've liked the opportunity to speak with Joshua first, but this might be just the chance he needed to share his message directly with the American people.

Go there if it flows naturally but don't force it.

"Yes. I'd be glad to address your questions. Go and get him. I'll wait right here."

—៣—

Adira set to work reviewing the locations of the digital dead ends to see if she really could start mapping out the city—but found herself worried about Travis and the physicist's wife. Travis was in no way prepared to deal with a situation like this.

You never should've let him leave here alone. You should go down there with him to room 408.

No. You can't second-guess yourself. Never ask what might have been. Always go with what is.

She would wait. She would trust Travis. He would call her if he needed to.

As she scrutinized the links he'd left open for her, she turned on the television to see if there was any news coverage about the shootings at the manufacturing plant outside of DC, or anything on the investigation regarding Nathan Lassiter's murder. Both were high-profile enough that she thought they would make national news.

Nothing yet.

A quick online search of news headlines gave her an update on both stories, but didn't tell her anything she didn't already know.

She turned back to her Red Team research.

Think, Adira. What could get you the answers you need?

Nathan had been looking into her previous assignments and left a printout of her past protective details. Because of the nature of the Red Team duties, testing airport security wasn't a full-time gig, and it allowed her a chance to pursue other work as well. She assumed it would be the same for the other Red Team members. Since Nathan's printouts had listed her previous jobs, she decided to explore the angle of additional work responsibilities for the rest of the team.

Not something that someone would have accessed or erased in the last twenty-four hours. Start back farther. Something from the past.

Rather than begin with the recent files Travis had been investigating, she took the opposite approach and started with ones that'd been altered since the date of the fire seventeen months ago, figuring she would begin there and work her way up to the present.

—※—

I arrived at room 408.

Hanging on the door handle was a *Privacy Please* sign.

I knocked.

No answer.

Leaning close, I called softly, "Dr. Yong?"

He didn't open it. I couldn't hear anyone moving around inside the room.

I studied the hallway in both directions.

Empty.

I gave it another shot, knocking and calling his name again, raising my voice a little this time, but still heard nothing from the other side of the door.

Based on how worried Dr. Yong had been when I spoke with him, I did not take his absence here as a good sign.

Although I didn't see any security cameras, I suspected that a hotel like this would have them trained on every hallway. Still, I wasn't sure I wanted to go to hotel security to ask for help just yet.

He's worried about his wife's safety. He would answer the door if he could, or he would've left you a message about where he went.

I studied the privacy sign hanging on the doorknob. Flipping it over, I saw one word scribbled in black marker on the back: *Hemlock.*

I reviewed my short exchange with Dr. Yong on the phone, but couldn't identify anything having to do with the word *hemlock.*

What had Adira said earlier about never underestimating what the obvious affords us?

"Sometimes the toughest thing to notice is the significance of what's right there in front of you."

A hemlock tree?

Hemlock as a poison?

No.

Maybe an acronym or an acrostic like earlier?

I assessed what I knew about Nathan Lassiter, his library, and the order of the books on his shelves, but couldn't come up with any meaningful connections to a hemlock.

A park?

No—wait.

Yes. I had it.

A room.

Recalling the locations of the seminars listed in the conference booklet that Mr. Alvarez had left behind, I realized that, though I hadn't noticed any rooms named Hemlock specifically, there were meeting rooms named after other trees—Oak and Aspen, for instance—where breakout sessions were going to be held.

Looking for a Hemlock conference room was my best bet here. Those rooms were on the conference center's third level, which was accessible from the other wing of the hotel.

To keep anyone else from following me there, I folded the privacy sign in half and slid it into my back pocket.

For a moment, I wondered if I should go back and pick up Adira, but since Dr. Yong had emphatically told me to come by myself, I decided that I didn't want to chance getting off on the wrong foot or losing his trust by having her along. If I did locate him, maybe I could convince him to come back to Alvarez's room with me.

Repositioning the Russian's gun beneath my belt, I left to search the other end of the conference center for Hemlock, urgently hoping that I could reach Dr. Yong in time to help save his wife.

CHAPTER 44

Adira found a hit.

It was so oblique that even if Travis had come across it, he might not have realized its significance. Regardless, she felt a smidge of pride from finding something that the DOD's head redactor hadn't been able to uncover.

The info was buried in an obscure personnel file from late last year, and while it didn't reveal the identities of the other team members, it did delineate what work they pursued in addition to their Red Team assignments: Venus, security consultant; Sapphire, firefighter; Bard, investment broker; Typhoon, police officer; and Flower Girl, executive protection.

Yes, she still accepted protective detail jobs. They paid well for what they required. Usually they were something small—a female musician or business exec was coming to town and her handlers wanted low-profile protection. They hired Adira because she wasn't physically threatening or intimidating. Since she didn't look imposing, she didn't attract attention. Also, she could walk into the bathroom or dressing room with the woman she was protecting, which a male bodyguard couldn't surreptitiously do.

Sometimes she would travel overseas in her work, but not so much in the last year or so.

Hang on.

Jobs and careers.

She turned her attention to the list again.

One of the Red Team members, Bard, was an investment broker? Really? The rest of the jobs made sense for a Red Team member to moonlight in, but a *broker?*

Travis was interested in this Patmos Financial Consortium being involved somehow. A broker might just be the guy they were looking for.

Maybe the Red Team really *was* the key to everything. If Nathan's death was related to the Patmos group, that was probably the case.

Track down Bard. Find the connection.

But how?

Though it looked like a step in the right direction, without the team members' actual names, Adira didn't know how helpful any of this information was going to be.

Thinking of Travis and how he'd gone to help the physicist alone, she glanced at the phone.

Seven minutes had passed.

Stay focused here. He'll call when he calls. Find out what you can in the meantime.

She took a moment to study Travis's map of the US with the Patmos Financial Consortium's land acquisitions highlighted, but nothing jumped out at her. As she was debating how to move forward, a segment on television caught her attention. A news helicopter was filming the protests here at Oak Ridge from a few hundred feet above the parking lot.

Adira dialed up the volume. The footage shifted to an attractive reporter who was onsite outside the building, near the protestors. Despite the clouds, a few strangled shafts of sunlight illuminated her and the man beside her as if they were being spotlit for all the world to see in the overcast day. He wore a tailored navy-blue suit and looked at ease being on camera.

The words at the bottom of the screen announced that they were *Live from Oak Ridge, Tennessee.*

"I'm Haniya Nishapuri, here at the International Nuclear Association Safety Summit, speaking with Senator Richardson from California," the reporter said pleasantly, then turned to address him. "Senator, thank you for joining me."

"Of course. My pleasure."

His name and party affiliation appeared onscreen: *Senator Cliff Richardson, (D-Ca.).*

"Can you tell us a little about this symposium and why you're here?" Haniya said.

"First, I'd like to take a moment to offer my condolences to the family of my colleague, Senator Presnell, who passed away last night. My thoughts and prayers go out to all of his loved ones."

"Oh, yes." Haniya looked a bit shaken by Richardson's response. "All of us were shocked by the news of his passing."

"Though we didn't always see eye to eye, Bill and I were committed to the same set of values. He worked tirelessly to serve the best interests of the American people. He will be dearly and deeply missed . . . In regard to the summit here, I know that assuring the protection of our infrastructure was a priority for Bill," the senator said, pivoting back to the question regarding the symposium.

Haniya nodded. "And that's the goal of the conference?"

"Some of the world's leading scientific minds and security experts have joined together to address a matter that affects us all—the safety of our nuclear power plants and reactors. I'm here because one of the greatest threats to innocent life is the potential of cyberattacks against our energy grid and infrastructure. I'm looking forward to all that Dr. Yong has to say, and I'm doing all I can to lend my support to his efforts and those of the International Nuclear Association in working to address cybersecurity at nuclear research and reactor sites worldwide. In addition, I plan on meeting with Janice Daniels while I'm here. I want to address ways that the public sector can better work with Big Tech toward those ends."

Haniya looked at him curiously. "The billionaire who purchased TalynTek from you?"

"Janice and I share a similar vision for using advancements in technology to protect people from radiological events."

They went on, but Adira wasn't listening. Her ears had perked up when Janice Daniels's name was mentioned.

Just over a year ago, she'd served as executive protection for Janice when the billionaire was attending a global climate change summit in Brussels. Janice had made hundreds of millions in tech and in real estate. She was known for buying properties in depressed Rust Belt cities, and then infusing them with cash to rejuvenate them, increasing the property values as well as her subsequent profits when she resold them.

Janice was a target for both the Right and the Left as they each accused her of kowtowing to the other end of the political spectrum for her own benefit. She was a bit of an enigma: Too much of a venture capitalist to please the Left; too much of a democratic socialist to please the Right.

Several times now, Travis had brought up the land purchases. If anyone had the resources, contacts, and expertise to decipher what this Patmos Financial Consortium was investing in, it was Janice Daniels. And, having worked protection for her, Adira figured she might be able to get an audience with her. If so, she could ask her about it in person.

That is, if she would agree to meet.

When Adira shifted her attention back to the television, Haniya was asking the senator about his political future. "What do you say to those who claim you're using your involvement here simply for political purposes, to attract support for a future presidential bid?"

"I'm not here for political reasons."

"Is that a no, then? The rumors aren't true?"

"I'm not interested in either confirming or debunking unfounded rumors. I can just tell you that I'm currently focusing all of my energy on the needs of my constituents and the well-being of the American people."

Well, Adira thought, *that wasn't exactly a no about running.*

Rather than press him further about a potential presidential bid, Haniya let the matter go, thanked him for his time, and then signed off. To Adira, it looked like he had more to say, but even though he leaned toward the mic as if he were going to add something, he ended up simply smiling and offering a brisk nod.

As the feed went back to the anchor in the studio, a BREAKING NEWS icon flashed dramatically across the screen while a riff of intense-sounding music played.

"Now, to our developing story. A suspect is wanted for questioning in regard to the deaths of three Army Intelligence Officers at a federal installation outside of Washington, DC, yesterday. The police have released this image of her, taken from security footage in a parking garage at Knoxville's McGhee Tyson Airport earlier this morning."

Oh. Not good.

Adira watched as a photo of her holding the toddler and facing the camera in the garage filled the screen. The existence of the screenshot snatched from the CCTV camera didn't come as a complete surprise, but it wasn't exactly what she was hoping for right now, either.

They'll be coming for you. It's just a matter of time.

She couldn't shake the thought that Janice Daniels might be able to help, and realized that she probably still had the billionaire's contact information in her address book in the Cloud.

Access it, call her, then go help Travis find the physicist's wife before someone tracks you down in here.

She went online to pull up Janice Daniels's mobile number while the news anchor mentioned a $75,000 reward for anyone who had information that led to the apprehension of the armed and extremely dangerous fugitive from the law, Adira Halprin.

CHAPTER 45

N̲ot wanting to startle Dr. Yong by waving a gun around, but also not certain I should enter the Hemlock room unarmed, I repositioned the innocuous-looking jacket around my waist so the bladed zipper was within reach of my right hand.

I pressed the door open and stepped into the room.

It wasn't set up as a main session ballroom, but rather prepped for a smaller breakout seminar. Fifty-four chairs waited behind strict rows of tables facing a podium that stood centered at the far end of the room. The lights were low, with none of the overhead fluorescents on, just the sparse, dimmed globes inset in the ceiling.

An expansive projection screen hung from the ceiling behind the podium.

My eyes were still adjusting to the dim lighting when one of the double doors just to the right of the screen edged open. I reached for the gun.

I'd attended enough conferences to know that those doors would lead to a rear access hallway that would allow hotel or conference center staff to remove and store chairs, tables, and sound equipment that wasn't in current use in the seminar rooms.

As the door opened the rest of the way, an Asian man came into view. He was a few inches shorter than Adira and stood backlit in the doorway. "Are you the man I spoke with on the phone?" he said. It was the same voice I'd heard on the call.

"Yes." I held up the privacy sign. "You left this for me."

Leaning forward, he peered past me, perhaps to confirm that I'd come alone as he'd asked, then signaled with urgency for me to join him.

I let go of the gun's grip. As I pocketed the sign and walked toward him, I wondered what his wife's kidnappers wanted from him.

How does her abduction fit in with everything else that's going on? Does the timing of that FOIA request relate in some way to the kidnapping? And what makes you think you'll be able to help find her, anyhow?

Truthfully, I had no answers.

I joined Dr. Yong in the access hallway and closed the conference room door behind me.

The clinically white, brightly lit passageway offered a stark contrast to Hemlock's muted beige colors and faintly illuminated walls. Tottering stacks of conference room chairs stood piled high in the narrow corridor, while a dozen folding tables leaned against the wall. An orange extension cord crept out from beneath them and coiled, snakelike, near Dr. Yong's feet.

To my right, the hallway stretched a hundred feet or so along the back of the neighboring conference rooms before angling out of sight. On my left, it terminated at an exit door about forty feet away, which, based on the layout of the conference center, I guessed would lead to a stairwell.

Dr. Yong was sweating profusely and his hand was twitching. "Tell me who you are."

"As I said before, my name is Travis Brock. I work for the Department of Defense."

"The Department of Defense? So you can help me?" Hope had found its way into his voice. "You can help me find her?"

"Dr. Yong, tell me what happened."

"They must have had it on the flight with me," he muttered. "That means they took her before I left Taipei."

"I'm sorry, slow down. What was on the flight with you?"

He shakily produced what appeared to be a white linen handkerchief from his pocket, then carefully unfolded the fabric to show me the ghastly item that'd been wrapped inside it: a severed human finger. A wedding ring encircled it.

A chill ran through me, ending at the base of my spine, right beside the gun that I'd planted beneath my belt.

"It is Su-wei's," Dr. Yong whispered. He wrapped the white cloth over the finger again and slid it into his pocket. "They warned me not to tell anyone, but when you called, I did not know what else to do. Maybe I should have told the senator, but I thought that maybe you . . . I cannot let them know I am speaking with you."

"Who are they? Who took her?"

"I do not know."

"Which senator?"

"Richardson. From California. I met with him last night."

"Have the kidnappers made any demands yet?"

He held up a USB flash drive. "They want me to insert this into my computer when I speak at ten."

"What'll happen if you do?"

"I am not certain," he admitted, his voice quavering. "I will be connected directly to the center's network. I am guessing the drive will upload a virus of some sort onto their system. I cannot chance that, but I also need to do whatever I can to save Su-wei. What should I do?"

"If there is a virus," I said, "is it possible that it could infect the Oak Ridge National Laboratory or Y-12's servers?"

"Yes, yes." A quick nod. "That is what I am afraid of."

Without question, any sort of cyber intrusion into Y-12's internal network could be catastrophic. I didn't even want to think about the kind of damage unfriendly actors would be able to precipitate if they gained access to the system files. They could obtain passwords, alter security settings, release radiation—just about anything they wanted to.

I thought of the time in 2013 at the Davis-Besse Nuclear Power Station in Ohio when the safety parameter display system, or SPDS, in the control room went down when the Slammer worm infected it. The SPDS was offline for more than four hours. The technicians weren't able to monitor the state of the reactor core and it could have melted down, but for some reason the plant wasn't running that day, and the core wasn't in operation—a fortunate coincidence, a chance happening that saved hundreds of thousands of lives.

Gulping, I set thoughts of that incident aside and refocused on Dr. Yong and the situation at hand.

The next question was one I didn't really want to ask, but I knew I had to. "Doctor, do you have any assurances that your wife is still alive? A proof-of-life picture, anything like that?"

His eyes were beginning to tear up as he shook his head. "I do not know how to get in touch with the people who took her."

"Have you tried contacting her?"

He nodded. "There was no reply to my texts or voice messages."

We definitely needed to return to Alvarez's room so I could get Adira's take on this.

Down the hallway to my right, a man wearing a hotel staff uniform emerged from the Aspen room. He began making his way toward us, past the tables and chairs in the passageway.

Dr. Yong stared at me quizzically. "Why did you contact me earlier if you did not have anything to do with Su-wei going missing? Why did you call my room?"

"I wanted to find out if you knew anything about Project Symphony." I was distracted by the man coming our way. "And the murder of a Department of Homeland Security supervisor named Nathan Lassiter."

Dr. Yong gasped. "Deputy Director Lassiter is dead? I had not heard."

"You knew him?"

"Only through a mutual acquaintance."

I ventured a stab in the dark. "Colonel Clarke?"

"Yes."

"You know about Project Symphony, then?"

"I . . . cannot say."

That was good enough for me.

"Listen," I said, thinking of the date on the FOIA request, "do you know anything about a fire a year and a half ago on November nineteenth?"

"No. I do not."

Because of the lighting and the angle of the baseball cap that the hotel staff member wore, I wasn't able to see his face, but something about the fact that he hadn't actually looked up at us yet—which I sensed would've been the natural thing to do—made me uneasy.

"We should go back to my room," I told Dr. Yong resolutely. "There's a woman there who I think will be able to help you."

At last, the man, who was now only thirty-five or forty feet away, lifted his gaze and peered directly at us. I recognized him immediately: the Russian who'd aimed his gun at me back in the basement of L & L Manufacturing—the same gun I had with me now, jammed beneath the back of my belt.

"Hello, gentlemen," he called. "I'm going to need you both to come with me."

I yanked on Dr. Yong's arm, directing him back to the Hemlock room. "Go. Hurry!" Then I whispered so the Russian couldn't hear, "Get to room 513."

Though I was worried the physicist might not listen to me because of his concern for his wife—and because this guy might be involved in her kidnapping—Dr. Yong didn't argue with me or hesitate, but immediately scrambled through the open doors and disappeared.

At that, the Russian started running toward me. I reached over, toppled the stack of chairs beside me to block his path, and dashed down the hallway in the opposite direction. How he'd tracked me down back here was a mystery, but what mattered right now wasn't how he'd found me, but how to lose him. Leaping over the folded-up tables that partially blocked the hallway, I sprinted toward the exit door. As I did, I heard the Russian tossing the chairs aside and clattering them fiercely against the wall.

The gun. You have his gun!

True enough, but I was no marksman. Besides, he might very well have armed himself with another gun since yesterday.

Probably had.

Almost certainly had.

Though I had that gun, I wasn't sure I was prepared to aim it at another human being, let alone pull the trigger.

My heart was racing and my thoughts were cluttered, hard to corral.

Did he and his partner take Su-wei? Are they behind all this?

It would've made sense for Russia to be interested in gaining access to Y-12's system files. With the hacker syndicate connection that Adira had mentioned, the flash drive could be their way in.

I maneuvered past a stack of boxes and, a few strides later, reached the exit door. I threw it open and found myself in a tightly enclosed stairwell.

Anticipating that the Russian would expect me to flee via the ground floor, I went up one floor instead, then squeezed my back against the wall, out of his line of sight. I heard the door below me smack open and heavy footsteps pound downward. A moment later, a second door banged against the wall and then began to creak shut as he left the stairwell.

I let out a breath I hadn't even been aware I'd been holding in, but my relief was short-lived. It wouldn't take him long to figure out I hadn't exited through that door.

From our encounter at L & L Manufacturing, I knew that this guy was working with at least one other man. They hadn't been the ones to kill Nathan, but they might be working with the person who did—Sapphire, if Nathan's acrostic really did identify his killer. At the moment, I felt like I was in a mirror maze, trying to find my way out using clues that reflected endlessly off each other and revealed no clear path forward.

But right now, helping Dr. Yong was the number one priority. That much *was* clear.

I'd sent him to Alvarez's room.

Get up there. Find Adira. Protect the doctor.

I took the stairs two at a time toward the fifth floor, hoping to catch up with him before the other Russian did.

CHAPTER 46

Senator Cliff Richardson still hadn't heard from Joshua, though he'd texted him twice, telling him that he was on his way to the main convention hall.

The television interview had gone reasonably well, but hadn't afforded him the opportunity to directly address the supply chain vulnerabilities like he'd been hoping.

If he could get to the auditorium, maybe he still had a chance to talk with Dr. Yong before the physicist went onstage. If not, he could hold a press conference later in the day and announce what he'd done, letting the world know about the compromised microprocessors that were now installed at the HEUMF on Y-12's campus. Whatever the consequences might be for him, the potential consequences of doing nothing, of ignoring this issue, were far worse.

As Cliff merged in with the other attendees walking toward the conference hall, Joshua angled in from a side hallway and joined him.

Though Cliff was curious about his associate's late arrival, he wasn't sure he wanted to probe too deeply into what he'd been doing. After a perfunctory greeting, he said simply, "You look tired."

"As it turns out," Joshua said, "I had to drive through the night. But I'm fine. I'm ready."

Cliff waited while two people walked past them, then whispered, "It was you, wasn't it?"

"Me?"

"The senator. Presnell."

"We discussed this. Measures had to be taken."

"But not—"

"It was a heart attack, Senator. That's all. It happens. It was sudden and unfortunate and had nothing to do with either one of us. You understand that, don't you?"

Cliff swallowed. He couldn't help it.

It seemed like the ground had tilted irrevocably beneath him. Because of his involvement in all of this, a fellow senator was dead. It was the exact opposite of what he'd wanted when he first began planning all of this. He was here to save lives, not see them get taken.

Joshua's a psychopath. No more people need to die. No more.

For a fleeting moment he thought about trying to cut ties with Joshua, about moving forward and announcing the news regarding the chips on his own. After all, what did he need Joshua for now? The wheels of their plan were all set in motion. He just needed to go through with the press conference announcing what'd happened.

Yet, as true as all that might've been, he couldn't help but think, *You're not in control of this any longer; Joshua is.*

He feared retribution from this man if things were not done according to plan. If Joshua had been the one to kill Presnell, who would be next? Better to move forward as planned, finish this, pay him off, and then be rid of him forever.

"Listen," Joshua said, "I was able to make arrangements with Y-12's public affairs director for us to visit the Highly Enriched Uranium Materials Facility. I told her I'm your aide. It helped tremendously that you're on the Senate's Subcommittee on Energy."

"When?"

"Now."

"What about Dr. Yong's speech?"

"It's nothing you don't already know, right?" Joshua lowered his voice. "This'll give you the opportunity you were looking for to point out the chips. Doing so after a visit to the facility will be even more convincing."

Cliff paused.

Go. You'll be safe. Nothing will happen to you in there. Plus, you'll be able to keep an eye on Joshua.

From what he'd been told, chips GA492 through GA500 had been compromised. He didn't intend for them to actually be *used* for infiltration; they were simply meant to demonstrate that the supply chain, as it was currently set up, contained vulnerabilities that could be exploited.

"Are you sure we'll be able to get into the facility?" he asked Joshua, who held up an ID card for a senate aide with his picture on it. The ID looked astonishingly genuine.

"Pretty sure."

———

On the fifth floor, I burst out of the stairwell and found myself in a laundry and supply room for the housekeeping staff. The air smelled of tart, overly fresh detergent.

Relieved to have made it this far, I opened the door leading to the guest rooms and ventured down the hallway. However, as I rounded the T in the hall, I saw the second Russian knocking on the door to 513, maybe fifty feet away from me.

I doubted that Dr. Yong could've made it up here this fast, so he probably wasn't inside, but Adira likely was. In either case, I couldn't let this man enter that room.

Grabbing the gun from my waistband, I aimed it down the hall and started toward the Russian. When no one answered the door, he unholstered a handgun of his own and directed it at the door handle. Rather than wait and let him get inside, I shouted, "Hey! Over here!"

He immediately faced me, swung the gun in my direction, and began stalking toward me. Thinking that I might be able to hide inside that linen supply room and get the jump on him, I backed up, edged around the T, and then flew to the door to open it, but found that it'd automatically locked when it swung shut.

I was cornered here, trapped at this end of the hall.

I spun around just in time to see the Russian come into view thirty feet in front of me. Without hesitation, he began closing the space between us, his gun pointed directly at my face.

In a rough Russian accent, he said, "Drop your weapon."

Instead, I leveled it at his chest. He was less than twenty feet away now, and I reminded myself of what Adira had said earlier: the Russians were trying to capture me, not kill me. Because of that, I doubted he would shoot first, and I thought that from this distance, I would certainly be able to stop him.

"Don't take another step," I warned him, "or I will fire."

He paused.

A flurry of thoughts whipped through my mind: *Would you really do it? Would you really take another man's life? Do you have it in you? Is that what you need to do to find peace?*

Justice. Revenge. Where was the line that separated them? Was there even a line at all? Were they really so different? Maybe there was a continuum between them rather than a line separating them. What if this man was the person who'd set the fire that killed Sienna? Everything seemed to be tied together here, so it wasn't out of the question.

Your mother hesitated. She pulled a knife on Dad and didn't use it. He might've killed her. She could have ended it once and for all. She could have acted. She held back.

The Russian studied me quietly, then took a confident step forward.

"Stop!" I had my finger on the trigger. All I had to do was squeeze.

Do it. Shoot him. He has a gun aimed at you. It'd be self-defense.

But then another voice: *No. If he doesn't want to kill you, then you wouldn't be defending yourself. You'd know the difference even if no one else did, even if you got away with it. You'd always know.*

"Did you set the fire?" I shouted.

"What?" Another step.

This is what it means to get your hands dirty, Travis. This is what justice feels like.

"The one that killed my wife. Did you set it?"

His only answer was to scoff at me and move closer, leaving him only two strides away.

"This is your last chance," I told him. "Do not move!"

But he didn't listen. Just approached me unwaveringly.

Act preemptively. Do it. Do it now.

I squeezed the trigger.

Nothing happened.

Jammed?

"Not all guns have safety," he said calmly, "but that model does."

I searched for the release, but it was too late—he lunged at me, raised his pistol above his shoulder, and brought the barrel down, striking it violently against the side of my skull.

And everything went black.

CHAPTER 47

THREE MINUTES EARLIER

Adira used the room phone to make the call to Janice Daniels's cell number. "Hello, Ms. Daniels?"

"I'm sorry, who is this?"

"Adira Halprin. I served on your protective detail last year in Brussels. Listen, I'm here in Oak Ridge and—"

"Yes, yes, I remember you, Ms. Halprin. Wait—you're in Oak Ridge? That's where I am."

"I know. I heard that on the news. I was wondering if I might speak with you in person."

Adira thought of the connections, of the physicist's missing wife and the threat to her well-being. She justified her next words by telling herself that they might be true. After all, at the moment, she couldn't prove that they *weren't*. "I have reason to believe you might be in danger."

"What kind of danger?" Janice Daniels's voice was marked with both curiosity and an understandable touch of concern.

"We really should speak in person."

"Perhaps I can set up a meeting later in the day. I'm afraid I have a speech to attend shortly."

"I can meet you beforehand. It won't take long, I promise."

A pause as the billionaire deliberated. At last, she said, "I'm staying in the presidential suite on the eighth floor. I'll send someone down to meet you at the elevator bay in the lobby."

—⁊—

NOW

Dr. Chia-hao Yong arrived at room 513, the one Travis Brock had directed him to, and knocked hurriedly on the door, but no one answered.

He rapped on it again, harder. Same result.

With everything that was going on, he wasn't about to wait around in the hallway for someone to come find him.

What had happened to Brock?

Was he captured? Is he dead?

There was no way to know. Chia-hao gulped in nervous fear at the thought of what might've occurred. He wondered if he should tell hotel security about the man in the back hallway who'd chased them, and decided that he needed to, even if it was just an anonymous tip. It was the least he could do for Brock, the man who'd reached out to try to help him.

Do that, then get to safety. Find a public place or a crowd as soon as you can!

He felt in his pocket: He still had the flash drive.

If there was even the slightest chance that inserting it during his speech might save Su-wei's life, he would do it. He had to.

Even if it means giving hackers access to Y-12's system files? How many lives are you willing to sacrifice for Su-wei's?

He buried those thoughts and used his mobile phone to call the front desk. He reported that a man from the hotel had been chasing them in the hallway behind the Hemlock room. The receptionist assured him that hotel security would look into it immediately.

When Chia-hao had left his room earlier, he'd dropped off his computer in the main convention hall with the audio engineer so the man could test the connection to the projector.

Now, he headed to the auditorium, his hand in his pocket, nervously clutching that USB drive, mentally preparing himself for what he had to do, and trying not to think about the people who might very well die as a result.

—⁊—

The security personnel at Y-12's outer perimeter didn't hassle Senator Cliff Richardson and his passenger, though they did use a mirror attached to the base of a retractable pole to check the undercarriage of the car for explosives, and brought out bomb-sniffing dogs to clear the vehicle.

Cliff identified himself, then mentioned that his aide was with him. The guards verified Cliff's credentials, and after learning who he was, barely gave Joshua's ID a second glance before waving them through.

Joshua had been right—it really did help that he was on the Subcommittee on Energy.

Cliff wrestled with how to handle things with him from here on out.

Just get through this visit. Then you can be done with him. You can make the announcement and you'll never have to see him again. But for now, act natural. Don't raise any suspicion that things aren't right.

They passed three separate levels of security fences, including concertina wire–topped ones rimming the lethal zone, where the heavily armed security personnel were authorized to use deadly force.

Because of his work on the subcommittee, Cliff knew about the campus's additional security measures: laser sensors, surveillance drones, heat and motion sensors, biometric access control systems, armored first-response vehicles, and even anti-aircraft guns. The defenses here were definitely formidable.

However, even with all of that in place, the facility was still vulnerable to intrusion through a compromised supply chain. Chips GA492 through GA500 being installed here were undeniable proof of that.

Currently, Y-12 had more than a hundred buildings on its 811-acre campus—although during its prime, at the height of the Second World War, it'd contained more than twice that many.

Cliff and Joshua drove past dozens of dilapidated, long-abandoned structures. No surprise about that, since cleanup of radiation-contaminated building materials was exorbitantly expensive. Some of the buildings on the original Oak Ridge site had been vast. In fact, the calutron building, known as K-25, was a single structure that, astonishingly, had covered forty-four acres, making it the largest building in the world at the time it was built.

Ahead of them, on the north end of the Protected Area, Cliff saw the gate for the construction zone for the new Uranium Processing Facility.

Cranes, bulldozers, and earthmovers were stationed around the skeletal steel framework of the new building.

At least two dozen workers clad in construction helmets stood scattered around the job site and on the high horizontal girders of the half-finished building. Cliff wondered briefly how much of a hassle it'd been for them to be cleared through the obligatory background checks.

Just beyond the construction zone lay the Highly Enriched Uranium Materials Facility.

Almost there.

—◇◇◇—

The lobby's elevator doors parted in front of Adira, and a towering man in an immaculate charcoal suit indicated wordlessly for her to join him. With his head stooped against the ceiling, he stood nearly seven feet tall and had quite impressive eyebrows. Or, well, eyebrow, if you wanted to be technical.

Adira decided on the spot that he would be called Lurch.

She stepped onto the elevator and took a moment to furtively reposition the fake cast that she wore on her right arm so the shiv hidden inside it wouldn't cut into her forearm—always be prepared. Always ready to act.

Which was also why she had the PSM tucked into the back of her belt, beneath her blouse.

She'd left her jacket and purse behind in Alvarez's room but had the tablet with the map showing the locations of Patmos Financial Consortium's land purchases with her. Hopefully, Janice would be able to offer some insight into what was going on.

Then you can get back to the room and wait for Travis's call—that or go to room 408 yourself.

The elevator doors closed and Lurch swiped a key card across the reader to take them to the presidential suite on the hotel's top floor.

—◇◇◇—

Dr. Chia-hao Yong entered the sound booth at the back of the auditorium, where the conference center's audio technician was fiddling with a headset microphone, checking the battery level.

"Test one, two, three," he said just before the doors opened and the first wave of attendees began to file in and find their seats. He tinkered with the dials and buttons on the sound board, tested the mic again, made a few final adjustments, and then assured the doctor that everything was set.

"Here's your mic, Dr. Yong. You should be good to go."

"Yes. Thank you." Chia-hao accepted the microphone.

"It's muted, but don't worry; I'll turn it on for you when you walk onstage. Also, I tested your laptop for the presentation, as you requested. All the adapters are in place. You're golden." He consulted his clipboard. "Do you have any other tech needs?"

"No. But I will need to be on the network."

"I'll grab the password for you," the man said without hesitation. "Give me one sec. I'll be right back."

CHAPTER 48

Cliff Richardson found himself tapping his thumbs and forefingers together rapidly, a nervous habit of his.

Relax. Settle down. Don't let Joshua see how twitchy you are.

He stilled his fingers as the HEUMF came into view: a stark white, concrete, rectangular box, 475 feet long and 300 feet wide, stanchioned by four guard towers manned by sentinels with automatic weapons.

Architecturally, it was not one of the wonders of the world, but in this case, form followed function. Its design had grown out of the need to construct a giant, veritably impenetrable box to entomb radiological materials.

They arrived at the final checkpoint at the edge of the construction zone, less than a hundred feet from the HEUMF's hulking, spartan exterior.

After parking, a guard carrying a tactical rifle strode toward the car to escort them to the building.

—⚓—

Adira followed Lurch into the suite where Janice Daniels and another bodyguard, dressed in a suit identical to Lurch's, were awaiting them.

The second guy wasn't quite as tall as Lurch, but he was bearded and brawny and must've been at least six foot six himself. Another giant. She would call him Goliath.

Adira knew that Janice was sixty-three years old, but apart from her arctic-white hair, she could have passed for twenty years younger. Though slim and small-framed, she didn't appear frail; rather, she radiated energy.

The suite was at least four times as large as Alvarez's room and contained a dining area for entertaining guests, a kitchenette, and a sprawling living space with bedrooms located at each end.

"Ms. Daniels," Adira said. "It's good to see you again."

"You as well." Janice motioned toward the cast on Adira's arm. "Is your arm alright?"

"Occupational hazard," she said dismissively.

"A fight?"

"You should have seen the other guy. He's not even out of the hospital yet." Janice smiled at that, but neither Lurch nor Goliath seemed to find it funny at all.

Okay, a bit light in the sense-of-humor department. Good to know.

"You've done something different with your hair," Janice noted. "From the time I last saw you."

"Good memory. I used to be blonde. I decided I was up for a change."

"Red becomes you."

"Thank you."

"I can't be too careful," Janice said. "With your permission, Reginald will search you for weapons. I'm sure you understand."

"Oh. Right. Sure. Have at it. I've got a gun, though. A PSM. I'm telling you now so he doesn't get startled when he finds it. It's behind my belt."

Adira set down the tablet. Lurch approached her and motioned for her to put her arms to the sides. She obeyed, and he started patting her down, without giving much consideration to the fact that she was a woman. When he located the Russian's gun at the back of her jeans' waistband, he slipped it beneath his own belt and nodded toward Janice.

He ignored the cast.

They always did.

"Now." Janice laced her fingers together. "You had something urgent you needed to tell me? That I might be in some sort of danger?"

"May I speak with you privately?"

Janice sized her up one more time, then asked the two bodyguards to give them a moment. "Follow me," she told Adira, indicating the balcony overlooking the valley.

Though they were on the top floor, an overhanging lip of the roof above them sheltered them from the slanting rain that had started to fall. Picturesque, bucolic hills surrounded the hotel and conference center, which now sat weary and wet under the downpour.

"I need to be perfectly honest with you," Adira said.

"Okay."

"I didn't come here because I think that you're in danger. I came here because—"

"You're in trouble."

"What?"

Janice held up her phone. A news article with Adira's face appeared on the screen. "After you called," Janice explained, "I did a little checking. It looks like you're in a bit of a bind. I understand that three people are dead at a federal facility near DC."

"I had nothing to do with that. It was . . ." Adira realized that explaining that it was the work of two Russian mercenaries who were trying to kidnap a Pentagon redactor with a superhuman memory might not sound all that believable. "It wasn't me," she reiterated at last.

A small pause. "What are you really here for, Ms. Halprin?"

"Long story short: A company, Patmos Financial Consortium, has been buying up land across the country. We think it's somehow related to a secret government program that's . . . listen, I know this sounds strange."

"We?"

"What?" Adira asked.

"You said 'we' a moment ago. Who is 'we'?"

"I'm working with someone from the Pentagon, and in order to clear my name, I need to get some answers."

The westerly wind began to spray droplets of rain toward them, and Janice stepped back to stay dry. "I *have* heard of Patmos Financial Consortium," she said thoughtfully.

"Everything's on my tablet. If you could just give it a look. I don't think it'll take you long. I just need to know why they would be purchasing those tracts of land."

Janice evaluated that. "You were very professional and treated me well when you were serving on my protective detail in Brussels. I trust that you're telling me the truth and I imagine that it won't be the end of the world if I miss the opening lecture. I'm hosting a roundtable after lunch, but let me see if I can help you in the meantime."

They reentered the suite, Adira pulled up the files, handed Janice the tablet, and said, "May I use your room phone?"

"Of course."

Janice led her to one of the bedrooms so she would have privacy for the call and Adira dialed room 513 to see if Travis had returned, but no one picked up. She tried 408. No answer there, either.

Okay. Decision time.

She could call the police as she'd agreed to do if she didn't hear from Travis in fifteen minutes—which had elapsed at least five minutes ago—or give him more time.

The physicist wanted Travis to meet with him alone. Notifying the police will alert the kidnappers, and maybe put his wife in more danger.

But getting the authorities involved might be precisely what she needs.

In the abductions Adira had worked in the past, she'd learned that you either stall or meet the demands of the kidnappers until (1) you have them in your sights, or (2) the victim is secure. And right now, neither of those was the case. In the end, though she was torn, for the sake of Su-wei's safety, Adira decided to give it another ten minutes, then try the rooms again.

She returned to the suite and found Janice seated on the couch, tablet in hand. "Give me a few minutes to explore this," the billionaire said. "In the meantime, can I have Reginald get you anything? Coffee? Tea? Water? Have you had breakfast? We can have some brought up."

"I ate already. Thanks." Adira's eyes landed on the minibar. "I could use a drink, though," she added candidly.

A touch of a smile. "A woman after my own heart." Janice gestured to Lurch, who crossed the room to the bar.

"Vodka?" Janice asked her.

"Perfect."

Lurch drew out two small bottles for her.

"Thank you," she said. She almost added, "Lurch," but caught herself just in time.

While Janice studied the map on the tablet, Adira went to the balcony to watch the rain lash the valley, debating if she was making the right decision by not contacting the authorities, and trying not to think about the dreadful consequences for the physicist's wife if she was making the wrong call.

CHAPTER 49

Cliff and Joshua passed through the metal detector at the HEUMF's entrance and retrieved their personal items from the X-ray machine's conveyor belt. However, as per facility guidelines, they had to leave their phones with the guard stationed at the entrance.

A sharply dressed woman with a wide smile and incredibly bright teeth handed them visitor badges and introduced herself as Mackenzie Everett. "I'm head of public affairs," she informed them cheerily. "I'm so pleased to meet you, Senator. It's not every day that we get members of Congress visiting us!" She turned to Joshua. "And you must be the gentleman I spoke with on the phone—Mr. Godfrey?"

He gave her a cordial nod. "Joshua. Please."

As they started down the hallway, Joshua asked her if they would need any special protective clothing or hazmat suits. She assured him that they would be fine, that those were only required in certain parts of the building.

"There's shielding all around us," she said, sweeping her arm in a wide arc. "In fact, you're being exposed to less radiation now than you would be in most urban areas and airline flights. You're actually safer here than you will be when you leave to drive back home."

"Naturally occurring radiation in the atmosphere?" Joshua said.

"Precisely. In fact, you can safely carry around u-235 in a plastic jar and be protected from the radiation. Your skin shields you from it! Of course, you'd want to be careful with the gamma emitters."

"Turn into the Hulk?"

"Not quite." A chuckle. "But even a tiny bit of those isotopes would ruin your day."

Cliff felt like he wanted to say something lighthearted, something to ease the tension that was building inside of him, but couldn't think of anything. Instead of focusing inward, on his anxiety, he directed his attention outward, onto his surroundings.

During his tenure on the Subcommittee on Energy, he'd seen classified pictures of the inside of the HEUMF, but they didn't do justice to what he saw here now.

The shimmering, spotlessly white floor and walls were hospital-operating-room clean. Vast, towering shelving units stretched back toward the far end of the extensive facility. Workers driving specially designed forklifts maneuvered up and down the aisles of stored uranium, removing or replacing steel racks as large as a kitchen table, each holding six containers of uranium that were about the size of gallon paint cans.

"What do you already know about the HEUMF?" Mackenzie asked them.

"It opened in 2010," Cliff said, using the opportunity of answering her question as a way of distracting himself. "It has a ten-meter-thick base that's built directly on underlying bedrock. The walls, the floor—even the roof—they're all constructed with reinforced concrete."

"Very good." She smiled, pleased. "It's built to withstand earthquakes, tornados, lightning strikes, floods—even the impact of aircraft. And the doors are secured with the latest intrusion deterrence technology."

"That's why it's known as the nuclear Fort Knox," Joshua noted.

"Yes," she said. "That's right." She pointed to the soaring shelves and slipped into lecture mode. "Since uranium is the heaviest element, each container weighs about a hundred and fifty pounds. Those steel racks you see are called rackable can storage boxes, or RCSBs. They're carefully designed to keep the uranium containers the proper distance from each other to avoid criticality."

The term *criticality* caught Cliff's attention.

Avoid criticality.

Yes, that's what you need to do. Avoid letting things with Joshua go critical here.

The objective was clear; how to do it was not.

With the weight of the uranium and the rack itself, it wasn't tough to calculate that the whole unit would weigh close to a ton. The RCSBs were stacked on shelves rising all the way from the floor to the ceiling high above them. No wonder they needed custom-made shelves and forklifts.

"So, this is where it's all kept," Joshua observed, studying the shelves. To Cliff, it sounded like there was true admiration in his tone.

"This is the place!" Mackenzie said. "We're looking forward to the new Uranium Processing Facility, of course." Then glancing in Cliff's direction, she quickly added, "Thanks to the Department of Energy's generous funding."

"Yes, of course," Cliff said.

A glint formed in Mackenzie's eyes. "Do you want to hold some enriched uranium?"

"Yes," Joshua answered for both of them. "We would."

"Follow me."

To kick off the conference, the president of the International Nuclear Association took the stage and gave Dr. Chia-hao Yong a glowing and flattering introduction, but Chia-hao was barely listening. Instead, he was thinking about the two items in his pocket: the flash drive and his wife's finger. If he obeyed the instructions, thousands of lives could be endangered, and she might still lose her life.

But if he didn't obey, she would almost certainly be killed, something he couldn't even bear to think about.

He wiped the back of his hand across his sweaty forehead, but it did little to help calm him.

At last, with the questions cycling mercilessly through his mind, and despite his reticence, he decided what he was going to do during his speech.

It would save more people. It was for the betterment of all.

He would show the attendees Su-wei's finger, and tell them the truth about what was happening and what had been done to his wife.

CHAPTER 50

I woke up slowly in the darkness, my thoughts weedy and thick.

I'd only been knocked unconscious once before in my life, and that was in a car accident in college, not from being smacked in the temple with someone's gun. Now, the throbbing in my head seemed to pulse in time with my heartbeat.

Doing my best to press the drumbeat of pain aside, I focused instead on trying to figure out where I was.

The building's high, grimy windows let in only a leaky daub of muted light.

I was seated on a concrete floor—I could tell that much—with a steel support pole behind me. My arms had been drawn back around it and my wrists were tied together. A rope of some sort. When I attempted to stand, I found that I couldn't. The rope must have been looped around the pole somehow to keep me seated on the ground.

I tried to wrest myself free, but the bonds were too tight.

The pounding coming from my temple wouldn't leave me alone and I could feel myself getting bleary-eyed and fuzzy-headed.

Stay awake, Travis. Come on. Concentrate.

Earlier, Adira had told me that I could use parachute cord to saw through plastic cuffs. That might have worked here—if only I could've reached the cord woven into the bracelet I now wore, but considering how my hands were secured, there was no way I'd be able to get to it.

Fighting to stay alert, I blinked and concentrated on discerning what else was around me, but I found myself drifting away. I struggled to stay focused, but in the end, despite my best efforts, a deep oppressive blackness, like a living thing, descended over me and swallowed me up again.

—⁂—

Mackenzie led Cliff and Joshua past the massive steel shelves containing the RCSBs to the smaller shelving units on the west side of the building.

As they walked, Cliff reminded himself why he was doing this, why he'd arranged for the modified microprocessors from Hyderabad. All for his country. All for America, the land that his brother had died to protect, a beacon of light in a dim and ever-darkening world.

Yes, despite what the historical revisionists claimed, the United States had done more good for the world than any other country in history. And yet, there was still so much left to be done in the fights against global terrorism, the effects of climate change, the rise of anti-Semitism, and the increase of income inequality worldwide.

As a nation, we could do more.

And we would.

But progress, like freedom, came at a price. Cliff was willing to pay that price with his choices and even with prison time, if it came down to that.

You're working toward what's best in the long run. You'll help future generations be safer. Once you announce what's happened, change will come.

When the new Uranium Processing Facility was finished, it would almost certainly include additional layers of security, but the supply chain risks wouldn't go away. The vulnerabilities in that realm would remain.

This week, with the eyes of the world on Y-12, was the time to act. There'd never been a more opportune time to make a statement about the vulnerabilities of our infrastructure and the porous security of the nation's nuclear reactors and weapons facilities supply chain.

Cliff just needed to figure out how—and when—to announce to the world that a shipment of microchips from India to one of the country's most heavily guarded facilities had been compromised.

Do it as soon as you leave here. Before lunch. Don't put it off any longer. Don't trust Joshua with any of this. It needs to be you.

"How's your back?" Mackenzie asked him, jarring him out of his thoughts.

"My back?"

"I don't want you to throw it out," she said half-jokingly. Or maybe she wasn't joking at all. "I'll tell you what—let's go with something a little smaller and more manageable." She indicated a shelf of cylinders slightly larger than a paper cup. "Those are each about eighteen pounds of u-235. Go ahead. Pick one up."

Joshua went first, carefully hefting one of the canisters. "That's crazy."

"I know!" Mackenzie seemed to take his words as a personal compliment. "Amazing, isn't it?"

"A little goes a long way."

"Yes, yes, it does."

When Cliff picked up the uranium cylinder for himself, he was reminded once again of how precious our country's fissile material is—and how vital it is to keep it secure.

In his hand, he was holding enough uranium to lay waste to a city. It was humbling—and a little unsettling—to consider the unfathomable power of even this limited amount of the enriched isotope.

"And that is why," he mumbled, "we can't allow our nuclear facilities to be hacked into."

"Speaking of hacking into something," Mackenzie interjected somewhat excitedly. "True fact: Back in October of 2013, former Vice President Dick Cheney revealed that he'd had his heart's defibrillator altered to avoid it being hacked into, in order to prevent terrorists from assassinating him."

"But that's ridiculous," Joshua said. "I mean, right?"

Cliff wasn't sure if Joshua was faking incredulity or not. He tried to read his face, but found it impossible to guess what might be going through the man's mind. Joshua was polite and yet heartless. Both kind and coldhearted. An enigma.

Yes. A psychopath.

Mackenzie shook her head in response to Joshua's question. "Actually, no, Mr. Godfrey. Hacking into cyber-physical devices could *absolutely* have happened. A lot of people mocked the vice president and laughed off the idea at the time, but anything that's connected to the Internet can be compromised."

"The more connected we are," Joshua said introspectively, "the more vulnerable we become."

"That's right! C'mon. I'll show you where our nuclear engineers work with the hot boxes to study our synthetic isotopes. It's just down the hall!"

—∼∼—

Before they left, Joshua Godfrey debated trying to take the uranium with him now. Mackenzie was busy chatting with the senator; it wasn't the way he'd planned it, but it might be just the chance he needed.

The cylinders were small enough to be easily handled. Easily hidden. In fact, the jacket he was wearing had two reinforced interior pockets that were just the right size for them.

Bring them with you. It'll be—

"Coming?" Mackenzie turned and called to him from ten yards ahead.

"Yes," he said. "Sorry. I got distracted there for a second, thinking about the destructive potential of what surrounds us here."

"It can be a little humbling."

Joshua carefully memorized the location of the smaller u-235 canisters so he could retrieve them in the confusion later, when the paramedics were rolling the senator's body past here and out of the building.

CHAPTER 51

D r. Chia-hao Yong stood at the podium, heart thumping, hands sweating. "For the last four decades," he said haltingly, "I have dedicated my life to assuring that radiological accidents and nuclear tests are things of the past. Our future as a race depends on it. Today, I stand here to tell you . . ."

Save her. Don't betray her. She's your wife. You have to trust that she's still alive. You have to!

"Um . . ."

He clicked to the first slide.

"On January 13, 2018, a man at the Hawaii Emergency Management Agency sent a false alert at 8:07 a.m. that there were incoming ballistic missiles: BALLISTIC MISSILE THREAT INBOUND TO HAWAII. SEEK IMMEDIATE SHELTER. THIS IS NOT A DRILL. This was sent to cell phones as a text, and was also broadcast through radio and television. Hundreds of thousands of people were terrified, frantic, panicking . . . The notice cancelling the alert did not get sent until nearly forty minutes later."

The slide showed a screenshot of someone's phone containing that second message.

"In that instance, human error resulted in two people attempting suicide. Imagine if the warning had gone out to the general population of the contiguous forty-eight states as well."

Click.

A map appeared, showing, with different-colored shading, the threats posed from various weapons of mass destruction in different parts of the world.

"We have all heard of WMDs—weapons of mass destruction—but I would like to recommend that we start referring to them as WMDDs, that is weapons of mass destruction *and disruption*. I am by no means the first to introduce this terminology, but I would like to place my name beside those who are already suggesting we use it. By doing so, we are including the four conventional kinetic WMD threats—chemical, biological, radiological, nuclear and . . . now, also, cyber."

Click.

The entire map turned red to show the universal threat of cyberattacks.

Chia-hao scanned the auditorium for any sign that the people who'd taken his wife might be here, just as he'd scrutinized the hotel's bar the night before. Once again, he saw nothing suspicious. Just an engaged audience waiting for him to continue.

Put the flash drive into your laptop as the instructions directed you to do. Mount it now!

No!

Yes, you have to!

He clicked to the next slide. This one showed a simulated missile attack.

"You might ask, 'How can we place cyber alongside these more conventional WMDs?' Well, cyber threats strategically carried out could cause any one of those other disasters. Also, by disrupting communications, cyber-attacks could be used to spoof a missile attack by another country and require the spoofed nation to make a response, similar to the incident in Hawaii."

Trembling, he told himself to decide and do it.

Do.

It.

Now.

He reached into his pocket and, bypassing the drive, drew out the fabric bundle containing his wife's severed finger.

Yes, he would hold it up, explain that she had been abducted and that he was being blackmailed. The truth would set her free.

Or it wouldn't.

Or it would seal her fate.

Is the truth worth her life? Think this through!

His racing heart just wouldn't slow down and he feared his breathing was becoming so quick and shallow that it would signal to everyone that something was wrong.

He held the finger in his palm. All he had to do was unfold his hand and hold it up and the attendees would know. Everyone would.

While his internal debate raged on, Chia-hao continued speaking from the podium. "Nongovernmental groups, nation states, and hacker syndicates are using the same AI to create viruses and facilitate intrusion that we are using to try to keep them out. It brings to mind the fabled monster from Greek mythology, the Hydra: as fast as we stop one threat, two more rear their heads. The attackers are more sophisticated than ever, have more tools at their disposal, and are motivated to do us harm through their attacks. Every year, cyberattacks grow exponentially in both sophistication and frequency. Cyber intrusion is a rapidly evolving threat, and our security measures must evolve faster."

No.

He couldn't show them Su-wei's finger. Whether it was cowardice or some rare breed of courage, he could not bring himself to do it.

At last, he replaced the finger in his pocket and tremulously pulled out the flash drive.

With all the love in the world for his wife, he slid the drive into his computer's USB port to mount it.

Alright.

It was done.

Now, to see what happened next.

CHAPTER 52

As it turned out, upon reflection, Adira had decided against the early morning vodka out of concern that it might dull her senses. She was getting ready to call the two rooms again to try tracking down Travis when Janice announced, "I think I've got it."

"The sites?"

"Yes. Their significance. What do you know about them so far?"

"Just that they're scattered all over the country. Travis—the guy I'm working with—is convinced they have something to do with . . . well, with the other things we're looking into."

"Travis?"

"Doesn't matter," Adira said dismissively. "What did you find?"

"At first I was thinking maybe mineral rights," Janice explained, "or coal, or even oil pipeline permits. But none of those things really added up." She gave Adira a triumphant smile. "It's natural gas. Those locations are sites either for natural gas extraction, production, or transport. We're talking unprecedented access to natural gas reserves and delivery capabilities."

Adira evaluated that, her thoughts winding through their fact-finding mission and the questions she and Travis had been asking. *How does natural gas relate to Project Symphony? Is that what this is all about? Is the Department of Energy involved with this?*

"It does make sense," Janice said. "Natural gas is the fastest-growing sector of the domestic energy industry. I've thought about investing in it myself, actually. According to projections, natural gas will continue to rise as an export over the next twenty years, even as it provides more energy for domestic markets."

She patted the tablet. "With these investments, if you take nuclear out of the equation, you're talking about billions of dollars of income during what could be an exponential rise in demand."

"Wait." Adira cocked her head. "What do you mean, 'take nuclear out of the equation'?"

"Nuclear energy provides about twenty percent of our country's current supply of electricity. I just mean that without it, something would need to take its place as a source of energy. Natural gas is the perfect alternative."

As Adira let all of that sink in, even though she couldn't immediately pinpoint why, a red flag had gone up.

And she trusted her red flags.

Janice went on. "It looks like Patmos Financial Consortium is owned by a Russian oligarch by the name of Ivan Popovic. Does that name mean anything to you?"

"No."

The Russians again.

If you control the gas, you control the energy. And if you control the energy, you control the economy. The Russians could be trying to cripple our energy grid, attack our infrastructure, or maybe manipulate world markets.

But only without nuclear.

Goliath consulted the time. "Ma'am, we should be getting down to the lecture hall. The opening address has already started."

"Yes, yes. Let me grab my purse."

Outside, a bolt of lightning ripped through the rain-ravaged sky, sending a boom of thunder shaking the sliding glass doors to the balcony. "Looks like there's quite a storm building out there," Janice said.

"Yes," Adira agreed. "It does."

That red flag had not gone away.

Ask her about Bard, the Red Team member, the investment broker. Could he be working with Popovic?

Adira mentally slid the pieces of the puzzle together and carefully observed the two men as she said to Janice, "Do you know what Bard does?"

"Bard?" She was sorting through her purse. "Bard who?"

In some cases, it wasn't about certainty. It was about evidence. And sometimes your gut realizes something before your mind does.

"What about the Walther at Lassiter's place?" Adira asked. "Did Sapphire plant it there?"

The look on Janice's face spoke volumes. "What?"

"That's it, then, isn't it?"

"What is?" Janice asked quizzically, as she slung her purse strap over her shoulder. "What are you talking about?"

"It wasn't the conference in Belgium," Adira muttered. "It was the person I was protecting there—that's why Nathan highlighted it . . . That's . . ." Then she eyed Janice again. "You know, don't you? You know all about us."

"About who? I'm afraid you have me at a loss here."

"When I asked if you knew what Bard does, you averted eye contact with me when you replied. Why? Because you do know about him—or her. Whoever it is. And the Red Team. You know about that too. And Lassiter's name rang a bell, didn't it? Also—how did you come up with the natural gas connection so quickly? You're involved, aren't you?"

There are moments in life when everything tips, when the gears lock into place and the wheel turns, and this was one of them.

Janice was quiet.

"You're the one," Adira said.

"I'm one of the ones," Janice acknowledged slowly. "There are many of us concerned about the potentially cataclysmic effects of a radiological disaster. By creating a controlled event, we can stop a much bigger one."

A chill. "What do you mean *a controlled event*? At Y-12?"

"Ma'am," Goliath said. He had drawn a Glock on Adira and was aiming it at her chest. "Should I—?"

"Just a moment." Janice held up a hand, signaling for him to wait, then said to Adira, "We take Isaiah 2:4 literally: 'And they shall beat their swords into plowshares, and their spears into pruninghooks: nation shall not lift up sword against nation, neither shall they learn war any more.'"

"We?"

Janice revealed a necklace that she was wearing. The emblem dangling on the delicate chain was shaped like a pruninghook.

Adira recognized the symbol from the signs the protestors had been waving around when she and Travis first arrived at the hotel—the same symbol she'd seen on Nathan's papers and then found online. "The Pruninghooks Collective," she said to Janice. "That's who's behind this?"

"We're a group of like-minded souls. Adherents to a doctrine of peace. We will sacrifice whatever is necessary for our children and for their children's children—stopping nuclear use once and for all."

"And with the natural gas deposits," Adira said, "you stand to make billions. That's what's behind all this."

"You still don't understand, do you? I already have more money than I could spend in a lifetime. It's not about money. It's about what money can buy."

"What's that? Power? Influence?"

"As I said, peace. Our goal is to assure that our world never again experiences a radiological disaster. Another Fukushima. Another Chernobyl—or God forbid, another Nagasaki or Hiroshima. We're only human, after all. There are just too many things that might go wrong with nuclear power or weapons—whether it's a software glitch or human error."

Stunned, Adira recalled what Janice had said earlier and referred back to it. "You're trying to take nuclear out of the equation."

"Are you aware that in 1961, a B-52 carrying two four-megaton nuclear bombs broke apart in midair? One of the bombs had a release mechanism tear loose when it dropped onto Goldsboro, North Carolina. The bomb was armed and only failed to detonate because a trigger the size of a light switch failed to engage. It very nearly devastated the state."

"I don't see what—"

"The simpler the system, the easier it is to monitor, to update, and to fix problems as they arise." Janice sighed in dismay. "But as it is now, our nuclear systems have been patched and then re-patched together over the course of decades, with very few plant operators even aware of how the systems integrate with each other. In some cases, there are thousands of digital overlays—any of which could be hacked into. Each one of them introduces a vulnerability, and that makes it more likely that one link in the chain will fail. But when we're talking about nuclear programs, we cannot afford *any* link failing, anywhere on the planet. Ever."

"A radiological incident would erode confidence in nuclear power." Adira found herself speaking her thoughts aloud. "People will turn from it. Legislation gets passed. Plants get closed. Natural gas becomes even more valuable."

"Yes."

"You're going to create a disaster to avoid a disaster? That's what you're saying? That's insane. You're crazy."

"Far from it. It's crazy to create seventy thousand nuclear weapons, as the countries of the world have done over the last eight decades, and then expect that every one of those weapons systems will work perfectly, all of the time, *ad infinitum.*"

Janice held the necklace's emblem in her hand, rotating it affectionately between her thumb and index finger. "Humans make mistakes," she said. "Machines are not always 100 percent reliable. Several times, we've only narrowly avoided a disaster of unimaginable magnitude. And it can't be attributed to anything other than luck. Those who create these weapons of extinction are the crazy ones. I'm just trying to bring some sanity back into the world."

Adira cradled her fake cast. It was designed to come off when twisted a quarter-turn clockwise at a very specific angle, but it was touchy sometimes—and she couldn't afford for that to be the case today, since releasing it was the only way she could get to the shiv and at least have a chance against Janice's bodyguards.

"Why did you have Nathan killed?" Adira folded her arms and, as discreetly as possible, endeavored to apply torque on the cast. "Because he found out about your plans? Because he reached out to Travis?"

"I'm afraid that after Nathan's father passed away his allegiance shifted."

Adira shuddered as Janice's words sank in—Nathan had been working with her and her radical collective.

He sold out his country! He betrayed everything he stood for, everything he taught you!

Adira tried to make sense of it. Nathan Lassiter was the last person she would have ever guessed could be compromised. A seismic shift happened inside of her, unsettling her confidence in her ability to read people.

Thoughts raced through her mind as she tried to regain her footing: *His dad's death was the impetus to all of this, but in the end he tried to make things right, to uncover what's really going on here. He was planning to fly down here. He knew about your background with Janice . . .*

Despite how hard she was tugging at it, the cast was still refusing to come off.

"The Russians who're after Travis," she said to Janice, "is that your doing, or is that Popovic?"

"That's enough questions for now."

A faint, muffled cry came from the bedroom down the hall.

"What was that?" Adira asked, although she thought she might already know.

Lurch and Goliath exchanged glances. Janice sighed, then lowered her gaze, almost apologetically. When she looked up, she was scrutinizing Lurch. "You assured me that she was taken care of."

"She was. She is. We drugged her. Gave her more than enough tranquilizer to knock her out for the rest of the day."

"Evidently not."

The person in the other room struggled to cry out again.

Someone took the physicist's wife.

"It's Su-wei," Adira said, even as she tried to calculate how to take out the two giant bodyguards, both of whom were armed, if she couldn't get the cast off.

"I was hoping it wouldn't come to this." Janice's tone expressed what sounded like genuine regret. "It doesn't please me that things have to end this way. If Nathan had only left things alone, you wouldn't even be involved. But we must play with the cards we've been dealt."

Adira assessed the situation.

Goliath still had that Glock pointed at her. It wasn't the first time she'd had a gun pointed at her face, but it was something you never really got used to and, despite herself, she felt a shiver of fear lace its way down her spine.

Lurch moved to block the door to the hotel hallway. Janice nodded toward him and said, "When we're gone, kill her. Then get to the hospital in Knoxville. I want you to be ready when the children start to arrive at ten thirty. They'll be seated by eleven. Time is ticking."

He pointed toward the bedroom where the cries were coming from. "And the Asian lady?"

"You know what to do. But make it as painless as possible. She's suffered enough already." Janice turned to Adira and tucked the pruninghook necklace beneath her shirt again. "Goodbye, Ms. Halprin."

"Oh, it's not goodbye yet," Adira said coolly. "I'll see you soon."

At that, the billionaire left, with Goliath lumbering after her.

As the door closed behind them, Lurch locked his gaze onto Adira. She still hadn't been able to make any progress with the cast that hid the shiv.

He began striding toward her, covering more ground with each step than should've been humanly possible.

"You should've known better than to wear a tie," she said.

"A tie?"

"Why cinch a liability up around your neck?"

"What are you talking about?"

"I'm going to make you sorry you wore that today."

A sniff of mockery as he held both hands to his sides, inviting her forward. "Let's see you try."

CHAPTER 53

Adira grabbed the necktie and yanked fiercely downward, hoping to tug the man's face down toward her knee, or at least tighten the tie enough to choke or control him.

It snapped free.

"Clip-on," he informed her unnecessarily.

"Right," she muttered, then flung the tie behind her as she backed up slowly, still trying to get the stupid cast off. "Reginald, is it? I'm just wondering: do you prefer the term *thug* or *goon*? Because I'm good with either one."

"You have a smart mouth, you know that, sweetie?"

"Call me sweetie again and see where that gets you." She cranked the cast to the side to try to free her arm from it, but the hinge refused to engage.

Seriously?!

When he was about a yard away, she leapt forward, swinging the cast toward the side of his head, but he was quick and flicked out a hand, grabbed the cast, and held it solidly. Then he lifted her off the ground, seemingly with no effort at all.

Well, at least that was something she could work with.

Grabbing his shoulder with her free hand, Adira swung to the side, twisting her right arm as she did. Now that he was securing the cast in place, and with her weight rotating against it like that, the latch at last unsnapped, freeing her.

She dropped to the floor, caught the shiv as it fell, and swept it forward, slicing it toward his leg. Although she was going for his femoral artery, he turned at the last instant and she ended up simply grazing the outside of his thigh instead.

He hardly even winced, but he did step back toward the couch, apparently to reassess things now that she was armed. He tossed the cast aside.

"Go on, get out of here," Adira said, waving the shiv toward the door and thinking primarily about helping the woman in the other room. "This is a one-time offer. If you come at me again, I'm going to have to defend myself. And I'm telling you right now: that's not going to end well for you."

"I'll take my chances."

"Suit yourself—actually, you know what? I was kinda hoping you'd say that."

He responded by smirking and pulling out her gun from behind his back. He was only three yards away. No way would he miss from that range.

She steeled herself, but instead of firing, he laid the PSM onto the couch and tipped his head sideways, cracking his neck on one side, then the other.

Apparently, he wanted to do this without a gun. Well, good for him.

And her.

Before edging closer, he flicked out an automatic knife that was at least twice the length of her shiv. She reassured herself that in knife fights it wasn't so much the size of the blade that mattered, but the training of the person wielding it.

As spacious as the suite was, it gave her room to back away from him. She angled back past the reclining chair that faced the expansive wall-mounted television and then moved toward the glass countertop spanning the wall beside the balcony doors.

However, as he came at her, he skillfully flipped the knife around into a reverse grip, angling the blade back toward his forearm rather than a traditional saber grip. Clearly he knew what he was doing.

He feinted toward her with the blade. No real commitment. Probably just trying to feel her out, test her reflexes. There's no reason to give your adversary more information than necessary, so to make him overconfident, she hesitated a little as she stepped to the side.

But then, one enormous step at a time, he came toward her, furiously swiping the blade at her while keeping his body out of reach with his impossibly long arms, forcing her backward, nearly to the balcony doors, driving the knife at her abdomen. She raised her left arm to protect her stomach as she danced backward, but he was close enough to leave a streak of red behind on her forearm.

Sure, she was quicker than he was, but with his inhuman wingspan and kick radius, she was at a serious disadvantage. When someone can veritably kick or punch you from across the room, you're gonna be in trouble.

Noted.

"Tell me where they're going," she said. "What's Janice going to blow up? Is it a hospital?"

He didn't reply.

"She wants you to meet her in Knoxville. Is that the target?"

He just sneered at her.

Reaching behind her, she tossed the balcony doors open and stepped back into the savage downpour.

He followed her, and all at once, pivoted and landed a solid sidekick against her left thigh, barely missing the deep bruise.

She stumbled backward, struggling not to cry out.

He grinned. "You were limping when you entered the suite, favoring that leg."

Nice situational awareness, she thought. *Not bad.*

Rain pelted her relentlessly as she struggled to keep her footing on the balcony's slick deck.

When he tried kicking her again, she deflected his foot with hers, but this was the ankle she'd rolled in the parking garage and that didn't feel too great either.

Girl, you're in rough shape here.

He came at her again, this time leading with a punch that he followed up with the blade, forcing her to the railing of the balcony. Her shiv was doing her no good.

As the rain flew in beneath the roof and lightning blistered the sky to her left, Adira thought about trying to headbutt him, but he was too tall for that and she didn't really want to get that close to his blade.

Well, height can be a liability too. The taller you are, and the longer your limbs are, the more vulnerable your joints are—especially your knees. She went for his left one, aiming a swift kick at it, trying to take it out, to make him crumple. But her heel caught his knee in the back instead of the side. His leg bent forward, but he didn't go down—although it did throw him off balance.

She targeted him with the shiv, stabbing it into his shoulder, but then losing control of it as he twisted to the side, tugging it from her grip.

With the shiv embedded in his shoulder, he lunged at her, gliding his blade at her neck, but she ducked, grabbed him by the shoulders, and threw herself backward across the floor of the balcony, rolling onto her back and tugging him with her, trusting that the momentum would carry him forward as she dropped down and ducked beneath him.

And it did.

He went crashing overtop of her into the railing. When he stood, wobbly and off-kilter, she landed a high kick, this time to his chest.

At first it looked like he might be able to stop himself from tipping off the balcony, but he was so top heavy that when the back of his legs hit the railing, he careened backward and, arms flailing, went over.

Adira rushed to where he'd fallen and saw him dropping through the piercing, dark rain toward the pavement eighty feet below.

She turned away so she wouldn't see him land. A moment later, the deep, crunching thud told her all she needed to know.

She closed her eyes and a surge of grief hit her, something both heavy and hollow at the same time. Every life has worth. Every life matters. But there were other things to worry about right now, so she slid her feelings to the side.

Box them up. Compartmentalize them. Deal with them later.

Story of her life.

She hurried to the bedroom where the cries were coming from.

Throwing the door open, she found a woman in a mauve pantsuit tied to the bed. She was gagged and looked terrified. One of her hands was bandaged up, but even with the thick wrappings around it, Adira could tell that she was missing her ring finger.

Gently, Adira removed the gag from the woman's mouth and immediately she began speaking in a language Adira didn't understand. She wasn't certain, but guessed it was Taiwanese. She knew a little Russian from her work overseas but had never picked up any Asian languages.

"Su-wei?"

The woman nodded, then began to speak again.

"English?" Adira asked. "Do you speak English?"

Su-wei looked at her quizzically, then began to speak frantically once more in that unfamiliar language.

Adira patted the air softly with her palms to show that she meant no harm. "I'm going to get you out of here," she said, more for her own benefit than for Su-wei's.

Then she set to work freeing her from the bed, wondering how she was going to stop Janice, and what had ever happened to Dr. Yong and to Travis.

CHAPTER 54

Eyes open again, I scanned my surroundings, evaluating my situation. A crooked splinter of lightning outside the window illuminated the interior of the building.

Debris lay on the floor all around me: radio transmitter paraphernalia, a stack of long-abandoned gas masks and grim-looking black rubber gloves, piles of vacuum tubes from early-generation computers, and World War II–era radiation suits that didn't look like they would've offered a whole lot of protection against anything.

Slowly, my eyes grew accustomed to the gloomy light, which was punctuated by the intermittent spasms of lightning.

A damaged instrument panel hung on a nearby wall, a snarl of wires oozing from its base, making it look like it'd been a living thing and someone had slit open its belly, releasing its corded insides to spew out.

Three stories above me, moldy ceiling tiles drooped in tatters from leaks in the roof. Saturated from the storm, they dribbled a thin but steady trickle of water down onto the concrete not far from my left foot.

The remains of manufacturing machines loomed large in the darkness. Rusted pipes snaked through gargantuan metal chambers that had served some secret purpose in the hidden past. Even with all that I knew about Oak Ridge, I had no idea what these immense machines would have been used for.

The warehouse-sized building had clearly been mothballed for decades.

I had to be either at Y-12 or on the nearby campus of the Oak Ridge National Laboratory, in one of their condemned or vacant factories. Based on how hard it would've been for the Russians to get me—and themselves—onto the Y-12 Security Complex, I guessed that I was probably somewhere on the ORNL campus instead.

Either way, I needed to get out of here.

Earlier, in the hotel room, Adira had emphasized threat assessment. Well, here's what I was aware of: There were at least two Russian assailants. The good thing was, we had evidence that they didn't want me dead.

What they wanted me alive for . . . well, I wasn't too thrilled to dwell on that. If they were Russian operatives and had identified who I was and what I knew—Defense Department secrets that even the president hadn't been briefed on—they would likely resort to whatever means they deemed necessary to extract the information they were after.

The phrase *enhanced interrogation* came to mind, and I was suddenly not so sure that being kept alive was such a desirable thing.

Once again, I tried to torque my wrists free, but it was no use. I couldn't snap the ropes and I wasn't going to be able to wriggle free from the bindings.

I studied the debris nearby but didn't see anything that appeared sharp enough to use to cut through the rope.

Another burst of lightning lit up the sky, and I caught sight of the wind jacket that Adira had given to me. It was out of reach but nearby, off to the right, where the Russians must've discarded it when they tied me up.

Though I couldn't get to the parachute cord I wore on my wrist to saw my way to freedom, if I could draw the jacket close enough with my foot, maybe I could use its razor-sharp zipper to cut through the bindings.

With the rope looped around the pole the way it was, rotating myself to the side wasn't easy, but finally I managed to face the jacket and stretch my leg out toward it.

—⁂—

It'd never bothered Joshua Godfrey that he wasn't handsome. In fact, he was grateful that he was so easily forgettable.

He was the type of person other folks simply overlooked or ignored—like that anonymous coworker whose name you can never remember, even though he's been stationed in the cubicle across from you for years. That was how it'd always been for Joshua—unceremoniously slipping through the cracks, moving through life unnoticed. An anonymous fixture in an all-too-conspicuous world.

It made getting away with his assignments that much easier.

Yesterday, two jobs in the DC area.

And now, today, here in Tennessee, potentially his last one.

If all went as planned, he would survive, but if necessary, he would be giving his life this morning to see this mission through to the end. He was doing it for his foster mom, the most significant person in his life, the woman who'd been there when he needed her the most back when he was an adolescent.

She'd helped him find his true self, his true calling, and now he'd vowed to help her—whatever that might require of him.

After his biological parents were killed in a car accident when he was five, he'd been passed from one foster family to the next, shuffled through nearly a dozen of them by the time he was a high school freshman. It'd made it nearly impossible for him to develop a deep connection with any authority figures, let alone a set of parents.

A certain proclivity toward violence hadn't helped.

But then, at last, when he was fifteen, it'd finally happened. He'd been placed with a couple who treated him with a mixture of fierce love and genuine compassion. They wouldn't take any nonsense from him, and they wouldn't accept anything less than his best. They didn't bail him out all the time, but they also didn't set him up for failure. He finally came to understand that they loved him. They truly did. And, to the extent that he was able to, he loved them as well.

Eventually he'd started addressing them as "Mom" and "Dad."

His mom, Janice Daniels.

His dad, Lancaster Daniels, now ten years gone because of pancreatic cancer.

Joshua had entered the military just out of high school and spent eight years as a Marine before leaving the service to pursue other interests—ones that his mom had convinced him mattered even more. "Given the short lives that we have," she'd told him, "it is better not to train for war but to stop it from happening in the first place." After Dad died, the message had sunk in enough for him to leave the Marines.

Now, he and the senator followed Mackenzie to an area where Y-12 researchers sat on the far side of thick, protective glass enclosures, using robotic arms to pick up and manipulate containers about the size of a quart jar that contained radioactive isotopes, including uranium-233 and cobalt-60.

No personal electronic devices were allowed in the building, but Joshua checked the time on his analog wristwatch.

If the physicist hadn't inserted the drive by now, he would be doing so shortly. The algorithm would do its work and because of the encoded microchips that Rakesh had shipped, no perimeter sensors would go off when the containers of uranium-235 were taken out of the HEUMF.

No warning sirens or klaxons would sound.

That is, if all went as planned.

While the senator and the public affairs officer were focused on the researchers working in the hot cells, Joshua took out the medicated patch he'd been carrying and surreptitiously attached the adhesive side to his right palm. Then, wary to keep his fingers from touching the saturated portion, he slowly peeled off the protective covering.

All he had to do was briefly press his hand against the senator's skin, just for a couple of seconds—two, three, tops. The drug would be absorbed percutaneously, and the end would begin.

—⁂—

After untying Su-wei, Adira helped her to the bathroom, where the woman promptly vomited into the toilet. Adira ran a glass of water for her, which Su-wei then used to rinse out her mouth.

The next step was not clear to Adira. While she wanted to reassure Dr. Yong that his wife was alright, she also needed to make sure that she stopped Janice from following through with whatever plan she'd put into play regarding a "controlled" radiological event.

It had to be some sort of radiological dispersal device.

A dirty bomb.

Janice had mentioned a hospital in Knoxville, but Adira wasn't certain which one that might be.

She said something about children arriving at ten thirty. The note from Lassiter yesterday mentioned eleven o'clock.

A children's hospital? Maybe. It was a place to start.

Okay, so what to do with Su-wei?

The shaking woman wiped off her face with a damp washcloth, refilled the cup Adira had given her, and gulped the water down. Then she gazed into the mirror at her bedraggled appearance and her bandaged hand and burst into tears.

Adira took her in her arms to comfort her—admittedly not her strong suit, but you do what you have to do, and she really did feel sorry for her. Su-wei wasn't in any condition to be left alone right now—and after what she'd been through, that was totally understandable.

But you can't just wait around here with her either! Not when Janice is planning a radiological attack!

Su-wei clearly needed medical attention, not just for the severed finger, but also for whatever the goons had drugged her with. However, Adira reminded herself that if she called in paramedics, they would undoubtedly ask her what'd happened, and that would require an awful lot of explaining and eat up an awful lot of time.

She tried calling both rooms 513 and 408 again.

No answer.

Don't worry about Travis. He'll be alright.

As much as she wanted to leave in search of Janice, she couldn't just abandon Su-wei here alone, not after what she'd just experienced.

Get Su-wei help and then get to Knoxville.

Adira phoned hotel security and said, "There's a woman in the presidential suite who needs immediate medical attention. Also, send security personnel to room 408. There's a man missing and that's the last place he was heading. His name is Travis Brock." She gave them a detailed description of Travis, then hung up before they asked any additional questions.

Using improvised sign language, she tried to convince Su-wei that she was going to be okay and that the people who'd taken her weren't coming back, but she wasn't sure how much, if any, of that got through.

In the end, she helped Su-wei to the suite's couch, took the Russian's gun from where Reginald had left it before doing his fatal backflip off the balcony, and tucked it into the waistband beneath her blouse.

Then, Adira placed a gentle hand on Su-wei's shoulder and waited restlessly for medical help to arrive.

—⁂—

When a staff member who was distractedly consulting a clipboard came ambling down the hallway toward them, Joshua took the opportunity to gently grasp the senator's wrist and guide him out of the way.

There. Done.

The drug was fast-acting. It wouldn't be long now.

"Thank you," Senator Richardson said to him.

"Of course, sir."

"I didn't even see him."

"Yeah, he kind of came out of nowhere."

Mackenzie was prattling on about Y-12's workforce. "Nearly forty-eight hundred people work here. Did you know that? And we have an amazing retention rate. Average age—forty-nine. Average years of experience—thirteen."

As the senator turned to listen to her, Joshua carefully removed the medicated strip from his palm and slid it into his back pocket.

He checked the time again and saw that, according to what his mom had told him, the drive should have certainly been mounted by now.

All he had to do was keep an eye on Richardson and wait for the drug to take effect, and then get the two canisters onto the ambulance to Knoxville.

CHAPTER 55

The man who'd followed the van away from the hotel to the decrepit factory here on the southern edge of the Oak Ridge National Laboratory campus stood beneath a tree to shield himself from the driving rain as he tried to figure out when—and how—to make his move.

He'd been able to identify two entrances to the building—one on the north side, the other on the east. Near the east entrance, sections of the roof had caved in and rainwater was funneling into the building.

No one was in sight at the moment, but two men had transported Brock into the building through the north door. Then one of them had left in the van again. From his vantage point, the observer had not been able to see their faces, but if he was right in what he was surmising, one of them would have been Ilya Vasiliev.

A razor wire–topped fence surrounded the grounds. Warning signs commanding people to *Keep Out* appeared every fifty meters or so, although there were occasional gaps in the fence that a motivated person could use to access the property.

Weeds and thick brambles grew everywhere inside the fence and thorn-snarled branches guarded the ground floor windows on the closest wing of the building.

He made sure that the auto-injector syringe was ready, then proceeded toward the east entrance.

—∞—

When Adira heard the knock at the door, she drew the gun, peered through the eyehole to confirm that it was medical staff, then hid the gun again and yanked the door open for the security officer who stood there. "You were supposed to go to 408! We need medical help here, not—"

"Ma'am, we had a call that—"

"Listen, there isn't time to explain everything. All I can tell you is that you need to help this woman. She was attacked, drugged, and who knows what else."

The trim man, who sported a voluminous mustache far too large for his narrow face, shifted his attention to Su-wei, who held up her bandaged hand and spoke in frantic, rapid-fire Taiwanese.

"A man leapt from a balcony on this side of the building just a few minutes ago," the guard said in a curious yet concerned tone. "Does that have anything to do with this?"

He didn't exactly leap, Adira thought.

"Yeah," she said. "It's all connected."

"What on earth is going on here?"

Adira pointed at Su-wei. "The only thing that matters right now is this woman in front of you. She needs medical assistance—and you need to make sure Dr. Yong from the conference knows that his wife is alright. And check 408, like I said."

"Wait. *The* Dr. Yong? The Nobel Prize winner?"

"Yes."

"I can't just interrupt his speech and—"

"That's exactly what you're going to do."

Before he could argue with her, Adira left with the tablet, jogged down the hall, and entered the elevator.

She pressed 5, the doors closed, and the elevator began its descent.

—∞—

Ever since inserting the drive, Dr. Chia-hao Yong had been fretfully waiting for something, anything of consequence, to happen.

No coding or cryptic messages had come up on his laptop's screen. Nothing dramatic had occurred.

He still didn't know if Su-wei was alive or dead.

He fumbled through his lecture, trying his best to stay focused, but his worry about his wife and about what might happen because he'd mounted the drive would not leave him alone.

"A nuclear event anywhere in the world," he said, "would also inevitably affect the surrounding nations. It is not just a matter for countries to address individually. The international community must tackle it collectively. Our unity today is essential for securing our peace for tomorrow."

Tell the attendees what happened. Show them Su-wei's finger. Do it now. It might not be too late to get the truth out there!

But he didn't.

Click.

Another slide: Two computers sitting side by side with an interposed arrow pointing from one to the other.

"As you may know, I have spent the last two years working on processes to help shield computers against hacking and cyber intrusion."

He didn't mention Project Symphony by name. Yes, in a forum like this he could speak about his public work, but he couldn't reveal anything about the handheld device he was helping the Pentagon develop that could hack into air gapped computers from up to one hundred meters away. It was one of the DOD's most highly guarded secrets, and was only a few months away from completion.

He went on, "By studying the tactics of the adversaries of freedom, we can learn to defend ourselves against them."

But that's precisely what you failed to do. You mounted the drive. Whatever happens now is all your fault.

Just six more slides and his presentation would be over. He would get off the stage. He would find someone to help him. He would find a way to undo what he had done.

Back in room 513 again, Adira quickly cleaned up and regrouped.

Travis was still missing, no new messages were waiting for her, and she wasn't certain what to do.

The blood from the wound on her forearm where Reginald had sliced her during their fight was seeping through her sleeve, but thankfully—although the cut was nearly four inches long—it didn't appear to be too deep. No nerve damage.

Another call to 408.

Still nothing.

Though she was worried about what might've happened to Travis, right now locating and then stopping Janice was the priority.

A hospital.

Children.

A dirty bomb.

All coming together somehow later this morning.

Once again, the text she'd received yesterday at the Knoxville airport came to mind: **11 am tomorrow. Be aware.**

Nathan knew something was going to happen today. That might be what got him killed.

After doing her best to bandage her arm with a strip of fabric torn from a bath towel, she called the New Haven Children's Hospital in Knoxville and asked if they were having any special programs for children today.

"Not that I'm aware of," the receptionist told her curtly.

"Are you sure? Because my nephew, he's a patient there. I wanted to make sure he doesn't miss out on anything. I heard someone mention there was something for the kids this morning? At ten thirty? Maybe eleven?"

"No, ma'am. We don't have any events scheduled. I hope your nephew starts to feel better." But it didn't sound like she hoped that very much at all.

"Check again."

A pause. "Okay. Still nothing."

"Yeah. Thanks."

Adira followed up with calls to all six hospitals in the region but came up short, without locating any children's programs.

What next?

She always thought better when she was chewing bubble gum, so she popped some into her mouth and then went to the window.

Two ambulances and three police cruisers were stationed down below, no doubt investigating the dead Brobdingnagian in the worsted wool suit under the presidential suite.

Adira rebuked herself for not setting up a time and a place to meet with Travis if they got separated.

He'll be okay. Stop the attack. It's what you need to do. It's what he would want you to do.

She phoned the Knoxville Police Department, got on the line with a lieutenant, and, trying to convince herself that she was doing the right thing, told him everything she knew about the bomb threat.

"Let me get this straight," he said when she'd finished. "You're telling me that you have information that there's going to be *a nuclear bomb* going off at a hospital in Knoxville today?" He sounded understandably dubious.

"Not a nuclear bomb. Some sort of radiological event. Something controlled. An RDD, probably."

"An RDD?"

"A radiological dispersal device," she said impatiently. "A dirty bomb. You need to—"

"And how do you know this?"

"The person behind it told me. She's linked to a domestic antinuke terrorist group who—"

"Antinuke terrorists who want to set off a nuclear bomb?"

"All you need to worry about right now is that they're terrorists."

A short pause. "Which hospital?"

"I don't know."

"When?"

"Eleven. I think. Maybe ten thirty."

"And who is this woman who's going to set it off?"

"Janice Daniels."

"The billionaire philanthropist."

"Yes."

"Uh-huh."

"You're going to be looking for a woman in her early sixties," Adira explained quickly. "White hair. A royal-blue blouse. She has a bearded man with her, approximately six-six, two hundred eighty pounds. Designer dark-gray suit and obsidian tie. Black hair parted on the left. I don't know his name, but he—"

"An old lady and a giant. Got it. Does she live in a shoe?"

"Listen to me, this is—"

"No," he snapped, "you listen to me. Making a bomb threat is a serious matter, and—"

"You're not hearing me. This is Adira Halprin. I'm wanted for a triple homicide outside of Washington, DC, yesterday. Take me seriously, or you will regret it."

"What? You're—"

She hung up.

There are already cops onsite. If he traces that call—which he probably will—they could be up here within the next two minutes. Get to Knoxville. Go.

Hurriedly, she threw on a new outfit, transforming herself into a neo-Bohemian brunette with the driver's license name of Eve Ella Hazelwood.

Even if the cops wouldn't do anything, she could.

She grabbed her car key and the tablet, stuffed Eve's wallet into her purse, and headed for the CR-V to leave for Knoxville.

She would figure out which hospital it was on the way.

CHAPTER 56

OAK RIDGE NATIONAL LABORATORY

SOUTH CAMPUS

I let out a tight sigh of frustration.

Though I'd been able to brush my heel across the top of the jacket twice, I hadn't been able to drag it any closer. As I was going for it again, the echo of footsteps approaching from the far side of the darkened warehouse caught my attention.

Time to make some progress here, or bail on the whole idea.

Taking a deep breath, I scrunched as low as I could and kicked my leg toward the jacket. It took three attempts, but finally, as my heel landed on it, I was able to draw it slightly toward me before my heel slid off the slick fabric.

The footsteps grew steadily closer. A flashlight beam bobbed along with them.

Come on. You can do this.

Gritting my teeth and pinning the jacket down with my heel, I began inching it my way. It seemed to take forever, especially with the sound of whoever was walking toward me getting closer and closer.

Finally, once the jacket was within reach, I rotated around the pole again, grabbed it, and then dialed myself back to face whoever was coming my way.

The flashlight looked to be about fifty feet from me.

As I repositioned the zipper to try pressing it against the rope, it scraped cruelly across the back of my left hand. I grimaced as the skin tore open and hot blood trickled down between my fingers.

Careful. Slicing your wrist open right now would not be a good move.

Trying to avoid any more cuts, I managed to get the zipper tucked over the rope with the jacket gripped in my hands. At last, I was able to draw it somewhat clumsily back and forth across the rope. As honed as the zipper was, I expected that I'd be able to cut through the bindings relatively quickly—as long as I kept pressure on it and kept my wrists and fingers out of the way.

The man who'd been striding toward me stepped into view.

He positioned the flashlight next to some sort of tactical rifle on a 1950s-era gray metal desk about twenty-five feet from me. As the light illuminated the warehouse, I identified him as the Russian who'd somehow tracked me down in that back hallway behind the Hemlock conference room.

"Where is she?" I asked him.

"I was about to ask you the same question."

"Why did you take her?" I pressed him. "What do you want from Dr. Yong?"

"Dr. Yong?" The Russian angled his head to the side and looked at me curiously. "I was speaking about the woman you've been traveling with."

Good. He doesn't have Adira. He doesn't know where she is.

"You're saying you didn't take Su-wei? You didn't cut off her finger?"

"I'm afraid I don't know anything about a missing woman or her missing finger."

Maybe I shouldn't have believed him, but with me tied up like I was, I couldn't think of any good reason why he would be lying to me.

But if the Russians didn't kidnap Su-wei, who did? And why?

At least, from what he'd said so far, it seemed that Adira was still safe.

While I worked at slicing through the rope, I continued talking, hoping to keep the guy distracted so he wouldn't notice what I was doing behind my back. "Who are you?" I asked. "Who do you work for?"

"My name is Sergei Sokolov. My employer is of no consequence."

Sokolov? Wait—I knew that name from my work at the Pentagon.

"You're a diplomat," I said. "You work at the Russian embassy, don't you? You've been there for nearly five years."

STEVEN JAMES || 307

He shook his head in admiration. "You really do have a gift. That memory of yours." He tapped his temple. "Extraordinary."

It struck me that, as an embassy employee, Sokolov would have diplomatic immunity. That was a get-out-of-jail-free card for just about any crime—even murder. He could do virtually anything he wanted to me in here and never have to face justice for it—not a very reassuring thought.

I felt a sweep of anger for the families of the three security personnel at L & L Manufacturing who would never see justice carried out for Sokolov's involvement in their deaths. He would walk.

As I thought about someone getting away with murder, of justice not being meted out, Sienna's death immediately came to mind.

"Did you set the fire?" I asked. "The one that killed my wife?"

"That's how you got your scars? From the fire?"

"Did you start it?"

"No," he said candidly. "Sapphire would be my guess."

"Sapphire? From the Red Team? Who is she? What's her real name?"

Sokolov just eyed me silently.

I'd been on the hunt for this person for so long that his words left me uncertain exactly how to proceed. Now that I had a name—even if it was just a code name—what did I do with it?

Sapphire likely killed Lassiter—so, both him and Sienna?

I thought of justice and vengeance once again and the words from Romans chapter 12 came to mind, words I'd recalled countless times over the last seventeen months: "Vengeance is mine; I will repay, saith the Lord." A famous verse. A classic sentiment. Well, if the Lord is in the business of vengeance, then it can't be all bad, right? If God's actions are pure and just, then vengeance must fall under the auspices of justice as well. It isn't a line that separates justice from vengeance, after all; they're two facets of the same thing—divine equity.

Retributive action in the service of holy wrath.

But God's the one who repays wrongs, not you. You shouldn't repay evil with evil, but evil with good. He's the Judge. The Avenger. You're not.

Yet shouldn't we each do whatever's in our power to see that justice is carried out? Isn't it a cause worth sacrificing everything for?

"Are you going to tell me who Sapphire is?" I demanded.

"How's your head?" Though it might've been an act, his concern sounded authentic. "Ilya told me that he hit you pretty hard."

I must have been distracted enough by concentrating on the conversation and my escape attempt with the zipper to not notice my aching head, but now, when Sokolov asked me about it, the pain immediately climbed to the top of my awareness again.

Pulse, pulse, pulse, pulse . . . pulsing in time with my heart.

"My head is fine," I lied.

"You didn't answer my question from earlier," he said. "Where is Adira Halprin?"

"What do you want from me, Sergei? Did you bring me here to kill me?"

"By no means. You're no good to us dead." His gaze became a fine-toothed comb raking over me. "I brought you here to recruit you."

"That's not going to happen. I've been trained to keep my secrets to myself."

While it was true that I had some training in that regard, I was no field operative or super spy. I wasn't sure how long I'd be able to hold my silence if Sokolov really did start pulling off my toenails or breaking my fingers one at a time.

I felt one of the loops of rope begin to fray. The bonds loosened slightly, but not enough for me to pull free.

Come on. Keep going. Just a little more . . .

As I continued working the zipper back and forth, I kept a careful eye on Sokolov. "Where's your partner? Where's Ilya?"

"Picking up a package. He'll be here shortly." Then he said, "How well do you know Adira Halprin? I mean, how well do you *really* know her?"

"What are you talking about?"

"Are you aware of her work in Almaty?"

When we were in Fairfax she'd mentioned something about a night in Almaty, Kazakhstan, but I couldn't see how that had anything to do with what was happening here.

He's trying to turn you against her. Don't listen. Don't give him anything he can use.

"I know that I trust her. And I also know I'm not going to help you, no matter what you do to me."

"I'm sorry to hear that." He picked a piece of lint off his shirt. Tossed it away. "I've asked nicely, but we can move to other ways of asking if that's what it's going to take."

Behind my back, a coil of rope gave way.

I tugged, but it still wasn't enough.

"I'd like you to tell me about Colonel Clarke," Sokolov said. "About the current budget allocations he's proposing for the continuation of a program known as Project Symphony. How far along is the prototype? Is it really being stored at Y-12?"

"I'm not sharing anything with you about my job."

He held up the tube of super glue that Adira had given me earlier. He must have gotten it from my pocket while I was unconscious.

"Do you know what the main ingredient in this is?" he asked. "It's *cyano-acrylate*. Do you have any idea what that compound will do to a human eye when it's squirted in beneath the eyelid?"

Don't get rattled. Stay on task here. Get yourself free.

I said nothing.

"Project Symphony," he replied. "All the notes of the song coming together. Sound familiar?"

Still, I didn't respond.

A small sigh. "This can go one of two ways, with the same result in either case. I'm going to persuade you to help me, Mr. Brock. You must realize that by now. We can take the long road to get there, or the short one."

"I'm not really interested in taking any trips at the moment," I said. "I haven't packed my swim trunks."

It sounded like something Adira might have said. She would've been proud.

Sokolov unscrewed the cap of the super glue while I aggressively sawed the zipper against the rope, burying my fear under the urgency of what I was doing.

Almost free. Almost . . .

CHAPTER 57

As Cliff followed Mackenzie through the HEUMF, his thoughts seemed to
be somehow racing and slowing down at the same time. He fumbled
to loosen his tie. "I don't feel so well," he muttered.

"You do look a bit flushed, Senator," Joshua told him.

"I think I just need to sit down."

"Follow me," Mackenzie offered. "There's a break room just down the hall."

"I don't know what's come over me. I'm . . ."

*You need to reveal the fact that the chips have been compromised. You need to
show how easy it was, to prove to the subcommittee and to the American people
the vulnerabilities inherent in the way things are currently structured.*

You have to . . .

But even as Cliff told himself that he needed to get the word out, he
couldn't find the right things to say because his focus had shifted to how difficult it was becoming to breathe.

"Yes," he managed to tell them. "I think I do need to sit down."

I watched as Sokolov repositioned the light in my direction so he could more
clearly see what he was doing with the glue. The glare was powerful and pene-
trating and I had to blink my eyes against it and turn away.

Leaving the flashlight beside his gun, he strode toward me.

I tugged at the bindings.

Nope.

Not yet.

Not quite.

I remembered what Adira had told me earlier: *"Stay attentive. Give nothing about your intentions away."*

Sokolov leaned over me, removed my glasses, and, holding my head in place, pinched the flesh beneath my right eye, pulling it out slightly to make room for the tube's nozzle.

"Hold still, now," he said. "Unless you're ready to chat about Project Symphony."

—⁓—

Just moments ago, in order to get to her SUV, Adira had needed to pass two cops who were stationed in the hotel's front lobby. While they hadn't appeared to be interested in speaking with her, she'd averted her gaze anyway, avoiding eye contact as she slipped past them and made her way through the rain and toward her car.

She found the SUV and climbed in, breathing a sigh of relief.

But in her exigency to enter the vehicle and get out of sight of law enforcement, she didn't look in the backseat.

So she didn't see the man who was lying there in wait for her.

—⁓—

There.

I was free.

Whipping my hands out from behind my back, I grabbed Sokolov by the shoulders. In one rather uncoordinated yet committed move, I yanked him toward me and thrust my head up at him, doing my best to headbutt him from the awkward position I was in as I lurched forward.

It wasn't a very good headbutt—I ended up slamming the top of my head into his jaw, and I doubted that I did much damage, but it did catch him off-guard, buying me enough time to scramble away from the pole and leap to my feet.

From where he stood, just two yards from me, Sokolov rubbed his chin and appraised me. "What happens now, Travis? What's your move? There's no getting out of here."

My plan hadn't really worked its way past just freeing myself from the ropes and avoiding that super glue.

"I don't want to hurt you," I said as intimidatingly as I could, eyeing that rifle on the desk.

"I do," declared a stern voice from somewhere off to my right.

In surprise, both Sokolov and I turned toward the voice. As we did, a burst of gunfire sent the Russian diplomat running. He dove behind the desk that held his flashlight, inadvertently knocking it off. The flashlight went skittering across the concrete in swift circles, sending disorienting cycles of light and shadow cycloning around the room.

Sokolov snatched up the tactical rifle and tipped the desk onto its side to shield himself from the bullets blazing toward him from the darkness.

I wasn't sure if the rounds would be able to pierce the metal, but it looked like a pretty formidable barrier.

When I tried to see who was shooting, I couldn't make anyone out, but the voice hollered, "Hit the ground!"

With bullets flying, I didn't need to be asked twice. I dropped down and flattened myself against the concrete.

"I'm here to help you," the man called to me.

Another spitfire of bullets. This time Sokolov responded with a barrage of his own.

"Crawl this way," the voice shouted urgently.

Staying as low as I could, I started toward him, whoever he might be.

—⚏—

While her bodyguard, Turo, drove her toward Knoxville, Janice Daniels checked a weather app.

Although thunderstorms were still moving through Oak Ridge, twenty-five miles away in Knoxville the rain had held off. It looked like the storms would skirt around the city's downtown, missing it entirely.

Good. Rain would've washed away the residue from the explosion and doubtless weakened its results.

Earlier in the day, Turo had set the RDX explosives in the Sunsphere and positioned a camera on the bridge for her to remotely watch everything unfold. He assured her that he'd hidden the explosives and detonator out of sight along the edge of the glass in the sphere's tower. Still, to cut down on the chance of anyone discovering the wires, she'd had him leave the *Maintenance in progress* signs up to stop people from visiting the observation deck.

Now he asked her, "To the townhouse?"

"Yes." She'd rented one on the outskirts of the city for this occasion. Just far enough from the blast radius to remain safe, yet close enough to monitor the city's response. "Then head to the hospital. When Reginald and Joshua join you, the three of you can transport the uranium to the Sunsphere. You won't need me there."

"Yes, ma'am."

"You'll have plenty of time to get to safety. Just don't dawdle."

"I understand."

The process of beating spears into pruninghooks was not an easy one. It took effort. It took courage. And it took some mighty blows of the hammer.

Today would be the mightiest and most effectual blow of all.

Yes, this would work. From the townhouse, she would watch as tomorrow's worldwide headlines unfolded, as a new chapter for humanity was written and a new reality began to unfold.

—⁓—

Locating the man in the shadows, I finished army-crawling toward him while a volley of bullets *zinged* above me.

He sat crouched behind the towering carcass of one of the mammoth machines. Black fatigues. Midfifties. Scruff. A medium frame. Thick, corded muscles.

"Get behind me," he commanded.

I hustled to take cover. "Who are you?"

"Name's Gunnar Bane," he said. "Colonel Clarke sends his regards."

"So, you're on our side."

"I'm on his."

I sorted through the thousands of names I'd come across in my work, but couldn't come up with anyone named Gunnar Bane. "Are you part of Project Symphony?"

"Are you?"

"I'm—never mind. How does this play out?"

"I have a syringe in my left vest pocket. An auto-injector." His eyes were trained on the desk Sokolov was hiding behind, which was about forty feet from us. "Go ahead and pull it out."

It seemed like a weird request. As far as I knew, auto-injectors were only used for drug overdoses, allergic reactions, or nerve agent exposure. I retrieved the syringe from the vest of his body armor and uncapped the protective cover.

"Alright," he said. "Now comes the tough part."

"I've never given anyone a shot before."

"There's a first time for everything."

"Where do you need me to inject it?"

"In your leg."

"In *my* leg?"

"Yep. Do it now, or I'm going to have to shoot you dead."

CHAPTER 58

Why on earth would I inject this into my leg?" I said, stunned. "And why would you shoot me?"

"You could do your arm instead. I don't really care."

This is crazy. What's going on here?

"But why threaten to kill me?" I said. "Aren't you here to rescue me?"

"I'm here to stop you."

"To stop me?"

"From sharing anything with Comrade Super Glue over there."

Gunnar leaned around the side of the hulking metal cylinder that we were using for cover, fired several shots, then squatted beside me again.

This time there was no return of gunfire. No sounds except for the distant echo of rain on the sheet metal roof overhead and the thin whisper of dripping water nearby.

"He might've slipped off," Gunnar mumbled. "We need to hurry. I don't know when his partner is gonna get back. Time for your shot."

"Wait. Hang on. What's in this needle?"

"Nanobots. Tracking sensors to show me where you're at. Like I said, Clarke wants me to stop you from having a sit-down with the Russians."

Of course the colonel couldn't afford for me to be compromised; it was something I'd understood from my first day on the job at the Pentagon a decade and a half ago. "Let me guess," I said. "You're authorized to stop me by whatever means necessary?"

"The colonel only wants what's best for the country."

"We all want the same thing here, Gunnar. Listen, I'm working to make sure our country's interests are placed first. You have to trust me."

"That's not my call to make."

"Is this where I tell you I'm innocent and you say, 'I don't care'?"

"I just have one job today, Brock, and that's to guarantee that what you know doesn't fall into the wrong hands. You come with me, well, that's the most favorable outcome for everyone. You take off, I can't promise you anything."

"Except that you'll come after me."

"And I will find you. And I will stop you. It's what I do, and I do it better than anyone."

"Well, I'm with you, so let's get out of here."

"I can't have you disappearing. Thus, the needle."

"Nanobots? Seriously?"

"Trackers, like I said. We inject 'em into you, and I can find you again. You don't let me tag you, I'm gonna assume you don't want to be found."

I debated what to do. At the Pentagon I'd read about the types of trackers he was talking about, but as far as I knew they were still in the experimental stages. Still not approved for human use.

Gunnar scanned the darkness. "We don't have much time. Your choice: I end this now with a bullet in your head to make sure you don't talk, or I bring you with me with the bots in place."

"You drive a hard bargain." I eyed the syringe.

"Just slam the end of it against your thigh and it'll do the rest," he said. Then he added helpfully, "And just so you know: It's gonna hurt."

"With your bedside manner, don't ever become a nurse."

"I'll keep that in mind." He was surveying the area, probing the shadows for Sokolov, who still hadn't resurfaced.

Taking a deep breath, I rather ungracefully stabbed the needle into my left thigh and plunged the nanobots into my leg. Gunnar was right about the pain. A sharp flare shot through me and I needed to close my eyes and clench my teeth to hold it in check.

I tossed the auto-injector into the darkness while he checked an app on his phone that showed him the nanobots' location. He patted my shoulder. "Let's go."

"One sec." I held out my hand. "Let me see that phone."

"Why?"

"To figure out the best way out of here."

After a brief hesitation, he placed it in my palm.

I studied the screen. A pulsing red dot indicated where I was, here in the south wing of the warehouse. I zoomed out. There were dozens of other buildings on the campus, plus a maze of twisting roads. I memorized it all, then handed the phone back to him.

"Got it."

He looked at me curiously. "Got what?"

"I know how to get us through the building, off the campus, and back to the hotel. It's about six miles from here."

"All that from just glancing at the screen?"

"I tend to recall details pretty well. It's my . . . I guess you could say it's my gift."

"Alright, let's—"

Sokolov shot at us again, a rapid battery of bullets clanging off the nearby machinery. Clearly, he hadn't slipped away after all, although I had no idea what he'd been up to while Gunnar and I had been talking.

"I have some photographs coming through," Sokolov announced loudly, "that you're going to want to see."

"What are they?" Gunnar called.

"I'll show you in a moment."

I didn't like this, and by the way Gunnar tightened up, it didn't look like he was too keen on the idea either. "Steady," he said to me. "I need to see what this is all about."

—∾—

On the way to the break room, Cliff's balance left him. He felt himself slumping to the floor, but Joshua was quick to support him, lowering him gently onto his back.

"Is he alright?" Mackenzie asked concernedly.

"I'm not sure." Joshua felt Cliff's pulse. "Sir, do you have pain in your chest?"

Cliff nodded faintly. He really was not feeling well at all. "It's this crushing pressure, spreading out into my arm."

Joshua leaned over Cliff to check his breathing, then said anxiously to Mackenzie, "I think he might be having a heart attack."

"Oh, mercy."

"Call an ambulance."

"I don't have a phone," she said, wringing her hands. "We're not allowed to have mobile phones in here. I'll have to use the landline in the office."

"Go. Hurry. I'll stay with him."

—m—

"I need to show you something," Dr. Chia-hao Yong said into his microphone.

His hand trembled as he unpocketed his wife's finger.

In the balance of all that mattered to him, he'd realized that if Su-wei knew that her safety might endanger thousands or tens of thousands of people, she would want them protected, no matter what it might mean for her personally. And, once Chia-hao came to that conclusion, he knew what he needed to do: He needed to get the truth out there.

And he would have done it.

He would have held the amputated finger up. Yes, he would've shown it to the conference attendees and told them everything. But just as he was about to do so, a woman leapt to her feet in the middle of the auditorium and shouted, "The blood of the innocents is on your hands! The Pruninghooks Collective declares it so!"

She lifted a bottle filled with dark red liquid, unscrewed the cap, and splashed the bottle's contents out across the audience.

Cries and screams erupted as the attendees discovered what it was.

"Blood!" someone shrieked. "It's blood!"

Security personnel hastened down the aisle to stop the activist, but she was in the middle of her row and with so many people surrounding her, there was no good way for them to reach her.

Chia-hao watched helplessly as the crowd near her pushed and shouldered their way toward the aisles, scrambling frantically to get away.

Then another protestor rose in the back of the room and started shouting invectives against the nuclear industry and the United States' military-industrial complex, condemning all who worked for the government. He ended by chanting, "Ban nukes; wage peace! Ban nukes; wage peace!"

Don't these people know we're on their side? Chia-hao thought as he stared in shock at the chaos spreading across the lecture hall.

A security guard made it to the first protestor and tried to subdue her, but she resisted violently, kicking at him and splashing a second bottle of blood into his face.

As the frenzied scene unfolded before him, Chia-hao tried to figure out what to do. It might already be too late, but, hoping to disrupt anything he might have already initiated with the USB drive, he tore it from his laptop.

Two thickset security officers hustled toward him from the side of the stage. "We need you to come with us," one of them said insistently.

"I did not mean to," Chia-hao said, fumbling for what to tell them. "I just . . . I . . ."

"Your wife, sir. She's alright. We have her."

"What? Where? Where is she?"

"Come with us. We'll take you to her."

—∞—

As the school buses arrived at World's Fair Park in downtown Knoxville, hundreds of middle-school students poured out of them, glad to be missing class for whatever reason, even if it was just some lame speech about how you're not supposed to bully people.

Totally predictable.

Totally boring.

Didn't matter. They weren't in a classroom. It was a good day.

One bus after another dropped off the students, who shuffled in loose lines behind their teachers through the sunny, gusty day toward the seats of the open-air amphitheater at the base of the glistening and historic Sunsphere, oblivious of the RDX explosives and the ticking timer planted in the observation deck two hundred and fifty feet above their heads.

PART V

Damp Earth

While Gunnar and I waited to hear from Sokolov again, I studied the route I was planning to take to get us out of here.

Narrow steel ladders rose above us and hitched themselves to the rusted catwalks that spanned the dark expanse of the vast building. Railed walkways arched over the maze of pipes that wandered around the tanker truck–sized turbines and containment units.

As I mentally charted our course to the far side of the warehouse, Gunnar said, "Do you think this place is contaminated with radiation?"

"I wouldn't lick those pipes."

"That's not quite what I was thinking, but thanks for the warning. Point is, we should be alright?"

"As long as we don't spend too much time in here."

"You think Sokolov's trying to inveigle us into giving up?"

When I didn't reply, he must've thought I wasn't tracking with him. "It means to induce someone to do something," he told me.

"Yes. Kind of an uncommon word."

He looked past me in Sokolov's direction. "I'm a writer. I'm using it in my book."

"What do you write?"

"Romance novels."

I blinked. "Romance novels?"

"Well, I'm still on my first one. The heroine's love interest, Donovan, is try-ing to inveigle her into the bedroom. If we get out of this alive, I'll share some of it with you." He scrutinized the desk. Sokolov hadn't spoken since promising us that he had photographs coming through that we would want to see.

What are they? I wondered, trying not to let my imagination get the best of me. *What sort of photos would a Russian assassin have with him, and why would he think we needed to see them?*

"This isn't right," Gunnar said under his breath. "He's stalling. We need to get out of here. Besides, I'm almost out of ammo."

"Didn't you bring extra clips or magazines or whatever?"

He shrugged. "I brought enough to kill you."

"Right," I said. "What do you propose?"

"We move. Get low, and stay close."

We edged out, but as soon as we did, Sokolov's head popped up from the other side of the desk and he fired a salvo of bullets in our direction. They dinged off the nearby metal and ricocheted off the concrete just three or four feet from me. Gunnar and I both scrambled back to our spots.

I was about to ask him what other options we had when I saw him cring-ing and holding his left shoulder, just beyond the reach of his body armor's protection.

"Okay," he muttered. "Adrenaline's gonna help for a little while, but then that sucker's gonna hurt like hell."

"You're hit?" I caught my breath.

"Just my shoulder. Nothing vital. A little shrapnel."

He tapped his body armor.

He'd been hit at an oblique angle and the ballistic plate protecting his chest had taken the brunt of the round, which had fragmented into his shoul-der. Blood was dampening his shirt.

"You good?"

"Looks worse than it is."

I wasn't so sure about that.

"And your gun's almost out of ammo?"

He held it up. "Two rounds left." I thought he might add something like, "One for you and one for me," but instead he said, "Unless I didn't count right. And I tend to be pretty good at math."

—∞—

Cliff tried to process what was happening. A heart attack? It couldn't be, could it? His dad had died of a heart attack, but that was when he was seventy, not fifty-two.

So had Presnell.

So . . .

Involuntarily, he clutched at his chest.

If you die, they won't know about the microchips. Joshua won't tell them. He'll . . .

Mackenzie had gone to the HEUMF's front door to wait for the paramedics to arrive. Before leaving them, she'd assured them she would be right back. "The ambulance is one of Y-12's. It should be here shortly."

Now, Cliff said weakly to Joshua, "We need to tell her about the chips."

"Don't concern yourself with that. I'll take care of everything. You just rest. It won't be long now."

"Before they get here?" The room was swimming around him.

Joshua was silent.

"What?" A sense of dread began worming its way into Cliff's consciousness. "What is it?"

"I need to tell you something." Joshua took a deep breath. "I'm sorry, Senator, but it was necessary. There's a much bigger plan at work here."

"What do you mean? What was necessary?"

"You're dying, Cliff."

"What?" His voice was faltering. It sounded like someone else speaking. "What did you do to me?"

"The same thing I did to Senator Presnell. It'll be recorded as natural causes. A heart attack."

"No . . . I . . ."

"It's started. It's taking effect. It's already too late."

"That's not—"

"Shh." Joshua placed a calming finger against Cliff's lips. "It's almost over. I need to say that we couldn't have done this without you. Your contacts and the help you provided regarding the supply chain vulnerabilities for the microchips was invaluable. I wish you could be around to see the results of your handiwork, but I'm afraid that's not going to be possible."

Cliff's thoughts were becoming blurrier and more difficult to rein in, but even as he started to lose track of everything else, one thought remained clear in his mind; one thought would not stop plaguing him: *You're responsible for this. Joshua is doing something with the chips, and you're the one to blame.*

"You should be thankful." Joshua patted Cliff's forearm gently. "There's no greater honor than to die in the service of a cause that will live beyond you, to give your life for the betterment of humankind. You can take comfort in that. All too many people die without ever knowing their purpose. Yours was to effectuate change, to usher in a more sustainable, compassionate, and peaceful world."

—m—

"I'm prepared to offer you a deal," Sokolov called to us.

I was surprised when Gunnar replied, "I'm listening."

"What are you doing?" I whispered.

He held up a finger. "Shh."

Sokolov slid a cell phone out from where he was hiding behind the desk. It spun across the pockmarked concrete in our general direction, but hit a divot and came to a rest about fifteen feet from me.

"I think you'll want to see what's on there, Travis," Sokolov said.

Gunnar grabbed my arm. "You can't go out there. It might be a trap. That phone could be wired to explode."

"By all accounts," I said, "he wants me alive more than you do. He's not going to kill me."

"I don't like it."

"That makes two of us, but what options do we have? You're shot. We're almost out of ammo. He's got that rifle, and as far as we know, he has reinforcements coming. Let's at least find out what's on that phone."

Gunnar chewed his lip for a second, then held out his gun to me. "Take Saundra. You get close to him, you take him out."

"Saundra?"

He shrugged. "Ex-girlfriend. Long story." He gave me a quizzical look. "You ever shoot anyone before?"

"I tried to. Earlier today. Safety was on, but—look, I'm sure you're a far better shot than I am. You keep her. I'll try to draw Sokolov out, get him to show himself. And when I do, take him out."

Gunnar nodded.

"Well?" Sokolov called. "The longer we wait, the—"

"I'm coming," I replied.

I eased out of hiding and held up my hands to show that I wasn't carrying any weapons.

Sokolov had said he was offering us a deal. I had no idea what that might be.

Easy, Travis. Easy.

Anxious about the photos and hoping that neither of these two guys would shoot me, I headed warily toward the phone to find out what types of pictures it might contain.

CHAPTER 60

When the paramedics arrived, Cliff tried to tell them what was happening, what Joshua was doing to him, but as hard as he tried, he couldn't seem to form any actual words.

And then his opportunity was gone. The EMTs positioned an oxygen mask over his nose and mouth and told him *to be calm* and *not to worry* and that *everything was going to be alright*.

He tried to point to Joshua, but found that both of his arms had been strapped down to keep them from tipping off the sides of the gurney.

"Take him to Knoxville," Joshua told the paramedics. "Advent Regional Medical Center."

"Oak Ridge has a hospital that's closer," one of the men offered.

"We have protocols in place," Joshua said vaguely. "He's a senator. You need to transport him to the most advanced care facility in the area."

Cliff watched, helpless and terrified, as the man who'd poisoned him held up the fake congressional aide ID. "I'm his aide."

But the paramedic wasn't convinced. "He could die on the way there."

"He could die while you're standing here arguing with me. Let's go."

"Alright." A sigh. "It's your call."

Please, no, Cliff thought. *It can't end like this.*

"It's fastest down this way." Joshua pointed, and without questioning his directions, the EMTs wheeled the gurney past the shelves containing the smaller uranium containers.

Forgive me, Keith. Cliff wanted to say the words aloud, but all he could do was think them and hope that somehow, somewhere his brother heard them. *I wanted to do what was right. To help our country. I wanted to. I tried.*

He craned his neck and just managed to see Joshua pick up two of the smaller u-235 canisters and slide them inside his jacket. As stealthy as he was, Cliff doubted that anyone else noticed.

And he was right. No one else saw a thing. Everyone was too focused on the man who was dying on the gurney, the United States senator they were rolling toward the exit.

But there'll be sensors at the door, Cliff reassured himself. *They'll go off. He won't be able to get those out of here.*

Unless . . .

The microchips.

—∞—

Carefully, and without making any sudden moves, I bent down and picked up Sergei Sokolov's phone.

When I saw the first image, I swallowed hard.

Adira. She had on the brunette wig that she'd worn earlier. Even though her face was partially obscured, it was definitely her. There was no doubt about it.

She was approaching her CR-V. The photo had been taken from inside the vehicle.

"There are more," Sokolov called to me. "Swipe through to the end."

—∞—

Joshua Godfrey hesitated slightly when they reached the HEUMF's exit. If the alarms went off, everything would be for naught.

Steeling himself and trusting that his mother had taken care of things, he walked forward.

Silence.

No klaxons.

No sirens.

Nothing.

Though he felt a wash of relief, things were not over yet. He still needed to deliver the canisters, still needed to make sure the RDD in the Sunsphere went off.

After retrieving his cell phone from security, he climbed into the back of the ambulance. The senator's wide eyes stared up at him as he tried to say something, but the words were lost to his fatigue and the oxygen mask over his face.

"Don't worry, sir." Joshua took his hand. "I'm here. I'm not going anywhere until this is over."

—⁂—

The series of fifteen photos showed Adira climbing into the vehicle, setting her purse on the seat next to her, and then keying the ignition. She didn't appear to have any idea that she was being photographed. The final picture revealed the tattooed arm of the person who'd been taking the photos. He was gripping a serrated hunting knife and holding it firmly against the front of her neck.

No, no, no. You have to stop him. You have to save her!

"He has Adira, Travis," Sokolov said to me. "Ilya does. And he's waiting to hear from me. If I don't contact him in the next two minutes, he's going to kill her."

I processed everything, tried to sort out if there was a workable alternative here, a solution that could bring a positive outcome, but every scenario I thought of ended with someone dying. An ache in my throat made it tough to speak. "What do you want from me?"

"The man who's with you, have him slide his gun out and step into view. Then you come with me, and she walks. Either she lives or she dies. The decision is up to you."

"And this man here?" I pointed toward where Gunnar was hiding. "The one you've been shooting at?"

"I think you know what needs to happen."

I half-expected one of Gunnar's final bullets to hit me as he made sure that I wouldn't betray our country by helping the Russians.

But it did not.

Instead, Saundra came skidding out of our hiding place and ended up just a few yards from my feet.

What's he doing?

"Hands where I can see them!" Sokolov commanded Gunnar.

"I was hit in the left shoulder," he replied from the shadows. "I can't raise that arm."

With that, he emerged, his right hand held high, his left arm hanging limply at his side.

Sokolov stood, his rifle aimed at Gunnar. For a moment, all was still. Just the two men staring stiffly at each other. The rain peppering the roof high above us.

Gunnar looked my way. "Just remember. Saundra's not safe."

"What?" Sokolov said. "What's—?"

"She likes to be lit up."

"What are you talking about?" Sokolov demanded.

It was clear to me that Gunnar was telling me in his own way to go for his gun, that the safety was off, that I should take the shot.

You already tried to kill one man today. You can do it.

Saundra was just two quick strides away. I wasn't certain I could get to her and fire at Sokolov before he could kill me, but I decided there was no more time for debate. I needed to act.

Sokolov doesn't want you dead. He won't shoot you.

Without another thought, I made my move, rushing toward the gun. But Sokolov's self-preservation instinct must have kicked in or else he'd changed his mind about wanting me alive, because he fired at me.

I couldn't tell how close the bullets were to my face, but it seemed as if they whizzed directly past me before sparking off the machines just ten feet to my right.

As I ducked low to grab Saundra, out of the corner of my eye, I saw Gunnar reach behind his back with his injured arm, whip out another pistol, and fire three rapid shots into Sergei Sokolov's chest.

The Russian fell heavily to the ground.

"I thought you were unarmed," I said to Gunnar, catching my breath.

"So did he." He cradled his left arm, clearly in pain.

"Another girlfriend?"

"Yeah." He patted his gun affectionately. "Maureen."

—⁂—

Dr. Chia-hao Yong held his wife as she wept in his arms.

They were in a security suite bustling with nearly a dozen police officers and hotel guards. A paramedic was attending to Su-wei's hand.

Chia-hao felt a wave of relief that she was safe at last and beside him. He gently brushed her tears away and wished that he could make it so that she would never cry again.

The drive—what did it do? What have you set into motion here today?

One of the police officers said to him, "Sir, can you ask your wife if she can tell us anything about her abductors? How many there were? It could help us tremendously if we had a description of them."

Chia-hao translated the questions to her. She responded at once, asking urgently for a conference program.

"Do you have a schedule of the summit?" he asked the officer.

The man retrieved a printed conference booklet containing the schedule of events and list of presenters. Su-wei quickly flipped through the pages until she came to the photographs of the guest speakers. She located Janice Daniels's picture beside the description of a breakout session she was scheduled to facilitate and planted a finger directly on the billionaire's face.

The officer stared at her, aghast. "You're saying it was this woman here? I know you were in her suite, but . . . You're sure she's the one behind all this?"

Chia-hao translated and Su-wei nodded, then spoke to him again.

"And two men in suits," he told the officers, relaying what she'd said. "Very tall."

—⁂—

As Adira studied the man in the rearview mirror who held the knife to her throat, she berated herself for not checking the back of the SUV before getting in.

A stupid mistake. One that might prove to be fatal.

He hadn't asked her to drive anywhere yet, and she didn't know exactly what he wanted, but she recognized him as the Russian from the interrogation room at L & L Manufacturing yesterday.

A few moments ago he'd disarmed her when she closed the car door, then tossed the PSM that she'd taken from the hotel into the back of the vehicle, far out of reach—which surprised her, since she thought he would've kept it for himself, since it'd been his to begin with.

You were handcuffed the last time you fought this guy. At least that's not the case now.

She thought about asking him how he'd found her but decided not to bother. The footage that the police had released of her in the airport parking garage might've been all he needed.

Stay calm. The more tense you are, the more mistakes you'll make.

"Where does this leave us?" she asked him, careful not to move too much with the knife's blade pressed against her vocal cords. "What do you want from me?"

"We go to Knoxville."

He knows. He's involved. It's all connected.

"The hospital," she said, piecing two and two together.

"Advent Regional Medical Center. Yes."

"Why?"

"Just drive."

She debated whether to reach down and release the seat and jam it backward. Maybe she could surprise him, knock him back in his seat, go for the knife . . .

No.

Only as a last resort.

With the blade securely in hand, he still had too much of a tactical advantage. He was behind her. He had the ability to easily take her out. She needed to wait, to bide her time.

He's taking you to the right place. Stop this once you get there.

Two credit cards with sharpened edges were in her wallet, which was currently in her purse on the seat beside her, but she couldn't reach into it without attracting attention.

"You drive," he said again in his thickly accented English. "I tell you where."

She decided she needed to go for the cards and slowly reached for her purse.

"No!" he ordered her.

"I need some more bubble gum," she said truthfully.

He tightened the blade against her throat with one hand and, to her surprise, fished through her purse with the other hand to get her the gum. He retrieved it, gave it to her, and then set the purse beside him in the back rather than placing it in the front again.

Crap. That didn't quite work.

She unwrapped a piece, popped it into her mouth, and started to chew.

Then, evaluating all of her options, she pulled out of the parking lot and hopped onto Highway 162 toward Knoxville.

If she could retrieve those credit cards and get her assailant out of the car, she just might stand a chance.

—⁂—

"I have to say," Gunnar admitted, "I didn't think Sokolov would fire at you." He was bent over the Russian, checking his pulse to ascertain that he was not going to be a threat to us anymore. "I didn't see that coming."

"Neither did I." It took me a moment of scrounging around in the shadows until I found my glasses. I slipped them on. "I was the decoy? By going for the gun?"

"We needed to flip the script. You did good."

Sokolov had told me that if he didn't contact Ilya within two minutes, the man would kill Adira. I checked the phone with her photos on it and saw that the last message was a text, written in English rather than Russian. Based on that, it looked like Ilya was expecting a written reply, not a spoken one. **Get Brock**, it read. **Text me when done.**

That played in our favor, because even though I knew a little Russian from my years of living with Sienna, I was glad I didn't have to translate anything here with Adira's life on the line.

I have Brock, I texted Ilya. **Wait for me at the hotel.**

"Now what?" Gunnar said.

"I go to the hotel and see how well Ilya follows instructions. And we get you to a hospital so you can get that shrapnel out."

And we do whatever's necessary to find Adira and make sure she's safe.

While I drove Gunnar's car toward the conference center, he sat beside me, doing his best to keep pressure on his wounded shoulder to quell the bleeding. He leaned back against the seat to keep pressure on the exit wound as well.

He quickly filled me in on his background, how he'd come up through the Rangers and then gone to Warrant School at Fort Rucker so he could fly helicopters—then in the same breath he reminded me that I still had those nanobot trackers in my leg, so I'd better not try to run off.

I wasn't sure if he was rambling a bit and jumping from topic to topic because he was feeling loopy from the pain, or if this was normal for him, but I let him talk without interruption.

I was caught up in my own thoughts about Adira. I could hardly believe all that'd happened in the last twenty-four hours—the roller-coaster ride of emotions and how important she'd already become to me. Although I was certainly worried about Dr. Yong and his wife and the consequences if he'd inserted that flash drive during his speech, it was this enigmatic and beguiling Red Team member who was foremost on my mind. Rescuing her. Stopping Ilya from harming her.

"Hang on," Gunnar said to me abruptly, leaving an account of his helicopter exploits in Colombia behind. "Did you know a Detective Caruso? From Metro PD?"

"Yes. He's investigating the arson at my house. He tried contacting me yesterday." Then I added, uneasily, "Why did you put that in the past tense? Did something happen to him?"

"Sokolov and his partner, Ilya Vasiliev, they got to him," Gunnar said between gritted teeth. I didn't know if it was because of pain or rage. Maybe both. "Caruso is dead."

A wave of grief surged inside me. Here was yet another casualty, another tragic example of the violence orbiting around me this week. "The case is still open," I told Gunnar, "but . . . wait—Sapphire. Sokolov mentioned that he thought she might've been responsible for the arson."

"Sapphire who?"

"It's a code name. That's all I know. I think she's also the one who killed Lassiter. Someone from the Red Team."

When I mentioned the Red Team, it brought my thoughts circling around to Adira again and I accelerated down Bethel Valley Road toward the conference center, telling myself that we were going to get there in time.

Yes.

We would make it.

She was going to be okay.

—⁂—

Over the years, Janice Daniels had discovered that people typically acquired tastes in correspondence to their means. The more they earned, the more they bought—but then, rather than resting in contentment, they continued moving along the same trajectory of frantic acquisition again every time their income level rose. Each time telling themselves that they needed just a little more to be happy.

Always just a little more.

Yet never quite enough.

As her own wealth had multiplied, she'd noticed that the types of things that brought her satisfaction had shifted—at first becoming more and more expensive. For instance, when she realized that she could fly to her favorite restaurant in Sicily for dinner and return home to the States during the middle of the night, she'd done exactly that.

But, one day, all of that changed. Her tastes actually became more pedestrian. All because of an auction twelve years ago.

It involved a Gustav Klimt painting that she'd wanted to add to her collection. As the bidding passed $95 million and she contemplated placing another bid, she looked out the window of the auction house and noticed a homeless man going through a dumpster, searching for food.

In that moment, she'd had an epiphany.

That painting was a sheet of canvas—that was all—and she was about to spend nearly one hundred million dollars on it. Simply a piece of fabric—one that she was planning to keep hidden from the world, tucked away behind a pane of glass in her bedroom.

After a quick calculation, she realized that she was bidding on a chance to deprive half a million starving children in Ethiopia of meals for a year, all because she wanted to hang something famous but completely useless on her wall.

The revelation had made her physically ill. She'd needed to excuse herself from the auction and find her way to the washroom to collect herself.

After that day, she'd started to take less pleasure in luxury and more pleasure in the things that didn't cost a dime—sunsets and starlight and the laughter of children.

When you finally got serious about reclaiming your life from the clutches of the urgent, you realized that happiness wasn't found by adding more material goods to your life—more clothes and cars and boats and planes. Those things only made happiness more evanescent and elusive, keeping it continually out of reach.

She'd begun to embrace a simpler way of life: Walking in a spring rain, sipping an unhurried cup of tea, reading mystery novels, unplugging from the Internet for a weekend.

Yes, temporary happiness might come from acquisition and consumption, but true joy only came from simplicity and sacrifice.

In time, she'd stopped looking only at the bottom line and had redefined what she was living for. As the Teacher put it in Ecclesiastes, chapter 5, verse 16, "What profit hath he that hath laboured for the wind?"

She'd been laboring for the wind all of her life, but after that auction, she'd started laboring for the future. For peace. For humanity. For what was best for the planet.

At any cost.

Though Janice had never met Ivan Popovic in person, she'd partnered with him on the natural gas project. He was interested for financial reasons; she had other motives in mind, but together they'd found it to be a mutually beneficial arrangement. Still, she knew what he was capable of, and being in bed with him, so to speak, made her uncomfortable.

In truth, he frightened her. She couldn't prove it, but she'd come to suspect that he was involved in human trafficking and international arms smuggling. Because of that, she'd already decided that when this was over, their relationship would be as well.

From what she understood, Ivan had told the two men, Sokolov and Vasiliev, about the u-235. The plan had never been to have Travis Brock turn up here in Tennessee, but for the time being, that was Popovic's issue to deal with, not hers.

Now, as she stood at the townhouse's living room window gazing out across Knoxville, a text came through from Joshua Godfrey, the young man she'd cared for back when he was a teenager—a son to her in all of the ways that mattered most: **We're en route.**

She could trust Joshua. Despite a number of admittedly uncharitable characteristics, he was reliable and had vowed, because of his love for her, to help her cause, even if it meant offering up his own life in the process—not something she would've ever asked of him, but sacrifices needed to be made for the good of the human race, for the good of the planet, and he'd committed himself unreservedly to that goal.

A soldier who was now fighting for peace.

Turo was on his way to the med center as well. She hadn't heard from Reginald, whom she'd left to take care of Su-wei and Adira at the hotel, but she wasn't worried. Even if Reginald didn't make it to the hospital in time, Turo and Joshua would be able to get the u-235 to the dome of the Sunsphere.

The explosion would occur. Trust in the system would erode, reliance on nuclear power would dissipate, and all of the glorious inhabitants of this fragile, magnificent, miraculous world would be better off and safer than they had been in more than half a century.

CHAPTER 62

At the hotel parking lot, I drove past the spot where Adira and I had left her SUV, but it was gone.

I tried to keep myself from speculating what might have happened to her. Tried to.

But failed.

Gunnar's voice was strained as he said, "You know how I mentioned that the adrenaline would only help for so long?"

"You're starting to feel that shoulder."

"Roger that."

Keeping Saundra on my lap, I dropped Gunnar off at the front of the hotel so he could speak with the security personnel about what was going on and hopefully get some medical attention. Then, I drove through each of the five interconnected parking lots for the hotel and the conference center, but saw no sign of Ilya, Adira, or her car.

How are you going to find them?

I had Sokolov's phone with me, but I didn't think I should chance sending another text to Ilya. He hadn't replied to my earlier message instructing him to meet at the hotel, so maybe he hadn't even received it—or maybe he'd figured out that I wasn't really Sokolov.

Tense and troubled, I returned to the hotel's main entrance to regroup and figure out the next step.

A police officer was waiting for me when I arrived. "Please come with me, Mr. Brock," he said, his voice stoic and impossible to read. "I'm here to escort you to the security suite. You'll be briefed when we arrive."

I had no idea how much trouble I was in, but whatever happened to me was secondary to my concern for Adira's safety. "Have you found her?" I asked him urgently. "Did your team locate Adira?"

"Not yet, no."

It's okay, I thought. *They will. You will.*

The state-of-the-art suite was teeming with police officers and a knot of harried hotel security personnel.

Dr. Yong stood beside a woman who had a blood pressure cuff on her arm and was being monitored by an EMT. Her bandaged hand testified to what'd happened to her finger, but apart from that, thankfully, she appeared to be unharmed.

A satellite feed had been set up in the corner of the room. Two officers were on the phone while they consulted a search grid on an expansive video screen. I couldn't immediately tell if they were trying to pinpoint Adira's location or find the people who'd abducted Su-wei.

Gunnar sat shirtless on a chair in the corner. A paramedic was carefully bandaging his shoulder and arguing with him about going to the hospital. When the former Ranger saw me, he said, "It's Janice Daniels. She's behind this. That's why they took Su-wei—to get Chia-hao to put the drive in while he gave his talk."

"Janice Daniels?" I said quizzically. "That makes no sense."

"I know, right? What's that they say about power corrupting people? No one's immune."

I'd never met the billionaire before, but she was well-known for her philanthropic endeavors around the world and for her work battling homelessness and childhood hunger.

Why would she be involved? Is someone forcing her to help?

While the EMT helped Gunnar slip on a green scrubs top, I asked Dr. Yong if he'd inserted the drive. He nodded. "Did anything happen?" I asked.

"Nothing that I know of."

But something *had* to have happened. Why else would they have threatened him and kidnapped and then attacked Su-wei the way they did?

The cop who'd shepherded me into the room led me to the officer who appeared to be in charge. Early forties. Wiry. Buzz cut. Focused. He nodded a brisk greeting to me rather than offering his hand. "Detective Hauer."

"Travis Brock," I said. Then, as Gunnar joined us, with his left arm draped in a sling, I added, "I'm with the Department of Defense. Is there any word on Adira Halprin? Anything at all?"

"Doing all we can to find her," Hauer told me in a quick burst of a sentence. "We know she helped Su-wei. In the process, one of Daniels's bodyguards took a dive off the eighth-floor balcony. We're not sure if your friend had anything to do with that. We're still trying to sort everything out."

"Ilya Vasiliev has her," I explained quickly. "We have to find him before he . . . Well, we have to find them. Now."

"I told him already," Gunnar said to me. "They've got Highway Patrol out looking for the SUV. We've got SAR sats on the job as well."

"What about Y-12?" I asked Hauer. "Did anything happen there while Dr. Yong was giving his speech?"

"As far as we can tell, the flash drive didn't adversely affect their system files. Their techs are analyzing them as we speak to make sure. We do know that Senator Richardson was in the HEUMF during the speech. He had a heart attack."

"Wait—what?"

"Richardson, the senator from California. I know. It's been a crazy morning."

"Is he alright?"

"Last I heard, he was in critical condition and was being transported to Advent Regional Medical Center in Knoxville."

I processed that. It was a lot to take in.

Janice Daniels is involved. If you find her, you might find Adira.

"What else do we know about Daniels?" I said. "I mean, I know she's a billionaire, gives away millions every year, but what's her motive? What's behind all this?"

"We're not sure," Detective Hauer admitted. "And so far, we haven't been able to locate her or her other bodyguard."

I placed Sergei's cell on the table and explained that I'd texted Ilya but hadn't heard back from him yet. "Maybe we can track his phone?" Then I had a thought.

"And let's analyze any other numbers that've called or texted this phone in the last twenty-four hours. See where that leads."

Hauer nodded and got started studying the cell.

"Let me check the room Adira and I were using," I said. "Maybe she left some indication of where she's gone."

Taking one of the hotel's security personnel and a police officer along with me, I headed to Alvarez's room on the fifth floor.

―⁂―

As the ambulance carrying Senator Richardson raced toward the hospital, Joshua watched the paramedics busy themselves with monitoring the vital signs of the dying senator.

Look concerned, he reminded himself, *then make the delivery, and ensure that the explosion occurs.*

―⁂―

The hotel guard unlocked 513 for us and we found Adira's suitcase beside the bed, but her purse and the DHS tablet were missing. If Alvarez had been back to the room, he hadn't left any indication of his presence. Everything appeared to be just like I remembered it. No clues pointing to where she might be.

Frustrated and empty-handed, we made our way back to the security suite. I shouldered past the other officers and found Hauer near the phone, which was on the table.

"What do we know?" I asked him.

"Someone named Ivan texted Sergei about an hour ago. Besides his exchange with Ilya, that's all we have. Every other name and number has been erased. The message is, 'He'll have two cylinders. Acquire one of them.' Looks like it was a group text that was also sent to Ilya. Does that mean anything to you? Acquiring a cylinder?"

I shook my head. "No, but let's search for anyone named Ivan who might've worked with Sergei Sokolov at the embassy. And maybe we can find Adira's tablet. She told me it was untraceable, but it's from Homeland. We'll probably need their authorization to track it, but we can at least try putting that into play." I could hear an edge of desperation climbing into my voice. "We've got to do something."

He nodded. "Let me make some calls."

At the moment I wasn't sure what else I could do.

Come on, Travis. Think. How can you find her?

I met up with Gunnar again. He had his cell phone to his ear, and when he saw me coming, he tapped the phone and said to me, "There's someone on the line who'd like to speak with you."

"Who's that?"

Instead of answering, he simply handed me his cell.

"Hello," I said. "This is Brock."

"Travis, it's Colonel Clarke."

CHAPTER 63

C "olonel. Hello."

"It's been a hell of a ride these last twenty-four hours."

To say the least.

"Yes, sir. It has."

"Gunnar brought me up to speed." I thought that Clarke might berate me or question what I'd been doing since I'd left his office yesterday afternoon, but he didn't. Instead, he just said, "I want to do all I can from this end to help you out. What do you need?"

"Can you see if someone from Homeland can trace Adira's tablet? I'm not sure if it'll lead us to her, but it's not here. She might still have it."

"Got it. What else?"

"Sergei Sokolov is dead. He was a Russian diplomat. You might have some explaining to do to the Russian embassy, but he's deeply involved in all this, so we have that on our side. He tried to kill me."

"Gunnar told me. We're on it."

I thought for a moment and realized that, as long as I had the colonel on the line, I might as well ask the question: "Sir, can you get me a list of the TSA's Red Team members? I think one of them is involved with this and might be responsible for Nathan Lassiter's death. Someone known as Sapphire."

"I'll do some checking."

"Also, I don't know how to . . . Sokolov was asking me about Project

Symphony. He was very curious. It keeps coming up. I know it has to do with air gap hacking and Paraden. Is there anything else I need to know?"

"I can't go into it over the phone, but there is a prototype. We—"

And that's when Sokolov's phone vibrated on the table. The cops nearby began to huddle around it.

"Hang on," I said to the colonel. "Something's up. Let me call you back."

—∞—

Sirens blaring, the ambulance screeched to a stop outside the emergency room doors of Knoxville's Advent Regional Medical Center and Joshua watched as the EMTs rolled the gurney out of the back of the vehicle and rushed the senator into the hospital.

The Sunsphere rose proudly above World's Fair Park just two blocks away. Joshua's mom had informed him that he would be meeting with someone named Turo here at the med center, but she hadn't given any more details about what he looked like.

"He'll find you," she'd said.

Now that he was here, Joshua sent her a text that he'd arrived and was ready to deliver the package.

Then he headed inside to wait in the hospital's lobby for a reply.

—∞—

I read the text from Ilya aloud: "Meet me at hospital in twelve minutes."

"Which hospital?" Gunnar asked.

I shook my head. "I don't know. Somewhere close enough for them to have driven to by now. At least that narrows it down." I turned to the officers who were busy at the computer screen in the corner. "Pull up a map of the area."

How would Sokolov reply? What can you write that won't give away that it's not him sending these messages?

Praying that this wouldn't backfire, I texted Ilya: **Change of plans. Brock won't talk. Where are you now?**

So far, we hadn't been able to track Ilya's phone or Adira's tablet, but we did have a way to figure out when the photos were taken. The pictures that Sokolov had shown us had been snapped here, just outside the hotel. By analyzing the hotel's security footage of Adira leaving the lobby, we could nail down precisely when she'd walked to her car.

I paced the room. "Show me all the hospitals within a thirty-minute driving radius of the hotel."

"Oak Ridge's is the closest," Detective Hauer announced.

"How far?"

"Five minutes. Ten tops."

"No." Gunnar shook his head. "Considering the timing of the texts and when she left, that doesn't fit."

I calculated the time between the text messages. "Knoxville would make more sense."

"If they were driving to K-Town," Hauer said, "we're probably looking at either Advent Medical or the children's hospital. They're not far from each other. Both downtown."

"Twelve minutes isn't enough time to get to Knoxville," I said, stating the obvious, "so if the meeting is there, Ilya must have been assuming Sokolov was already en route."

"If he gets to a hospital and Sergei doesn't show up," an officer nearby asked, "he's not going to let Adira—"

"Don't say it," I cut in. "We're going to get there. We'll stop him."

I turned to Hauer. "Send officers to that hospital in Oak Ridge and the two in Knoxville. Look for her vehicle, but do it discreetly. The last thing we want to do is provoke or spook Vasiliev."

While Hauer and his team turned their attention to contacting the local authorities about the hospitals, Gunnar said to me, "We need to get to Knoxville."

"It's too far. Half an hour—and that's with no traffic. We'll never make it in time. Unless . . ."

"Unless?"

I was staring out the window. "We don't drive."

CHAPTER 64

Gunnar followed my gaze to a news helicopter resting on the helipad located on the conference center's roof at the far end of the complex.

I figured that the chopper might very well have been grounded because of the storm. Rain was still coming down in sheets and the wind was still tossing the branches of some nearby trees around, but at least there didn't seem to be as much lightning as there had been earlier when we were in the warehouse.

"You were telling me earlier about how you fly," I said.

"That I was." A quick nod. "Let's do this."

While the officers analyzed their data and made their calls, I grabbed Sokolov's phone. Then, Gunnar and I slipped out of the suite and hastened toward the elevator.

"Okay, listen," I said, "I'm going to play devil's advocate for a second."

"Go ahead."

"First—the obvious—there are thunderstorms in the area."

"I've flown through worse. That model's not ideal for what we need, but we should be alright—as long as the downdrafts don't exceed our lift capabilities."

"What happens then?"

"They slam us into the ground."

"But you can handle that? Avoid that?"

"Absolutely."

"Are you just saying that to reassure me?"

"Yes."

"Great."

We arrived at the elevator.

Once inside, we realized we couldn't get to the top floor without an executive suite key card, but we could get to the seventh floor and take the steps from there. I punched the button.

"Next?" he said.

"You've been shot."

"And you wanted to get me to a hospital to have someone treat it. This is the fastest way to do that. Hospitals have landing pads. It's a perfect win-win."

"Authorization to fly that bird out of here? Will that be a problem?"

"I won't turn on the transponder. Anything else?"

"That about covers it."

"So we do this thing." It sounded more like a conclusion than a question.

"We do it."

As we rode past the first few floors, I asked, "How long do you think it'll take us to fly to downtown Knoxville?"

"In these conditions, hard to say. Probably eight to ten minutes."

That would be cutting it tight.

"You just focus on getting us there," I said. "I'll find out which hospital we're heading to while we're in the air."

The elevator dinged on the fifth floor, and a mother and her son joined us. The boy looked about five or six and immediately started enthusiastically pressing the buttons one at a time. Looking at us apologetically, his mom shooed him away from them.

"Two things are true wherever I've been in the world," Gunnar said, loud enough for the woman to hear.

"What are those?" I asked.

"A smile means the same thing, and kids love to push elevator buttons."

The woman gave him a kind look. Whether they were heading up further or had gotten onto the elevator mistakenly, hoping to take it down, I wasn't sure. Either way, when we reached seven, we left them behind, found the steps, and bounded up them toward the roof.

—∞—

Calculating how she was going to get the jump on the guy seated behind her, Adira turned off the highway toward downtown Knoxville.

If she made a wrong move, all he had to do was jam the blade of his knife through the seat, or reach up and slit her throat and she would be meeting her maker a little before she was ready to.

She angled the rearview mirror toward the purse lying on the seat beside the Russian.

Just get to those credit cards. At least that'll help level the playing field.

—∞—

Joshua watched as four police officers swarmed into the hospital's lobby. They didn't appear to be looking for him; in fact they hurried past without paying him any attention. As they did, he heard one of them say something to his partner about a bomb threat, but they must not have been taking it too seriously, because they weren't ordering the hospital to be evacuated.

Apparently, they didn't know everything, but clearly it was time to move.

Turo hadn't shown up yet and Joshua hadn't heard from his mom, but he realized it wouldn't be wise to wait around here for her contact any longer. Even without him, he could make sure the message was sent.

In honor of his mother and all she believed in, he was going to see this through to the end. He would deliver the u-235 to the Sunsphere himself.

Zeroing his focus in on what lay ahead, he eased past the other people in the waiting room, left the hospital, and started walking directly toward World's Fair Park.

—∞—

The chopper's pilot stood on the roof waiting beneath an overhang, watching the stubborn rain and keeping an eye on his bird.

As we approached him, Gunnar put a hand on my shoulder. "Let me take this. You can back me up." He removed his hand and called to the pilot, "Hey, there. We're going to need to borrow that helicopter."

Borrow. The same term Adira had used yesterday when we were trying to get a car.

Maybe it was a thing.

"What?" the guy said to Gunnar. "Who are you?"

"Name's Bane. I'm a pilot."

He studied Gunnar's scrubs and the sling supporting his left arm. "Right. And I'm the king of France."

As I was reaching for my Pentagon creds to help make our case, Gunnar said to him, "I hate to do this, buddy, but I'm not asking for permission. I'm telling you what's going to happen. We're taking that helicopter."

Agitated, the guy straightened up and took an aggressive step toward Gunnar, but before he could do anything else, Gunnar hauled off and punched him in the jaw hard enough to torque him around backward.

He collapsed, unconscious.

I stared at Gunnar in disbelief. "I thought that only happened in the movies."

He tossed the sling aside and stepped toward the chopper. "Gotta know where to hit 'em."

"Adira would love to know how to do that."

"She probably already does."

Yeah, he was right. She probably did.

"Come on." He hefted himself into the bird with his one good arm. "Let's fly."

—∞—

Children milled around the stands of the open-air amphitheater, texting each other as they waited for the program to begin. Their teachers stood to the side, doing their best to ignore the students' blatant abuse of the schools' cell phone use policies.

In truth, the teachers were as thankful as the kids were to be out of their classrooms.

An emcee walked onstage and shouted into the microphone, "Everybody ready?" When the students responded less than enthusiastically, he went through the, "I can't hear you . . . !" routine several times until they finally made enough noise to satisfy him.

Everyone settled into their seats.

"Our speaker today appears *all over the country*," he gushed, "sharing his message of hope, humor, and inspiration with more than *two hundred thousand* students every year! Let's all welcome former NFL Pro Bowl tight end Jamaal Koban!"

—∞—

Joshua was halfway down the block when an SUV pulled up beside him. A man in the backseat lowered his window, revealing that he had the blade of a tactical knife pressed against the throat of the woman who sat behind the wheel. Joshua didn't recognize either of them.

"Do you have it?" the man asked him roughly.

"Have what?"

"Cylinders. From facility." The guy spoke with a distinctive Russian accent.

"You Turo?"

"I'm his associate. I'll need one of them."

"That's not gonna happen. Who sent you?"

"Popovic."

Joshua paused, studying the man and then gazing down the street toward World's Fair Park. Popovic was working with his mom. Only people who were involved knew that, and that meant his mom trusted them.

Maybe it *would* be better if there were two of them separately delivering the canisters. Otherwise, if he got caught on his way to the Sunsphere, everything would be lost.

Divide and conquer.

He handed one of the cylinders to the Russian and said, "I'll meet you on the observation deck." Then he turned his steps toward the Sunsphere again and hurried on his way.

—∞—

Adira wasn't sure who that man outside the car was or what he was carrying, but when the Russian accepted the canister from him, she knew she needed to act, *now*.

With the blade angled against her windpipe, she didn't dare lean forward—but backward was still an option. As she slipped her left hand down toward the seat release lever, the man behind her bent close to her ear and whispered, "Goodbye, Adira."

"I told you yesterday . . ." She released the seat and threw her weight backward even as she swept her right hand up to grab his wrist to keep the knife from slicing her neck. "It's Flower Girl!"

The blade grazed the bottom of her chin, but she could live with that. Her throat, that would've been a different story.

As he struggled to reposition himself, she went for the knife's handle, but he managed to hold on to it and twist his arm free from her grip. He tumbled out of the car, scrambled to his feet, and bolted down the street, canister in one hand, knife in the other.

Adira blanched as she realized that securing whatever was in that cylinder was more important to him than killing her was. That could not be good.

The two men had taken off in opposite directions.

Of the two, the Russian was closer. She had the best shot at stopping him.

Snatching up her purse with the credit cards, she exited the car and chased him toward a Cuban restaurant at the end of the block. He briefly glanced her way as he pushed open the door and burst inside.

As she pursued him, Adira tugged out her wallet and tossed the purse. She pocketed the cards in stride, then shoved her way past two pedestrians, blew through the door into the restaurant, and saw the Russian escaping into the kitchen. She sprinted toward him and caught up with him before he could exit.

The cook and other kitchen workers fled, leaving the two of them alone.

Moving forward slowly, Adira cornered the Russian near the stove. Soup was boiling on the front burner. A knife block waited near the sink. Both were close. Plenty of options for her, if she needed them.

The guy white-knuckled his knife. "Been looking forward to this."

"Good to know I've been on your mind. A girl hates being ignored." She indicated the canister he was holding in his other hand. "You're not leaving here with that."

"Only one of us will walk out of here," he replied.

"Well, I'm not gonna carry you, but I'm glad to let you crawl. In fact, if you want to get on your hands and knees right now, it could save us both—"

And with that, he went at her.

CHAPTER 65

Turbulence from the wind rocked us as we soared toward Knoxville. Lots of noise as well—both from the engine and the storm.

When we'd first boarded, Gunnar had looked around, impressed by the helicopter's capabilities. "Sweet." He'd tapped the control settings. "I've only seen this once before."

"What is it?" I'd asked.

"This baby's got Bluetooth. You can use Sokolov's phone through the headsets. It'll be a ton easier to make calls if you need to."

Now, using that Bluetooth connection with Sokolov's phone, I heard from Detective Hauer, who was not very excited about our little excursion in the helicopter. However, I could deal with the fallout from our decision later. I just wanted to find Adira in time.

Hauer informed me that a police lieutenant in Knoxville had just told him that a woman had called the department earlier in the morning, warning them that someone was going to set off a dirty bomb at a Knoxville hospital.

I smacked the console in front of me. "How come we didn't know this earlier?"

"Good question." Hauer's words were laced with the same anger I felt. "But we know it now."

Maybe it was Janice and her bodyguard who had the dirty bomb. Maybe it was Vasiliev. Either way, I advised Hauer to evacuate the two downtown hospitals. "We need to do it. At this point we don't have a choice."

He agreed and told me he would get it rolling.

End call.

A bolt of lightning punctured the sky near us and the nearly instantaneous *boom* of thunder rattled my teeth. The navigational needle dialed around to point in the direction of the electrical activity. Gunnar muttered something unintelligible under his breath, took us lower, and piloted us through the whipping wind and driving rain toward Knoxville.

—◊—

Adira had a lot to overcome.

It wasn't just the Russian's size and strength, but also her own injuries—her forearm, cut and tender from her fight with Lurch. Her bruised leg. Her tweaked ankle.

This had not been her day.

The Russian set down the canister and, knife in his right hand, cocked back his left fist, telegraphing his intentions. Adira poised herself, but when she ducked out of the way of the blade coming at her, he punched her hard, landing a brisk and stunning uppercut to her gut, catching her by surprise.

He'd driven her backward, away from the stove, but a fire extinguisher was within reach. She snatched it up, aimed it at him, and depressed the trigger.

Nothing. Expired.

Brilliant.

She tried to smash it against his skull, but he expertly deflected it, nearly knocking it from her hand. However, she held on and was able to use it to block the knife as he sliced it at her throat.

She threw her elbow up, connecting solidly with his jaw, and drove him back a step.

From where she stood, the knives on the counter were still out of reach. When he saw her eyeing them, he slid the knife block even further back.

She took advantage of the moment to kick him in the groin. As he buckled forward, she kneed him violently in the face, sending him reeling backward.

He composed himself faster than she thought he would and straightened up. She swung the fire extinguisher toward his temple to end this, but he blocked it with his forearm, one-handedly wrenched it from her, and launched it furiously across the room.

She collected herself. Assessed her position. Her assets.

And his.

He has a combat knife.

Her training kicked in: *Stop the attacker first. Worry about disarming him second.*

Most of the time when someone has a sharp weapon, you want to keep your distance. However, when they have a blunt weapon, you move in closer to take away their ability to swing it at you.

Blunt, rush in. Sharp, stay away.

She backed up around the counter toward the stove again.

A weapon could actually become a distraction.

If you knew what you were doing in a fight, you could take advantage of the inclination that someone with a weapon has to keep ahold of it, even if that puts them at a momentary disadvantage. Knives, guns, nightsticks—it was instinct to attempt to hold on and regroup rather than take out the person you were fighting by another means.

Knowing that, she grabbed the handle of the soup pot and was about to throw the boiling liquid in his face, but he kicked her sore leg out from under her, making her drop the soup and slip on it, toppling her onto the steaming linoleum.

When she tried to press herself up, she burned her hand and had to scuttle sideways and roll to her feet to evade his kick. As she did, she went for her back pocket and retrieved the credit cards.

When the Russian saw her holding them, one in each hand, she thought he might scoff or laugh at her, but he didn't. Instead, he seemed to focus more intently on what he was doing and, as he drew nearer to her, he appeared to do so warily.

Then, he swooped in, and she went at him, one hand toward his throat, the other toward his arm. He'd raised the knife and, though she couldn't get to his neck, she swept the second card up against the underside of his right arm, near his armpit, then leapt back.

He licked his lips once, then gave her a curious look as his sleeve began to turn red where she'd sliced him.

"What is—?" he began.

"That's your brachial artery. It's not going to take you long to bleed out."

After a short internal debate, she made a decision. "Take off your belt and cinch it around your arm above that cut if you want to live."

Instead, he shambled unevenly toward her.

"I'm telling you, with your elevated pulse you don't have much time. Do it now."

He swung a meaty fist at her and she ducked and tried to swipe one of the cards against his ribcage, but he made it out of the way before she could reach him.

He fumbled a little as he walked her way and she doubted he would have much fight left in him after a few more seconds.

All at once, he stumbled to his knees and toppled heavily forward. He quavered there on the linoleum as the blood surged from his slit artery and pooled around him.

Kicking the knife away from his hand, Adira went for his phone and the canister, which she found to be astonishingly heavy.

One container down. One to go.

The Russian stopped quivering and the flow of blood eased to a trickle.

She ran to the restaurant's dining area, where four people remained, huddled in the corner. "There's a man hurt in kitchen. He's bleeding really badly. Get a doctor in there right away!"

Outside on the street again, she scanned the area but saw no sign of the man who had possession of the remaining canister. She studied the one in her hand and saw from the label that it was u-235. A radiation warning symbol appeared on the side.

Oh.

That was bad.

Very bad.

Turning her attention to the Russian's phone, she read the most recent texts from someone named Sergei and thought, *Screw it*.

She punched the call button.

—m—

Through the chopper's Bluetooth, Sokolov's phone rang in my headphones.

I hesitated before answering. It could be Ilya, and my Russian wasn't nearly good enough to fake being Sergei. If it was him, he would realize right off the bat that I wasn't his contact—but maybe I could offer a trade. My life for hers. I went ahead and accepted the call. "Hello?"

A questioning voice: "Who is this?"

"Wait—Adira? Is that you?"

"Travis?"

"Yeah!" *She's alive!* "Are you okay? Are you safe?"

"A little beat up," she replied. "Bleeding. Burned. Bruised. Other than that, intact. And you?"

"Good. Where are you?"

"Downtown Knoxville. Listen—if I'm right, Janice Daniels is going to set off an RDD here in the city. I thought it was at a hospital, but I'm not sure anymore. The guy with the canister said something about an observation deck and he was on foot, heading away from the med center."

"Canister?"

"It's u-235, Travis. He's got at least fifteen pounds of it. Janice said something about eleven o'clock and so did Lassiter's text to me yesterday. This could go down at any time."

Glancing out the window, I could see that we were nearing the city.

"I need to talk to Colonel Clarke," I said. "I'll call you back."

Uranium-235? It was an odd choice for a dirty bomb, but depending on the type of detonator and explosive device, it could be devastating in a highly populated area. There was even a DOD program that'd been developed to find ways to disseminate it using a new type of detonator with RDX as the conventional explosive.

The compromised plans from Paraden Defense Systems. That's it. That's how it's all related.

I entered the colonel's number and my access code. Clarke picked up. Quickly, I summarized what was happening.

"Do we know the target?" he asked.

"No, sir, but apparently it's somewhere with an observation deck."

"Terrorists try to make statements. They go for show, for symbolic importance. If it's a dirty bomb, they'll very likely look for something emblematic or iconic."

"I don't know the city well, but I'm on it. Colonel, you need to have NSA send a text to everyone in downtown Knoxville to shelter in place." Only after

I said that did I realize we'd already ordered the hospitals to be evacuated. "Everyone. Even people on the streets. They need to find protection. It's u-235, so any sort of solid deterrent or physical barrier will help."

"Got it. Done. Still working on that list of Red Team members for you. I should have it in the next few minutes. I'll text you what I find."

"Thanks."

He hung up.

Gunnar asked, "Is that something NSA can actually do? Text everyone in a certain location regardless of their cell phone carriers?"

"Oh, yeah," I said. "They don't advertise it, but they can do it."

I had no idea how Gunnar was managing to control the pain in his shoulder while piloting the chopper. He might've taken some pain meds before I arrived at the security suite, but since paramedics aren't typically authorized to prescribe medicine, I doubted it.

This guy was starting to seriously impress me.

"So," he said, "we're no longer heading to a hospital?"

"No. But I'm going to find out where we need to go."

I started searching online for an iconic site with an observation deck within walking distance of the med center.

CHAPTER 66

"I meet students all over this country," Jamaal Koban intoned to the nine hundred-plus middle-school children in the amphitheater. "Students who've been mocked and made fun of and hurt. Who've been belittled and cut down and teased just for being who they are. Cyberbullying is unacceptable! It has no place in our world today. How many of you have ever had someone share something about you online that you didn't want shared? Hands up." He encouraged them to join him by holding his own hand high. "Let's see those hands!"

Nearly every hand eventually went up, although not all at once, as if the students were waiting to see if it would be cool to raise their hands too.

As Jamaal continued, explaining how to report cyberbullying, students throughout the crowd started looking at their phones, comparing them to each other. When the teachers followed suit, he realized that something was up.

He tried to go on, but the students and teachers began to rise. Some started crying. Some were shrieking. Then droves of them began running from the amphitheater and toward the buses parked just beyond the bridge that spanned the street bordering the Sunsphere.

Pandemonium.

—‌m‌—

When Joshua arrived at the base of the Sunsphere, a broad-shouldered, hulking man probably six and a half feet tall stopped him.

"You're Godfrey, aren't you?" the guy said.

"Who are you?"

"Turo. I work for Janice. Do you have it with you?"

"Prove it."

Turo pointed to his lapel, where he wore an emblem for the Pruninghooks Collective. Joshua produced one of his own from his pocket. "You were supposed to meet me at the hospital."

"Plans changed. Your mother approved everything."

Joshua noticed children fleeing the open-air amphitheater and gathering near the buses across the road. Somehow, word must have gotten out about what was happening.

He reminded himself that the radiological dispersal would still affect them. Even if they weren't directly below the tower, the radiation would still reach them. In fact, being out in the open and not under the canvas overhang might cause even more severe exposure.

"Where is she?" Joshua asked the man claiming to be Turo.

"At the townhouse." He told Joshua the correct address.

Satisfied, Joshua confirmed that Turo was armed.

A Glock 20 Gen4.

That would do.

Having come directly from the HEUMF via the hospital, Joshua had no weapons with him. However, he figured it was more important to have an armed sentry here on the ground than to take the Glock with him up into the tower, so he let Turo keep it.

The man handed him a pair of wire cutters. "In case you need them up there when you're getting everything set."

"Right. You wait here," Joshua told him. "Once I get to the top, disable the elevators. Shoot anyone who comes anywhere near those elevator doors."

"And we're gonna be able to get out of here in time?"

"Of course," Joshua said as convincingly as he could.

Turo nodded and Joshua entered the elevator beside the stairwell and began his ascent.

—⁂—

As Gunnar flew us toward Knoxville and I worked at narrowing down possible targets, I received a text from Colonel Clarke with a list of the five Red Team members' names:

Venus – Ramona Tamara Carmen
Sapphire – Joshua Bryant Godfrey
Typhoon – Justin Noel Dawes
Bard – Conrad Donnell McAllister
Flower Girl – Adira Chrysanthemum Halprin

There it was. Sapphire's real name: Joshua Bryant Godfrey. It wasn't a woman after all, like I'd been assuming, but a man. And if Sokolov was right, he was the one who'd started the fire at my home; he was the person responsible for Sienna's death.

And Nathan Lassiter's, as well, if the acrostic means what you think it does.

A torrent of emotions flooded through me—pounding waves of anger and resolve and fear mixed with a strange breed of relief. This was the name I'd been searching for all this time. If I found him, I could finally right the scales.

But then the terrible irony struck me—he'd taken Sienna and now he was part of this plot that was endangering Adira. He might very well take her life too.

Although I wanted to find Godfrey and confront him, at the moment, the priority was stopping the potential dirty bomb attack. Still, I'd been consumed with the search for the arsonist for almost a year and a half and I couldn't stop thinking about my own personal quest for justice.

How did Sokolov know it was him? Why would a Red Team member set fire to my house?

"What is it?" Gunnar asked. "What do we know? Is that from Clarke?"

"Yes," I replied. "It's the names of the people on the Red Team."

"Do you have a location yet?"

"No."

We were entering the city itself. My thoughts were jumbled. Hard to pin down. Too many things tugging me in different directions.

The weather had broken. Though the sky was partially overcast, the ground was dry, so the storms had apparently missed Knoxville.

"Something's up," Gunnar said. "What is it?"

I knew we needed to find the location where Janice's people were taking the uranium, but the thoughts of the arsonist distracted me.

When I didn't reply to his question, he said, "Spit it out."

I rattled off an answer. "A year and a half ago, my wife was killed in a fire. It's how I got my scars. I think I just identified who started it."

"Seriously? From the Red Team?"

"Yeah."

Focus here, Travis. Observation deck . . . Where are they taking that uranium?

Downtown Knoxville stretched before us. As I studied the skyline, I considered my search for something recognizable and iconic, somewhere that would make a statement and was within walking distance of a downtown hospital.

A dirty bomb . . .

A location that would be efficacious for spreading the radiation . . .

There was only one logical choice, shining before us, golden and glorious in the day.

"There." I pointed. "That sphere. Get us close."

"Alright. ETA two minutes."

I immediately conferred with Adira, we established that the name of the tower was the Sunsphere, and she said she'd head toward it ASAP. Then, I mentioned Godfrey to her. "You ever meet him?"

"No."

"See you in a few."

I went online. Though there was no trace of a Joshua Bryant Godfrey on social media, it didn't take me long to locate a photo of him posing with the rest of his fire crew at a local charity fundraiser. Shock and resolve wrestled inside me. "It's him," I muttered. "It's Godfrey. He killed Sienna."

"How do you know?" Gunnar asked.

"He's the guy who carried me out of the fire," I said. "He even showed up at Sienna's funeral." It was agonizing saying the words, and I almost couldn't get them out. "It was all just a game to him. That's why he didn't go back inside for her."

"What are you talking about?"

"She was still alive when he helped me out of the house. I always wondered if he might've been able to save her if he'd gone right back in."

He could have, but he wanted her dead.

Gunnar spoke up. "You seriously think a Red Team member started the fire? That this guy, Godfrey, is responsible?"

"I'm going to ask him when I find him. And if he is, I'm going to kill him."

"Revenge, huh?"

"Justice."

"Gotcha."

I waited. When Gunnar didn't go on, I said, "What do you mean, 'Gotcha'?"

"I just mean I get it. Who am I to tell you not to want revenge? I can't imagine how it would've affected me to have my wife killed."

"Yeah." I was a bit surprised he was being so supportive, but felt, in a way, vindicated. "That's right."

"Just remember, killing someone is something you can never undo. There's no walking it back. You tell yourself it won't affect you, that you'll be the exception, but you won't be. It'll change you. There's no way around it."

That doesn't matter, I told myself. *At least justice would be carried out.*

We soared across the city, the Sunsphere clearly visible as we came in from the northwest.

Retribution was one of those four goals of the justice system, as I'd spoken about with Adira on our drive down to Knoxville. It was by far the trickiest one to make sense of and implement. The one that could swallow you up whole.

"'An eye for an eye,'" I reminded Gunnar. "Isn't that what they say? 'A life for a life'?"

"That's what they say."

I didn't love how this was going. "You wouldn't understand," I told him stiffly. "This is justice and it's personal."

"Justice is never personal. It's universal. *Vengeance* is personal. And trust me, it always opens more wounds than it heals."

I'd never heard it put quite like that. I fumbled for a reply. "You've killed people," I countered. "You killed Sokolov back in that warehouse."

"Yes."

"So you're not really the one to lecture me."

"That's right. I'm not."

He left it at that and pointed to a field about a hundred yards from the Sunsphere. "I'm taking us down."

—m—

From the observation deck, movement off to the right caught Joshua's attention as a news helicopter landed on a strip of grass just across the bridge near the base of the tower. It was providential—the crew would be able to broadcast everything live, as it happened.

As they themselves died.

He verified that the elevators were disabled, then unscrewed the plate that covered the RDX's detonation device to secure the u-235 canister and confirm that the timer was operating properly.

—m—

Gunnar and I leapt out of the helicopter and tore across the field toward the Sunsphere. I had Saundra with me. Two bullets. He was carrying Maureen.

At the base of the tower, a hefty man stood beside the elevators. No sign of Adira.

As we approached, I called to him, "Listen, have you—" But that was as far as I got. He flashed out a handgun and fired at us. I dove to the side behind a concrete bench and Gunnar slid deftly behind a telephone pole.

"I'll cover you," Gunnar said, his voice crisp, direct.

But even if he did, the guy with the gun was so close to the elevators that I'd never be able to get to them unless he was out of the picture. Either he'd need to be incapacitated or I'd need to use the stairs.

I looked up at the imposing height of the Sunsphere. While it was true that I ran half-marathons to keep in shape, this tower was another animal altogether. It had to be at least twenty stories to the observation deck. None of my races had prepared me for anything like this.

But I could make it. I could do it. I had to.

"You good?" Gunnar asked me.

"Yeah," I said. "I'm taking the stairs."

He leaned around the side of the telephone pole and exchanged fire with the man. While he did, I took off for the stairwell on the north side of the Sunsphere and started up the steps as fast as I could take them.

CHAPTER 67

B y the time I reached the observation deck, my legs were burning and I was literally gasping for breath. Aiming Saundra in front of me, I did my best to steady my hand as I pressed open the door and entered the glass-enclosed deck that encircled the tower.

The city lay below me. Setting off the device up here would be terrifyingly effective, especially on a gusty day like this. The wind would disperse radioactive contamination all across the downtown area.

A touch of dizziness from overexertion crept up and took hold of me, fuzzying my vision. Dots everywhere. I had to mentally focus on my breathing to avoid being too light-headed.

Breathe, breathe, breathe.

I saw no one, but with the stairwell and elevator bay to my back, I had only a partial view of the tower's doughnut-shaped interior. I could hear faint, echoing movement somewhere out of sight.

So.

Situational awareness.

The six-foot-wide deck extended out from the tower's center. Just beyond the walkway, thick panes of glass were held in place by a network of slim steel girders angled both upward above the deck and downward below it, enclosing the circular walkway and providing a full 360-degree view of downtown Knoxville and the surrounding area.

Trying my best to quiet my breath, I listened, hoping to make out where the sounds were coming from, but the echo was disorienting. All I could really tell was that the sounds' origin came from the other side of the sphere, whose diameter must have been at least seventy feet.

With the gun in my left hand and my right hand against the center tower to steady myself, I edged around to the right of the stairs, catching sight of the downtown skyscrapers as well as the convention center just east of here.

Heading clockwise around the tower, I ended up going in almost a complete circle before I found the man, kneeling on top of one of the angled glass panels just beyond the walkway, bent over a set of wires that stretched out of sight beneath the observation deck's floorboards.

He had a pair of wire cutters in his hands.

A three-foot-high glass barrier designed to keep people on the deck and off the windows stood between us.

When he turned and looked at me, I recognized his face immediately.

"Joshua Godfrey," I said.

"Travis. It's been a long time."

Yes. This was the man who'd carried me out of my blazing living room on the night of the fire, the firefighter who hadn't gone back in to save my wife but had later showed up at her funeral. Seeing him here brought it all back: the smoke in my lungs, the burns, the image of a blackened hand from a burning woman on the stairs, reaching out to me through the flames.

"It was you," I said through clenched teeth. "You started the fire, didn't you?"

"Yes."

"Why? For what possible reason?"

"I was hired to do it, Travis. It was a job. That's all."

A job?

"Who was it?" I demanded. "Who hired you?"

He didn't answer.

"Sienna died because of you," I said.

"Things are not what they seem, Travis."

"What's not what it seems?" I felt surprisingly at ease leveling Saundra at him. Maybe I was getting used to aiming guns at people, or maybe it was just because of who he was. What he'd done. I had two bullets. That would be enough. "It all seems pretty clear to me."

His gaze shifted toward his feet and I wondered if he had a weapon, but as I stepped closer, I realized he was checking a digital timer on a black rectangular device not much larger than a laptop computer. I stood less than ten feet away, but because of the angle, I couldn't make out the numbers. However, I could tell that they were changing with every passing second.

"Shut it down," I ordered him.

A headshake.

"Disarm it, Joshua."

"That's not going to happen."

Shoot him. Be done with this.

No. You need him to stop the timer!

"Back away." When he refused to move, I realized that he wasn't going to help me. I needed to stop this detonator myself.

"I said move away from the bomb."

He moved slightly closer to me, then stopped.

I stalked toward him until I was about ten feet away and was finally able to make out more of the device. Though I'd read hundreds of pages of explosive ordnance schematics, I'd never been this close to one in real life.

A cluster of wires threaded into a series of brick-sized blocks of plastic explosive. From my reading and research at the Pentagon, I identified it as RDX, a military-grade explosive that was favored by the British and had similar qualities to C-4. Even though we weren't at the tower's base, I anticipated that with that much of it, the explosion would likely take off at least the top half of this structure and maybe, if it affected the internal integrity of the tower, topple the whole thing.

The design for this device came from a top secret DARPA program that'd been running for the last two years. I'd read up on it. Studied it. Remembered it. Yes, it was from Paraden Defense Systems. These must've been the plans that were compromised. I didn't know how to fully disarm this bomb, but I thought I could maybe stop the timer, stall things out, buy some time until a bomb squad could get up here.

But to do that, I needed to get past Godfrey.

Kill him. Finish this. Then stop the bomb.

"You could have gone back in and saved her." My eyes were burning with tears. "You killed Sienna."

"No." He shook his head. "I didn't."

"Who then? The person who hired you?"

"You still don't understand, do you?"

"Oh, I think I do. Now, get away from the bomb!"

He climbed over the railing and stood on the deck before me, pocketing the wire cutters and holding up his hands.

Eight feet away.

"Set any weapons you have on the floor in front of you," I said. "Slow and easy."

He didn't move.

"Do it!"

He just said, "It's too late, Travis. You can't get away in time."

Godfrey might've been armed, might not have been, but I wasn't trained on how to frisk someone while keeping a gun on him.

"Get on your knees." I tried to sort out what to do. "And keep your hands where I can see them."

He remained momentarily still, but when I peered over the railing to check the digital timer, he spun and darted out of sight around the other side of the sphere.

I cursed myself for not squeezing the trigger when I had the chance.

Get him later. He can wait—those children down there can't. You can't let this detonator blow. Stop the timer, then go find him.

Climbing over the railing, I cautiously moved out onto one of the glass panels. Because of the angle, I was barely able to keep my balance. I couldn't help but look down at the city two hundred and fifty feet below me. Standing there on the glass and peering through it at the vast open space beneath me gave me a sense of vertigo.

Steadying myself, I knelt beside the device.

First, I tried to remove the cylinder of uranium, but it was locked in place and wasn't going anywhere. However, the detonator's casing was loose and I thought I might be able to get inside it. Carefully, I unscrewed the wing nuts, lifted the cover, and found a nest of tangled wires of various colors.

I checked the digital readout.

One minute and fifty-three seconds.

Setting down the gun, I studied the pattern of wires, then closed my eyes to focus on what I'd seen of this design at the Pentagon.

With the schematics in mind, I opened my eyes again. Steadying my hands, I began to sort through the wires, but out of the corner of my eye, I saw Godfrey hurtling toward me. Awkwardly, I fumbled for the gun, but he was quick and vaulted over the railing before I could draw on him.

He dove forward, tackling me.

Together, we fell backward and I landed solidly on my side, flat against the glass. I heard a sharp crack from beneath me, but, thank God, the glass didn't give way.

He punched me in the face, mangling my glasses and sending them flying. He cocked his arm and was about to swing again, but I threw a desperate hand up to his throat and managed to push him aside and squirm out from beneath him. He ended up closer to the gun and whisked it up, aiming it at me.

"I didn't kill Sienna," he said adamantly.

Why did he keep reiterating that, especially if he was just going to kill me too? I hated that he was toying like this with my pain, but right now I was more concerned with stopping the timer than seeking revenge for Sienna's murder or playing guessing games about Godfrey's motives. I had to be. Thousands of lives were at stake.

The fractured glass beneath me was not going to hold my weight for long.

If I went straight at him, he would shoot me. I needed some sort of advantage.

In one desperate move, I leapt up, grabbed the ridge of one of the girders, and drew myself up, then I kicked off the glass and launched myself at him.

It wasn't very graceful, but it did the trick.

I landed heavily on him and the glass beneath us spiderwebbed into a network of intimidating fissures. I heard the high, tinny sound of glass cracking and would have scrambled to the side, but I had my hand on the gun as I tried to wrench it from his hands.

We were both struggling for control of the weapon when it went off.

CHAPTER 68

Godfrey stumbled backward and we stared at each other. Fresh blood stained both of our shirts, but when I felt my chest and stomach to see if I was hit, I found no wounds. No seeping blood. No bullet holes.

I eased carefully away from the cracking glass onto a fully intact panel as he collapsed, blood leaking out of the gunshot wound in his abdomen. "You can't stop it," he stammered. "If you find Lena, it'll all be clear."

Lena? Who's Lena?

Whoever she was, it didn't matter right now. I needed to disable that timer.

If Gunnar was right, there was one bullet left in the gun. Godfrey still held it. I braced myself for him to shoot me.

He was breathing heavily, the blood on his shirt thickening, growing darker. "You know the person who hired me to start the fire," he said.

"Who's that? Lena?"

He was kneeling unsteadily.

The arson, his denials that he was responsible, even avenging Sienna's death—all of that paled in comparison to what I needed to do now, here, with this bomb.

"You have some wire cutters," I said. "Throw them to me." I started toward him. He shook his head. He tried to aim the gun at me, but couldn't lift his arm. "You're dying, Joshua," I said as gently as I could. "You're bleeding out. Give me the wire cutters."

He'll go unconscious, then you can get them.

But time—is there enough time?

However, he must have been thinking the same thing, because, with what little strength he had left, he tilted the gun downward, angling the barrel at the cracked glass panel beneath his feet. "The future begins now."

"No!" I cried. "Help me, Joshua. Disarm this. There are kids down there. You can—"

He squeezed the trigger.

The glass blew apart, raining down toward the pavement hundreds of feet below us. He disappeared from sight as the sound of the gunshot reverberated sharply around the Sunsphere.

Wind swirled in, curling around me, disorienting me.

He was gone. He was dead. Justice, retribution, revenge—definitions and continuums and theories didn't matter right now. The only thing that mattered was the bomb.

I rushed toward it.

Forty-nine seconds.

I knelt. No one else was going to make it up here. There wasn't time to call for help.

There was only time to remember.

I reviewed the schematics for this device one more time.

"It's the red wire," I muttered. "Why is it always the red wire?"

It's easier to remember that way. Red goes boom.

Thirty-eight seconds.

Crouching next to the device, I pressed the tangle of wires aside, trying to find the place where they were attached to the detonator itself—which was made all the more difficult without my glasses.

I needed something to snip the wire, but had no knife with me and the wire cutters had gone down with Joshua. I wished I'd kept Adira's razor-zippered jacket with me—it might've just done the trick. But it was still back in that building on the Oak Ridge National Laboratory campus.

Glancing around, I considered what I had available, then scrambled over to the broken window, where some of the shards remained embedded in the frame like angry teeth.

Prying one loose wasn't as easy as I'd hoped it would be, but I finally managed, slicing halfway through two of my fingers in the process.

As I hurried back to the detonator, I tried to isolate the pain in a back corner of my mind, but my hand twitched from the dripping cuts.

Twenty-three seconds.

With my good hand, I dug through the wires and came up with the red one.

Nineteen.

Cut this and those kids down there live. You do too.

Eighteen.

By now, both of my hands were slick with blood as I took in a nervous breath and drew the glass against the wire.

It remained intact.

With blood smearing everything, I tried again, but either the wire was too thick or the glass shard wasn't sharp enough.

Twelve.

I combed through all I knew about this device, mentally flipping through the schematics, but couldn't come up with anything else to do. Blood everywhere. Which was the red wire? They were all red!

Nine.

Okay. Wing it.

I grabbed the wire that I trusted was the correct one.

Seven.

Tried to pull it from its fitting.

Six.

It resisted, and I leaned back, yanking at it, praying this would work.

Three.

It tore loose.

I closed my eyes, waiting. Trembling.

Nothing.

Heart hammering, I let out a deep breath and looked at the timer. It'd stopped with two seconds left.

I gazed down to where Joshua Godfrey had fallen. His body lay sprawled and motionless on the concrete far below me.

For nearly a year and a half, I'd thought that I would be relieved to see the death of the person who'd started the fire, but I wasn't. The goal I'd had for so long was accomplished, but I felt only remorse, not relief.

The fruit of justice might be peace; I wasn't so sure what the fruit of retribution was. But it wasn't peace.

I held my sliced hand against my shirt, putting pressure on it to stop the bleeding.

Would I have killed an unarmed man? Could I have squeezed that trigger? I didn't know for certain. I thought I could've done it, but maybe that wouldn't have been justice. Only vengeance. And they weren't the same. I could see that now. Gunnar had been right.

Vengeance is personal. And it always opens more wounds than it heals. Justice is universal.

But now wasn't the time to sort all that out.

Now we needed to get a team up here to permanently and completely disarm this bomb.

And I needed to make sure Adira was okay.

CHAPTER 69

I reached the bottom of the stairs and saw that a bevy of police officers was encircling the tower, moving in. As I emerged, they snapped their weapons up, aiming them at me, but Gunnar shouted adamantly for them to lower their guns.

The titan of a man who'd been in the gunfight with Gunnar was on the ground, cuffed beneath three burly officers. He was alive. I couldn't tell if he was injured or not, but he did not look happy.

"We need a bomb squad up there!" I called out. "Now!"

One of the cops spoke into his radio, and I turned to Gunnar. "Is Adira okay? Have we heard from her?"

He pointed to a crowd of people who'd gathered nearby. She stood just outside the line of police tape that'd been hastily stretched between a couple of telephone poles. At first, I felt a wave of relief, but then I saw a bloody strip of cloth tied in a makeshift bandage around her left forearm.

"Adira!" I hurried toward her.

Behind me, Gunnar directed the officers to clear the civilians out of the area.

Adira's eyes widened when she saw my own blood-splattered shirt and bleeding hand. "You okay?"

"I'm fine. You?"

"Still alive and kicking."

"Your arm?"

"Just a flesh wound." She brushed off my concern. "So you stopped him?"

"He stopped himself. He took his own life. He was the one."

"The one?"

"Who started the fire. The arson at my house. It was Joshua Godfrey— Sapphire. The same guy."

She let that sink in. "So it *was* all connected."

I still wasn't entirely certain how all the threads wove together, but I said, "Yeah. It looks like it was."

"You finally found the justice you were looking for."

I didn't know if that was the right way to put it or not. "I'm just glad it's over."

To my surprise, Adira leaned forward, into my arms.

Holding her felt right, like a step in a new direction, one toward the future, but any sense of peace or completion eluded me. I couldn't shake the thought that things weren't really over after all. Joshua had insisted that he hadn't killed Sienna, so maybe justice hadn't been meted out yet at all.

He'd also said I knew the person who'd hired him.

Lena, I thought, recalling the name he'd mentioned. *Who in the world is Lena?*

—∞—

Adira eased back from her embrace with Travis.

Yesterday morning she hadn't even known this man, and now, already, she'd started to fall for him in a big way. She didn't always exhibit the best judgment when it came to guys—no question there. Maybe this time it was finally different.

Yes, it is. Of course it is.

She was about to ask him to come to the hospital with her while she got her burned hand and sliced arm treated, when a video call came through on the phone she had with her—the one she'd taken from the Russian in the restaurant. She looked at it curiously, then answered it.

Janice Daniels's face appeared. "Hello, Adira."

"Janice." Adira angled the phone to the side, pointed to it, and mouthed to Travis, *Trace the call.*

He hurried off to speak with an officer, raising a phone of his own to his ear as he did.

"Congratulations to your friend there," Janice said. "He saved all those children."

Turning in a slow circle, Adira studied the crowd that the police officers were currently dispersing, the windows of a neighboring hotel, even the faces of the paramedics stationed beside a nearby ambulance. No sign of the billionaire.

"Where are you, Janice?"

"That doesn't matter. He killed Joshua. I cared for that young man when he was a teenager."

That's news, Adira thought.

"Joshua killed himself," she said to Janice. "You can't lay that on Travis." She kept up her search, but still saw nothing to clue her in on Janice's location. "He's the one who murdered Nathan for you, isn't he?" The words caught in her throat as she remembered her mentor. Her friend.

"I didn't call you to talk about your former boss."

Still no sign of her. There was nothing on the phone's screen to reveal a specific location, but now Adira noticed a wall in the background, establishing that she was inside a building.

"Why *did* you call?" she said.

"To caution you."

"You won't get away with this. The FBI will freeze your assets, shutter your businesses, interview everyone who's ever worked with you. They'll find you. There's nowhere in the world you can hide. Turn yourself in."

"I'm afraid that living on the run sounds more appealing to me than dying in prison." Janice's face gave no indication that she was either afraid or intimidated. "Besides, there's still work to be done."

"The Pruninghooks Collective?"

"This is just the beginning."

"I'm coming for you."

"A word of warning, Adira: you never know what might be waiting for you if you do. Be careful."

"Careful isn't in my repertoire. And I'm no Bible scholar, but I can tell you that your little verse about plowshares and pruninghooks doesn't justify trying to kill children in the name of ending war. That much I'm sure of."

"Don't you see?" Janice replied. "We've done what we set out to do. We managed to get the enriched uranium out of Y-12. Yes, Knoxville narrowly avoided a major radiological event, but the result will be the same as if the bomb had actually gone off. The public will lose their trust in nuclear power. They'll turn from it. We'll have a safer world as a result."

Adira scrambled to keep her talking, to get as many answers from her as she could. "And the Russians? Popovic? Was he the one who hired the men to abduct Travis and—"

"Goodbye, Adira."

"Wait—"

The video screen went blank as Janice ended the call.

Adira shouted to Travis, "Do they have anything? Could they trace it?"

"Clarke put NSA on it. We have a site north of the city. SWAT's en route."

—◊◊◊—

The camera that Janice had sent Turo to position on the bridge beside the Sunsphere earlier that morning gave her a clear view of everything that was happening, and now as she gathered her things from the townhouse, she considered what she'd been able to accomplish. In the end, the outcome might not have been exactly what she'd had in mind, but it'd still proven her point, still accomplished her goal.

Yes. Waking people up. Not a massacre but a message. Change on the horizon. Creating a world where nation would not rise up against nation. *And no one would study war anymore.*

Today she'd lost Joshua. She would mourn him, but she would also celebrate his life and his sacrifice. He did what was necessary for the good of all. And because of that, he was a hero in the truest and most noble sense of the word.

—◊◊◊—

FIFTY MINUTES LATER

ADVENT REGIONAL MEDICAL CENTER

Gunnar and Adira were being treated for their injuries. My sliced fingers were stitched up and my left hand was bandaged where the bladed zipper had cut into it.

While a nurse attended to her burned hand, Adira informed me that Joshua Godfrey had a connection to Janice Daniels. "She cared for him when he was a teen. They were responsible for Nathan's death. I don't know how much Nathan knew about the uranium, but in the end he did what he could to clue us in on what was going down."

"And since Joshua was a Red Team member," I said, "Nathan would've let him into the house. And with the computer logged in to Nathan's account—"

"Joshua could've corrupted the Red Team files after he killed him," she said, finishing my thought for me.

Although we'd need to confirm it, the facts did fit.

Right now I wanted to explore the connection between Janice Daniels and Senator Richardson, who, from what I'd heard, had pulled through and was in intensive care. I recalled that she'd purchased his tech company from him when he moved into politics.

After I got word that the SWAT team hadn't caught Daniels, I went to the hospital's other wing to see if the senator knew anything that might help us locate her.

I found him in the Cardiac Unit with an IV and connected to a panel of beeping machines that were monitoring his vitals. He wasn't intubated and was conscious and aware.

"Senator Richardson?" I showed him my ID. "My name is Travis Brock. I work at the Pentagon. How are you feeling?"

"Tired," he responded feebly. "What happened out there?"

"It's okay. There was a bomb. We stopped it."

"Thank God," he muttered. "I never intended for any of this to happen."

A touch of ice in my spine. "What do you mean? What didn't you intend?"

"There were microprocessors," he said, his voice strained, "that shouldn't have been installed at Y-12. A compromised supply chain."

"Is that how they got the uranium out?"

He was quiet.

"Why, Senator?" I didn't know if he would answer me or not, but the question seemed to hang there in the air between us. It needed to be asked. "Why would you even get involved with any of this?"

"My brother died for this country. I owed it to him to make things better. It was all for the greater good."

The greater good.

That was the rationalization of all dictators, of all despots, of all tyrants and those who precipitated the greatest atrocities in human history. From the countless battlefields strewn throughout the landscape of the past, drenched in the blood of the young, to the gas chambers and the Gulag and the prison camps of North Korea. It was the cry of the machete-wielding Rwandans hacking their neighbors to death by the thousands and the goal of Hitler and Stalin and Mao Zedong and Pol Pot. Of Genghis Khan. Of Chiang Kai-Shek. Over and over again it was the oppressor's justification that echoes endlessly through the raw, bloody chambers of hell: *The greater good. This is all for the greater good.*

Injustice always begins with rationalizing a wrong.

Justice begins with righting one.

Maybe that was the answer I'd been searching for.

I could've pressed the senator, but I figured that, for the time being, that could wait. Right now, Janice Daniels was the priority. However, when I asked about her, he wasn't able to tell me anything we didn't already know.

A doctor came in. "We really thought we were going to lose you, Senator." She patted his shoulder as she shook her head in amazement. "But you're a real fighter. I can't explain it any other way."

After she'd checked his vitals and left, Richardson asked me to fill him in. I told him what'd gone down at the Sunsphere and about the death of Joshua Godfrey, who'd been a Red Team member and had confessed to starting the fire at my house. A look of deep sadness crossed the senator's face when I mentioned that my wife had been killed in it. When I finished, I said, "Senator, do you know anyone named Lena?"

"No. I'm afraid not."

"Are you familiar with Project Symphony?"

"I think I need to rest now," he said somewhat delusively, then he closed his eyes.

When it became clear that he wasn't going to offer me any more information, I went to check on Adira and Gunnar, and to search for who Lena might be.

Two weeks later

TUESDAY, MAY 10

CHAPTER 70

THE PENTAGON

ARLINGTON, VIRGINIA

8:14 A.M.

A lot had happened since the events in East Tennessee.

Janice Daniels was still at large. Though we'd questioned her body-guard, Turo Pärnänen, the man Gunnar had been in the shootout with at the base of the Sunsphere, he hadn't provided anything solid about her location or her future plans. Truthfully, with her connections and resources, I suspected it would be tough, even for our intel community, to locate her.

Ilya Vasiliev had died in the Cuban restaurant following the fight with Adira. Further research revealed that he and Sergei Sokolov were in the pocket of a Russian oligarch named Ivan Popovic—the same Ivan who'd texted their phones, directing them to acquire the u-235. We'd also learned that Popovic was working with Janice Daniels on the Patmos Financial Consortium land purchases, so at least we finally had some answers on that front. The State Department was investigating the connection, and it looked like they might expel some Russian diplomats in response to the actions of Sokolov and Vasiliev on US soil and the involvement of Popovic on the energy scheme.

Senator Richardson had identified the compromised chips, which had been altered to allow unauthorized access to Y-12's system files and allowed Godfrey to leave with the enriched uranium. The facility was in lockdown while their technicians checked the other microprocessors and inventoried their stock of radioactive isotopes. The senator was facing a slew of state and federal charges related to what he'd done, but it wasn't clear yet how much time he might serve since he was cooperating fully with the authorities. His rumored presidential bid, however, appeared to have been stopped in its proverbial tracks.

The Pruninghooks Collective claimed responsibility for the attack and was officially designated a domestic terrorist organization by the FBI, a move that allowed more federal funds and resources to be channeled into fighting them and their agenda—and to finding and stopping Janice Daniels.

Dr. Yong and his wife were doing well, considering all that they'd been through.

Adira's injuries and Gunnar's wounded shoulder were on the mend. The cuts and abrasions on my hands were healing.

In addition to Lassiter's and Senator Presnell's deaths, and the arson at my house, the authorities were taking a deep dive into Joshua Godfrey's past to see what other crimes he might have been responsible for.

I was still processing what he'd told me when we were alone in the Sunsphere.

He'd alleged, repeatedly, that he had not killed Sienna. He'd even gone so far as to tell me that I knew the person who'd hired him. I still wasn't sure if I should believe his words, but I couldn't think of any reason why he might've been lying to me. And he was so determined in his denials that I felt he was probably telling the truth.

But if not him, then who?

He was in league with Janice Daniels—did she hire him? Was she behind all of this? I couldn't see why that might be the case, and I didn't know her personally, but at this point I wasn't about to rule anything out.

Godfrey had mentioned someone named Lena. After coming up short looking into anyone by that name in relation to Nathan Lassiter, I'd tried another approach.

Figuring that there had to be a reason why Detective Caruso was killed on the same day he texted me that he might know a reason for the date of the fire, I turned to his current caseload for answers.

With Colonel Clarke's authorization and Metro PD's approval, I was granted access to Caruso's files. I studied what he'd come up with during his investigation into the arson at my house and found that a State Department employee named Lena Rhodes had gone missing shortly before the fire, and so had some classified files she had access to. Caruso had written a cryptic note on one of the papers in his files—a photo of our burned house. Just six words: *Were you there? Were you watching?* Next to it he'd jotted the initials *L.R.*

Nothing as solid as I would've liked, but it was something. A first step, if nothing else. Rhodes was single. No children, no spouses, either present or ex. Metro PD put out a BOLO on her, but there was still no sign of her. No current leads.

Why would she have hired Joshua to start the fire? And, if Caruso was right in suspecting that she was present, why hadn't anyone seen her that night? And once again, Joshua had said I knew the person who hired him— but how was that true when, as far as I could tell, I'd never met Rhodes?

I didn't want to get lost in speculation, so over the last two weeks, I'd tried to hold myself back from making too many assumptions, but it wasn't easy. I dug, I researched, I scanned thousands of online and physical files about Lena and her work, but found nothing solid that I could use—and with each passing day I became more and more frustrated and impatient for a final resolution on her possible involvement.

Now, Adira adjusted her visitor badge as we walked down the corridor toward Colonel Clarke's E ring office. Gunnar and I flanked her. Clarke had asked to see the three of us together. Though I didn't know what the meeting concerned, I expected that it was to follow up on our previous debriefing sessions at Y-12, and to make sure we were doing alright.

On the drive over here, Gunnar had told Adira about the romance novel he was writing. They'd been discussing it ever since, and she'd been asking him to read her some excerpts. Now, she pressed him again: "You have to let me hear it. I really like romances. What section are you working on now?"

"The love scene."

"Oh, that's my favorite part. Let's hear it."

"I'm not sure it's quite ready yet. Still tinkering with it."

"Come on." She gave his good shoulder a friendly slug. "You have it with you?"

"It's synced to my phone, but—"

"Pull it up." We came to a drinking fountain beside the restrooms and she approached it. "I won't take no for an answer."

While she bent to take a drink, he peered my way for support.

I shrugged. "Don't look at me. I'd listen to her when she says she won't take no for an answer. She's got some mad fighting skills."

"Mad fighting skills, huh?"

"I'm just saying."

At last, with a sigh, he gave in and scrolled across his phone's screen until he came to the manuscript, then explained, "The heroine, Jessie, is falling for this cowboy named Donovan."

Adira straightened up and unwrapped a piece of bubble gum. "Donovan's a good romance novel name."

"Thanks." Gunnar seemed more nervous now than I'd ever seen him, even when Sokolov was aiming that rifle at him. He took a deep breath. "Okay, here goes. 'Jessie's face blushed with pleasure at the thought of Donovan's fingers caressing across her skin, the largest and most visible organ on her body.'" He looked up and informed us, "It's true, you know. Your skin is the body's largest organ."

"I've heard that," I said, unsure how else to respond.

Gunnar went on. "'And then, her fantasy became true reality as he touched her bare forearm with skin of his own.'" He looked up from the phone. "What do you think so far?"

Adira and I shared a glance. "Well." She popped the gum into her mouth. "I didn't expect you to put it quite like that."

"Exactly." Gunnar held up a knowing finger. "I didn't want it to be too predictable." He continued, "'Donovan pointed with his outstretched finger toward the bedroom. "Come with me, my vixen," he said, waggling his eyebrows. They dipped and dove below his forehead like two dead caterpillars made of hair, wriggling longingly with unbridled desire.'" Gunnar paused. "I'm trying to get the word *bridled* in there since Donovan's a cowboy. It's all about the subtle use of imagery."

"I see," I said.

"So?" he asked innocently. "Your honest opinion?"

"I . . . I've never heard anything quite like it before."

"I know." He grinned broadly. "Pretty original, right?"

"It's not exactly my genre, but—"

"Wait," Adira said to him. "His *eyebrows* had unbridled desire? And they were wriggling like *dead* caterpillars?"

"If they weren't dead they might crawl across his face."

"True," she conceded.

"Anyway, I'm still tweaking that sentence. Then Donovan turns toward Jessie, throbbing with desire, or maybe heaving with passion. I'm not sure. Maybe she's throbbing and he's heaving. I also want to get the word *titivate* in there."

"Titivate?" Adira said.

"It means to dress smartly. To get yourself ready for a big night. You can titivate yourself, or titivate someone else. I'm hoping to have Donovan titivate Jessie."

I patted his shoulder. "Give that a little more thought."

"Right."

"I'm anxious to hear what happens next," Adira told him. "Especially if there's mutual titivating going on."

"I'll let you know."

As we continued toward the colonel's office, Adira said to me, "There are a couple of things I still don't understand about what happened when we were in Oak Ridge."

"Such as?"

"How did Sergei find you and Dr. Yong behind the Hemlock room? And how did Ilya know to go to Alvarez's room to look for me?"

"There's evidence that someone hacked into the hotel's CCTV security cameras. From there, it would've been easy to track us."

"And Popovic was working with Janice the whole time?"

"From what I can tell, she wanted the uranium, and he wanted me."

Adira nodded in acknowledgment. "And they both benefitted from obtaining control of the natural gas sites."

"Yes."

"Huh," she said thoughtfully. "And the nuke safety summit in Oak Ridge, that's why the timing mattered, why all of this came together when it did?"

Gunnar was preoccupied typing some notes on his story into his phone.

"I believe so," I said to Adira. "After his father's funeral, Nathan must have decided to do what he could to stop the stolen Paraden schematics from being used. He obviously had his suspicions about what was happening, but didn't know all that Janice had in mind—he couldn't have known the whole plan or he would've contacted others at Homeland or the FBI's Counterterrorism Division."

"Agreed," she said. "At least in the end, he turned back to what he believed in. He tried stopping things. He lost his life trying to bring you and me together." Then she was silent, and I had the sense that her thoughts had shifted back to his death. To losing her friend.

Over the last couple of days we'd speculated that Nathan had brought Adira in because of her past with Janice, and that he'd reached out to me because he knew that with my access to the archives I could pinpoint the connection between Paraden and the Pruninghooks Collective.

However, there was still the date on the FOIA request that was puzzling. Clearly, he'd chosen the date of the fire to get my attention, but was there more to it? Did he know something regarding the fire that we hadn't been able to discover yet? He'd been planning to meet Detective Caruso the day before everything went down in Tennessee. Now, both of them were dead, so the question of what he'd learned was still lingering out there, still something I needed to untangle. And I didn't know where else to even begin looking for answers.

We passed the apex of corridors 3 and 4, and as we neared the colonel's office, Adira asked me in that frank manner of hers, "By the way, what exactly did Sienna do?"

"She was a linguist. A translator. She worked for the intelligence community."

"'The intelligence community' is a broad category. For whom, exactly?"

"Mostly the CIA, although she consulted with other government agencies when needed."

"Inside the State Department."

"Yes," I said. "Sometimes."

Gunnar looked up from his phone. "The same place Lena Rhodes worked?"

"Well, yes."

Adira considered that. "Maybe you've been asking the wrong question this whole time."

"What do you mean?"

"What if you weren't the target of the fire? What if Sienna was?"

Over the last year and a half, I'd wondered that very thing several times, but it'd never led me anywhere. However, hearing Adira put it so bluntly now made it seem like more than just a hypothetical.

Gunnar spoke up. "If Godfrey and whoever hired him—Lena Rhodes, for instance—were after Sienna, it would explain why there haven't been any other attempts on your life in the intervening months since the fire—except, of course, for what went down in Tennessee."

Maybe Adira was right. Maybe they both were. The possibility of Sienna being the target of the arson was an angle I needed to explore more in-depth and take more seriously.

We arrived at the glass doors and were ushered into Colonel Clarke's office. After greeting us, he addressed Adira first. "Is this your first time in the Pentagon, or were you ever here when you worked for the Secret Service?"

"First time."

"Well, what do you think?"

"Very 1940s. I keep expecting Captain America to show up."

"Beyond that?"

"It could use a little variegation in the color scheme, but it does have a certain Spartan appeal that seems militarily appropriate."

"Would you be interested in spending a little more time here?"

A head tilt. "In what capacity?"

I glanced at Gunnar, who was smiling slightly. I wasn't sure what was up, but evidently he'd been let in on whatever this meeting was about.

"You've done a great service for your country," Colonel Clarke told Adira. He strode toward the window and gazed outside pensively. "I've been thinking about starting a new team. Something, shall we say, not exactly on the books." He directed his gaze at her again. "Ms. Halprin, I believe your skills will be put to better use in the program I'm putting together here than on the Red Team."

"I'm interested."

He eyed me. "And I'm thinking about getting you out of the basement."

"No more redactions?"

"Let's just say you won't *only* be doing redactions from now on. That is, if you say yes."

It sounded intriguing. "Go on, sir."

He returned to his desk and laid out three red file folders, one for each of us. "Here's what I'm thinking."

THAT EVENING

6:58 P.M.

Adira couldn't get the job opportunity off her mind. The chance to work with Gunnar and Travis in the search for the Pruninghooks Collective and other select projects that the colonel had in mind was fascinating and inviting. She always enjoyed new challenges and adventures, especially ones with guys she was interested in.

Like Travis.

So, a win-win.

And Gunnar seemed like quite a character too. It would certainly prove interesting working with him and hearing his rather unorthodox romance novel unfold.

She was more than a little curious about Project Symphony. Colonel Clarke had promised he'd read them in on it and give them a demonstration next week of what it could do, so she was looking forward to that and to seeing what the prototype was actually capable of.

She lit some lilac-scented candles in the living room of the DC apartment the colonel was temporarily providing for her. With the open floor plan, it wasn't far to the kitchenette, and with only one subdued living room lamp on, the whole space had a nice, quiet ambiance.

Okay, romantic ambiance.

Why not just own it?

She wasn't exactly the world's greatest chef, but you can make frozen pizza taste pretty great if you just add some jalapeños and sliced pickles to it before you pop it in the oven.

As she was putting on some gentle mood music, she heard a knock at the door.

She answered it and found Travis standing there holding a vase with a floral arrangement of red and white chrysanthemums.

"Hello, Flower Girl." He held out the vase for her.

"How sweet of you, Duck Boy," she said, as she accepted the flowers and invited him in.

"As I mentioned to you in Tennessee, we're going to need to choose a different secret agent name for me."

"I kinda like it."

"Mm-hmm."

She closed the door and, back in the cramped kitchen again, placed the vase on the table and removed the pizza from the oven. "I assume you like it hot?"

"Hot?"

"Your pizza."

"Oh. Yes."

"Good timing, then."

She grabbed two beers, sliced up the pie, and motioned for him to have a seat at the kitchenette's table.

He eyed the pizza. "Pickles? Really?"

"Don't knock it 'til you've tried it. Trust me."

"For you, I'm willing to expand my culinary horizons."

"That's good to hear."

As they started eating, he acknowledged that the pizza was better than he'd thought it would be.

"Pickles and all?" she said.

"Pickles and all."

Hoping to quiet the burn of a slice with a few too many jalapeños piled on it, she downed some of her beer, then asked him if he'd come up with anything more on the whereabouts of Lena Rhodes.

"I spent all afternoon exploring the link between her and Sienna. The only connection I could make was a reference to a translation project Sienna was involved with—an energy treaty with Russia that the State Department was drafting. A week before the fire, Lena named Sienna in an internal communique regarding some work she'd done on it. She was concerned about Sienna's contribution. That's it. After Sienna's death and Lena's disappearance, it doesn't appear that there was ever any follow-up on Lena's memo."

"But Caruso's notes indicated that she was there the night of the fire?"

"Not conclusively, but they do point in that direction. It's worth looking into more closely, but I have the feeling that we'll need to locate Lena to ultimately discover the answers we're looking for."

"But she's still nowhere to be found?"

"I'm wondering if she might've assumed another identity. That could explain why it's been so hard to track her down."

Adira pondered that while the two of them made their way through the pizza. "As far as the fire goes," she said, "there really aren't that many reasons people commit arson."

"To hide something or to gain something."

"To gain something?" she inquired. "You mean like insurance money?"

"Yes." He nodded. "The problem is, no one benefitted from this fire. Neither Sienna nor I had any substantial life insurance policies or anyone else listed in either of our wills."

"To hide something, then. To cover up another crime or destroy evidence."

"There isn't any evidence that I can think of that was destroyed. It was my house, not my office."

"And you never brought work home?"

Travis tapped his head. "I can't help but bring it home."

—⁂—

As Adira went for a bite of the last slice of pizza on her plate, I said, "Now that you have your mouth full, let me ask you a question."

"Sure," she said, chomping heartily. "What's that?"

"What happened in Almaty?"

More chewing. "What do you mean?"

"When I was in that deserted factory and Sergei Sokolov was about to torture me, he started asking about you."

She swallowed. "Did he?"

"Yeah. He was trying to get information from me, mainly about Project Symphony, but he also asked if I knew about what happened with you in Almaty."

"Okay."

"I told him that I trusted you and that—"

Before I could finish, she reached over and placed a finger gently against my lips. "Shh. That's not a story for tonight. It's a story for another time."

"What's the story for tonight?" I asked. The words sounded strangely squished with her finger pressed up to my lips like that.

She leaned close and whispered, "It's still being written. But I think there's a good chance it's going to have a happy ending."

Then she kissed me.

And I returned the favor.

After a few rather memorable and not unpleasant moments, she sat back and asked, "Are those nanobots you injected into your leg still working?"

"That's a good question. Why do you ask?"

"Maybe I want to be able to keep tabs on you, Mr. Redactor."

"Maybe?"

"Almost certainly."

"I suppose that could be arranged. Nanobots or not."

"Hmm." She quieted her voice. "By the way, there's something I probably should have told you earlier."

"What's that?"

"I like your scars. They make you unique."

No one had ever told me before that they liked my scars. "I guess it's just the shape of my skin," I said a bit uncertainly.

"It's the shape of your life," she replied. "It's your story. It's all part of who you are. And I like who you are."

She gave me a diminutive smile, and in the warmth of her acceptance, I felt my scars on the inside—the deeper ones, the invisible ones that'd marked me since the night of the fire—begin to soften. Maybe even begin to heal.

And when I smiled back at her, I meant it.

Two days later

THURSDAY, MAY 12

It took Janice Daniels nearly twenty minutes to find the grave marked with Sienna Brock's name, but at last she located it on the east end of St. Andrew's Cemetery, on the outskirts of the city.

The morning was drizzly, but that didn't stop her from kneeling in the damp earth and laying a bouquet of flowers beside the headstone.

After whispering a short prayer, she stood and noticed a woman wearing a black dress and dark veil approaching her. Based on all that she'd discovered and all she'd been told, Janice suspected she knew who it was.

As she brushed the moist soil off her pants, the woman joined her by the gravestone, and then, keeping her voice low, said, "You've come to pay your respects."

"I thought it was appropriate," Janice replied.

A small pause. "It was a terrible tragedy, the fire."

"At least there was only one casualty."

"Yes."

Janice was quiet for a moment. All around them, misty rain soaked through the day.

The woman adjusted a necklace with an emblem that Janice hadn't noticed until now.

The Pruninghooks Collective symbol.

And she wore a wedding ring.

But that doesn't make sense. She wasn't . . . unless—

And then, it all came together for her. It hadn't been as she'd first supposed. Caruso, the detective who'd been investigating the arson at Travis Brock's home, might not have been able to definitively link the cases, but he'd been on the right track. The connection to Lena Rhodes. It was there. It had been since the beginning.

Janice gazed at the woman beside her. Yes, she was a true master of deception, a true broker of lies.

Janice said softly, "You needed to disappear, so you had Joshua start the fire."

"He was always faithful to the cause."

"And you've been hiding all this time."

"I've been preparing for what's next. With Ivan."

With that, she signaled to the town car she'd just left. As the window lowered, Ivan Popovic stared out at them. Bald. A gaunt face. Late sixties. Unflinching eyes that could bore right into you, right through you. For the first time in as long as Janice could remember, she felt a chill of uneasiness. "How long have you been working with him?" she asked, her voice catching.

"Since college."

"And that's why you pursued Travis Brock like you did? And why you killed her—to avoid being discovered?"

The report. The missing files. If the State Department had dug deeply enough, they would've found out everything, who she was working for. That's why . . .

The woman took her hand. "It's time for you to come with me."

Before walking anywhere, Janice reached up and lifted the veil from the woman's face.

And yes, it was just as she'd suspected.

It wasn't Lena Rhodes beside her—she'd been the one to die in the fire. The one killed and never missed. The one who was buried here, now, beneath their feet.

No more Lena, no more questions. There was no reason for Travis or the authorities to suspect that anyone other than Sienna had been in the house on the night of the fire, so they wouldn't have tried to identify the body by dental records or anything.

The woman with the veil was the linguist, the translator, the traitor.

Sienna Brock.

And now she smiled. "Let's go, Janice. We have a lot of catching up to do."

Note to Readers

Thanks for the gift of your time, and for journeying with me through this story. After spending the last several years with these characters roaming around in my head, it's been a blessing (and a relief) to finally set them free on the page. As always happens with my stories, they surprised me by their choices as they took on a veritable life of their own. I look forward to seeing what mischief they get into in their next adventure.

A few thoughts:

First, I've done my best to respect the locales and technical information related to this story, but since this is a work of fiction, I sometimes needed to take liberties in describing specific locations, historical references, and government oversight responsibilities and facilities.

Second, concerning the RDD in this story: It's true that isotopes other than u-235 would likely be more efficacious, from a terrorist's point of view, for use in a dirty bomb in a metropolitan area. I considered using them in the book, but eventually, choosing to err on the side of prudence, I decided not to include more details on them, how to access them, or how to actually construct a bomb that would effectively disperse them.

Third, I'm indebted to Gary A. Haugen for his insightful discussions about justice and oppression in his book *Good News About Injustice*, and for his list of atrocities and despots on page 47 that inspired my similar list in chapter 69.

Finally, a word of thanks. Many people assisted me with the research for this book. Although I'm not able to list all of my resources and contacts by name, you folks know who you are and my sincere thanks and gratitude go out to each and every one of you. The story would not have been possible without your help.

This book is dedicated to all those in our government who serve as the keepers of secrets and the arbiters of truth. You work in the shadows so that we can live in the light. Thank you. This book is for you.

—Steven James

Steven James is a critically acclaimed author of eighteen novels and numerous nonfiction books that have sold more than 1 million copies. His books have won or been shortlisted for dozens of national and international awards. In addition, his stories and articles have appeared in more than eighty different publications, including the *New York Times*. He is also a popular keynote speaker and professional storyteller with a master's degree in storytelling. Since 1996 he has appeared more than two thousand times at events spanning the globe, presenting his stories and teaching the principles of storytelling to writers, speakers, teachers, and leaders. When he's not writing or speaking, he hosts the weekly podcast *The Story Blender*, on which he interviews some of the world's leading writers and storytellers. In 2020 he was inducted into the Christy Award Hall of Fame for excellence in fiction writing. *Publishers Weekly* has called him "[a] master storyteller at the peak of his game."

TYNDALE HOUSE PUBLISHERS
IS CRAZY4FICTION!

Fiction that entertains and inspires

Get to know us! Become a member of the Crazy4Fiction community. Whether you read our blog, like us on Facebook, follow us on Twitter, or receive our e-newsletter, you're sure to get the latest news on the best in Christian fiction. You might even win something along the way!

JOIN IN THE FUN TODAY.

 crazy4fiction.com

 Crazy4Fiction

 crazy4fiction

 @Crazy4Fiction

CP0021